The Magus of Sicily

Also by Philip Gwynne Jones

The Venetian Game

Vengeance in Venice

The Venetian Masquerade

Venetian Gothic

The Venetian Legacy

The Angels of Venice

The Venetian Candidate

The Venetian Sanctuary

To Venice with Love: A Midlife Adventure

The
Magus
of
Sicily

Philip Gwynne Jones

CONSTABLE

CONSTABLE

First published in Great Britain in 2025 by Constable

Copyright © Philip Gwynne Jones, 2025

Map on page vi by David Andrassy

1 3 5 7 9 10 8 6 4 2

A CIP catalogue record for this book
is available from the British Library.

ISBN: 978-1-40871-996-1

Typeset in Adobe Garamond by Initial Typesetting Services, Edinburgh
Printed and bound in Great Britain by Clays Ltd, Elcograf S.p.A.

Papers used by Constable are from well-managed forests and
other responsible sources.

MIX
Paper | Supporting
responsible forestry
FSC® C104740

Constable
An imprint of
Little, Brown Book Group
Carmelite House
50 Victoria Embankment
London EC4Y 0DZ

The authorised representative
in the EEA is
Hachette Ireland
8 Castlecourt Centre
Dublin 15, D15 XTP3, Ireland
(email: info@hbgi.ie)

An Hachette UK Company
www.hachette.co.uk

www.littlebrown.co.uk

*This book is dedicated to my dear friend Krystyna Green,
without whom none of these books would ever have happened.*

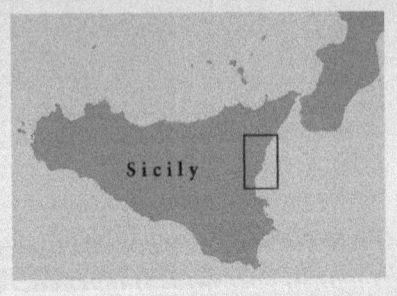

Sicily

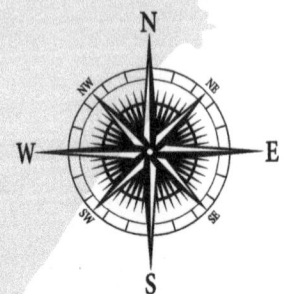

N
NW   NE
W   E
SW   SE
S

● Mount Etna

Sicily

● Santa Maria La Scala

● Acireale

Aci Trezza
●
Aci Castello ● ● Faraglioni dei Ciclopi

● Catania

Ionian Sea

There are approximately one hundred and fifty thousand psychics practising in the Italian peninsula. Thirteen million citizens consult them every year.

It is a business that generates about six billion euros.

(Figures provided by the *Guardia di Finanza*, the Italian financial police)

Prologue

Perhaps the first thing to learn about Acireale is what to call Acireale. Sicilians would call it *Jaciriali*. Locals would call it *Jaci*. Apart from those that call it *Aci*, of course.

Its origins date back to the fabled Greek city of Xiphonia, a city so lost to memory that nobody is quite sure where it was or even if it ever existed. And so, the reasoning goes, it might as well have been here as anywhere else.

The shepherd boy Acis, they say, fell in love with the nymph Galatea. This had the unfortunate effect of angering his love rival, the cyclops Polyphemus. In terms of a contest, shepherd boy versus cyclops was always likely to be an unequal one, and Acis was unceremoniously squashed under a boulder, his blood flowing out and becoming the river that the Greeks called *Akis*.

Acireale looks out upon the Ionian Sea, and the *Ciclopi* off the coast of postcard-pretty Aci Trezza, the Cyclopean Isles hurled into the sea by the blinded, enraged Polyphemus in his attempt to kill the fleeing Odysseus. The bay sweeps around to Aci Castello, dominated by its black basalt fortress, and all the way to the city of Catania, its baroque *centro storico* surrounded by a grubbier, grittier urban sprawl. Catania has been buried under lava no fewer than seventeen times in its history, which has bred in its residents a curious mixture of fatalism and optimism.

Greeks and Romans, Arabs and Normans and Spaniards all passed through here and left their mark. Christianity and Islam, Judaism and ancient folk-myth have roots that lie deep within its soil.

Acireale rebuilt itself following the great earthquake of 1693. It raised the Italian Tricolour for the first time in 1860, as part of Garibaldi's 'Expedition of a Thousand'. In the twentieth century it survived Mussolini's fascism, Allied bombing and the best efforts of the *Cosa Nostra*. Still it remains, optimistically clinging to the lower slopes of Mount Etna.

A land and a city with deep roots, a troubled past and an uncertain future, Acireale lies there, under the volcano, hewn from the lava and wedded to the sea.

A land with a violent past and, occasionally, a violent present as well. . .

Chapter 1

March 2023, somewhere outside Turin

Never try and con a con man.

It was just an hour to Milan, and then the Magus planned to change to the sleeper to Catania. Now, that might seem as if he were going back on himself, and Genoa might have seemed the more obvious station at which to change, but there was a method to it. If he took the service from Genoa, he'd have to share a sleeper compartment with up to four people. And he really, really didn't want to have to do that. Whereas, by taking the service from Milan, he could have a cabin to himself and sleep all the more soundly.

There were fewer people in the carriage than he might have expected. He'd figured he could afford to treat himself to first class. He leaned out of his seat, just a little, and took a look at the other passengers. Just three of them, in various forms of standard business attire. One of them hunched over a laptop. Another leaning back in his seat, eyes closed, listening to something on expensive over-ear headphones. The third was watching a film on what might just have been the largest phone the Magus had ever seen.

The thought struck him that perhaps he could now afford

something similar. But then he'd need to buy jackets and trousers with bigger pockets and that seemed like a waste of money.

There was a hiss from the door opening behind him, and the gentle thunk of it closing. The conductor, he assumed, or the drinks trolley. In either case, he'd be needing his wallet. He balanced his briefcase on his knee and reached inside his jacket.

'Can I sit here, my friend?'

He was startled for a moment. The speaker was a big man, completely bald, his skin burnished a deep nut brown. There was the faint smell of sweat, smoke and stale booze about him. Not enough to be immediately objectionable, but more the sign of someone who's been burning the midnight oil even though it was barely past eight in the evening.

'Erm, this is first class,' said the Magus, and immediately hated himself for sounding like the sort of person who says things like 'Erm, this is first class.'

'I know,' said the other man, with a look in his eyes that accused him of making a judgement. Which was true.

The Magus tried to recover the situation. 'It's just that the seats are reserved,' he said. Which sounded feeble but was at least an attempt at not being obviously rude.

The big man looked at the illuminated LED strip above the seats. 'Oh, that's okay. Nobody's sitting here until Bologna. And you're getting off at,' he squinted at the strip again, 'Milan.' He looked down expectantly at the seat opposite, which had a copy of the *Corriere della Sera* on it.

The Magus tried not to sigh, moved the newspaper, and positioned it on top of his briefcase.

The big man smiled and sat down. 'Long journey ahead of you?'

'Quite a long one. Rome,' he lied.

A near-empty coach and this guy had decided to sit face to face with him. Worse, he seemed in the mood to talk. All he really wanted was a large glass of wine and to switch his brain off but that, it seemed, was not going to be an option. Oh well. It was only an hour to Milan. That was manageable.

'Rome, eh?' The Magus nodded. 'Holiday?'

'Business.'

The big man nodded at the briefcase. 'Oh yes. Of course. You go there a lot?'

'Sometimes.'

'Couldn't live in Rome. Chaos, isn't it? Mind, Bologna's not much better. I blame the politicians, myself.'

There were two options, thought the Magus. Either he was the unluckiest man in the world because the most boring man in the world had chosen to sit opposite him, despite there being an almost completely empty carriage to choose from. Or there was more to it. Someone had been sent to find him. Which, he supposed, also made him the unluckiest man in the world.

'Politics, eh?' he said, in order to fill the dead air between them.

Next stop Chivasso flashed up on the information screen. What did he know about Chivasso? Nothing. But it was just ten minutes away. It was a shame to break his plans. He'd been looking forward to a leisurely train journey overnight. Still, if it had to be done. . .

He checked his companion over as discreetly as possible.

Physically bigger, and definitely muscles there. A straight fight might be hard work. There was nothing to indicate the presence of a gun, given the way his jacket was hanging. A knife or a knuckle duster would be another matter. Still, he'd have to take that chance.

A shame. Turin had been a nice job. He'd heard about a private gambling club where proper money was changing hands. And there was one guy there who was doing ever so well. Just a little *too* well.

He'd sat in on a few games. He lost a little money. Just enough to keep them interested. Just enough to draw them in.

They were all counting cards. Casinos don't like it, but it's not the same thing as cheating. It's the one thing that everyone can do if they have the patience and time, which, to be honest, most sensible people don't. If they spot that you're counting cards – and most places are wise to it by now – you get asked, politely, not to return. If you're found to be cheating, well, the conversation will be less polite.

He watched the main guy over a few nights and started to notice the shifts and hops and passes. Cards being shifted from the top of the pack to the bottom and vice versa. He was good, very good. He'd have to give him that.

So the Magus started to bid higher and higher, losing more and more. Eventually the table was left to the two of them; the Magus dabbing at his forehead and sipping from the glass at his side and pretending he'd drunk more than he had.

And then he reeled him in. He spotted the cards that his opponent was shifting on the deck and adjusted accordingly. The greatest danger, the biggest gamble, was the possibility that his opponent would decide to cut and run. But as he looked across the table, he could tell exactly what the other man was thinking: that he'd found a sucker, someone with more money than sense, an amateur who makes the classic mistake of doubling every stake in the hope of finally coming good.

Which, of course, is what happened. Except this time it actually worked. There was an awkward silence around the table. All the more so when the Magus immediately decided it was time to call it a night. He packed his winnings away, keeping an eye on the exits. He was expecting there to be trouble – there often was – but there was nothing more than an angry silence. He was away to the station and on the next train to Milan within minutes.

Except, of course, it wasn't as easy as that. His travelling companion, he was certain, had been despatched to get his boss's money back. Time, then, for a Plan B. And fortunately, he always had a Plan B.

He took out his phone and tapped away. Five minutes after arriving in Chivasso he could be on a train to Genoa. Genoa. He smiled. It seemed like that was his destiny after all. Oh well. Sharing a compartment it would have to be.

'You seem happy,' his new friend said. The Magus's phone plinged as the transaction cleared on his new rail ticket.

He smiled back. 'Just some good news, that's all. Nothing major. Just a few logistical issues to sort out. You know what travelling's like.'

He looked up at the information screen again. Five minutes to Chivasso. He got to his feet, bracing himself. The next couple of minutes were going to be crucial. Timing was everything, in magic as in life.

He scanned the compartment. Laptop man was still engrossed in his spreadsheets. Headphones guy was leaning back in his seat, his mouth slightly open. The other still had his eyes fixed on his cellphone. If they were getting off, they'd be moving by now. He checked behind him. No conductor. No trolley service.

He took down his suitcase and folded his *Corriere* away inside his coat. 'Nice talking to you,' he said.

The big man frowned. 'My friend, we're still a long way out of Milan.' He craned his head around to check the screen. 'We're coming into Chivasso.' He shook his head. 'Wherever the hell that is.'

He'd taken his eyes off him. Just for a fraction of a second. And, in magic, that's all you need.

Get this wrong, and he'd have started a fight in the middle of a train.

Get it right and – well, there would another set of problems to unravel, but he could deal with those as and when necessary.

His fist lashed out and caught the big man square on the chin, his eyes rolling back in his head. He hit him again just to be sure, sending him slumping back into his chair.

He checked the screen once more. Four minutes.

He dragged his new friend over to the window seat and leaned his head against the glass. Unless somebody took a very close look, they'd assume he was just sleeping.

He went through his pockets.

Mobile phone. He'd have that.

Wallet. He flicked through it. Some money. He'd have that as well.

Cigarettes and a lighter. He left them. Whoever this guy was, he was going to want a smoke when he woke up. And when he had to tell whoever had sent him that he'd lost his target.

He collected his luggage and briefcase. Then the train halted at Chivasso, the door hissed open, and he stepped down into the cool night air.

Five minutes later, he was on the train to Genoa, patting the case at his side.

Don't try and con a con man.

He tried to piece together what had just happened. His gambling buddies, it seemed, were sore losers. It might be good to lay low for a while. More than that, it might be good to be somebody else for a while.

He flicked through the ID cards in his wallet. Some of them were paper, some of them laminated. None were biometric. All were expiring within a few years, but that was fine. That was tomorrow's problem.

Domenico Rossi. Marco Riva. Simone Lucarelli. Calogero Maugeri.

Maugeri. A good Sicilian name. A good *Catanese* name.

Calogero Maugeri.

He smiled to himself.

Now, there was a name to conjure with.

Chapter 2

'How much longer until John the Baptist turns up?' Nedda Leonardi dropped her empty bottle of *birra Messina* into the recycling bin at the side of the kiosk and glanced at her watch.

Stefano Gallo stretched his arms wide, enjoying the feeling of the summer sun on his skin, and yawned. 'It starts when it starts, Nedda. You should know that by now. These things never begin on time.'

She rolled her eyes. 'I'm kind of bored of this, you know? They could just have reprinted last year's report and nobody would have been any the wiser. That's if anybody reads it at all.'

'It's local colour, Nedda. Part of the local pageantry. Part of our history. *Your* history, I should say. But more importantly, it'll fill half a page.' Nedda half-checked her watch. 'And if you're wondering about the time, it's about thirty seconds on from when you last checked.' She looked back towards the kiosk. 'And no, you're not having another beer.'

'What is this, have I come out to work with my dad or something?'

'I just don't want you killing yourself on your scooter on the way home.'

'Why, Stefano, what a kind thought. And I keep telling you, it's a bike not a scooter.'

'I'm not being kind. I just don't want to have to explain it to your dad, that's all. Neither do I want to tell the boss that I've managed to kill one of his reporters.' He glanced at his watch.

'Ah-hah!'

'What does that mean?'

'You checked the time. You're getting as bored as I am.'

'Not at all.' He gave up trying to pretend. 'Okay, it's dragging on a bit, I admit.' He closed his eyes, his lips moving as he ran through the timings in his head. 'Okay, *U pisci a mari* should be starting any time now. Operative word being *should*. We take a few photos of that. Then they start parading Johnny the B through the streets. We take a few photos of him as well. Get a shot of his hand, that's the important bit, the relic. Then I write my copy, you write yours, and we should be able to file this early evening. And everyone will be happy.' He opened his eyes. 'So which bit do you want to cover?'

'Which do you recommend?'

'*U pisci a mari* is probably more fun. Properly bloody that can be, at times. Fishermen waving terrifying-looking knives. And a man pretending to be a swordfish being hacked into pieces.'

'Thanks. I know what it is. I've seen it often enough.'

'So do you want to do that?' Nedda said nothing. 'Look, I'm offering you the most interesting one. It's that or talk to the priest.'

'Okay.' She wasn't convinced. 'But does that leave you with enough to do?'

'Sure. I'll talk to the *padre* about John the Baptist. Plenty of material there, I'm sure.'

'I'm never quite sure when you're joking, Stefano.'

'Oh, I'm serious. That's what you've got to do in this job. Boss sends you out to cover a school football tournament, your job is to make it sound as exciting as the *Azzurri* winning the World Cup. At least, that's what I try to do. So I'll let the *padre* talk about John the Baptist, the importance of saints, traditions, family – all that stuff. And try and make it interesting. Admittedly that's kind of a big ask.'

'You could always ask him about the hand?'

'Like what?'

'You know. Ask him if he thinks it's real or not.'

'What's the point? "Priest says relic is real" isn't a story.'

'What if he says it isn't?'

'He won't. Trust me on that.'

'Do you think he believes it?'

Stefano shrugged. 'I think he believes he believes it.'

'Do you?'

He rubbed his forehead. 'Okay, I give in. I'll buy you another beer as long as you promise to stop asking questions.'

Nedda smiled. 'Deal.' Then she paused. 'Oh, hang on, I think they're about to start.'

June the twenty-fourth. The *sagra* of San Giovanni Battista, patron saint of Aci Trezza. Saints Venere and Sebastian may have held sway in Acireale, while further along the coast Aci Castello had long been the domain of St Mauro; but Aci Trezza was now firmly established as the realm of John the Baptist.

It hadn't always been that way. St Joseph had served

perfectly well as their patron until he was unceremoniously replaced in 1750. Little now remained of poor Joseph in the town, save for his commemoration on March the nineteenth, when his statue was paraded around the town before being placed back in its niche, in a side chapel in the church now dedicated to St John the Baptist. Joseph's statue had been one of the few things to survive the great earthquake of 1693. It was only right that there still remained a place for him, no matter how small.

But the great celebration, of course, was reserved for the Baptist himself, on the twenty-fourth of June. His effigy and relics, enthroned amongst red anthuriums, would be paraded around the town before being returned to his eponymous church, and then – devotional duties all taken care of – the party could really start, with fireworks, eating and drinking long into the night.

The terracotta-coloured houses were now draped in red and gold silks, as, indeed, were the people. The streets were filled with the aromas of coffee and cigarettes, of sweet and savoury pastries and of good, fried things. A brass band stood outside a *gelateria*, enjoying the respite of something cool upon their lips instead of brass instruments heated white-hot by the blaze of the sun.

Sicily has long been a land where the sacred and profane have existed side by side, and the ancient, folk-horror pantomime of *U pisci a mari* comfortably co-existed with the veneration of the Christian saint. Before the Baptist's statue was carried around the town on his golden throne, people would gather by the shore to watch and commemorate their town's long and precarious relationship with the ocean.

Nedda remembered the very first time she had watched it with *papà*. He'd explained it all to her beforehand, about how they were about to watch a simple tale – a pantomime, if you like – about the fishermen who had plied their trade along the shore for centuries. Three men in a boat would head out to sea in search of a swordfish, played by one of the young men of the town. They would then pretend to spear him, haul him on board and prepare to slaughter him. But just as the *ràis* – the captain – was about to apply the killing blow, the young man-fish would slip into the water leaving the distraught crew to mourn the loss of their catch. A reminder that a simple mistake might mean the difference between putting food on the table and going hungry.

Triumph and disaster walked hand in hand. It was always the same in Sicily. And on the feast day of St John the Baptist, this was their very own Passion Play.

Papà had told her that it was just pretend. That nobody would be really hurt. But he hadn't told her quite how much blood would be involved. When the man-fish was hauled on board the boat, and the *ràis* held a huge rectangular knife above him, both blade and boy soaked in crimson gore, Nedda had screamed and buried her face in her father's shirt.

The next term at school had been a bit difficult after that. Nedda with the red hair, Nedda the outsider, was now Nedda who'd sobbed all the way through *U pisci a mari*.

'Nedda?' Stefano was waving his hand in front of her face. 'Earth calling.'

She shook her head in annoyance, shaking the memories out. 'Sorry. Head in the clouds.'

Stefano sighed. 'All right, I'll go and talk to the priest. You stay here and watch, talk to locals, and take photos. The bloodier the better.' He checked his watch. 'And I'll see you here in about thirty minutes, yeah?'

She nodded, staring out to sea to gaze at the *Ciclopi*, the Isles of the Cyclops, rising from the sea. So different from the urban sprawl of Catania. So beautiful the way they rose out of the deep blue sea. So . . .

'Nedda?'

'Sorry?'

'Did you hear a word I was saying?'

'No. Head/clouds thing again.'

'Oh for Christ's sake. I said I'll meet you back here in half an hour. And don't miss anything.'

'Stefano, it's just a pantomime about swordfish. It's not the last helicopter out of Saigon.'

'"Just a pantomime about swordfish."' He grinned. 'Photos, plenty of gore, remember? That's what the old man wants.' He looked more closely at her. 'Are you okay?'

'I'm fine.'

'It's just you don't look one hundred per cent.'

She shook her head. 'Probably just the heat. Don't worry. Go on, go and talk to the priest about relics.'

He smiled. 'Okay. I'll see you in a bit.'

He made his way through the crowds, and up the steps of the church of San Giovanni Battista, where fishermen, dressed in the traditional bright red and gold, were dancing and capering to the strains of a brass band.

Even at a distance, Nedda could see the priest was smiling yet thin-lipped, as if thinking that there was perhaps a little too much dancing, a little too much capering, than was properly reverent.

She looked out at the deep blue sea once again, and then turned through a full circle, taking in the brightly coloured dancers, the pilgrims waving their red handkerchiefs, the deep gold of the throne carrying the Baptist, and the reds and yellows of the boats.

Sicilians did nothing in black and white. *Bianconero* was for Milan and Turin and the cold cities of the north. Sicilians lived in the brightest Technicolor.

'Midsummer's day and the nativity of St John the Baptist – a celebration where the old and new religions come together and the veil between these opposing worlds is thin.'

Would she use this? Perhaps not.

The priest was still smiling, but dabbing at his forehead. She felt sorry for him. It was only late June, yet it must be fearfully hot under a cassock. In a month's time it would be almost unbearable.

Cheers rose from the crowd, as the fishing boat set out into the harbour for *U pisci a mari*. The woman next to her hauled a small boy into her arms so that he could see properly. The fishermen, gaily dressed in red shirts and gold sashes, waved back at the crowd.

The boy cheered and clapped, and then turned to waggle his hand at Nedda. She was never quite sure how to react to small children, but smiled and waved back. He reached out for her, his hand tangling in her hair.

His mother gently pulled him away. 'Leave the nice lady alone, Tonio.'

Nedda smiled. 'It's all right.'

'He's very excited. Aren't you, Tonio?'

The little boy pointed towards the sea. 'That's my brother. *Mamma* says he's the best swimmer in the world.'

She laughed. 'Maybe the best in Aci Trezza, *trisoru*.' She hugged him closer to her. 'Now, you remember what I said? This is all just pretend, understand?'

'I understand, *mamma*.'

Nedda shielded her eyes against the glare of the sun, and looked out to sea, the mournful drone of every boat siren in the harbour echoing in her ears. A slim, dark-haired boy – presumably this year's swordfish – was hauled out of the sea and splayed out across the prow of the boat as the *ràis* prepared him for the ritual slaughter. His legs – one ankle wrapped in a yellow ribbon, the other in red – thrashed helplessly at the water as the *ràis* held a wicked rectangular blade high above him, whilst discreetly rubbing the lad's chest with a rich red dye.

'This is all just pretend, remember?' repeated the child's mother.

The *ràis* passed the blade over the body of the young man. Once, twice, three times; as cheers rang out from the crowd.

The bloodier the better.

This is all just pretend.

'*Signurina*, are you all right?'

She put her hand to her forehead. 'I'm sorry, it's just the heat. I think perhaps I need to sit down.'

The noise. The smell of the sea and the stink of fish and petrol. The boatmen capering and singing. And the blood. The stale taste of the beer was rank in her mouth, and for a moment she was afraid she was going to vomit, as she fought her way through the crowd and sat down, unsteadily, on the quayside, breathing deeply.

'It's just pretend,' she heard the child call out.

Plenty of gore, remember? The *ràis* lifted his blade, which, she struggled to remind herself, was merely made of wood with the ends sprayed crimson. He pretended to hack and saw at the young man's limbs. Just pretend. But horribly realistic.

The young man-fish slipped over the side of the boat and into the sea, the blood-red dye spreading out around him. The story should have ended there, with the fishermen cursing their luck and paddling back towards shore, all the while thinking that they'd earned a few beers from their friends in the crowd for providing the afternoon's entertainment.

Instead, a cry came up from the *ràis*. Not the practised, slightly forced cry of a non-actor in a play, but one of genuine alarm.

'There's someone in the water.'

The man-fish splashed around, turning himself through a circle.

'There's a man in the water. To your right!'

He turned a little more, and then gasped, swallowing water and spitting it out. Something, someone, was almost on top of him. A body, arms and legs spread wide, face down.

'Get him out!'

The crew tugged at the body, their arms straining against the weight of clothes sodden with water, and hauled it into the boat.

'We need a doctor!'

The crowd were quiet now, the silence only broken by the sound of an occasional murmured prayer or gentle crying, as the crew hauled on the oars and rowed, as if through treacle it seemed, back towards the shore.

'It's only pretend,' cried the little boy, but Nedda was no longer convinced.

She pushed her way towards the front, holding out her journalist's card and shouting *Scusate! Scusate!* against a background chorus of *Ois!* and *Cazzos!*

The crew dragged the body onshore, and laid it face down on the jetty. The *ràis* knelt by him, turning his head to the side, and letting water drain from his mouth and nose.

'A doctor?' he cried, again.

Nedda looked over her shoulder, back at the church. The dancing had stopped, and the bearers of John the Baptist gently lowered him to the ground. One by one, the crowd fell silent as the church bells chimed the quarter-hour. She had no idea if Stefano could see her, but waved an arm back and forth in the hope of attracting his attention. Then she saw him on the church steps, shielding his eyes against the sun, and he broke into a run. One of the fishermen grabbed Nedda by the arm as she pushed herself further forward.

'No, *signurina.*'

With her free hand she jabbed her journalist's card toward his face. 'Nedda Leonardi. *Catania Nuova.*'

He shook his head, and a look of distaste flashed across his face, but he let her pass.

Another young woman had pushed her way through the crowd, and was bent over the figure, compressing his chest. She paused to check the pulse then shook her head and repeated the operation. Again, she paused, this time to pinch the nose shut and breath into his mouth.

Nedda snapped away with her telephone, trying to ignore the shouts of *Che vergogna. Shame on you.*

The woman got to her feet, shaking her head, and glared. 'Happy now? Got all the photos you need?'

'I'm a journalist.' Nedda waved her card again.

'And I'm a doctor. And this man is dead. Would it kill you to show a bit of respect?'

'I'm sorry.' She was about to continue, but her voice was drowned out by the sound of ambulance sirens.

Someone pushed her roughly out of the way as the boat crew moved to encircle the body and shield it from prying eyes, their faces flushed as scarlet as their garments. Red dye dripped from them; a macabre crimson drizzle that spattered around the dead man.

The *ràis* ran his stained fingers through his hair as he looked down. Then he crossed himself. '*Gesù*,' he said. 'It's him.'

Nedda was about to ask him what he meant when two burly paramedics pushed their way past and through the circle of men.

Just one hundred metres away, the church bells were chiming out in veneration of John the Baptist.

Chapter 3

'Didn't hear you come home, last night.'

'Actually, *papà*, I didn't. I've just come back to pick some things up for work.'

Angelo Leonardi put down his paper, and adjusted his spectacles in a way that Nedda had come to understand signified 'A Conversation' was about to be had.

'Oh, yes?' he said.

She yawned and stretched. 'You heard about what happened?'

He nodded. 'I did. A horrible business. But don't think that even a tragic accident is a good way of changing the subject.'

'We – that's Stefano and I – hung around with the fishing crew. Hoping we'd get some photos and the chance to talk properly to them.'

'And did you?'

'We had to buy them a lot of beer, but we did.' Her face fell. 'Or, at least, they talked to Stefano. They more or less ignored me.'

'More or less?'

'One of them asked for my phone number. Anyway,

Stefano decided we deserved a drink as well after all that. And then it became more than one. And it was late, and I didn't want to take the bike home and so—'

Angelo waved his hands. 'Stop. Please. I don't need to know any more, thank you.'

Nedda continued. 'And so, I spent the night on his sofa.'

'Mm-hmm. The sofa, yes?'

'Yes, a long upholstered seat with arms at each end, suitable for two or more people. Also sleeps one person in reasonable comfort.'

He pretended to read the paper for a few moments, and then raised his eyes again. 'What's he like then, this Stefano?'

'Quite good at his job, I think.'

'That's an even worse way of avoiding the question than talking about the accident. You know what I mean.'

She ran a hand through her hair. 'He's all right, I suppose. On occasion he crosses over into "quite nice" territory.'

'Really?'

'Really. That's as far as it goes. "Quite nice" and no further.'

'Well, maybe you should bring him along one evening. I'll cook for us all.'

'*Papà!* Don't start all this again.'

He got to his feet, and limped across the room, ruffling her hair along the way. 'Joking, *trisoru*, joking.' He picked up the newspaper again. 'So, my little girl makes the front page for the first time, eh?'

She grabbed at it. 'I've not seen it yet.' She scanned the first paragraph, and then tossed it back on the table, swearing under her breath.

'Something wrong?'

'You could say that.' She jabbed a finger at the headline. '"By Stefano Gallo and Nedda Leonardi".'

'Mm-hmm?' Angelo kept his voice neutral.

'Stefano was up at the church talking to the priest and some dancing fishermen. I was there on the spot. I saw that body floating in the water. I saw the doctor giving him the kiss of life.'

'So you're worried about not getting top billing?'

'No.' She frowned. 'Well, yes. Is that pathetic?'

Angelo sighed. 'No. No, it's not pathetic. But, *trisoru*, here's the hard truth. Do you think anybody is looking at either of the names under the headline? Seriously? A man was found dead, floating in the water, during Aci Trezza's biggest celebration of the year.' He reached over to take her hands. 'Nobody – *nobody* – cares about who wrote that story. The dead man floating in the water. That's all they care about. But still, you're on the front page. Be proud of that.' He tapped his chest. 'I am.'

She brightened. 'Well, maybe I should get this framed? Perhaps this might be the start of better things?'

'Better things?'

'You know what I mean. I'm tired of all the local colour and lifestyle stuff. I don't think there's a carnival or festival in the whole of the Catania region that I haven't covered by now.'

'Well, they're part of our history. They're important too.' She opened her mouth, but he shook his head. 'But I understand. So tell me, Nedda. What do you want to be doing instead?'

'Oh, *papà*, I think you know.'

He nodded. 'Mm-hmm. You want to be doing something like your *mamma*. Yes?'

'That's right. Does that make you angry?'

He shook his head. 'No.'

'But the reason I'm not getting to do anything beyond colourful local culture is because of her, isn't it? People think I got my job because of her.'

Angelo smiled. 'Well now, Nedda. This is Sicily, after all. I imagine there were people saying that Andrea Camilleri only got a head start because his parents knew Pirandello.'

'So, what would *mamma* have done? She'd have kicked her editor's arse and demanded she got something better. Wouldn't she?'

'She would. And she'd probably have lost her job in the process.'

'But she'd just have gone out and got another one.'

'She would.'

'So, maybe I should do that?'

'And if it doesn't work out?'

'Then I'll stay in Acireale and fix motorcycles.'

'That's a wonderful idea, Nedda. I can't think of any profession in Sicily better on gender equality than motorcycle mechanic. Look, you're thirty years old—'

'Twenty-nine!'

'Twenty-nine. You know what I'm like with birthdays. Twenty-nine with a journalist's card and a job on a proper newspaper. As I said, you should be proud of that.'

She was about to speak, but her phone trilled. '*Ciao*, Stefano. Yes, I'm with *papà*. I've kind of lost track of time.' She checked her watch and swore, causing Angelo to shake his head. 'Okay, when do I need to be there?' She swore again. 'I'll do my best.' She hung up and turned to her father. 'Sorry, *papà*, got to run.' She gave him a kiss on the cheek.

'You'll be back for dinner?'

'I don't know. Leave me something in the fridge just in case, maybe?'

'Maybe I should leave something for Stefano as well?'

'And maybe you shouldn't. *Ciao, papà.*'

'You be careful on that thing!'

'I'm always careful.' She picked up her jacket and helmet from where they were hanging on the back of the door. It wouldn't be long now until leathers became unbearably hot but, for now, the rush of the wind would keep her cool.

As for the helmet, well, wind in the hair was all well and good. Being pulled over by the police, less so. They were still turning a blind eye to scooter riders without any protection, but motorcycles were another matter and red-haired girls on Royal Enfields tended to be recognisable. Besides, she told herself, helmet-hair was something that only pretend bikers worried about. *If you have a ten-euro head, wear a ten-euro helmet.*

She swung a leg across the bike, gunned the engine, and sped off down the hill through Acireale, past the *pasticcerie* and coffee bars and out onto the main road that led to Catania. She smiled to herself as she passed first a Ducati and then a Harley-Davidson dealership along the way. Harleys, she thought, were made for going in straight lines. Ducatis were fine in summer. Less so when trying to start them on a cold January morning. But Enfields you could fix with a spanner. In the unlikely event they ever needed fixing at all.

On she sped, parallel to the railway line, and past the dull commercial centres and industrial estates at the side of the road. Then down, down towards Aci Trezza, the vegetation at the side of the road already looking bleached and scrubby in the heat of early summer. The sea ahead of her, Etna to her right, and the smell of saltwater and petrol in her nostrils.

Along the coast, past Aci Castello, and then into the outer sprawl of Catania itself. Past the mural of Falcone and Borsellino, down past the fish market and the outskirts of the *centro storico*, and finally to the garage on Via Leonardi, where she kicked the stand down, and dismounted.

She always felt ungainly and heavy whenever she got off the bike. Everything, even walking, felt more difficult, as if she were once again subject to the laws of gravity and pulled earthward; her gait as clumsy as that of the pigeons scavenging for food outside the bars of the *Piazza del Duomo*.

'*Ciao*, Nedda,' said Marco, already hot and sweaty from the morning's work. 'Just leaving the bike here again?' He wiped the oil from his hands on a greasy rag, and smiled.

'As always, Marco.'

'What are you doing with that crappy bike, Nedda? I know someone who could sort you out with a lovely Moto Guzzi. Good price, reliable, no rubbish.'

'This "someone", Marco, is this your cousin again, by any chance?'

'There is a small family connection. Second cousin, I think.'

'Okay. But if I buy a Guzzi I'll be here every couple of months giving you money, won't I?'

He crossed himself. 'No, no. I swear. He doesn't sell any old rubbish.'

'Thanks. But if it's all the same to you, I think it's best if we continue with our arrangement, don't you?'

He grinned. 'If you say so, Nedda.'

She tucked the Enfield away in the corner.

'Be careful, Nedda. We've had a couple of antiques dealers in here recently. They might be interested in that.'

She stuck her tongue out at him and went on her way. They'd had the same conversation every morning for months.

When she was little, *papà* used to tell her that the building in the middle of via Leonardi was the family *palazzo*, which they'd lost years ago. So she had promised him that when she was grown-up and rich and famous she would buy it back for them.

The building had long since served as a garage and there were days when she suspected *papà* had not been one hundred per cent honest with her, but she still told her colleagues that she'd been *parking the bike in my palazzo* every morning.

Catania Nuova was based on Via Etnea, the great lava-paved street that swept up from the *centro storico*. Editor-in-chief Aldo Lentini made great play of the fact that you could see Etna from his office and it was therefore the best one in the city. In truth, he'd have to be leaning out at a perilous angle and the odds are the volcano would be obscured by clouds, heat haze or pollution, but, technically, he was correct.

She made her way up the stairs, into the office, and smiled at the young man on reception.

'*Ciao,* Ciccio. How's *il vecchiu* this morning?'

'*Ciao,* Nedda. Hardly seen him. He's been cloistered away with Gallo for the past half-hour.'

'Thanks.'

The door to Lentini's office was open, but she thought it polite to give a half-knock before he called *Avanti*.

Aldo Lentini was not a bad man. In the past, she'd been told, he'd been a great newspaperman. But he'd grown pink and plump with the passing of the years and now seemed happy to quietly serve out his time whilst waiting for retirement. His staff all seemed to like him and not a few to genuinely love him. If *Catania Nuova* never seemed to break the big stories that *La Sicilia* did, it was seen as being a comfy, decent place to work. The sort of place where you were unlikely to be shouted at. Or shot at.

No, Aldo Lentini was not a bad man at all.

The trouble was, he never seemed likely to give her anything resembling a decent job.

'*Buongiorno*, Nedda.' He smiled at her. 'Stefano and I were just finishing up.'

'Finishing up? Sorry, I got here as quickly as I could.'

Aldo smiled. 'No problem.'

Stefano cleared his throat. There was something about the look on his face, an awkwardness that in other situations she might have called an 'about last night' expression.

'Nedda, there's been a development. The pathologist's report will be out today. Late afternoon, most likely. So, in time for us to hit the morning editions for tomorrow.'

'Us?' she said.

He flushed. 'The newspaper.'

Aldo tapped the side of his nose. 'I've got an old friend at the *Questura*. He gave me a heads-up on this. Gallo's heading off to see him now.' He wagged a finger at him. 'Now, you remember what I said. This one enjoys his food. And his drink a little too much. So buy him lunch but take it easy, eh?'

'We'll be very good. I promise.' There was still an awkwardness to Stefano's expression.

Nedda looked at the two of them. 'And so – where do I come in?'

Aldo smiled at her. 'I've got something else for you, Nedda.' He scribbled on a notebook in front of him, tore off the front sheet and passed it to her.

'What is this?'

'New *pasticceria* opened near the *Teatro Antico*. Lovely family involved, so I'm told. Get along there and have a chat with them, photo of all of them smiling together, that sort of thing. Lots of photos of cakes. You know how it works. It's a feel-good story."

'You what?'

'It's a feel-good story,' he repeated. He turned to Stefano. 'You still here, Gallo?'

Stefano shrugged and mouthed the word *sorry* at her, but she just stared at him.

There was silence in the office as Lentini went back to scribbling on his notepad. He looked up at her. 'Sorry, is there anything else you need?'

Mamma wouldn't take this. Mamma would call him out.
Mamma would probably get fired.
But do you really care anymore?

'Why are you doing this?'

'Doing what, Nedda?'

'All this. I never get anything beyond the crap jobs here.'

'You're new here, Nedda.'

'Not new enough to be fit for nothing beyond the girly jobs. Tell you what, why don't you give me fashion? Or knitting? Or how to look fabulous at fifty?'

Lentini removed his spectacles and polished them on his sleeve. 'If you like, Nedda. But right now, what I want you to do is file me half a page on a pastry shop. I want a photo of a happy smiling family. I want photographs of cakes. Can you do that?'

'Fine. Tell you what, would you like me to bring you back a *cannolo* while I'm at it?'

'That would be lovely. Have one yourself while you're there.'

Mamma would have told him where to stick his job and stormed out. But Nedda set out to photograph a cake shop and buy a pastry for her editor, and settled for merely slamming the door.

Chapter 4

The Magus looked at the cards on the table, closed his eyes and took a deep breath. He sat there in silence for several minutes, so still that the young woman in front of him scarcely dared to breathe for fear of breaking the silence.

He muttered something under his breath and his hands shook for a moment. Then he jerked his head to the side and his eyes snapped open.

'Is everything—?' she began.

He held up a hand and smiled. 'Everything is fine.'

'*Papà*. Is he there? Can I speak to him?'

He shook his head. 'I'm afraid that's not possible. But he wants you to know that he is happy.'

Her face fell. 'I'm glad, of course. But can't I speak to him?'

'I'm sorry. Sometimes it's just not possible. Today is one of those days. But perhaps if you were to return?'

She looked uncertain for a moment, doubt flashing across her face. He'd seen that look before. Everybody in the business knew that when a mark became suspicious you had to put them at their ease immediately or any chance of them becoming a regular client would be lost. You needed to pull a rabbit out of the hat.

'*Mamma* would be angry if she knew I was here,' she said.

'I understand.' He paused. 'But your *papà* is happy. He had a good life in your world and he's watching over you now.'

The girl took a deep breath and dabbed at her eyes.

'He wants you to be happy as well, you know?'

She said nothing, but the tears were flowing now.

'It's the young man, isn't it? Gigi. The basketball player.' The girl started from her seat, but he waved a hand and, slowly, she sat down, breathing deeply. 'You're worried that *papà* might not approve. That he might not want you to be together. That you'd be letting him down in some way. Am I right?'

She nodded, silently.

'And *papà* wishes only for you to be happy. And if this young man can help you to be so, well, he thinks it is right that you should be together.'

'Did he really say that?'

The Magus nodded. 'My dear young lady, all he wishes is for you to be happy.'

She sat back in the antique chair, lowered her face and wept, silently. He smiled. 'Take all the time you need. Please.'

She blew her nose and dabbed at her eyes. 'Thank you,' she said, her voice raw with emotion. 'Thank you.'

'It's my pleasure.'

She fumbled in her purse for money. 'As we agreed?'

'Just so. In cash, if you would.'

She nodded, and pushed five twenty-euro notes across the table to him. He swept them up with a practised movement and tucked them into his jacket pocket. He noticed a fleck of grey hair dye on the tips of his fingers. Clumsy of him. The streak in his hair was part of the image, after all. He put a hand to his moustache and stroked it. Had he curled it properly? That was the problem, doing this job day in, day out. You became lazy.

He got to his feet. 'Could I make you a cup of tea? Coffee? Perhaps just a glass of water? I'd offer you something stronger but I don't drink. I find that gets in the way of communication.'

She shook her head. 'No, I need to be going. *Mamma* will be wondering where I am. And then tonight, I can see Gigi and tell him—' The tears started to flow again, and she threw her arms around him in an awkward embrace. 'Thank you,' she said.

He returned her hug with a gentle pat on the shoulder.

'Not at all, my dear. Come back any time, as I said.'

She nodded and did her best to smile against the tears and sobs.

The Magus turned to the audience. 'And that's how you do it!'

The lights went up and the audience, such as it was, started to clap. He bowed, and then stretched an arm out to the young woman, pulling her over in order to share the applause. He kissed the back of her hand, and she smiled back at him.

The *Teatro Giovanni Verga* was smaller than the more modern *Teatro Turri Ferro,* but that suited him just fine. Renting the space was reasonable enough and he could usually count on half-filling it. He looked out at the audience, taking a brief headcount. Well, perhaps a third if it was a matinee.

'Thank you. Thank you all. There we have it, ladies and gentlemen. I think that was about fifteen minutes' work for one hundred euros. In cash, of course. People in this business do so love to be paid in cash. And there's every possibility of the young lady turning up again next week for the same amount of money.' He spread his arms wide. 'Any questions?'

There was a murmuring among the crowd, but nobody raised a hand.

'Come on, come on.' He smiled. 'Don't you want to know how it's done?'

Someone stood up. 'She's a plant. The girl, I mean.'

'Well, of course she is. After all, what you've just seen would be a terrible thing to do to a normal member of the public, wouldn't it?' He turned to his accomplice. 'Why don't you introduce yourself, my dear?'

The young woman stood up. 'My name's Maria Giulia, I'm an actress from Siracusa, and I'm still waiting for Steven Spielberg to call, which is why I'm here tonight.'

There was a ripple of laughter. 'You're very good,' came a voice from the back.

'Thank you. A lot of it had to be improvised. I didn't quite know exactly what the Magus was going to ask me.'

'It's not scripted?'

'Not at all.' She paused. 'And here's a thing. My parents are alive. But I do have a boyfriend called Gigi. And he's a basketball player. But the Magus didn't know that.'

'Seriously?'

'Absolutely not.' She sat back down again, and turned to the Magus, smiling and clapping her hands.

He took another little bow and spread his arms wide

again. 'She's telling the truth. She didn't tell me anything about her boyfriend at all. So, my question to you all is simply this. How did I do it?'

'There's a thing called cold reading, isn't there?' A young man in the front row, this time.

'There is, yes. Do it properly and it's very effective. Your mark won't even realise you're doing it. But that's not how I found out.'

'No?'

'No. It was even easier than that.' He turned to the young woman. 'Maria Giulia Rizzo. A young actress living in Siracusa.' He raised a finger and smiled. 'With an Instagram page and Twitter account. Showing pictures of her hand-in-hand with a handsome young basketball player called Gigi.'

Maria Giulia put her hands to her face and laughed. 'Oh, so that's how you did it.'

'As easy as that, my dear. And by the way, he seems like a fine young man, you're very lucky.' She blushed, and he continued. 'So, I just threw him into the conversation and the rest of it – well, I knew she was a good enough actress to improvise her way through whatever I came up with.

'And this is what makes it so easy for the fake medium. All this information is out there, and it's easier to find than ever before. All you need is an internet connection and a name.'

'What if your client isn't on social media?' came a voice from the crowd.

He joined in with the laughter. 'Well in that case, sir, you fall back on the time-honoured "the spirits aren't coming through tonight".

'Just remember. It's all in the act. The people who come

to see a,' he made quotation marks with his fingers, '"psychic" – they want to believe. That's the important thing. They want to believe.' He shrugged. 'Let's face it, who wouldn't? They're easy to persuade because they want to be persuaded. The information is easy to find. And so all that remains is the performance.' He touched the streak of grey in his hair. 'All this? Just for show. Just part of the act. If you want to be a Magus, you need to look the part. Just like this.' He tugged at his moustache and, wincing slightly, pulled it from his face. 'There must be less painful ways of doing this, I'm sure.'

There was a ripple of laughter.

'Okay, I think there's time for just one last question.'

'Yes, I've got one.' A man stood up at the back. 'Why are you doing this?'

'To give you all an entertaining afternoon, I hope. Oh, and to put a little food on the table for Maria Giulia and myself.' He paused for a moment. 'But the main reason is that I hope every person that comes to see me is someone who won't waste their money – or worse – on one of these crooks.'

'Isn't that a bit harsh? I mean, do they really do much harm? Isn't it just a bit of harmless fun at the end of the day? Like checking your horoscope, that sort of thing.'

He shook his head. 'No,' he said. 'It's many things. But it's not much fun. And it's never harmless. And just remember – it's only magic to you. It isn't magic to me. And that's a bit sad, really, isn't it?'

And with that he took two steps backwards, raised a staff above his head and clicked the button set into it that he knew would set off the pyrotechnics. There was a flash as the lights briefly flickered on and off in the auditorium. Then there was a puff of smoke and a slight smell of sulphur. Well, of course there was.

There came raised voices from the audience. A moment of distraction. Sometimes that was all you needed. Then the lights came back on, and the smoke began to disperse. The audience murmured in confusion, heads pointing this way and that as they searched the auditorium for him. And then someone shouted and pointed as they spotted the Magus sitting in the back row and eating popcorn from a paper carton.

'What?' he said, trying not to smile as the applause swelled.

He gave the carton to the small boy sitting two seats away from him, got to his feet, and bowed modestly.

'Just remember,' he said, as the applause died away. 'It's only magic to you. Good night, everyone.'

Chapter 5

'Thank you, Maria Giulia, you were wonderful.'

The Magus stood in front of the mirror, carefully touching up the dye in his hair. Then he dabbed at his upper lip, slightly red from where he'd torn his moustache away with an excess of theatricality, removing the last of the spirit gum.

Maria Giulia smiled. 'Thanks. It was fun. I mean, it was a bit weird. But fun at the same time.'

'Would you be free? If I needed to use you again?'

'Sure. I mean, there's always the risk I'll be on TV by then and everyone will recognise me, but if that doesn't happen,' she shrugged, 'I'll be there.'

'Good. Excellent. And don't worry about being recognised. We'll go a bit further afield next time. Perhaps Taormina. Good tourist crowd there, we could do very nicely.'

'That man at the end. The one who asked you why you're doing this. I still don't know. Why *are* you doing this?'

He sighed. 'As I've said. Because everybody who comes to see me is somebody who isn't going to sign their life savings over to a charlatan in the future. That's why.'

'But aren't you worried? Some of these people might be angry with you.'

He shook his head. 'These are sad, inadequate men and women, Maria Giulia. Not *Cosa Nostra*. No, I'm not worried.' He brightened and reached into his pocket. 'One hundred euros, as agreed. And,' he hesitated for a moment, 'in recognition of a job well done, why don't you let me buy you dinner?'

'Oh.' She blushed. 'That would be lovely. It's just that Gigi and I have plans tonight.'

'Gigi? Oh yes, of course.' He'd forgotten about the basketball player. 'Well, you'd better be on your way then.'

'Okay. It's just we really have arranged things and so—'

'Of course. I'll be in touch. Goodbye, Maria Giulia.'

She hurriedly stuffed the notes into her handbag, gave him a quick smile, and was gone.

He sighed and stared into the mirror. Sometimes he wished he really did have the ability to read minds.

There was a knock at the door, and the face in the mirror looked back and raised an eyebrow. He hadn't expected this. She'd forgotten something, presumably. Or perhaps Steven Spielberg had just called that very minute.

'Maria Giulia?'

He pulled the door open. The man who stood before him looked sweaty and nervous.

'Calogero.'

'Salvatore? What are you doing here?'

'Calogero, we need to talk. Can I come in?'

He shrugged and stepped back from the door. 'Are we on first-name terms, then?'

'Have you anything to drink?'

'This is a dressing room, not a cocktail bar. I think there's a bottle of some bad *grappa*. Or I could make you some terrible coffee, if you like.'

'Grappa, please.'

Calogero nodded and took down a half-empty bottle from the shelf above the mirror. 'Supermarket grappa. Nothing special.'

'That doesn't matter.' Salvatore reached for the bottle, his fingers shaking as he twisted the cap off. 'Have you got a glass?'

Calogero looked around and saw an espresso cup on the table in front of the mirror, coffee dregs still clinging to it. 'Hang on, I'll rinse this out.'

'Doesn't matter.' Salvatore snatched the cup and filled it to the brim. Then he knocked the contents back in one. Then, following a gentle cough, he filled it to the brim again.

'Better?'

'Much.'

'Good. I'm glad to see you haven't lost your dignity, Salvatore. Now, what's this all about?'

Salvatore, his hands still shaking, reached into his jacket and pulled out a sheet of newspaper which he smoothed out on the table in front of them. He jabbed a finger at it.

'This.'

Calogero ran his eyes over the story and nodded. He'd read it that morning. Some sort of terrible accident at the feast of John the Baptist.

'Yes?'

'This is Gianmaria Lombardo.'

Calogero frowned but said nothing.

'Don't piss around. Gianmaria Lombardo. One of us. . .'

'Oh yes. "The Mystical Lombardo", wasn't he? Or was it "Lombardo the Mystic"?'

'This is serious.' He scowled. 'And don't pretend you didn't know him.'

'Mm-hmm.' Calogero refilled the cup and slid it across the table. 'Tell me more.'

'We both have history with Gianmaria, Calogero. And yesterday they pulled his body out of the sea at Aci Trezza.'

'Gianmaria enjoyed a drink, Salvatore. It was a public holiday. Too much sun. Too much of this ,' he made a drinky-drinky motion with his right hand, 'and he ends up in the sea.'

Salvatore reached for the bottle again. 'I know you don't like what we do, but do you have to be so fucking logical about everything?'

Calogero shrugged. 'It seems a more reasonable response than getting drunk on cheap grappa in my dressing room. Anyway, I'm sorry. I know you were close.'

'Close? We weren't close.'

'Oh, really? Well, if you weren't, I suppose this might turn out to be quite convenient for you.'

Salvatore narrowed his eyes. 'What do you mean by that?'

'One less person in a similar field of work to your own. That's all.'

Salvatore slammed his hand on the table and Calogero leaned across to steady the cup. 'Listen to me. I don't think this was an accident.'

'No?'

'He had enemies, Calogero.' He narrowed his eyes. 'Lots of them.'

'Well, of course he did. Given his line of work it would have seemed a bit odd if he hadn't.'

'For Christ's sake, you prick, are you just going to sit there and take the piss?'

Calogero put his head to one side. 'You know, that's an idea. . .'

'As I said, I know you don't like what we do—'

He waved a finger at him. 'No, no. I *despise* what you do. There's a difference.'

'I just want to know: do you know anyone who might have a grudge against us? The psychic community, I mean.'

'"The Psychic Community."' Calogero drawled the words out. 'Well now, that's a grand description. As to anyone with a grudge, I could probably name a few dozen. But that's a fragment, of course. Scratch the surface and you'll probably find hundreds, Dig a little deeper and – oh, I don't know – thousands? Tens of thousands? People defrauded of their inheritances. Of their life savings. Relationships broken, health destroyed. Plenty of motivation there, I imagine.'

'So, you won't help us?'

'Even if I wanted to, what could I do?'

'Go to the cops. Give them names. Anyone you've been in touch with who might just have a motivation for this.'

'I can't do that. Client confidentiality and all that. Besides, why are you so worried? This is, in all likelihood, an accident. If not, it's a personal vendetta. A one-off.'

Salvatore screwed up his eyes and shook his head. 'Okay, then. Maybe I'll go and see Mater Morgana later. Maybe she'll be more helpful. She sure as hell couldn't be any less.'

Calogero was silent for a moment, and then burst out

laughing. He reached for the bottle. 'You know, Salvatore, I think I'll have to join you.'

'What's so funny?'

'Why, you are. You've been doing this for so long now that you've started believing it yourself. Look at you. Terrified and cowering and heading off to see a mad woman pretending to be a witch for protection.'

'She's not pretending.'

'Oh Salvatore, yes she is. And as for the Mystical Lombardo, the only things he ever saw coming were his victims. A mile off.' He got to his feet. 'Go home, Salvatore. Keep the bottle if you like. And sleep well. Whatever happened to Gianmaria is nothing that's going to affect you. I can guarantee it.'

Salvatore stared at him for a moment. 'Okay, Calogero, I'm going. But you know something? This is convenient for you as well, isn't it? Very fucking convenient. And I know that.'

He grabbed the bottle and staggered from the room.

'Remember that, Calogero.'

Chapter 6

Photograph of happy, smiling family in front of *pasticceria*.
Check.
Photograph of cakes.
Check.
Cannolo for Aldo.
Check.

Nedda looked down at the untouched *cannolo* wrapped in a napkin next to her computer. Aldo had assured her that they were excellent and suggested that perhaps if she were ever to pass by there in the future she should make a habit of picking up a box for the office. She had fixed a smile to her face and managed not to slam the door on her way out.

She stared at the screen and tapped, without enthusiasm, at the keyboard.

How did you get a killer headline out of a new pastry shop opening? The answer was you didn't. But the sub-editor, she was sure, would think of something.

She'd grumped her way through the interview with the owners, two nice young men who'd taken over a historic bakery from their uncle, and now she felt guilty. They'd been smiley and cheerful, and not just a little excited at the prospect of a feature in *Catania Nuova*. Nedda, by contrast, had been visibly bored and irritable and the fact they'd given her a box of pastries to take away had, if anything, made things worse as the guilt preyed on her mind.

Okay then, she could still make it up to them. She'd write the best pastry-related article of her life. After the story hit the front pages tomorrow – or, more likely, by the time it snuck on to page thirteen – people would be queuing round the block at the Buscemi Brothers.

She picked up the *cannolo*. A cylindrical tube of fried pastry, dusted with icing sugar and filled with a sweet mixture of ricotta. The ends, as traditional in Catania, had been dipped in pistachio nuts. One of the lads – either Alessandro or Antonio, she couldn't remember – had stressed how committed they were to traditional Sicilian recipes and that were any unfortunate tourist to wander in and ask if they had any chocolate ones they would be ejected on to the street immediately. She'd thought he was kidding. Probably.

She bit into the pastry, and allowed herself to smile as the *scorza* crisply crunched between her teeth. She'd been a bit of a shit to the Buscemi brothers and leaving the pastry uneaten at the side of her desk had been a sulk of truly monumental proportions, but it wasn't too late to put things right. The next time she was passing by she'd pick up a few for *papà*. He would, of course, complain that Catanese *cannoli* were never as good as those from Palermo. He'd still eat them, though.

It was, perhaps, her earliest memory. Sitting outside *papà*'s favourite bar in Palermo, her legs swinging back and forth, unable to reach the ground. *Papà* with a *cannolo* moustache of icing sugar and ricotta caused by over-enthusiastic eating. *Mamma* tutting away as she dabbed at his top lip with a napkin, and then smiling and kissing away the speck of cream from the tip of his nose.

Before Nedda and Angelo had left Palermo for Acireale.

She shook her head, and took another bite of the *cannolo*. Concentrate on the good stuff, Nedda.

The story kind of wrote itself. She did her absolute best but ultimately had to concede there was little more that could be brought to it. It was a pastry shop owned by two nice young men. That would have to be enough. She added a final line about how she'd be rushing back to the Buscemi Brothers for *cannoli* which made her die a little inside, but she felt it needed to be done.

And that left the rest of the day for – what, exactly? Aldo could be depended on to think of something but it would probably involve cooking or soft furnishings or something similar.

Why was he doing this? In most other circumstances she'd have marked him down as a swaggering misogynist shit but Aldo wasn't one to swagger and neither, she had to admit, was he any kind of shit. There were other female journalists on the staff of *Catania Nuova* who seemed to get proper jobs. So why was she the only one who seemed to be stuck in lifestyle article hell?

Maybe he just didn't like her? It was possible, she supposed. Maybe she'd slammed the door just one too many times? Maybe she'd been just a little bit too eager to please? Maybe she just needed to wait her turn.

She shook her head again.

No.

It wasn't easy to get a journalist's card in Italy. A Master's in Journalism had taken two years at the *Università Suor Orsola Benincasa* in Naples. Then the internships. Then the state examinations. Then acceptance into the *Albo dei Giornalisti*. And finally, the day, the great wonderful day, of receiving her press card from the *Ordine Nazionale dei Giornalisti*.

No, it hadn't been easy. And for what? To review *pasticcerie* in a provincial Italian newspaper? She dabbed at the few crumbs that remained of her *cannolo* and licked her finger. Something would have to be done before she either died of boredom or chucked it all in to become a motorcycle mechanic.

She brought up the morning's headlines from the regional papers, and then searched further afield. The story of the death at Aci Trezza had spread beyond Catania, to Palermo, Messina, Reggio Calabria and even further afield, although – by the time she reached Rome – the tone of the coverage was one of tutting at the sorts of sorry accidents that happened in the uncivilised South. There was nothing in any of them to add to the story that she had filed with Stefano.

But the socials were always a good start for digging deeper on a story like this. Somebody on Twitter, Instagram, Facebook – wherever – would have recognised the man pulled from the sea. And they'd have stories about him.

Too many stories, perhaps. The dead man was identified, variously, as a *mafioso* killed in a gangland slaying, as a recently defrocked priest, and as an embittered member of the community who hadn't been selected for the pantomime and who had died in an act of revenge gone hideously wrong. One man suggested it was his cousin, a pizza chef in Aci Castello, but nobody seemed to be taking that seriously.

And yet the *ràis* had seemed to recognise him. *Gesù, it's him.* Had the police spoken to him? She couldn't remember.

She tapped away at the official website for *U pisci a mari*. *Ràis* for the year was Dino Torrisi, described as a fish merchant from Aci Trezza. He smiled out at her from the screen, nut brown and weathered with eyes crinkling in the glare of the sunlight. The last time she'd seen him he'd been bare-chested and covered in fake blood, but she was pretty sure he was the same guy.

If he was a fish merchant, then, the odds were he could be found at the *Mercato Ittico* in Aci Trezza. She frowned. The fish market kept, by normal people's standards, anti-social hours. Catering only to the trade, it opened in the small hours of the morning and closed sometime before eight.

She sighed. Okay. It would be an early start. But she might actually get something useful done. And then she could buy Aldo his precious *cannoli* on her way into work and everyone would be happy.

She shut down her computer. Perhaps it hadn't been a completely wasted day after all. And, so, perhaps, she could treat herself to a little celebration.

Chapter 7

Nedda the Elephant, its white tusks shining in the sunshine, smiled over at the cathedral of St Agatha as it had for centuries.

Technically, it was looking at both the cathedral of St Agatha and the church of the same name. It might seem that this overloaded the piazza, but, having treated Agatha most horribly during the Decian Persecution, the Catanese had turned to her for protection from Mount Etna. Agatha, seemingly, had agreed to let bygones be bygones and so two buildings bearing her name now encroached upon each other in the same part of the *centro storico*. For the *Catanese* at least, one could never have too many Agathas.

When Nedda was a little girl, *papà* would bring her to Don Pappalardo's for ice cream – his own parents, he said, would take him there as a special treat when he was a small boy. He said it was the best *gelateria* in the world and, having few points of reference outside Catania, she could only agree.

Sometimes he would sing her a silly song. Something about *Nedda the Elephant packing her trunk*. It was a nonsense song that he'd heard in London many years ago when he and *mamma* were on holiday. He'd sing it and she'd push at his legs and tell him to stop being silly even though it always made her laugh. And then when she was older, he'd tell her about *U Liotru* as the statue was really called, about how the sculptor had tried to preserve the elephant's modesty by making him/her gender neutral (pronouns were important, it seemed, even in those days). The men of the city, though, had taken great exception to this perceived slight to their virility and so the sculptor had seen fit to add a splendid pair of testicles to the animal in order to appease them. She'd asked *papà* just why people would find the sight of a bollock-less elephant a threat to their manhood but he'd just shrugged and said that men were strange creatures and they were like that. He also told her not to use the word 'bollocks'.

U Liotru went on to become the symbol of the city's football team. As far as she knew, they'd never done very much. She'd asked *papà* why they'd never been very good. But as dad said, elephants must find football terribly difficult, all the more so when weighed down with a large obelisk on their back. And then he suggested it might be best not to say this aloud either.

Nobody quite knew from where or when the original statue came. Carved from lavic stone in ancient times, the sculptor had made some interventions of his own by standing him (by now it was generally referred to as 'him') in a fountain, strapping a large Egyptian obelisk to his back, and adding the aforementioned testicles. And men (for it is usually men) have been using 'under the bollocks of the elephant' as a point of reference ever since. If, that is, they are allowed to use the word 'bollocks'.

Nedda was very close to having been an Agatha. Her

mother, Angelo had told her, had been a huge fan of the English writer Agatha Christie. It was also, she had said, a good Sicilian name. But *papà* got his way and called her Nedda, which, he said, was an even better Sicilian name and, more importantly, much prettier. As a little girl she'd once told him that she'd rather be a writer than be pretty, but he'd told her that she could be both, a solution that kept them both happy.

A ripple of applause came from a nearby table. A little girl, a tiny blonde angel with her hair in red bows, was being held up to the camera of a videographer by her beaming father as everyone else on the table cheered. He held her, kissing the top of her head, as her tiny hands fumbled with the ribbon that secured the enormous parcel on the table before her.

Her mother joined in to help and reached into the box to draw out a child's pedal car. But not just any pedal car. An Audi.

Someone else – an uncle, or just a friend of the family – came over with a box wrapped in paper with the Louis Vuitton logo and pressed it into her hands.

'*Signurina?*' The voice came from Nedda's side. '*Signurina?*'

The speaker was a young girl, not even in her teens.

Nedda looked around. Her mother, she knew, would be nearby, working the tables.

'*Ciao, tesoru,*' she said, knowing what was coming.

'*Signurina,* have you finished those?' The child pointed at the *stuzzichini* on the table.

'Yes, *cara*. You take them.' Nedda passed her a napkin and the girl gathered them together, before popping an olive into her mouth and skipping away happily. She turned to give Nedda a wave and mouthed the words 'thank you' at her.

Nedda waved back and smiled. She would, she was sure, see her again tomorrow. And the day after tomorrow. And, indeed, every day she chose to take a drink here.

In the adjacent bar, the girl's mother was trying and failing to beg money from the family of the golden-haired Louis Vuitton toddler, all of whom steadfastly refused to make eye contact with her.

Nedda sighed and sipped at her wine, which now tasted warm and sour. Were they *Rom*? Refugees who'd made their way from Lampedusa? Or simply Sicilians down on their luck? It made no difference. Whatever her background happened to be, the young girl would not be getting an Audi for her next birthday,

'Mind if I join you?' The words jolted her out of her reverie and she started.

'Stefano?'

'The very same.' He hooked a chair with his foot, dragged it out from under the table and sat down. The young girl she'd given her *stuzzichini* to skipped past again, this time on her way to another table. 'You've been meeting the locals, I see.'

'It makes me sad. She was here yesterday. She'll be here tomorrow.'

'It's a scam. But you know that, of course.'

'I know. But she's just a child.'

'Being run by somebody. Probably her mother.'

'I know,' Nedda repeated. 'But she's just a child.' She changed the subject. 'How did you know where to find me?'

He smiled. 'Well, I'd like to say my journalistic skills were honed to a fine edge during my years in Turin. But actually I just asked around where you liked to go after work, and they said you'd be spending time with your elephant.'

She laughed. 'Of course. But it's important to remember that it *is* my elephant. I feel very proprietorial about it.'

Stefano waved at the *barista*. 'What are you having?'

She shook her head and looked at the remains of her wine. 'I'm fine, really.'

'You don't want another?'

'I'd love another. But I've got the bike.'

'*Gingerino?*'

'No thanks.'

'*Crodino?*'

She shook her head.

'Lemon Seltz?'

'That only makes sense if you get one from a kiosk. It's never the same sitting down in a cafe.'

He spread his hands wide and grinned. 'Okay. I give in. I've exhausted my knowledge of non-alcoholic drinks.'

'You get yourself something, I'm happy just to sit around and chat.'

'Oh good.' He turned to the *barista*. '*Birra Messina* for me.' Then he turned back to her. 'Look, I'm sorry about what happened this morning. This was your story more than mine. You were there when it happened. I was just talking to a priest. I know it's not fair.'

'Well, it wasn't a complete disaster. I bought some excellent pastries. That seems to have put me in Aldo's good books.'

'He's one of the good guys, you know?'

'Sure. Apart from the whole "unreconstructed dinosaur" thing.'

'Trust me, there are a lot worse out there. I had to do all this shit in my first job as well.' The *barista* arrived with Stefano's beer and a plate of *stuzzichini*. Stefano gestured at the plate of snacks. 'Go on, tuck in. Given that you gave yours to the little girl.'

Nedda picked up a small *arancino* and popped it into her mouth, then gasped with pain. 'Ow! Shit!'

'Hot?'

She flapped at her mouth and nodded, before reaching for the dregs of her wine.

'Hotter than expected.' She gingerly touched her tongue. 'I don't think there's any permanent damage, though.'

'Oh good. *Death by arancino* would be a most undignified way to go.' He looked at her empty glass. 'And now you really have to have something else, or I'll be drinking on my own.'

'Okay then. I'll have a *crodino*. I don't really like them but you can kind of persuade yourself they're almost alcoholic.'

'And I'm amazed their marketing department hasn't snapped you up.' He waved at the *barista*. '*Crodino*, please.' He smiled. 'And maybe I should have asked for some non-molten snacks as well. Look, for what it's worth, do you want to know how my day went?'

'Does it involve pastries? If it does, I probably don't need to.'

'No pastries were harmed during the filing of my report. I stood around for hours and eventually the pathologist's verdict was – accidental death.'

'Really?'

'Slight wound to the back of the head consistent with having fallen.'

'I don't get it. Fallen where?'

'Plenty of rocks around there. What do you call them?'

'The *Ciclopi*?'

'That's it. They reckon he probably pulled his boat up to one of them and slipped and fell when he was tying it up. After which, poor guy drowned. Sorry, Nedda. It seemed exciting at the time, but it's a nothing story.'

She shook her head. 'No. That makes no sense. First of all, where's the boat?'

He shrugged. 'Anywhere, I guess. Probably drifted out to sea.'

'And those rocks. There are always people on them at this time of year. Kids tombstoning, all that sort of stuff. And it was the busiest day of the year. There's no way he could have fallen there. He'd have been seen.'

Again, he shrugged. 'Well, we'll see. His boat will probably be found sooner or later. Look, if anything comes in on this, Aldo will pass it on to me.'

'Oh, I think that's very clear.'

'But what I mean to say is, if anything comes in, I'll pass it on to you. We can both work on this. You go and get the old man his breakfast in the morning and the rest of the time you can spend fighting crime. If anything comes up. Which it probably won't.'

Nedda smiled. 'Okay. Thanks.' Then she frowned. 'Wait a minute, do we have a name?'

Stefano shook his head. 'Not yet. They're trying to contact relatives. Something like that.'

'Fair enough. Shame, though. We could have used that for tomorrow's edition.' She looked at his jacket. Something was poking out of the top pocket.

He caught her gaze. 'Something wrong?'

'Just wondering what that is?'

He looked down. 'Oh,' he said. 'Scratch card.'

'Did you win?'

He grinned. 'Never.'

'Anyway, it's kind of you. Cutting me in, I mean. Just one thing, though.'

He spread his hands. 'Ask away.'

'Why would you do this?'

'Oh, I remember what it was like when I started. Nobody ever really gave me a chance. All the hardened *scribachinni* would sooner sell their own mothers than give anyone else a break. I promised myself I'd never do that.'

'Thanks.'

He grinned. 'Okay, so now that's sorted, what say you let me buy you something genuinely alcoholic sometime?'

'This is all part of your mission to give young journalists a helping hand, yes?'

'Absolutely.'

She smiled. 'Okay. I'm not sure I approve of this behaviour. But I guess we can do that sometime.'

Chapter 8

Calogero navigated the elderly Cinquecento along the narrow single-track road of Madonna delle Grazie. Or was it Madonna dell'Aiuto? Hemmed in by dry-stone walls overgrown with thick greenery, he fervently prayed he wouldn't meet someone coming the other way. Santo the stage manager had been good about letting him use his car when it was free, but he imagined the deal was built on always getting it back in one piece.

As if reading his mind, a motorcyclist screamed towards him at terrifying speed, and he yanked the steering wheel to the right as the bike buffeted past him. He checked the rear-view mirror. The biker had his knee down, enjoying the twists and turns of the serpentine road.

Calogero pulled over to catch his breath. Silly bastard. All it would take would be one corner not taken exactly right, or a single car taking up just a little bit too much of the road and. . .

He shuddered, shook his head, stepped out of the car and took out a packet of cigarettes. Morgana, he remembered, disapproved of smoking. He looked around at his surroundings. Just ahead of him was a crumbling roadside chapel to the Madonna. He couldn't remember having noticed it before.

There seemed to be any number in this part of Italy; so many of them ignored and unloved and tumbling into decay.

He leaned against the Cinquecento and smoked away. The evening air was warm and filled with the chirping of cicadas. A car passed in the opposite direction, the driver making great play of yanking at his steering wheel, leaning on the horn and flashing his lights, angry at having to divert his route by a few centimetres.

Calogero was about to grind his cigarette underfoot, and then changed his mind. The land was parched and the risk of accidentally starting a fire very real. He walked along the road to the chapel and took a look inside. The figure of the Madonna was chipped and bleached by the sun, and the interior strewn with discarded cans and fast-food wrappings. Maybe kids came out here to party and make out until the great day came when the bars and *chioschetti* would no longer ask them for ID. The thought made him smile, but then he looked down at the detritus and felt a bit sad. He chose a clear patch of concrete, dropped his cigarette to the floor, and ground it firmly underfoot.

Mater Morgana's house lay a few kilometres further along Madonna delle Grazie. Or Madonna dell'Aiuto. Calogero passed by a few farmhouses, a small vineyard and a hopeful-looking *trattoria* until pulling up outside the rusty iron gates that barred the way to her house.

The roadside, as it had been the whole way, was strewn with debris presumably thrown from passing traffic. He shook his head. Jesus, why did people have to behave like this? Then he remembered the cigarette butt and that he, too, was part of the problem.

He locked the car, pulled at the gate which squeaked open, and made his way up the path. A few chickens pecked around in a ramshackle coop in the front garden.

The figure of a woman could be seen silhouetted in a window, and the strains of music came from within. Classical music. Opera of some kind. Something he felt he should recognise but didn't.

The ground crunched beneath him, and he looked down at his feet and smiled. He bent to wipe the dust from his shoes and dabbled his fingers in the crunchy white crystals that covered the earth, just as the door opened.

'Calogero.'

'Morgana.'

'I suppose you'd better come in.'

'Are you sure I'll be able to?' He touched his fingers to his lips. 'Salt, Morgana? To keep out the devil?'

'Whatever you may be, Calogero, you'd be a poor sort of devil.'

'I'm flattered.'

'Well, you shouldn't be.' He made great play of stepping over the salt circle in front of Morgana's door. 'Stop that,' she snapped, and led him inside.

The front room was warm in the evening sun and smelled of leather and old books. Calogero looked around and nodded approvingly at the dark mahogany bookcases that lined the room.

'Quite the collection.'

'My mother's. Most of it, anyway.' Morgana nodded at a photograph on the wall of a severe-looking woman in her late fifties. He looked to the opposite wall to where the image was reflected in a mirror.

'Captromancy, now?' He smiled. 'A new hobby of yours?'

Morgana rolled her eyes. 'I just happen to like the mirror. You think everything in here has to be linked with my job?' She nodded at a beaten-up leather armchair. 'Take a seat, why don't you? That's the uncomfortable one.'

'Thanks.' He lowered himself gingerly into the chair and felt the springs groaning beneath him. It would be comfortable enough – well, tolerable enough – in the short term. Opposite sat an identical chair, perhaps slightly less battered, next to a side table on which sat a ceramic teapot in particularly hideous shades of orange and yellow. Two equally unattractive cups were placed to the side, steaming away.

'You'll take a cup of herbal tea?'

His face fell. 'I will, thank you. Unless of course—'

'There's nothing stronger. And you need to drive home.'

'Of course.'

'You don't take sugar.' It wasn't a question.

She passed him one of the cups. The steaming brew smelled of ginger and lemon. 'Careful. It's hot.'

He looked up at her. 'You just made it?'

'Two minutes ago.'

'You were expecting a visitor?'

She smiled at him, for the first time. 'Yes. Now why don't you tell me why you're here, Calogero?'

He sipped at his tea and smiled back. 'Why don't you tell me? You seem to know everything already.'

She was about to speak, and then shook her head. 'Let me turn the music down.' She crossed to the opposite side of the room and turned the volume down on an elderly CD player.

'Pretty,' Calogero said. 'But I don't know it.'

'Bellini. *Norma*. I've been playing it a lot recently. I don't know much about opera, but this was my mother's favourite recording. Appropriate for a white witch, she told me.

Me protegge, me difende
Un poter maggior di loro.'

He smiled. '"A power greater than they protects me and defends me"? Or is that just the circle of salt?'

'You don't have to be quite so obvious in your scepticism, Calogero. There was a time that you were very happy to buy into all of this.'

He shook his head. 'You're wrong, Morgana. I may have bought into it. But unlike you, I was never a believer.'

She scowled at him. 'Which makes what you did all the more cynical, doesn't it?'

'Perhaps. But in a way I'm trying to put things right.'

'And how's that going?'

'Slowly.' He sighed. 'Come on then, Morgana. Let's talk. You know why I'm here.'

'Because of Gianmaria Lombardo.'

'It is. Has Salvatore been to see you?'

'He has. Silly fool, stinking of cheap drink. Be lucky if he didn't kill himself driving back in the state he was in.'

'He came to see me as well.'

'And how was he?'

'Not good. To the extent that I let him keep the bottle.' He frowned. 'If I'd known he was coming out here I wouldn't have done that. So, what did he want?'

'He wanted to know if I'd seen anything. About Gianmaria.'

He sighed and rolled his eyes. 'Oh Christ.'

'And don't do that.'

'I'm sorry, but it's tiresome. I'm never sure with Salvatore if he ever believes any of this nonsense or not. He's been in the business so long I'm not sure he knows how to tell fact from fiction anymore.'

Morgana smiled and sipped at her tea. 'And what about me, Calogero? Do you think I believe any of this nonsense or not?'

He smiled back. 'Oh yes, I believe you absolutely do.'

'And so, you had nothing better to do on a warm summer's evening than drive out to see me?'

'Something's bothering Salvatore. I thought it might be worthwhile knowing what it is.'

'Nothing more?'

'Nothing more. I'd like to know. Even though Gianmaria and I were never friends.'

'No. You weren't, were you? And as to why Salvatore came out, he believes that Gianmaria was murdered.'

Chapter 9

'You don't seem very surprised.'

Calogero shrugged. 'I'm not. Gianmaria's death seemed to have hit him hard.'

'I didn't realise they were so close.'

'They weren't. Except, perhaps, financially. But he seemed genuinely shocked. And so it doesn't surprise me to hear that he thought Gianmaria was murdered.'

'And what do you think?'

'I think Salvatore was drunk and emotional when he saw me. And, as far as we know, there's no indication that Gianmaria did anything other than fall into the sea and drown.' He paused, sipped at his tea, and promised himself something stronger when he got back to town. 'Well now, what do you think, Morgana?'

'I don't know. I haven't *seen* anything. But Salvatore thought somebody had paid him a visit. Someone unknown.'

'I take it you don't mean as a client?'

'He said he woke up on the morning of Gianmaria's death and somebody had left a package on his doorstep.'

'Go on.'

'A Tarot deck.'

Calogero laughed. 'Is that all? He'd probably ordered one from Amazon and forgotten about it. "Psychic has Tarot Deck" is hardly a story, Morgana.'

Morgana sighed. 'Perhaps. Perhaps not. Anyway, he brought it over to me. And forgot to take it home again. Would you like to take a look?'

He sighed. He didn't really think there was a choice. 'Sure. Why not?'

Morgana took down a deck of cards from the mantelpiece and spread them out on the table between them.

'Notice anything?'

His eyes scanned the cards, and he frowned. 'Nice expensive pack. Someone spent proper money on this.'

'Try harder. Come on, cards are supposed to be your thing.'

'Gambling's my thing. Not Tarot.' He shook his head. 'One moment. Let's rearrange them.' His hands moved swiftly over the cards. 'Only sixty-three?'

Morgana smiled. 'That's right.'

'One missing. But which one?' He moved them into suits. And then his hands stopped moving and he looked up at Morgana. 'Oh, I see.'

'As you said, there's one missing.'

He nodded and rubbed his chin. 'The Five of Cups.'

'Describe it to me.'

He laughed. 'You don't need me to describe it to you.'

'Indulge me. I want to know you haven't quite forgotten everything you used to know.'

He sighed again. 'Okay. A cloaked figure stands overlooking a river. There are five cups at his feet, three of which are overturned. A bridge leads across the river to a castle in the background.'

'Meaning?'

'Loss. Challenge. Disappointment. Or, if reversed, the opposite of those – recovery, forgiveness, moving on.'

'Good.' She smiled. 'Or are we overthinking it? Perhaps it's more literal than that. Water. A castle in the background.'

'And Gianmaria was found drowned, just a couple of kilometres away from the castle in Aci Castello.'

'Exactly.'

'I think *you're* overthinking this, Morgana.'

'Possibly I am. Probably I am. But it was enough to spook Salvatore.'

'He's easily spooked.'

'He is.' She yawned and stretched. 'But he's worried about something, Calogero. And so are you.'

'Me?'

'You didn't just drive out here for a social call, did you?'

He shook his head. 'No.'

'So you think Salvatore is right to be worried?'

'I think there are people who might not wish him well. Certainly there were those who didn't wish Gianmaria well.'

'But not you, of course?'

'Me?' He shrugged, yet took his time answering. 'Why would I have anything against them?'

'Only you know that. But they, of course, might well have cause to be angry with you. Trailing your little act around the country. Showing the public how it's all done. More than enough reason to bear a grudge.'

There was silence for a moment, and then an owl fluttered

through the open window and sat on the arm of Morgana's chair. She stroked its ears as it snuggled down. Then it turned to look at Calogero and hissed, stretching out a talon with claws extended. He hadn't even realised that owls could hiss before.

He gave an apologetic half-shrug. 'I'm not really an owl person.'

'Menocchio can tell. He's a very good judge of character. Aren't you, *trisoru?*'

Menocchio hissed once more, and turned around, curling himself into Morgana's lap.

'What did he make of Salvatore?'

'The same as both of us. A weak, vain, silly man. As I said, he's a good judge of character.'

'And does he also think Gianmaria was murdered?' Calogero was only half-joking.

'Oh, he does.' Morgana smiled. 'I think we all do. Don't we?'

Chapter 10

Nedda had never been good with a lack of sleep and had passed another disturbed night at home. Angelo had told her that it was hardly surprising and it was nothing that a glass of warm milk with a shot of grappa couldn't sort out. To be fair, that was Angelo's answer to most things. He'd been a loss to the medical profession.

They'd also lost out when Dino Torrisi decided he'd rather make his life on the sea. He was wielding a terrifying-looking blade with perhaps just a little too much enjoyment as he worried away at the swordfish lying on the slab in front of him, separating the head from the rest of the body, before easing it away with a sigh and wiping his bloodied, gory fingers on his apron.

He smiled at Nedda. At least, she thought it was a smile.

'Thanks for agreeing to meet me,' she said.

'Not sure you deserve it,' he replied. 'Not after what happened two days ago. Photographing that poor bastard on the jetty, close up.'

'Just doing my job.'

'Sure. What was that headline in the paper? "Horror in the Sea of Blood"?'

'That wasn't me. That was the sub-editor. It's just the way it works.'

Torrisi nodded, but she couldn't be sure if that meant she was in any way forgiven.

She looked around the market. It stank of fish and fresh blood. By mid-morning, the stench would be unbearable without completely hosing down the interior. Prices, everywhere, were by the kilo. Thirteen euros for stockfish. Seven euros for the flesh from the head or tail of a swordfish. Eight euros for the more prized tranches from the central section.

What had she last paid for a fillet of swordfish? Twelve euros? Fifteen? For a couple of hundred grammes. Although, admittedly, there'd been chips as well. But there seemed little connection between what was served up in restaurants and the bloodied remains lying on these slabs. She understood why tourists were not welcomed here. If, indeed, any could possibly have been brave enough to step inside.

'*Signurina.*' Torrisi looked pissed off, as if she'd been ignoring him. Or, worse, the little woman was disturbed by seeing the gory reality of the fishing trade.

She shook her head. 'Sorry. My mind's elsewhere.'

'Hmph. Okay. Let me clear up and then maybe we can get a drink somewhere.' He swept some offcuts into a plastic bag and held them out to her. 'For your dinner. In the pan with tomatoes, capers. A little garlic. Not too much, mind.' He kissed his fingers. 'Fit for a prince. Or princess.'

She shook her head again. 'Sorry, Dino, I think that's going to be too difficult.'

A smile played across his face. Yet again, the young girl had let him down.

'I'm on my motorbike. I don't have a coolbox or anything. Which means it's going to be in the tank bag all day. After a day in the heat I don't think I'm going to feel like cooking it. For that matter, I don't think the guys in the garage in Catania will be keen on keeping my parking space any longer.'

His eyes narrowed. 'You've got a bike?'

'Sure.'

'What kind?'

'Royal Enfield.'

He smiled, properly this time. 'Good bikes.' Then he shook his head. 'But my wife won't let me ride anymore.'

'I don't understand?'

'Getting too old, she says. Come on then. It's time for breakfast.'

She had, evidently, passed some sort of test.

'*Signore, Signurina?*' The waiter, balding and tanned in singlet and shorts, looked as if he was already prepared for the blazing heat of high summer, even in the relative cool of the eight o'clock sun.

'I'll have a coffee,' said Nedda.

'Single or double?'

She looked over at Torrisi. 'Are we going to be long?'

He grimaced. 'I'd make it a small one,' he said. She had not been completely forgiven, then.

'How about you?' she asked.

'Spritz Etna, I think.' The waiter nodded and smiled. 'They're not just for tourists, you know. And even if they were, I wouldn't care.'

She looked around. There were just six tables outside the bar, practically in the street. The view across to the blue of the sea and the *Ciclopi* made the petrol fumes all worthwhile, however.

'You come here a lot?' she asked.

'Every day. When I'm at work. Not Sundays.'

'You live nearby?'

'Near enough.'

The waiter arrived and set down a coffee for Nedda, an Etna Spritz the colour of sunset for Dino, and a *cornetto* with pistachio. An unusual combination for breakfast, but, if it worked for him, who was she to criticise?

He caught her eying up the spritz. 'You want one?'

'No,' she said, a little too vigorously. 'I'm heading off to work, remember?'

'I remember. You remember that I've finished work?'

'I do.'

'So I can have a spritz. And then go home to bed.'

'Sorry, I wasn't, you know, suggesting anything bad.'

'Everybody thinks that. Tourists out for a coffee and a *cornetto*. All thinking the same thing. Look at the sad old man who needs alcohol to start the day. They never think that that same sad old man has been up to his elbows in fish guts for hours.' He sniffed at his shirt sleeves. 'Sorry, I probably don't smell too good. The guys here are used to it. And I don't notice anymore.'

She noticed the waiter wrinkling his nose just ever so slightly as he passed by and wasn't too sure about that.

'Right then,' said Torrisi. 'What would you like to talk about? And this is off the record, isn't it?' Nedda hesitated. 'If it isn't, then we can just sit here in silence, finish our drinks and go.'

'I don't understand why.'

'Because I don't want my name being in a headline like "The *Ràis* talks of Sea of Blood Horror". No matter who writes it. So you promise me that I'm not going to see anything like that tomorrow?'

She hesitated again, but this time only for a moment, and then nodded. 'I promise.'

'Okay then.' He took a large bite from his pastry. It's a difficult thing to eat a large *cornetto* overstuffed with pistachio cream with any degree of dignity, and the tips of Torrisi's moustache were now frosted with icing sugar and a touch of green. It was a bit horrible in many ways, but it also made her wish she'd had one as well.

He sipped at his drink. 'I was in Venice once, on holiday. You know, I saw people – tourists – drinking spritzes for breakfast up there. And they call us uncivilised.'

Nedda tried to drag the conversation back to the point. 'The man they pulled from the sea. You were the first person to see him. Properly, I mean.'

'I suppose I was.'

'The police are reporting that he fell into the sea, banged his head on one of the rocks and drowned.'

Torrisi nodded. 'Could be. There was so much blood in the water it was almost impossible to tell what was his and what was fake. But from what you say it sounds like he was unconscious when he hit the water.'

'So, you think it was just an accident then?'

He shrugged. 'No reason for it not to be. Surprised it

doesn't happen more often. Hot days, booze and people who can't swim or sail properly. It's a recipe for something bad happening.' He narrowed his eyes. 'Why do you ask?'

'No reason.'

'That's not true, is it? You went to the trouble of getting up early and meeting me in a room full of stinking dead fish. Oh, and buying me breakfast.'

'I'm buying you breakfast?'

'Sure. So, again, why do you ask?'

'The police haven't released his name yet. I think I can scoop them. You know his name, don't you?'

'Why would you think that?'

'I heard you. *Gesù, it's him,* you said.'

He grumbled into his spritz. 'He was covered in water and red dye and maybe even some actual blood. I couldn't be sure.'

'Did the police talk to you?' He shook his head. 'So go on, Dino. Who do you think it was?'

He sighed. 'Do I get another spritz?'

'Depends if I get a name.'

'Okay.' He clicked his fingers at the waiter. 'I think his name was the Great Lombardo.'

Nedda stifled a laugh. 'The what?'

'The Great Lombardo. Or Lombardo the Great.'

'What sort of name is that?'

'He was one of those magicians. Fortune tellers, whatever you want to call them.'

'How could you know that?'

'*Signurina*, you're a journalist, aren't you? Just keep your eyes open as you walk around the town. Here, Jaci, Catania. You see posters up for them everywhere.'

'So you're saying he was a psychic?'

He laughed. 'I don't think he was.'

'I mean a medium. Or whatever you call them.'

'I prefer to say con artist.'

'Whatever. So you think there might have been people with a grudge against him?'

'Oh, I can well imagine that.' He smiled, slyly. 'Why? Would you like it better if it were murder?'

'No, of course not.'

'Really?'

'Of course not,' she repeated.

'But it would be a big old story for a young girl like yourself?'

A young girl like yourself. She ignored the insult. 'It would. Yes.'

'Mmm. But I think you're going to be disappointed. Chances are he really just slipped and banged his head. A few minutes in the water would have done the rest. He might have been a psychic but he didn't see that coming.' He chuckled. 'Sorry. I probably shouldn't say things like that. He might have been a fraud, but it's also possible that he genuinely believed it.'

'Is that likely?'

He shrugged. 'Maybe. He was certainly tooled up with enough gear.'

'I don't understand.'

Torrisi's hands went to his throat. 'When the woman was giving him CPR I noticed his neck. He was wearing the *cornicello*. Maybe he thought that would help him ward off evil.' He shook his head. 'Didn't work. Obviously.'

Nedda frowned. 'But lots of people do that. I've think I've got one myself somewhere.'

'Not just that. He also had a nail on a leather thong. Iron, I imagine. And a silver amulet. The *mano figa*.'

'Meaning?'

'All signs of protection against evil. Now either it was just a fashion statement or he really was scared of something.'

Chapter 11

'Aldo, I've got a name for you.'

Lentini put down the newspaper he was reading, took off his glasses and polished them on his sleeve. 'I've got a name for you too, Nedda. Lots of them, in fact.' Then he smiled, a little weakly, and looked apologetic. 'No, that's not fair. But I have got lots of names – none of them complimentary – for those *cafoni* at *Stampa di Sicilia*. Take a look at this.' He tossed the newspaper across the desk.

And there he was. Gianmaria Lombardo. Single. Forty-five years old. No wife, long-term partner or kids as far as anyone knew. There were multiple photos: Gianmaria in a bar, playing football, at the beach in Speedos with hands on hips and an unfeasibly hairy chest. That one Nedda didn't need to see. He was described as a businessman and entrepreneur.

She frowned. 'Aldo, how did they get this?'

'I've no idea, Nedda. But I suspect one of the cops leaked it.'

'Why would they do that?'

He seemed surprised. 'Money, of course. Not very much. But probably enough for a pizza night out and a few beers. Even cops need the occasional treat, I suppose.'

'Why would they even want this? *Stampa di Sicilia* are based in Palermo, right? Do we not even get first dibs on our own deaths anymore?'

'I suppose it's a good story for them as well. No mobsters, no corrupt politicians. Just a tragic death on a local holiday. Hell, for them it practically counts as a Good News story.'

Nedda tapped the front page. 'They describe him as a "businessman".'

Aldo raised his eyebrows. 'That surprises you – why?'

'The guy I met this morning described him as, well, a psychic, I suppose you'd say. A medium.'

'Oh. Right.'

'Does that surprise you?'

'It does a bit. But I'm not sure it's relevant. I don't know if there's much more of a story in this, Nedda.'

'Aldo, I got up at an unholy hour and stood in a market full of stinking fish with a very grumpy man in order to get this name.'

'I'm sorry, Nedda. Would it help if I said that displays fine journalistic instincts?'

'A little. I had to buy him breakfast as well.'

'Oh well. In that case, the least I can do is buy yours.'

'Really?'

'Yes. Pop out to that place you went the other day – the Buscemi Brothers, something like that, wasn't it? – and pick up a box of something nice for the office. I'll pay you back.'

'Oh, so I still have to go out and pick it up myself?'

'If you would. Thank you. And don't slam the door,' he said, about a second before Nedda slammed the door.

***

Gianmaria Lombardo had drowned off the coast of Aci Trezza during one of the biggest festivals of the year. A festival during which quite a lot of booze was downed. It was perhaps not that surprising for a middle-aged man to have one too many and to have fallen from the rocks or from a boat and into the sea. There was, almost certainly, no story in this.

It was just that the alternative was pastry shops and lifestyle features. Nedda sighed, and scrolled further and further through the social media postings. Pages and pages of tributes and happy photographs.

I hope this prick is burning in hell right now.

She blinked. Whoa. That came out of nowhere.

There's a lot of happy people in the Catania area tonight.

The comments below were the expected mixture of 'Shame on you', *Che vergogna, Che minchia* and ever more creative abuse, but the original poster had not risen to the bait and had fallen silent.

She clicked on his profile. *'AngryinAci'* was the handle. She scrolled through his posts. The name seemed appropriate in that very few things seemed to make him happy. No name, but a photograph and, crucially, his place of work.

Well, now.

Nedda smiled. There was still breakfast to be bought, but the day might turn out to be more interesting than she'd thought.

Chapter 12

You really had to want to go to the beach if you lived in Acireale. Oh sure, you could take a car or you might be lucky enough to find a bus going in the right direction at the right time but, for most people, the main route was to take the stony path that snaked back and forth, back and forth all the way down the two-hundred-metre drop to the tiny seaside village of Santa Maria la Scala. The walk, slippery underfoot and mercilessly exposed to the sun on a hot day, took about fifteen minutes to descend. And considerably more on the way back. Holy Mary of the Staircase. It wasn't just a clever name.

Giovanni Dionigi Galeni had an unusually interesting career path for a farmer's boy from Calabria. Abducted by pirates at the age of seventeen, he served as a galley slave, worked his way up to become a corsair in the Ottoman Navy, served as Chief Governor of Alexandria and, by now calling himself Uluç Ali Paşa, became the commander-in-chief of the entire Ottoman Navy. Along the way he also managed to get himself mentioned in *Don Quixote*.

Yes, the farmer's boy from Calabria had certainly done well

for himself. The only reason, perhaps, that the Italians never tried to claim him as one of their home-grown heroes was his annoying habit of attacking them. He seemed particularly keen on having a go at Sicily, and Acireale in particular.

The Spanish, rulers of the island and tired of all this by now, built the *Fortezza del Tocco* to defend it. Ali was cold in his grave by the time they completed it but, still, you could never be too careful. There it stood, keeping watch over the seas, until falling into disuse in the nineteenth century. It stands there to this day, its crumbling walls sloping away into the vertiginous hundred-metre drop down to Santa Maria la Scala.

And here, it seemed, Mr Angry of Aci plied his trade as custodian of the museum.

'Mr Angry?'

'You what?'

'Sorry. I mean, *signor* Caruso?'

The man behind the metal gate nodded. 'That's me.' He sipped from a can of Moretti, but said nothing more.

'My name's Nedda. Nedda Leonardi. I'm from *Catania Nuova*.'

'Never heard of you.'

'No reason you should have. But I was down in Aci Trezza two days ago. When they pulled that poor man out of the sea.'

He snorted. 'Poor man, my arse.'

'I saw your postings on the socials. I thought maybe you'd like to talk.'

'What, you think maybe I did it?'

'I don't know. Did you? The police are saying it's an accidental death.'

Again, he snorted. 'Accidental death, my—'

'Your arse. I know. Are you saying he was murdered?'

'I'm not saying anything. And why should I talk to you?'

'No reason at all. But the fact you hope he's burning in hell tonight made me think you had strong opinions you might like to share with me.'

He looked her up and down. 'Why would I do that?'

Nedda sighed. 'You know, that *"AngryinAci"* handle really suits you.'

He grimaced but did his best to turn it into a thin smile. 'Yeah, well. Okay then. Come in for a minute if you want to talk.'

She was about to speak, and then paused. She looked him up and down. Early thirties, perhaps, with a shaven head and what might have been either designer stubble or just a heavy five o'clock shadow. An Inter Milan shirt, shorts and Crocs completed the picture. He looked normal enough, but still. She looked around, but there was no-one else on the path.

'Oh look, you think I'm some sort of psycho? Fine, let's talk here.' He rattled the gate. 'I'll keep this between us if you like.'

'It's not that, it's just—'

'Make your mind up. All the same to me.'

She hesitated and then nodded. 'Okay. Let's go inside.'

Mr Angry's office was something of a shrine to Inter Milan, with framed photographs – some in black and white, some in colour – covering almost every scrap of space on the wall.

Current players, ex-players, Nedda couldn't be sure. None of them meant anything to her. A jersey in a wooden display case held pride of place, and he nodded with satisfaction. He tapped the glass. 'Twenty ten replica shirt. Signed by Jose Mourinho.' He peered more closely at the glass, fearing that perhaps he'd left a smudge.

'Is he a player, then?'

'What?'

'Jose whatshisname?'

'I take it you don't work on the sports desk?'

'No.'

'Jose Mourinho. The legend. He took us to the Champions League in twenty ten.'

'Oh. Right. That's good?'

'Biggest prize in sport.' He nodded at the glass case. 'This was in my dad's restaurant. Jose came in one day, just like that, with his wife and kids. Just on holiday like everyone else. Not here, of course, this was up in Taormina.'

'Right.' Nedda paused. 'We're a long way from Milan down here.'

'You've just noticed?'

'Well, I'm wondering – why don't you support Catania?'

'Why would you support Catania?'

'I don't know. Just with them being local, I suppose.'

He laughed. 'You really don't know about football, do you?'

'Never really saw the point of it. As far as I can see it just seems to make people angry. It doesn't seem like much fun.'

'Ninety-nine per cent of the time it isn't. It's the one per cent that keeps us going.'

The conversation wasn't proceeding quite as expected and she was, perhaps, learning rather more than she wanted to know about football. 'Taormina,' she said. 'Nice place for a restaurant.'

Mr Angry's expression darkened. 'It was.'

'Oh, I'm sorry. He's not there anymore?'

'The restaurant's long gone. And *papà* – well, *papà* is gone as well.'

'I'm sorry,' she repeated.

'And they're both gone because of that piece of shit who died two days ago.'

'I don't understand.'

'Don't understand as in you don't understand football?'

'As in I don't understand the connection.' She got to her feet. 'I'm not sure if you want to talk or if you just want to be angry at something or someone. Up to you.'

He waved a hand at her. 'Okay. Sorry. Go on, sit down.' He sighed. 'You ever been to a psychic?'

The question threw her and she couldn't stop herself from giggling. Then she remembered this was the second time that day that psychics had come up in conversation, and she forced a serious expression onto her face.

'You're laughing. Of course you are. I guess most people would. But then *papà* wasn't most people. So, you've never been to a psychic?'

'No.'

'Medium, card-reader, astrologer, spiritual adviser. Anything like that?'

'No.' She frowned. 'Well, there was Don Biagio at Santa Maria, I suppose. But I was only seventeen at the time.'

'Yeah, well I don't imagine Don Biagio gave you financial advice on your business, did he?'

'No. It was more warnings about unsuitable boys. Which kind of meant all boys. I didn't really take them on board.'

'Thing is, *papà* did. Financial advice, I mean. Not unsuitable boys. It was difficult for us when *mamma* died. I suppose you could say he kind of went to pieces. Got into a bit of a state. That sort of thing. And then one night, he's watching television – well, he's not watching it, he's just clicking away at the remote control, surfing between channels – and he comes across one of these psychic programmes. One of Berlusconi's shit channels, you know? Then the next day he tells me he's going out to see one of these fortune tellers. And I think, poor *papà*, he misses *mamma* so much and if one of these people can make him feel better, then where's the harm?' He scowled as he saw the expression in her eyes. '*Papà* wasn't stupid, you know.'

'I never said he was.'

'You thought it, though. Everyone does. "How could you be so stupid." Can't remember how many times I've heard that. He never went to university, but he was smart.

'I don't remember exactly how many of these people he saw. One of them said she was a witch, her I do remember. Mater Morgana was her name, or at least that's what she called herself. She said she couldn't help him. Then there was Salvatore Someone. He read cards, things like that. Might still do for all I know.

'But the one he saw the most was Gianmaria Lombardo. The Mystic, he called himself. *Papà* came home one day and I hadn't seen him so happy in months. *Mamma*, he said, was looking down on us. And she wanted us to be happy. But just once wasn't enough, you understand? Every month he spent a little less time at the restaurant and a little more time with people telling him how much *mamma* loved and missed us both. Every month a few more bills would drop through our letterbox. At first he would tear them open. And then he stopped doing even that.

'Then one day he drove off to work. And late afternoon one of the guys in the restaurant calls me, because the boss hasn't turned up. And he starts shouting at me because they're all pissed off because nobody's been paid for weeks. So I put the phone down, and I call the cops.

'They found his car. He'd turned off the road, pulled into a car park and sat there looking down upon Taormina. And when he had looked all he wanted, he walked to the cliff edge. And he carried on walking.

'That place would have been mine one day, you know? It was a good place. Classy. Instead of which I'm acting as guardian for this crappy little museum that people only ever stop at because they think they might be able to get a bottle of water or an ice cream or a beer to break up the walk back from the beach. The rest of the time I do odd jobs wherever I can fit them in. But that's not what matters. What matters is that *papà*'s last few minutes on earth were spent in despair. And loneliness. But now Gianmaria Lombardo, Lombardo the Mystic, is dead. And I'm glad.

'So in case you're wondering: no, I didn't kill him. But I tell you this, I'd shake the hand of whoever did.'

'You said there'd be a lot of people celebrating in Catania tonight?'

He nodded. 'And elsewhere. The Great Lombardo was all over this part of the country like a rash.'

'I've never heard of all this.'

'Why would you? What if you've ended up losing your life savings to people like this? What if you've confessed all the nasty shit there is in your life to them? You feel stupid. You feel embarrassed. So you shut up about it. And even if you don't, the police aren't going to do anything. How can they?'

She got to her feet. 'Okay. Thanks for your time. And, well, I'm sorry about what happened.'

He nodded. 'Yeah, well. He wasn't the only one.'

'So what are you going to do now?'

'I thought I might get drunk tonight and raise a glass to *papà*. But it won't bring him back. All that'll happen is that I'll wake up in the morning with a stinking hangover and feel even worse. So maybe I'll just go for a beer and a game of cards with my buddies later on. And that's probably all.'

Nedda smiled. 'Okay. Well thanks for your time again. Listen, can I quote you on any of this?'

He shook his head. 'No deal. You mention my name and I'll say I've never met you in my life.'

'Okay. How about I just refer to Lombardo as "a controversial figure"?'

He nodded. 'I guess I can live with that.' He moved to the window, shielding his eyes from the sun shining out over the bay. 'I've only got one more week here until this place closes. Nobody comes here, as I said. They say it needs major work. The walls aren't safe. I know that. It's like everywhere in this damn country. Nobody spends any money until it's too late.'

He looked back over his shoulder and pointed at the wall,

where a large hunting rifle was hanging. 'You see that there? I've taken it down once or twice. Felt the weight in my hands. Wondering if it still works.'

He turned back, tapping the glass of the window. 'You know, some days I'd stand here and I'd look at people making their way down to the beach. All happy and smiling. And then I'd see them, hours later, sweaty and red-faced and their feet all torn up because they hadn't got proper shoes. And I'd think – all it would take would be one misstep. One slip on the rocks. And how long might you lie there, with the sun beating down upon you, praying for somebody to come? Wondering if anybody would. And I would think, perhaps I'd be the only one to notice. And what would I do if I saw him – Lombardo – lying there? Would I just watch him? Or would I take that gun down again?'

He grinned at her, and she stepped away from him, rattling the doorknob and yanking at the door, which scuffed its way across the floor.

He didn't move at all. Just continued to smile. And then she was out into the warm evening air. She turned and looked back, and he was still there, still smiling through the window. And so she ran, as carefully as she could, back up the slope to where the bike was parked.

Chapter 13

'Have you ever been to a psychic, *papà*?'

Angelo paused, a forkful of *caponata* and swordfish in his hand. 'That's not a question I'd been expecting, Nedda. Least of all over dinner.'

'Well, have you?'

'Why do you ask?'

'After *mamma* died. Did you never think about it?'

He frowned. 'No. Why would I?'

'But you missed her so much.'

'Of course I did. But I knew it wouldn't help. What's more, I know she'd have broken my balls if I'd done something so damn silly.' He frowned again. 'Hmm. Probably shouldn't have said that in front of you.'

Nedda smiled. 'It's okay.'

He jabbed a fork at her, before returning to his swordfish. 'But don't let me hear you using that around the house.'

'No, *papà*.'

'I don't want to hear that you've been using it in the office either.'

'I won't, *papà*.' She paused for a second. 'Did you like it there?'

'Where?'

'The nineteen fifties.'

'Cheek.' He flicked a napkin at her. 'I wasn't even around in the nineteen fifties.' He lowered his voice. 'Not quite, anyway. So why the sudden interest in psychics?'

'The man who died two days ago. It turned out he was a medium.'

Angelo shrugged. 'They can drown like anyone else, I suppose.'

'Yes, but. . . there was a man I found. Via the internet.' He raised his eyebrows, and this time it was Nedda's turn to flick a napkin at him. 'Not like *that*. He'd posted a message about hoping the guy was burning in hell and that there'd be a lot of happy people in Catania tonight.'

He rubbed his chin. 'Hmm. I can imagine that could happen.'

'Do you think somebody might have been angry enough to kill him?'

'Again, it's possible. Imagine that your *mamma* or *papà* have passed away and you discover that all their property has been left to the cat because the Great Zibibbo or somebody told them to. I imagine that might be motive enough.'

'But did you ever come across this? When you were in the *Guardia*, I mean?'

'Me, no. But I had plenty of friends who were always pulling these people in. For tax evasion, you know?' He smiled. 'They might have been psychic, but none of them ever saw the police knocking at the door in time for them to stash the money away.'

'Uh-huh.' She smiled. 'You've still got friends in the police, right?'

'I have.' He frowned. 'Oh no. What does this mean?'

'I just want to know more about the man who died. Gianmaria Lombardo.'

'And why, exactly?'

'Just in case he didn't drown.'

'Did Aldo Lentini tell you to do this?'

'Absolutely not. He wanted me to report on a new *pasticceria* and buy him some *cannoli.*'

'Nice. Were they good?'

'Very.'

'Hmph. You never buy me *cannoli.*'

'Next time I pass by I'll pick some up for us both.'

'Okay then.' He returned to his swordfish. 'I'll see what I can do.'

'Mamma. Mamma.'

The little girl pulled and plucked at her mother's hair.

'Mamma. Mamma. *Wake up, please.*'

She grabbed at her shoulders and tried to shake her awake. Her mother remained immobile, slumped over the steering wheel, the noise of the horn deafening in the closed space.

Again she grabbed at her mother, tears streaming down her face. Screams and shouts came from outside the car.

'The girl's alive.'

'Grab her. Somebody get her out, for God's sake.'

She felt something, someone, grabbing at her legs and pulling her towards the door. She screamed and kicked out, but then an arm was around her waist, dragging her backwards. She reached out towards her mother, stretching her hands into her hair.

And then she was outside, being carried.

'Run!'

She was carried towards a group of people, many in tears, some crossing themselves and praying.

'Child, come here. Don't look.'

They gave her into the arms of a woman. Perhaps mamma's age, perhaps a little older. She held her close. She smelled good, like mother. Yet the stink of petrol and burning rubber was overpowering.

There was a sound of thunder from behind her, but the woman held her tight to stop her turning round. And then she caught sight of her hands and saw that they were covered in blood.

'Nedda? Nedda?'

Angelo's hands were on her shoulders, shaking her. Gently at first, and then with increasing force.

'Nedda. Wake up, *cara.*'

She shook her head, trying to shake away the nightmare before slumber pulled her back down again.

'Come on, Nedda. Don't go back to sleep. The nightmare will only start again.'

She shuffled herself upright. Then she put her head in her hands and rubbed at her eyes. Her forehead was damp with sweat.

'Was I crying?'

Angelo nodded. 'And worse.'

'Shit.' She shook her head again, more violently this time, as if trying to physically shake out the images. 'Sorry. For swearing, I mean.' For once, her father seemed inclined to let it go.

'The usual?'

She nodded. 'It hasn't happened for so long. And now, in the last couple of days. . . ' Her voice trailed off.

'Because of what you saw. All that fake blood. And then the man in the sea.'

'Probably.'

He patted her shoulder. 'Come on, then. Only one way to deal with this.'

'Really, *papà*, I'll just go back to sleep.'

'No, you won't. If you do that straightaway you'll go back into the dream. Which will wake me up on the other side of the house and possibly the neighbours as well. Come on. Pull on a dressing gown. I'll see you downstairs.'

The bomb, it seemed, had not been aimed at Rosa Giorgianni but rather at a prominent anti-mafia judge in the car in front. Detonated by remote control, it had efficiently taken out the judge's car, those on either side and two police outriders. For want of neglecting the early-morning check underneath the car, five people were now dead.

No, the bomb had not been aimed at Rosa Giorgianni. But an investigative journalist was a nice little bonus.

Six years old is no age at which to become a celebrity. At first Nedda had thought that the second glances and double-takes that she received were merely due to her bright red hair, an inheritance from her grandmother. And then, when she was older, she realised that she would always be the little girl in the photograph, held in the arms of a stranger, her bloody hands held out towards the camera, screaming as the car containing the body of her mother exploded. The photo had swiftly become one of the *leitmotivs* for the brutality of *Cosa Nostra*.

But Angelo had not wanted his daughter to be a poster girl for anything and, within months, had moved the two of them as far across the country as possible. He'd moved to Palermo to be with Rosa, but now it was time to return home. Catania, he knew, shared the same problems as his adopted city, but it was at least a long way away. There would be no daily memories of *mamma* here. And, with time, perhaps the nightmares would stop.

Yet even in Catania, the rumours and the whispers would not go away. Little Nedda with the Red Hair was soon identified as Little Nedda the Girl in the Photo. She had thought the whispers and pointing in the playground made her special until she was in her early teens. Then she stopped wanting to be special, and just wanted to slap those who thought she was.

'Better?' said Angelo.

'Much.' She wrapped her fingers around the mug. The night was warm, but the heat was still comforting. 'Are you sure this is the right thing, though?'

He shrugged. 'Of course. We used to give you warm milk with honey all the time when you were a little girl. Sometimes I put a shot of grappa in there as well.'

'You gave me grappa when I was a kid?'

'Sure. Only way to get you to go to sleep at times.' He took a sip from his mug. 'Guaranteed to cure any cold or fever. So my mother said, at any rate.'

'And it works for bad dreams as well?'

'Of course it does. Warm milk, honey and grappa. It's like drinking a big hug.'

Nedda closed her eyes and breathed in the aroma from

the steaming drink. She certainly felt better but, given the ingredients, that was only to be expected.

'Did you ever have them?' she said. 'Nightmares, I mean.'

Angelo shook his head. 'No. But then I saw a lot of things when I was a cop. Bad things.'

'But this was *mamma*.'

'I know. But I never had any bad dreams. Perhaps because I didn't sleep very much at all. Not until we came here.'

'Do you think she'd have liked it here? In Catania or Acireale?'

'She'd have kicked my arse if I'd ever suggested leaving Palermo. But she always loved the sea, and so part of me thinks that she might have looked out upon the *Ciclopi* one morning and decided that she might just have been able to forgive me.'

Nedda gave a weak smile, and then changed it to a scowl. 'I hate this, you know?'

'You mean the dreams?'

'I mean the nightmares.'

'I know you do.'

'It's because they make me feel weak. And I hate that. And I think *mamma* would have hated it too. In some ways it makes me feel like I'm letting her down.'

'Now that's silly.'

'Is it?'

'She'd have been proud of you. Hell, she *was* proud of you. And she loved you very much.' He paused. 'Which isn't to say that she didn't think you were a colossal pain in the arse at times.'

'Oh.'

'I'm proud of you too, of course.' He cleared his throat. 'And I love you very much. And, yes, if I have to say it, I also find you a colossal pain in the arse at times.'

'Oh,' she repeated. 'And this is supposed to help me sleep better how exactly?'

Angelo grinned. 'I meant that in a good way.'

'There's a good way?'

'Of course. When you were a little girl you never stopped asking questions. But that's okay. That's what your mother did. And, yes, people found her a pain in the arse as well.'

'The wrong people, though?'

He sighed, and suddenly looked tired. 'Yes. The wrong people.'

Nedda yawned and drained the remains of her milk. 'Okay. I'm properly tired now. Can I go back to bed?'

'Do you promise no more nightmares?'

'No more nightmares. Promise.'

'Okay then.'

She bent to kiss the top of his head. 'Goodnight, *papà*.' He showed no sign of moving. 'You're not going to bed?'

'Not just yet. I think I'll stay up for a bit. Maybe read a little.'

'You're not going to get all sad or anything, though, are you?'

'Maybe just a little. But not in a bad way. Sometimes that's all right.'

'If you're sure.'

'I am. Now stop being a pain.'

She smiled. 'I'll stop. Goodnight, *papà*.'

'And Nedda?'

'Yes?'

'I meant what I said. I really am most proud of you, you know?'

She kissed the top of his head once more, rubbed his shoulders, and made her way upstairs.

Chapter 14

'Stefano?'

Nedda had spotted him, hunched over the counter, in the *tabaccheria* across the road from *Catania Nuova*.

'Stefano?'

He showed no sign of having heard her, so she reached out and grabbed his shoulder.

'Stefano? It's me, Nedda. We used to work together, oh, about forty-eight hours ago.'

'Nedda?'

'Oh how lovely. You do remember me!'

He rubbed his forehead. 'Sorry. I'm miles away at the moment.'

'I can tell.' She peered at him. 'You look rough.'

'I feel rough. I'm not sleeping well right now.'

'Why do you think that is?'

'Dunno. Just overwork, I guess.'

'So, what is it? Crafty cigarette?'

He looked pissed off for a moment but then smiled and threw up his hands. 'You got me,' he said. 'But I'm giving up next week, promise.'

She noticed a bunch of scratch cards in his hands. 'You

still playing those?'

'I thought I needed something to replace cigarettes.'

'Are they working?'

'No. I can't get the ends to light.' She laughed and he smiled at her. 'This joke was brought to you by the year 1975. Shall we go get a coffee from a kiosk?'

'That'd be nice.'

He made to walk away from the counter but the shop owner called him back. '*Signore*,' he called, rubbing thumb and forefinger together. 'You forgot something.'

'Ah.' Stefano smiled, and took out a twenty-euro note. 'Mug's game,' he said. 'Guess that means you're buying the coffees.'

'Is it the Lombardo story? Seriously, you look tired.'

He shook his head and yawned. 'Seen worse things than that. And what do you mean, "story"? It's not a story.'

'Are the police still saying that?'

'Autopsy showed the guy hit his head. They reckon he was tying up his boat on one of the *Ciclopi* and slipped.'

'What was he doing out there?'

'Trying to get a better view of the festivities, I guess.'

'But again, where's his boat? It's been nearly three days now. And why didn't anyone see him?'

He shook his head. 'I don't know. The boat will be some-where in the middle of the Med by now. It'll turn up at some point.' He yawned. 'I don't really care. It's a nothing story.'

'Wow. You're turning the charm on this morning.' She pointed at the box full of *cannoli* in the bag hanging on her shoulder. 'Have one of these. I think you need the sugar.'

'In the street?'

'Sure. If we leave them in the office Aldo will scoff them as soon as we take our eyes off them.' She opened the box and, even amongst the odour of cigarettes and petrol that permeated the baking hot streets, the smell of sweet pastry and ricotta filled the air.

He grumbled something under his breath but took one anyway. His eyes brightened as his teeth broke through the shell and into the soft filling.

'Okay. You might be right. These are good.'

'Aldo thinks so too. So much so he's given me a new job. Every day I'm supposed to pick up a box for the office.' She smiled at him. 'Better?'

'Much.'

'Good. Quick question. What if Lombardo's death wasn't accidental?'

'But it was.'

'But what if it wasn't?'

'Why would you think that?'

'There was a message on the socials. Somebody wrote that plenty of people in Catania would be celebrating. On account of the guy being a medium.'

Stefano shrugged. 'That's possible. It's an industry built on exploiting people. If someone finds out they've been played, I can imagine them bearing a grudge.' He scratched at his chin, and looked cross for a moment, aware that an inadequate shave had left a layer of stubble. 'What's this guy's name?'

'Caruso. First name Elio. He lives in Aci. Goes by the name of "*AngryinAci*" on the socials.'

'And is he?'

'Yes. Although he was willing to talk.'

'Wait a minute, you've been to see him?'

'Sure.'

'Was that smart?'

'What do you mean?'

'Guy expresses pleasure in somebody dying and you thought it was a good idea to go round to his house alone?'

'He's an angry middle-aged man living alone and working in a crumbling museum on the outskirts of Acireale. Not a serial killer.'

'Nedda, that pretty much sounds like the definition of a serial killer. Seriously, don't do that again.'

'Oh wait, you're going to tell me I need a big strong man to go around with me? I went to a *pasticceria* on my own as well. Should I have waited for you?'

He frowned. 'Yes. No. Maybe. It's just – well, just take care, that's all.' He took another *cannolo* from the box. 'You know, I wonder if we can finish these before we get back to the office?'

'Found anything?' asked Stefano. For a moment, his hand rested gently on her shoulder, but then she moved her chair forward, just an inch, and he removed it. 'You've been chained to that computer all morning.'

'I'm not sure. Gianmaria Lombardo seems to have kept his nose pretty clean. There's a story from *La Sicilia* a few years ago, when he was fined a thousand euros for tax evasion.'

'Only a thousand? I'm surprised they even bothered reporting that.'

'It was part of a wider piece. About how big the psychic industry is. I had no idea.'

'I suppose I can understand that. It must be one of those industries with hundreds of thousands of customers, but where no one actually admits to using their services.' He paused. 'You really do think there's something in this, don't you?'

Nedda shrugged. 'I don't know. But it's a compelling story, I think. And as much as I appreciate a good *cannolo*, it's more interesting than a new *pasticceria* opening up.'

Stefano nodded towards Lentini's office. 'And what does the old man think of you spending your valuable time playing detective?'

'As long as I bring him his coffee and breakfast goods in the morning, and supply a suitable number of feel-good articles over the course of the week, he seems happy enough.'

He rubbed his chin. 'Breakfast. That gives me an idea. Why don't we do a late brunch?'

'Brunch?'

'Yes. It's an exciting new concept our American cousins have thought up. And I know just the place.'

'Haven't you got work to do?'

'Nothing that can't be put off. Come on. It'll do you good to get away from that computer. Besides,' he grinned, 'I've got an idea for you. Something that might be even more exciting than tax evasion.'

'You have?'

'I have. I'll tell you over brunch.'

'Can't you tell me now?'

'Uh-uh.' He smiled and waved a finger. 'Over brunch. Come on, I'm hungry. I think the *cannoli* have made me feel like eating things again. If you don't come, I'll start wasting away.

Nedda sighed. 'Okay. Again, I'm not saying I approve of this. But on the other hand, I am kind of hungry.'

'Great. Let's go.'

Chapter 15

Nedda was vaguely aware that there existed a TV station called *Bella Catania* but only as one of those ultra-cheap local channels that lurked in the higher numbers of the TV guide.

She rarely needed to stop in Cannizzaro, a dormitory town outside Catania, halfway to Aci Castello. It seemed an unlikely place to house a TV station but that was the address Stefano had given her.

He'd been infuriatingly vague over what he insisted on calling brunch, merely saying that there might be something worth checking out. A number of people on the psychic circuit, he said, occasionally turned up on *Bella Catania* in the late-night slots when fools and their money were more easily parted.

She sped through dull streets lined with duller shops and malls and petrol stations. She must have ridden this way hundreds of times in the past and yet had barely any memory of it. Cannizzaro just seemed like a place in-between places, between the urban sprawl of Catania and the seaside charm of Aci Castello. No reason to stop here, she thought, and then sped past the hospital. Unless, of course, you had to.

She stopped and kicked the stand down outside a row of

shops advertising phone unlocking services, vapes and computer repairs. She reached into her jacket, and pulled out the scrap of paper on which Stefano had scrawled the address. It didn't look like a TV studio. Nevertheless, there it was on the doorbell panel. *Bella Catania.* Unless he'd just got the address wrong and this was an Airbnb. She looked around at the traffic whizzing past and breathed in the petrol fumes. No, that didn't seem any more likely.

She pressed the buzzer and immediately the *citofono* sprang into life.

'*Chi è?*'

'Hi there. My name's Nedda Leonardi. I'm a journalist with *Catania Nuova.*'

There was a pause and then the *citofono* buzzed and the door clicked open. 'First floor.'

The interior felt for all the world like a typical apartment block, to the extent of two kids' bicycles being tucked away in a stairwell, and the stairs led up to a plain wooden door with the words *Bella Catania* fixed to it with a white sticky label.

Again, she thought, it didn't look much like a TV studio.

The door opened before she could knock or ring the bell, pulled open by a young guy wearing an AC/DC T-shirt.

'Hi.'

'Hi there. I'm Nedda Leonardi and I'm—'

'A journalist. Yeah, you said. Come in.'

He ushered her through into a room lined with thick black curtains. The only sources of light were two heavy arc lamps on tripods, blazing out heat. It was hot enough in late June. In the height of summer, she thought, it must be unbearable.

At the far end of the room, in front of a green screen, stood a man in a lab coat holding an enormous toothbrush in one hand and a similarly large set of teeth in the other. He smiled and nodded at her.

AC/DC put a hand on her arm, making her jump. 'Listen, there's only room for one person in the soundproof booth so I just need you to sit down here for five minutes and keep quiet. Is that okay?'

She nodded.

'Great.' He pointed to a grubby sofa next to the booth. 'Sorry, it's a bit of a state. I can't keep Toto off it.' He saw the expression on her face. 'My dog,' he clarified. 'Oh, and do you want a coffee before we start?'

'Yes, that'd be nice, thanks.'

'Sugar?'

'Please.'

His face fell. 'I don't think we have any. I could take a look,' he added, without enthusiasm.

She waved a hand. 'Without is fine. Really.'

He disappeared into the booth, and she heard the hum of a capsule machine. He returned with a steaming plastic cup, and Nedda winced when the heat reached her fingers.

'Sorry, it's a bit hot, these aren't really the right cups.'

'It's fine,' she repeated, passing it from hand to hand.

'Toto,' came a voice, 'are we ready to wrap this up? I've got to be back in the surgery by three.'

'Toto?' she said. 'I thought that was your dog?'

'And my name as well. Makes it easier for everybody to remember, doesn't it?'

'Oh. I suppose so.'

Toto looked over at the guy in the lab coat. 'Okay,

Giovanni. Just five minutes.' He closed himself away within the booth. 'Let's just do the bit about "Good Oral Health" once again and we can wrap this.'

The man in front of the green screen smiled and nodded.

Nedda sipped at her coffee, and winced at the bitterness of it. She switched the cup to her other hand. The plastic seemed to be crumpling under the heat. Unpleasant as it was, it might be wise to finish it off as soon as possible.

'And so, with the summer months approaching, it's more important than ever to think about our teeth. When we're out on a hot day, what better than a lemon *granita* with a brioche, eh? What could be better than a *cannolo* for breakfast and then perhaps a *torta cassata* mid-afternoon? Well, just remember that it might be a treat for us but not so much for our teeth. Remember to drink plenty of water – this is good advice anyway – or why not carry a travel toothbrush with you?' He tapped the giant toothbrush against the dentures. 'It doesn't have to be as big as this one,' he smiled. 'Your teeth will thank you, and happier teeth will make a happier you. I'll see you next week. In the meantime, this is Dr Giovanni Messina wishing you good oral health.' He held up the toothbrush, smiling broadly at the camera as he held his position.

'Okay, let's cut it there.' Toto's voice came from the booth. 'That's great, Giovanni.'

'Thank you, Toto.' Dr Giovanni smiled, and packed his enormous toothbrush and dentures away into a sports bag. Then he struggled out of his lab coat. 'Getting hot in here,' he said, dabbing at his forehead.

He stopped in front of Nedda, as if registering her presence for the first time. '*Signurina?*'

'Nedda Leonardi. Journalist.'

'Oh.' He smiled. 'Well, do give us a good write-up.' He looked at the empty coffee cup in her hand. 'I hope there's no sugar in that,' he frowned.

'Not a trace. Promise.'

'Good. Well done.' He smiled again, nodded at Toto, and was gone.

Toto gestured at her empty cup. 'Another coffee, *signurina*?'

She shook her head. 'No thanks. And you can call me Nedda.'

'Are you sure? I've found the sugar.'

'Really, it's okay.' She looked around the tiny studio. 'So, this is where it all happens then?'

He grinned. 'The magic of television. I know it's not exactly *Cinecittà* but it's all mine.'

She nodded her head in the direction of the door. 'And so, what was all that?'

'*Dental Hygiene with Dr Giovanni Messina*. It goes out at three o'clock on Sunday afternoons.'

'Right. Does it get much of an audience?'

Toto's chest swelled with pride. 'Highest viewing figures for any oral hygiene programme in the Catania area.'

'Wow. Well done.'

'We're very proud of it. I think Giovanni might be becoming a bit of a cult figure. Anyway, what can I do for you, *signu*— Nedda?'

'It's about that accident in Aci Trezza the other day. During *U pisci a mari*.'

'Oh, the man who died.' He frowned. 'Poor guy. Nasty.'

'I think you might have known him. Or at least met him.'

His frown deepened. 'I don't know. Remind me of his name.'

'Lombardo. Gianmaria Lombardo.'

He shook his head, but then his expression cleared. 'Oh yes. I remember now. We had him on a couple of times. Doing psychic TV stuff.'

'Tell me about that.'

He shrugged. 'You've not seen any of it?'

'I've managed to avoid it.'

Annoyance flashed across his face for a moment. 'It's great late-night TV. Always pulls in lots of viewers. Advertisers love it.'

'I don't understand. What's it all about?'

'We get a psychic in, and viewers phone them up. Tell them there's someone they need to speak to on the other side. Or say they're worried they've been cursed, something like that.'

'Really?'

'Absolutely.'

'And then what happens?'

'The psychic – whichever one it happens to be – tells them what they need to do.'

Nedda hesitated for a moment. 'And does this involve the exchange of money?'

Toto looked confused. 'Sure it does. Otherwise how would these guys make a living?'

'Uh-huh. I understand.'

'There's nothing illegal about it. As long as everybody's paying their taxes, that is.'

'Gianmaria Lombardo seems to have made a few enemies.

I was just thinking – did he ever receive, I don't know, any threats on air. Anything like that?'

Toto shrugged. 'Not that I remember.' He frowned. 'Are you saying what I think you're saying?'

'I don't know. But I do know there are people who are happy that he's dead. And so I just thought this might be something worth following up.'

'What are the police doing?'

'Nothing as far as I know. They've got something that looks very much like an accidental death and don't see any need to take it further.'

'So this could be a scoop for you?'

'That's not what it's about,' Nedda said, but her reply sounded unconvincing even to her own ears.

'Could we have first dibs on this? If it ever comes to anything. You know, the whole drama-documentary reconstruction?'

She thought, for a moment, that he was teasing but his expression was serious. She wasn't sure that Toto and *Bella Catania* with their one studio above a vape shop seemed entirely equipped for the production of drama-documentaries but she nodded anyway. 'I'd see what I could do.'

'Great. Now let me see what I can find.'

Chapter 16

'It's around here somewhere.' Toto ruffled through an index file on top of a filing cabinet in the back of the booth. 'We keep a card index on everyone, you know? Just in case we want to invite them back.'

He flicked through a few more cards, and pulled out a handful. 'Here we are. All the psychics you need.'

He spread them out upon the top of the filing cabinet. 'Ah, here we go. Paolo Bucinelli. Also known as *Solange*.' He held the card up for Nedda to see.

'He looks a bit like that guy – what's his name – the British guy from that punk band?'

'Johnny Rotten?' Toto laughed. 'Yeah, I said that to him. It really pissed him off. He was sick to death of people telling him that. We were lucky to get him, you know?'

'Really?'

'Yeah. He was a big name in psychic circles. But it turned out he was on holiday in Taormina and we managed to get him to do a couple of shows. The advertisers loved it, of course. Crazy guy, but in all the right ways.'

'What happened to him?'

'Died a few years back. Somewhere in Tuscany.' He looked

at her. 'So, just in case you were wondering, not linked with what may or may not have happened in Aci Trezza the other day. Now, let me see. Who else have we got? There's *The Great Alfons*, but I think he's in prison. *L'Indovino Duccio*. He's definitely in prison. *Nuccio il Chiaroveggente*. . .' He paused. 'I think maybe he and Duccio were the same person. They can be difficult to keep track of. All those aliases.' He leafed through a few more. 'Dead. Dead. *Bruno the Psychic Wonderdog*, probably not of much use to you.' He picked out another card. 'This guy, I think, is in prison. This one's disappeared, or at least never returns any calls. This one – definitely in prison.'

'This is sounding like a high-risk occupation.'

'It's up there with gangsta rapper or nineteen-forties jazz musician. This is a job with a high probability of pissing off the wrong people. Or of attracting the attention of the *Guardia di Finanza*.'

'But you give them space on your TV channel?'

Toto sighed in exasperation. '*Signurina*, this isn't RAI or Mediaset. It's me operating out of a crappy room above a vape shop. My biggest star is a dentist. I'll give anybody a break as long as I think they can pull in any sort of money from advertisers.'

'Sorry. But is there anybody on your books who isn't dead or in prison? Or a dog?'

'We've got four. There's Mater Morgana. She claims to be a white witch. A strange one. It's all herbalism and healing, all that mother goddess stuff.'

'Okay. Who else?'

'This guy. Salvatore Sipala. Otherwise known as *Salvatore the Seer*. We've had him on loads of times.'

'What's his particular game, then?'

'He removes curses. If something in your life isn't going quite right, it's probably because somebody has cursed you. And he'll remove it. For a price. Oh, and he's also pretty useful with Tarot cards.'

'Over the phone?'

'That's what he does. Now here,' he tapped one of the cards, 'is the guy you're interested in. Gianmaria Lombardo. Otherwise known as *Lombardo the Mystic*. Mainly dealt in putting grieving relatives in touch with their loved ones.'

Nedda shook her head. 'Christ.' She looked at the remaining card. 'Who's this one? *Il Mago*?'

'The Magus? Real name is Calogero something. Hang on, it'll be on the back.' He turned the card over. 'Calogero Maugeri. He's a strange one.'

'In what way?'

'He only appeared on the scene about six months ago. He's not like the others. He's not in the predictions game. Very much a sceptic. He says the whole psychic business is something anyone can learn. Any half-decent magician can do it, he says.'

'But you still used him?'

'Of course. It was dynamite. We put him on the same show as Morgana, Salvatore and Gianmaria. I thought it would be classy to have a proper debate on the subject. And there was always the chance they'd have a fight, of course, which would be even better.'

'And did they?'

Toto grinned. 'You want to watch it?'

'Sure.'

'Just give me a minute. I've got this on the server some-where. Ah, here we go.'

The recording crackled into life, the picture blurred at first before sharpening. The colours were a little washed out, and a line of interference crackled away at the bottom of the picture.

'It's not perfect. We don't keep every recording. Even we realise that there's a limited market for back episodes of Giovanni the Dentist. But we kept this one. Now watch.' The picture sharpened further, revealing five people sitting around a horseshoe-shaped desk.

'*Buona sera, everybody, and welcome to the first episode of* The Psychic Show *with me, your host, Toto Licata.*'

Nedda looked from the screen to Toto and back again. 'So, who's directing?'

He paused the recording. 'Can't remember the guy's name. A media student from Catania. He did a bit of work for us. I think he's now working in advertising in Milan. So, in a way, I gave him his first break. This meant I had to host the show, of course. I even put a proper shirt on for it. Oh, and that "first episode" thing?' He grinned again. 'Well, there was only one. You'll find out why.'

He restarted the player.

Chapter 17

Bella Catania TV studio, February 4th 2024

'*Buona sera*, everybody, and welcome to the first episode of *The Psychic Show* with me, your host, Toto Licata. I'm here with Mater Morgana, Salvatore the Seer, the Mystical Lombardo, and Calogero Maugeri, otherwise known simply as *the Magus*. Welcome everyone.'

There were general murmurings of *hello* and *good evening* around the table.

'You've probably seen all these good people before on our regular late-night *Psychic Specials*, and so we thought, what better than to bring them all together for a series of special programmes in which we ask the very pertinent question – do psychic phenomena actually exist?

'And we'll start tonight with Morgana. *Mater Morgana*, I should say. Now,' Toto chuckled, 'they tell me you're a witch?'

Morgana had been fiddling with her necklace and looked up as if only just aware of where she was. 'They do? Who do?'

Toto looked thrown by that. 'Well. People.'

'People. I see.'

'And are you? A witch?'

She nodded. 'Oh yes.'

Toto chuckled. 'Well, I'll be on my best behaviour, I promise. I don't want to get cursed or anything.'

'Is there any particular reason that I should do that?'

'No. It's just—'

'That I'm a witch?'

'Well, yes, and so—'

'I could curse you if I wanted to, is that what you want me to say?'

'Well, could you?'

'Yes.' She played with her necklace some more. 'Yes, I could.'

Toto had been expecting some late-night nonsense, possibly with a couple of arguments thrown in, in the hope of slightly higher than usual viewing figures, but Mater Morgana was making him more than a little nervous. He forced himself not to make the *corna*, put a smile on his face and turned to the other guests.

'We're also joined tonight by the Mystical Lombardo.' He smiled and waved at the thick-set man on the opposite side of the table with his shirt unbuttoned and a heavy gold medallion around his neck. He was already sweating under the studio lights.

'No.'

'No?'

'No.'

'I don't understand.'

'I'm Lombardo the Mystic. Not the Mystical Lombardo.'

'Oh. I see. I'm sorry. Well, it's still a great pleasure to have you on the show.'

Lombardo grunted, and sipped at the water in front of him. 'Hot in here.'

'Tell us about your experiences of the psychic world, Lombardo.'

He nodded and took some more water. 'It all started when I was a little boy. In the countryside. We lived in a small town outside Siracusa, you know? And one day my little sister went missing. My mum and dad, they went crazy, you can imagine. They called all our neighbours, then they called the police, the priest, everyone. The whole town went crazy. And then I just said to *mamma* that little Angelica had locked herself in a barn about a kilometre away and couldn't get out.

'And my father, he clouted me around the ear,' at this point Lombardo rubbed the side of his face, as if to indicate that the memory of it still pained him, 'and told me not to be stupid. But there was a cop there, a young guy, and he looked at me and made the *corna* and told me to speak up.

'And we went there, and we could hear Angelica crying from inside. She'd gone off on her bike and gone to look inside and somehow locked herself in.

'So my father shouted at her and then he burst into tears and then so did my mother, and the young cop was looking at me and shaking his head. I asked him what the matter was, and he told me he could see something in my eyes. There was a look, he told me, a look that his grandfather had. He told me I was a *chiaroveggente*, a clairvoyant.'

Toto nodded. 'Fascinating. Absolutely fascinating. Thank you, Lombardo. We'll come back to you later but first I want to go to the third member of our panel, who is Salvatore

Sipala, otherwise known as *Salvatore the Seer.*' He paused as if waiting for Salvatore to contradict him. 'I hope I've got that right.'

Salvatore merely nodded, his bald pate shiny under the lights, and refilled his glass with water.

'How long have you known you were psychic, Salvatore?'

He shrugged. 'Nearly all my life. Like Lombardo. It was just something that was always there, you know. Voices I could hear that nobody else could hear. People I could see that nobody else could.'

The fourth member of the panel, a man in perhaps his mid-thirties, with swept-back hair and a thin moustache, coughed something under his breath. Everybody turned to stare at him. 'Sorry,' he said, and sipped at his water. 'Something went down the wrong way. Carry on.'

Toto turned back to Salvatore. 'And those voices, those people. Can you hear them now? See them now?'

Salvatore smiled. 'Oh yes. They're all around us. There's one on your shoulder, for example.' Toto started, and looked at his left shoulder. 'No, no. The other one. But don't brush him off. Leave him there.' He smiled. 'That's your father.'

'You what?'

'Your father. He always said he'd be there to look after you, didn't he?'

'How could you know that?'

Salvatore smiled again, and gently tapped his ears. 'They told me.'

'You see this as being a gift then?'

He nodded. 'Of course. I feel very blessed. Wouldn't you agree, Gianmaria?'

'I would. I do see it as a blessing, I agree. I also think that it gives us a responsibility to help people as best we can.'

Mater Morgana stopped fiddling with her necklace for a moment and looked up, but said nothing before returning to her work.

'Over now to our final panellist tonight,' said Toto, 'Calogero Maugeri, who you might know better simply as *the Magus*. Calogero, would you like to tell us about your gifts and when you became aware of them?'

Calogero looked confused for a moment but then his expression cleared. 'Oh, I don't have any,' he smiled.

Now it was Toto's turn to look perplexed. 'I'm sorry?' he said, perhaps thinking he'd phrased his question badly.

'I don't have any. Seriously, I don't. No second sight or anything like that. I'm afraid I'm not even the seventh son of a seventh son.'

Toto scratched the back of his head. 'In that case, I'm kind of wondering why you came on the show?'

'Oh, just to show people how easy it is to do this sort of thing.' He turned to Lombardo. 'I did enjoy that story about finding your sister, Gianmaria. I can only imagine what a relief it must have been for you and your parents.'

Lombardo nodded. 'It was. Thank you.'

'It's a wonderful story. The thing is, though, when I heard it tonight – just as when I heard it for the first time – I started to wonder quite how difficult it would be to lock yourself in a barn.'

Lombardo grinned and spread his hands. 'You know what little sisters are like. They always find a way.' Salvatore chuckled and patted his companion on the back.

Calogero smiled back at them. 'She was a handful, I can imagine.'

The two men chuckled along with him.

'It's just that, when I first heard this story, six months ago, she was your cousin, not your sister.'

Lombardo didn't miss a beat. 'Ah, she was my cousin. But she lived with us, and so I treated her like a little sister.'

'That was kind of you. And how lovely for little Angelina to have a big brother to look out for her.' He paused and frowned. 'Sorry, is it Angelina or Angelica?'

Lombardo's smile was slowly melting. 'Angelica.'

'Cousin Angelica. Not sister Angelina. Or is it the other way around? Anyway, either cousin or sister, they somehow managed to find a way to lock themselves inside a barn.'

Lombardo scowled, sipped at his water, and turned to Toto. 'Is there any point to this?'

Toto wiped a bead of sweat from his forehead and yet he smiled, aware that this was going just as he'd hoped. 'Yes, Magus, I'd like to try and steer this conversation back on to the subject of psychic phenomena if I may.'

'Of course.' Calogero smiled at Lombardo. 'It's just that, if you're going to do this sort of thing, you really do need to make sure that story is bulletproof.'

'You've just misremembered, that's all.'

'It might be. But given the event I refer to is up on YouTube,' he turned to the camera and smiled, 'the viewers will be able to check it out for themselves.' He turned to Salvatore. 'And yes, how could you possibly know that Toto's father said he would always be there to look after him? I mean, it's not as if that's something that just any father might say to their children at some point in their lives, is it?'

Salvatore took a drink from his glass and slammed it down hard on the table. 'We're just trying to make an honest living here, you prick.'

'An *honest* living, you say? Why not just try some stage magic? A few years' practice and I think you might be modestly competent at it.'

'You son of a bitch.' Salvatore turned to Toto. 'You invited this prick on here just to show us up, didn't you?'

Toto raised his hands, hoping to calm things down. Just a little, and just for the moment. 'That's not true. That really isn't true.' He turned to Morgana in the hope that she might provide some relief.

'You're very quiet, Mater Morgana?'

She shrugged. 'Well, someone has to be.'

'Is there something you'd like to say?'

'Yes. I think there is.' She stared at the faces of the men around the table, all flushed and sweaty with anger. 'You brought us on here for one reason only, didn't you? In the hope that we'd end up like this. Or, better still, somebody would swing a punch.'

'That's not so, Mater Morgan—'

She waved a hand at him. 'Do be quiet, please. You asked me if there was anything I'd like to say. And there is. You don't need to be a witch to predict what was likely to happen. If I want to see a lot of very angry middle-aged men wanting to punch each other I can go to any number of disappointing bars in Catania. I don't need to switch my television set on to do it.' She jabbed a figure at Lombardo and Salvatore. 'You two – you two are just a pair of *cafoni*.' Both of them opened their mouths to speak. Morgana slapped her palms on the table and they fell silent. Then she turned to Calogero. 'But you? You I don't understand.'

He smiled. 'I'm flattered.'

'Don't be. I'm just wondering what your interest in this is?'

'I just want people to know the truth, that's all.'

'Is it?' she muttered almost to herself. 'I wonder.' Then she ran her hands through her hair, and shook her head. She got to her feet. 'I'm going,' she announced.

'Morgana?' said Toto, a note of despair in his voice.

'You don't need me here. I'm not going to start a fight and there's more chance of the rest of them doing so if I'm not here. Besides, I've got an owl to feed.' She turned and left, without saying goodnight to the rest of the panel.

Toto turned to the camera. There was, it seemed, not going to be any actual violence but a heated discussion and a guest storming off was almost as good. 'Well, there we go, ladies and gentlemen, this is an emotive subject as we all know and something we'll be exploring in weeks to come.'

'Like fuck we will,' said Salvatore and Toto winced. Salvatore took a drink from his glass. Toto was starting to realise that it probably held something other than water.

'You got this prick on here just to make us look bad, didn't you?'

Toto smiled a weary smile. 'Salvatore, I wonder if we could just watch the language a little bit?'

'It's past ten o'clock and no one's fucking watching anyway.' He stared at Calogero. 'Seriously, though – *seriously* – what the fuck are you doing here?'

Calogero smiled back at him. 'I'm enjoying being part of this edifying discussion, Salvatore.' Then, in a stage whisper, he murmured, 'I'd put more water in it next time' and made a drinky-drink motion with his hand.

Salvatore paused for a moment as his face slowly turned a deep shade of purple, then clenched his fists and launched himself across the table sending bottles, glasses and something that was probably not water flying through the air.

The camera shook for a moment, and then Toto cried out, 'Don't cut it! Keep filming!'

Salvatore's hands were around Calogero's throat, but then Calogero in one sharp movement boxed his ears and Salvatore rolled away, howling in pain.

Calogero took his seat again, smoothed his hair down, and righted the bottle of water. He poured the remains into his glass and looked disappointed at how little remained.

He held the bottle up to someone off camera. 'I think we might need another one of these,' he said. Then he smiled. 'Now then. Where were we?'

Salvatore, panting, pulled himself back into his chair, breathing heavily. He reached for his upturned glass and drained the few remaining drops from it. He glared across the table at Calogero. 'You're a fucking dead man, Maugeri.'

Calogero nodded. 'Well, in that case, this must be the first time you've genuinely succeeded in talking to one.'

For a moment Salvatore looked as if he were about to hurl himself at Calogero again. But then Lombardo put a firm hand on his arm and leaned across the table.

He smiled. 'Where were you this time last year, Magus?'

And Calogero blinked. 'I'm sorry?'

'I'll repeat it again, seeing as you missed it. Where were you this time last year?'

'I don't understand.'

'I'm sure the viewers would like to know.'

Calogero leaned back in his chair. 'If you must know, I think I was working on a cruise ship. Late-night entertainment, you know?'

'A cruise ship. Really?' Lombardo paused. 'You remember the name?'

Calogero shook his head. 'I don't remember.'

'Fair enough. I guess if you take enough cruises they must all roll into one.' He leaned forward and tapped his finger on the table. 'Except we know that's not true, don't we?'

Calogero made a show of looking at his watch. 'It seems we're running a little late.' He got to his feet. 'It's been a pleasure, everyone, but I need to be going.'

Lombardo grinned. 'Let me guess, you've got an owl to feed as well?'

Calogero turned and walked from the set.

And then the screen went black.

Chapter 18

Car park, Bella Catania TV studio, February 4th 2024
Calogero leaned back against his car, and sparked up a cigarette. He shook his head. Well, that had all turned out to be a bit of a waste of time. With a bit of luck he'd still get his fee, modest as it was, but in general he considered any evening where getting into a fight was a high point as being a bit of a waste of time.

He heard two sets of footsteps moving towards him, and shielded his eyes against the glare of the streetlamps. Two figures, half in shadow.

'Maugeri?'

Salvatore, of course. Well, he'd been expecting this. And Gianmaria.

He smoked away, then dropped his cigarette and ground it underfoot.

'Maugeri,' Salvatore repeated.

'Hello, Salvatore.' He held the packet out to him. 'Cigarette?'

Salvatore's hand lashed out and his fingers closed around Calogero's, crushing the cigarettes as if he wished they were his fingers. The packet dropped to the ground, and Calogero winced.

'Sorry. If I'd known you were trying to give up I wouldn't have offered.'

'Fucking clever bastard, aren't you? Just like in there. Clever boy thinks he can make a fool of me.'

'Look, Salvatore.' He reached out and patted him on the shoulder. 'I don't really want a fight. I don't think you do either. Not really.' He wasn't one hundred per cent sure about that, admittedly. 'Why don't you just go home and sleep it off?'

Salvatore balled his fist, and the other hand reached out to grab him by the collar. This, evidently, had been the wrong thing to say.

Calogero sighed. It seemed the only way out of the situation now was going to be through violence. Salvatore had the smell of cheap booze upon his breath and was already a little unsteady on his feet. He reckoned he'd be able to take him without too much trouble, unless Gianmaria wanted to get involved too. But this was going to end the evening in a proper fight. Not a drunk fight in a TV studio, but a proper grubby little fight with two men scuffling in a car park when all he really wanted was to be back home, perhaps with a little smoke before bedtime. Still, if it had to be done.

'Salvatore.' Gianmaria's voice lashed out. Sipala paused for a second, his fist poised in mid-air.

'Salvatore,' Gianmaria repeated, his voice quieter this time. 'Let's not do this, eh?'

'This fucker tried to humiliate us, Gianmaria.'

'I think you managed that quite well all by yourself, Salvatore. Now, just let him go, eh?'

Salvatore cursed, but dropped his hands to his side and

stepped back. Calogero straightened his jacket and shirt, and smiled.

'I don't know why you're so happy, Maugeri. Oh, sorry, would you prefer I called you "Magus"?'

'As you like. Calogero is fine, of course.'

'Whatever.' Gianmaria paused, and patted the car door. 'Get in.'

'What?'

'We're going for a little drive.'

For the first time, Calogero felt a stab of fear. Salvatore was just an aggressive drunk. He'd dealt with plenty of those. But Gianmaria was an unknown quantity.

'I don't understand.'

'You will. Salvatore, sit next to him. Don't do anything stupid. Either of you, but especially you, Salvatore.'

'Gianmaria, I don't understand either.'

Lombardo rubbed his face and sighed. 'Listen. It's late. He's got a car. We haven't. So, we either wait for a late-night bus or a taxi that'll rip us off, or ask our new friend the Magus here to give us a lift. Clear?'

Salvatore furrowed his brow, but went and sat in the passenger seat anyway.

'Well done. You live somewhere on the outskirts, don't you?'

'Yeah. But listen, I don't want this fucker to know where I live.'

'Oh Christ.' Calogero checked the rear-view mirror. Lombardo had his head in his hands. 'Look, Magus, do you promise never to go round to Salvatore's with the intention of doing him harm?'

Despite himself, Calogero smiled, and his heart rate began

to slow as the prospect of being shot in the back of the head seemed to recede. 'I promise.'

'You're not crossing your fingers, are you? I wouldn't like to think of you doing that.'

'Absolutely not.' He crossed himself. 'Look, I'm crossing my heart.'

'Very good. You see, Salvatore? Absolutely nothing to worry about.' Gianmaria yawned. 'Now. Tell the Magus where to go and, with a bit of luck, we can all be home before the sun comes up.'

They pulled up outside Salvatore's apartment. He got out of the car and leaned on the bonnet.

'You come looking for me, I'll be waiting for you,' he growled, pointing a finger at Calogero.

'Naturally. With your special powers you'll see me coming a mile off.'

Salvatore growled, and stalked around to the driver's side of the car, fists clenched. Just as he reached the crucial spot, Calogero pushed the door open as hard as he could, catching Salvatore in the balls and sending him sprawling.

'Didn't see that coming, did you?' he murmured.

He felt a hand on his shoulder. 'Just drive, please, Magus.'

'Anywhere in particular?'

'I'll tell you. For now, just drive.'

He guided the car back north through the suburbs of Catania then up towards Aci Castello. Then, on the outskirts of the small town, with the castle silhouetted in the moonlight, Gianmaria tapped him on the shoulder.

'You got plenty of petrol in this thing?'

He nodded.

'Okay. Let's go for a drive. Right up into *Parco dell' Etna.*'

'You sure?' Calogero fought to keep down another rising tide of panic.

'Sure I am. It's lovely at this time of night.'

He guided the Cinquecento along the long, sweeping roads that skirted the volcano and through the tiny villages that clung to its side.

'Do this at daytime and the sun's in your eyes, and it's a pain in the ass trying to avoid tour buses. But on a clear night,' Gianmaria sighed, 'you've got the sea spread out before you, and you're driving along the side of an actual volcano.' He chuckled. 'Imagine that. It's an actual fucking volcano, Magus, and we don't even think twice about it. That's just where we live. Under the volcano.'

'Uh-huh.' Calogero saw a passing place at the side of the road and pulled over.

'I didn't tell you to stop.'

'I just figured we needed to talk sometime and here might be good.' He removed the keys from the ignition, got out of the car and slammed the door. He shivered. 'Chilly. We must be higher up than I thought. Wish I'd thought to bring a better coat.' He looked at Gianmaria and smiled. 'So, let's talk.'

Gianmaria smiled back. 'What makes you think I want to talk?'

'Your prints are all over the car. We were on television earlier, having an actual fight. If anything happens to me now, the police will be paying you a call very soon. Also, I think if you wanted to shoot me in the back of the head you'd have a very long walk home. So come on then. Let's talk.'

Gianmaria nodded in the vague direction of Catania. 'He's an asshole, of course.'

'Salvatore? You surprise me. He seemed so well-adjusted.'

'It's not all his fault. He's like so many of these people. Got too much money, too quickly. It's made an asshole out of him. But you,' he reached out a hand towards him, 'smoke?'

He nodded, and proffered the crumpled packet. 'If you can find one that's not too squashed.'

Gianmaria sparked up, and smoked away in silence for a few minutes, looking out upon the ocean. Then he stubbed out his cigarette on the sole of his boot.

'I don't like leaving all this shit around but,' he shook his head, and pointed at the cans, bottles and garbage bags that littered the passing place, 'everybody else does it and so what difference does it make?'

He took a business card from his wallet and scribbled a number upon it. He tucked it into Calogero's jacket pocket and patted him on the chest. 'Now. You look after that, understand?'

Calogero shook his head. 'No. I really don't understand.'

'This is my address. No reason why you shouldn't have it.'

'Thanks. And the number?'

'That's the amount I'd like you to pay me every month. Send it in the mail if you like. Just be sure it's there by the third of the month. Cash is better than a bank transfer, obviously.'

Calogero rubbed the bridge of his nose. 'Okay, I've gone from not understanding to full-blown confusion here.'

'Not much to misunderstand, Magus. This is what you're going to be paying me every month, from now on.'

'Okay. And why would I do this?'

'Because there is a very angry man in Turin who'd very much like back the money you stole from him in a card game.'

Calogero looked him up and down and kept his face stony. 'I don't know what on earth you mean.'

Gianmaria smiled and leaned in towards him. He patted him on the back, and then whispered into his ear.

Calogero could not prevent himself from stiffening and, even in the chill air, he felt sweat breaking out on his forehead.

'How could you know that?' he said. There seemed little point in denying it now.

'Ah, *Magus* – let's use that for now, yes, or we'll be up here all night arguing about names – it's very easy in this line of work. You see, I've got a job where people want to talk to me. And the more you talk to them, the more chances there are to find things out about them. Without them even realising it. And the more you find out,' he smiled, 'the more opportunities there are. You understand now, right?'

'Oh, I understand perfectly. Corrupt businessmen. Guilty husbands or wives. Perhaps even the occasional priest with some terrible skeletons in the closet.'

'Exactly.'

'Not the easiest way to make a living, I'd have thought.'

'It is if you're good at it. And I'm very, very good at it.'

'An easy way to make enemies as well.'

'I hope I'm not counting you among them.'

'That depends.' Calogero nodded, thoughtfully. 'Now, am I being hopelessly naive in suggesting an old-fashioned "go to the police" isn't a practical solution?'

The two men laughed, and Gianmaria shook his head, genuine amusement in his eyes.

'No, it most certainly isn't. How closely do you really want the police to look at your credentials, eh?' He sighed. 'In my life I seem to be surrounded by idiots and assholes, or in the case of Salvatore, both. Now, you might well be an asshole, Magus, but I don't see you as an idiot. I've got a rough idea of how much money you might be pulling in. I've got a rough idea of how quickly you must be burning through that briefcase full of cash. So that figure I've given you there is, I think, pretty manageable.'

'Uh-huh. And when the money's gone?'

'Then we'll renegotiate.' Calogero opened his mouth, but Gianmaria waved a hand at him. 'No, no. Don't shout and swear. And please don't threaten me. I've heard all that before. From seasoned professionals. People whose job it is to make threats and to carry them through. Not stage magicians.'

Calogero looked at the card. He turned it over in his hands, giving himself time to think. Then, with a flick of his wrist, he sent it spinning through the air towards Gianmaria. The other man flinched, but Calogero's hand closed around it, just in front of his nose. He opened his fist to reveal an empty palm. A look of confusion spread across his face. 'Where can it be?' he said, scratching his head. 'Ah.' He reached behind Gianmaria's head. 'Here it is. It was behind your ear all the time.' He dropped it into his pocket. 'I'll take good care of it,' he said. 'Very good care.'

'Good man.' Gianmaria sat back inside the car. 'You're a clever and tricky fellow, Magus. Just don't be too tricky, eh?' Then he smiled. 'I was just thinking about what I said. About us living under a volcano. Thing is, Magus, you're kind of living on top of one as well.' He yawned. 'And now, I think, we should be getting home.'

The two of them drove to Aci Trezza in silence.

Chapter 19

Stefano clicked the window shut on his computer and ejected the pen drive. Then he put his hands behind his head, closed his eyes and smiled.

'What do you think?' said Nedda.

His eyes snapped open. 'I think it's absolutely bloody brilliant.' He spun his chair around to face her. 'Where's the rest of it?'

'There's no more. Toto – he's the guy at the station – said that the show overran. The last bit was never recorded.'

'Hmm. A shame. It might be interesting to know what happened next.'

'Apparently they cleared the set, Sipala tried to find a bottle of grappa, and Maugeri just disappeared.'

'In a puff of smoke?'

'Perhaps so.'

'Did this ever go out?'

She shook her head. 'No.'

'I wonder why not?'

'Toto said that almost immediately they started to get phone calls. Weird ones. Threatening, I guess you'd describe them as. Saying it would be better if it was never broadcast.

I can see why they thought it was easier to forget about it. It must have been frightening. So, what do you think, should I take this to the police?'

Stefano tapped the pen drive against the desk. 'No. I don't think so. Not yet. The police are happy to think it's an accidental death. And all you really have is two guys having an argument on a late-night show that nobody saw. No, you need more before it goes to that level. Have you spoken to Aldo yet?'

'No.'

'Okay. Do that first. Just tell him you think there's something worth checking out.'

'Do you think he'll listen to me? Or just send me out for *cannoli* again?'

'Honestly, I think he'll do both. But I think he'll take you seriously if you show him this.' He held up the pen drive.

'Then I'll do that. But I'll tell him that it was your idea – going to the TV station, I mean.'

'No, you won't.'

'What do you mean?'

'Tell Aldo that I gave you the idea and he'll take the story off you and give it to me. You'll be back down the *pasticceria* before he's even had time to eject the drive.'

'Are you sure?'

'Yes, I'm sure. This is your story, Nedda. You deserve it.'

'Well. Thanks.'

'It's not a problem.' He smiled. 'You could always let me buy you dinner to say thanks.' Nedda flushed. 'Come on. Just dinner.'

'God, you don't give up, do you? But okay.'

***

Calogero bought a bottle of beer and an *arancino* from the *chiosco*, called it lunch, and looked out upon the harbour. He pressed the bottle to his forehead, enjoying the cool against his skin. The bus journey had been hot and sweaty – he'd heard about parts of Sicily where the buses were air-conditioned, but they'd yet to reach Acireale – and the midday heat was now making it difficult to stand in the direct sunlight. A group of tourists, laughing and chatting, walked past in swimwear. They probably had the right idea. In jacket and trousers he felt overdressed.

He bit into the *arancino* and smiled. A good meaty *ragù*, tomato sauce, mozzarella and rice. A complete meal in itself for a couple of euros. And a beer to boot. All was well.

Then the base of the *arancino* collapsed between his fingers and trickled down the lapel of his jacket.

'Shit.'

In his hurry to grab a handkerchief and mop himself down, he lost his grip on the bottle of beer, which fell from his hand and smashed on the pavement.

'Hey!'

The kiosk owner, angry, sweaty and red-faced, came running out. 'Hey. What's the matter? Never drunk a beer before?'

'Sorry, my friend. My mistake. I'll clear it up.'

'No, you won't. You'll probably cut yourself and bleed to death. I'll do it.'

'Okay. Thanks. Sorry.'

The kiosk guy went back inside and returned with a dustpan and brush. He gave the ground a few cursory sweeps before depositing the broken glass in a bin.

'Do you want the same again?'

'I guess that wouldn't be on the house?'

'You guess correctly.'

'Ah, what the hell, let's go for it.' He looked down at his jacket. 'This is gonna need a clean anyway.'

'Could be worse. I remember some guy wandering over here from the *gelateria* on the corner. He's maybe in his sixties, white hair, white beard, white hat, white suit. Looks a million euros, which might be why he's with this babe in a bikini who looks like a model but he's probably saying is his niece. Anyway, they're walking down to the jetty, because he's got a boat there. And it's a hot day and he's eating a chocolate ice cream. She's not eating anything. In fact, she doesn't look like she's ever eaten an ice cream in her life. And then the wind changes direction and his entire ice cream disintegrates and he's sprayed head to toe in a fine layer of chocolate. And his "niece" is trying not to laugh, and he's trying not to lose his cool, but everybody – and I mean everybody – is pointing and laughing and I'm thinking, man, that *was* a nice Armani suit but there's no way that's coming out in the wash.'

Calogero looked down at his lapel. 'You know, I was thinking maybe I could go for an ice cream after this. Now I'm not so sure.'

'Stick with vanilla or lemon, my friend. Useful tip. Much easier to get out.'

'I'll remember that.' Calogero drained his beer and finished – carefully – the last of his *arancino*. He slid a few euros across the counter and was about to leave when the owner gently coughed.

'Two of each, remember?'

'Ah yes. Apologies.' He slipped another note across, gave a little wave, and made his way down to the jetty.

The wharf also served as a car park, the windscreens of the vehicles all lined with silver foil to reflect the sun and to ensure the owner would not be vaporised by the heat upon opening the door. Behind the cars were set a series of arches, supporting the road above. These served as cooler, shady spaces in which to repair boats and, on this occasion, for a group of three men to sit around an upturned beer crate to smoke and play cards.

Calogero shaded his eyes and looked out at the islands of the *Ciclopi*. A group of teenagers had taken a pedalo out to them and the two boys were taking it in turns to scramble up the rocks and tombstone from the top, presumably in the hope of impressing the girls. If, that is, one can ever be truly impressive in a pedalo. Then he turned back and made his way into the shadow of the arches. There were, he noticed, other upturned boxes upon which to sit, but he thought it best to wait to be asked.

The men, of course, stopped talking as he approached.

'Can we help you, mister?' said one. 'You want to hire a boat, something like that?'

He shook his head. 'Nothing like that. Just a question about a guy who might have done, a few days back.'

Another of the group lit up a cigarette. His eyes narrowed, as if in suspicion, but he offered one to Calogero anyway. He shook his head.

'His name was Gianmaria Lombardo. You might have heard of him.'

Two of them shook their heads, but the third nodded.

'The dead guy, right? The one pulled out of the sea during *U pisci a mari*.'

'That's the one.'

'Why do you want to know about him hiring a boat?'

'I don't. I want to know if he had a boat.'

'Sure he did.' One of the men nodded towards the jetty. 'He's got a mooring down there.'

'Is it still there? The boat, I mean.'

Another of the men laughed and cracked open a bottle of *Messina*. 'My friend, the police have been round and asked us all this already. And we can tell you what we told them. No, his boat is not there.'

'So where is it now?'

'Drifting somewhere out in the sea, I guess.'

'Police say it was an accident.'

'Guess it was. Guy goes out on a hot day. Maybe he's had a drink. Isn't paying attention. Maybe gets dizzy in the heat and falls overboard.' He looked over towards the *Ciclopi* and grinned. 'Or maybe he goes tombstoning like those crazy kids. Get that wrong, even by a few inches,' he clapped his hands together, '*whumph*. Game over.'

'Somebody would have seen him.'

'Everyone who's there is either watching *U pisci* or they're watching John the Baptist. Could easily happen.'

The art of distraction. Something in plain sight but on the busiest day of the year.

'Anyone been to look for his boat?'

'Police went out the day after.'

'They find anything?'

'If they did, they didn't tell us.' The man narrowed his eyes and took another cigarette. 'Why you so interested?'

Calogero shrugged. 'He was an old buddy of mine. Nothing more. You happen to remember the name of his boat?'

'He didn't tell you himself?'

'We weren't those sorts of buddies.'

Two of them shook their heads but the third frowned. 'Some kind of stupid name. Acanthus. Or Agadoo. Or Agabus. Something like that.'

'Thank you.' He smiled at them, and then turned and walked away, giving a jaunty little wave over his shoulder.

Agabus.

Of course.

Chapter 20

The only other red-haired girl in Sicily worked at a bar and *pasticceria* called *La Dolceria Bella*. In truth, it wasn't Nedda's favourite bar in Acireale but, given that it was owned by the only other red-haired girl in Sicily, it had become her regular.

A poster outside advertised a performance by someone calling himself 'the Magus' at the *Teatro Giovanni Verga*. Outstanding feats of magic divination were promised, and a strip pasted diagonally across the poster shouted out to the reader that the run of the show had been extended by 'popular demand'.

The Magus himself – all neatly trimmed goatee beard and moustache, and swept-back hair greying at the temples – could not have looked more like a stage magician had he been sawing a lady in half with one hand and pulling a rabbit from a hat with the other. She'd never heard of him before but, the more she thought about it, the more she realised that she'd seen posters about him throughout Acireale in recent weeks.

Torrisi, the *ràis,* had told her there were posters for mediums and psychics posted up throughout the region. She'd never noticed them until two days ago. But he was right. They were everywhere. On telephone poles, bins or pasted on to walls. Some bleached to illegibility by the sun and some as clear as if they'd been printed that morning. Some offering services at home or over the telephone and some, like the Magus, performing in person. They were everywhere. And yet she'd never noticed them before.

She went inside and ordered her regular prosecco – *La Dolceria Bella* had aspirations and served nothing so vulgar as beer – and stood directly in the flow of the air-con, enjoying the feel of it chilling her skin through her clothes.

'Long day?' asked the only other red-haired girl in Sicily.

'Very. Frustrating.'

'Want to tell me about it?'

'Men.'

'Oh dear. Work-related or love-life disaster?'

'My love life *is* a disaster, Adelina, but that's fine. I can manage that. In some ways growing old with my dad seems better than most of the alternatives. No, it's work. I'm going to spend the rest of my days reporting on the best pastry shops in Catania.'

Adelina brightened. 'You could do a feature on us, if you'd prefer?'

'Maybe I'll do that. Hey, maybe I'd actually be happier working here. It'd be a change from some superannuated old dinosaur telling me what to do.'

'Well, I'd be telling you what to do. And I'm not super-whatever-you-said.' She frowned. 'At least I don't think I am.'

'That poster in the window,' said Nedda, changing the subject. 'You know anything about this guy?'

'Oh, my mum went to see him a couple of nights ago. She said he was dead good. The things he found out about her. She was convinced it was magic. And then he went and spoiled it by saying it was all a trick. And that made her a bit sad.

'No, the one she really liked was at the same theatre a couple of months ago. Salvatore the Seer, he called himself. The things he knew about everyone!'

'So, what does he do?'

'Oh, he looks around the room and picks someone out and says something like, "Is there a man called Stefano in your life?" And then they say no and he says, "Well, there soon will be and—"'

Nedda frowned. 'That's weird.'

'What is?'

'Stefano. He's a guy at work. We're going for a drink tonight.'

Adelina flicked a bar towel at her. 'You utter tart. And you didn't tell me. You've got a date and you didn't tell me.'

'It's not a date. It's just a drink.'

'Whatevs. Come on, tell me all about him.'

'Not much to say. He's more senior than me.'

'Not good.'

'Also older than me.'

'How much?'

'Maybe ten years?'

'Hmm. So when you're ninety he'll probably be dead. Cross that bridge later. Is he nice?'

'Seems to be.'

'Good looking?'

Nedda stroked her chin.

'Ah-hah! So he *is* good looking.'

'I didn't say anything.'

'You were looking for the right words and couldn't find them. So I'm taking that as a yes. Where's he taking you?'

'Some place called the Fish Bar down in Trezza.'

'Hmm. Good place. Cheap date, mind.'

'And, as I said, it's not a date.'

'And, as I said, whatevs. You know, funny thing is the name "Stefano" just came into my mind.' She clicked her fingers. 'Hey, do you reckon that means I'm psychic?'

'Maybe so. So, what else did your mum say about the Magus?'

'Not much. Thing is, I said she was convinced it was magic. And she was right up to the end.'

'What happened?'

'The guy basically said everything he'd done on stage was a trick and any stage magician could do it. And so we needed to be careful. That it was very easy to find out almost everything about us. Things we'd rather keep hidden.'

'Wow.'

'Oh, and then he disappeared in a puff of smoke and mum went back to thinking it was all magic again.' Nedda, she noticed, had finished her glass and was reaching for her purse. 'Anyway, you come back tomorrow and tell me all about your d—'

Nedda glared at her.

'Your drink. I was absolutely going to say your drink.' She smiled. 'And remember, there are some things you're not going to be able to keep hidden from me.'

Chapter 21

'Seriously? You've not been here before?'

'I told you, I don't usually go out in Aci Trezza.'

'Any reason why?'

'Aci Trezza means having to take the bike. Which means I can't have a drink. And Acireale seems less busy somehow. I mean, I know it's busy, but Trezza just seems different.' Nedda pointed towards the road running parallel to the shore, with a steady stream of motorcyclists, car drivers and pedestrians. 'I mean, whenever I've been down here at night it's always like this.'

Stefano nodded. 'Sure. But I kind of like that. I always think Aci Trezza is just touristy enough. Loads of visitors but in a good way. And night time is the best time. The sun setting behind the *Ciclopi*, the moon coming up. It's magical, really.' He tapped the menu. 'As is the food here. Come on, what are you after?'

The Fish Bar seemed to have been built on an impossibly steep angle, so much so that the legs on the tables were of differing lengths. The bar itself was painted in a cheery blue and white, and looked out across the sea.

Nedda consulted the menu. 'Got to say, it's very good value.'

'It is. Which kind of makes it ideal for a first date.'

'Don't call it that, this is just two friends having a bite to eat, okay?'

'Whatever. Anyway, if I'd taken you somewhere posh I'd have looked a bit needy and maybe just a bit creepy. Also, I really don't earn all that much money. Whereas here – you're a cheap date.' He smiled.

'I am not a date, cheap or otherwise.'

'Sorry. Anyway, go ahead and choose something. Oh, mind you, we'll have to start with the tempura shrimps. That's non-negotiable.'

'That good?'

'That good. Order now and tell me I was right later.'

'Uh-huh. Okay, tempura shrimps it is. And to follow – what are the *scoppolaricchi* like?' She pointed at the entry for deep-fried baby cuttlefish.

'For the first five minutes you'll think they're the best thing you've ever had. Then you'll think you've ordered too many.'

'Uh-huh. Fish and chips?'

'Fish and chips? Isn't that kind of boring?'

'I don't know, I've never had it. But God forbid I should commit the cardinal sin of being boring on something which is definitely not a date. I'll have the anchovy burger. Is that exciting enough?'

'It certainly is. And to drink?'

'Just a beer.'

'Only a beer? You don't want to split a bottle of prosecco or anything?'

'Better not. I've got the bike.'

Stefano looked disappointed for a minute, but then smiled.

'Okay, I'll go and order. Two beers, tempura shrimps, one anchovy burger and fish and chips for me.'

'What?'

He shrugged. 'What can I say? It may be boring but it's also really good. Don't worry, I'll let you share.'

'Good?'

Nedda dabbed away the few remaining fragments of anchovy with a napkin. 'Mighty good.'

She looked out, across the line of traffic, to the sea. The moon had risen behind the *Ciclopi,* casting silvery patterns across the ocean. She smiled. 'This is some place, you know? I mean, it's just a little blue and white bar where people fry things, and the air smells of petrol and fried fish, and the legs on the table need to be at an angle otherwise your dinner – and you – would slide into the sea. And yet it works.' Then she frowned. 'Have you still got that sofa?'

'No, I decided that watching TV from the floor was the way to go, and so I didn't think I'd need it in the future. Yes, of course I've still got it.'

'Good.' She got to her feet. 'Let's go and find a bar.'

Stefano linked his arm in Nedda's as they made their way along the front. For a moment she thought about politely shaking it off but decided not to. He was being nice. And not pushy nice, just nice. Well, okay, perhaps just a little pushy but bearably so.

'Where's good?' she said.

'Well, there's the *Caffè del Porto.* Best negronis in Trezza. But I've got an even better idea.'

He led her along the *Lungomare,* a street that seemed to

consist entirely of bars and restaurants where a never-ending stream of waiters smiled hopefully and tried to usher them inside.

'Does this always happen?' said Nedda.

'It seems to. I guess I just don't look Sicilian enough. They're never going to stop treating me like a tourist. But if I'm having a night out, I'm good with fish and chips, followed by sitting on the steps with a beer.'

The bars and restaurants thinned out, to be replaced with a series of stalls selling sweet pastries and candy floss; and the air was filled with the chatter of excited children, the smell of warm sugar and the strains of a guitar from a busker sitting at the base of the black basalt steps that led down from the church to the marina. A serious-looking girl, her hair in ringlets, with a very non-serious-looking poodle with similar hair, sat at his feet.

'Isn't this a bit weird?'

'How do you mean?'

'Stefano, four days ago we stood here and saw a dead man being pulled out of the sea.'

'We did, but,' he grinned, 'today it's as normal as it ever gets.' He looked out at the happy chattering crowds, and the endless stream of teens on *motorini* passing by. 'I guess everyone mourns in their own way, is what I'm trying to say.'

'Ouch. So, where's this drink coming from then?'

'You grab us a seat on the steps along with everyone else. Just find a space for two. Oh, and if you see any spare plastic cushions, get one.'

'Is that important?'

'These steps have been baking in the sun all day.' He

rubbed his chin. 'I'm trying to find the right words here, but something to go between you and the stone is very welcome. Now, what are you having?'

'I'll just have a *birra Messina*. No, hang on, that's boring. I'll have a *Spritz Etna*.'

'Yeah, you know what? Maybe I'll have the same.'

He returned in a couple of minutes with two plastic glasses filled with a deep red liquid.

'Is this kind of your local then?'

'I guess it kind of is. Well, it might become it. I'm still finding my feet here.'

'You moved out here from Catania, right?'

He nodded. 'Just a couple of months ago.'

'Any reason why?'

He laughed. 'Why?' He spread his arms wide to emphasise the view that lay before them. 'Come on, is there any need to ask why?'

'Don't you miss the big city, though?'

'Not in the slightest. Anyway, how about you living up in Acireale? Which is just like being here only higher up. Don't you ever think about moving down to Catania?'

'I don't know. Aci suits me fine. It's good bike country when the weather's right. And as for dad, well, I don't think he'd want to move back to the city.'

'Why not?'

Nedda shook her head. 'Long story. But it's linked to his job.' She paused. 'He was a policeman. With the *Guardia di Finanza*.' Stefano said nothing. 'What's the matter? Oh, don't tell me, you're one of those people who doesn't like cops?'

'No, it's not like that at all. It's just—'

'What?'

'Well. You don't seem like a policeman's daughter.'

It was such a feeble response that Nedda could not help but laugh.

'Cheers, Nedda.'

'Cheers, Stefano.'

They were about to clink glasses – or as best as one can manage with a plastic beaker – when Stefano gazed right into her eyes. Nedda held his gaze for a moment before looking away.

'No,' he said, alarm in his voice.

'What?'

'You mustn't look away when we clink. Otherwise you'll have seven years of bad sex.'

She giggled. 'Oh, come on.'

'Seriously.'

'You believe that? Yeah, right.'

'I'm serious. I got this wrong six years and eleven months ago and I don't want to get it wrong again.'

She shook her head. 'Honestly. Anyway, as I was saying, dad's had enough of big cities.'

'Whoa now, BIG change of subject there.'

'Yes, BIG change. Let's just say he prefers to be tucked away somewhere like Acireale than Catania. Or Palermo.'

Stefano nodded. 'I know about your mother,' he said.

Nedda said nothing. She sipped at her drink, and then she sipped a little more. And then she looked out at the traffic going past and smiled at a little girl happily skipping along the pavement ahead of her family, as her father cried out for her to be careful and her mother tried to catch her up despite having to push a pram. Then she raised her glass again. 'One of these days I'm going to fucking dye my hair blonde, you know?'

'I'm sorry. It's just kind of difficult not to know who you are. Especially in a job like ours.'

'Oh, don't I know it? Aldo knows as well. He's never said anything to me, but of course he does. I think that's why I'm trapped in lifestyle feature hell. I think he sees it as being some kind of duty of care. Keeping me away from anything that might hurt me.' She took a deep breath and another draught from her glass. 'Oh look, this seems to be evaporating.

'I never knew my mother well. She was taken away from me when I was very young. But she worked hard, damn hard, to make her way in a field where men wanted nothing more than to pat her on the head and ask her to make the coffee. You know how many female newspaper editors there are in Italy?'

Stefano shook his head. 'Dunno. I've never really thought about it before.'

'Of course you haven't. You haven't thought about it because you haven't needed to think about it.' She held up three fingers. 'That's how many there are. Three. In the whole of Italy.'

Stefano shrugged. 'I'm sorry. I know it must be tough. Maybe it will change with a female PM. Meloni used to be a journalist, after all.'

'I can't see it myself. She doesn't seem to like journalists very much. Or women for that matter. But, as I said, my mother worked damn hard at her job. And she'd be horrified at the thought that I'm spending my life filing reviews of *pasticcerie*.'

'I'm sorry,' Stefano repeated, and the two of them sat there and watched the traffic go by.

Eventually he broke the silence. 'You'd suit it, though.'

'What?'

'Being a blonde.'

Nedda jabbed an elbow into his ribs.

'Ow.'

'You deserved that.' She looked at her glass. 'Get me another drink and maybe, just maybe, I'll forgive you.'

He looked down at his own – 'I'm not doing very well here, am I?' – and knocked it back.

'So,' he said, upon returning from the kiosk. 'What are you going to do about it?'

'Me?'

'Well, I'm pretty sure your mother wouldn't want you accepting any help from me.'

'Well, you have helped and I'm grateful. This might be nothing, but it's possible there's something more to Lombardo's death than a simple drowning.'

'What did the old man say? Did you show him the video?'

'Yes. I told Toto – that's the guy at the TV station – that I wouldn't show it to anyone. Of course, I've shown it to you as well but I'm telling myself that doesn't count.'

'Thanks. I think. What did Aldo say?'

'He ummed and ahhed and said *most interesting* and then he gave me a stack of lifestyle features to cover – "Baby joy for local singer mildly famous ten years ago" – that's not the headline, by the way – and then, and *then*,' she grinned, 'he only told me that I can go and cover Lombardo's funeral tomorrow!'

'Wow!'

'A funeral. I'm living the dream, Stefano.'

He scratched his chin. 'I wonder if they'll be there?'

'Who?'

'The other people in the video. It might be telling if they are. Or if they aren't.'

'So, either way is – telling?'

Stefano looked down at his drink. 'Yes. You know, that sounded so much more intelligent in my head. What did you think about them?'

Nedda's brow furrowed. 'Morgana's a strange one. She's either mad or very clever. Possibly both. She certainly seemed like the only grown-up in the room.'

'And if a witch is the sanest person in the room, then I guess we're talking about a very strange room.'

She nodded. 'Both Salvatore and Gianmaria seemed like shysters to me. Gianmaria seemed relatively switched on. He seemed to get under Maugeri's skin at the end. I don't think Salvatore is anything more than an unpleasant drunk. Oh, and violent as well, of course.'

'Maugeri was riling him, though.'

'Still, attacking someone on live TV does demonstrate a bit of a short fuse. But I think Maugeri is smart if maybe not as smart as he thinks he is. He pushed them too far. Not with the fight but with something Gianmaria said afterwards. Asking where he was this time last year. Gianmaria knew something about his past. Something Maugeri was afraid he was going to reveal. Anyway, after my pastry run and funeral duties tomorrow, that's something to look into.'

She drained her glass and got, a little unsteadily, to her feet.

'You okay?' Stefano took her elbow.

'Yes. Two spritzes on top of beer is my limit, though.'

'Ah well. Let's get you home.' He paused. 'My home, that is. You're okay with that, right?'

'Sure. It won't be the first time. Dad'll be wanting to have "A Conversation" tomorrow but that's okay. Hell, he'll probably be wanting to meet you.'

'Seriously?'

'He's kind of old-fashioned that way.'

'Why not? Maybe we should all go out together?'

She looked at his empty glass. 'I think maybe I'm not the only one who's drunk.'

'So, what does he like eating? Where shall we go? Got to make a good impression.'

'Whoa now, George Clooney. Let's not rush this, eh? Let's have a think on this tomorrow with a proper night's sleep behind us.' She paused. 'I was serious about the sofa, by the way.'

'And so was I.'

'Besides,' she smiled, 'six years and eleven months, right?'

'And a few days.'

'Still.' She patted his cheek. 'Better not to risk it.'

Chapter 22

A hot summer's day is no day for a funeral.

Nedda had grumped her way through the morning, fuelled by *cannoli* and too much coffee. Stefano, the bastard, looked as fresh as a daisy and had offered to go out and do the pastry run for her. Nedda, her back aching following a night on the sofa, had been only too willing to accept.

John the Baptist, still enthroned in anthuriums, had been reinstalled in his church as a sparse congregation waited to welcome Gianmaria Lombardo for the last time.

Nedda sat at the back and waited. Gianmaria, it seemed, had not wasted many of his earthly years in making friends. A small group of men, all roughly the same age, shared a pew together near the front. Family? Friends? Drinking buddies? Maybe, she thought, there'd be the opportunity to talk to them afterwards.

Two women sat across the aisle from them, occasionally dabbing at their eyes. Nedda tried to remember what she'd read from the necrology. No wife, or wives, or sisters had been mentioned. Cousins perhaps?

She heard footsteps behind her, followed by the scrabbling of paws, a little *woof* that made her jump, and a whispered admonishment.

'Excuse me, can I sit here?'

Nedda turned to the speaker and jumped again.

'I'm sorry, did Luna startle you?' Mater Morgana sat down without waiting to be asked. 'You're okay with dogs, I hope?'

Luna gave a tiny little *yap* and Morgana bent down to scratch her behind the ears. 'Shhh, *trisoru*. You need to be quiet.'

Nedda looked down at the miniature dachshund and Luna gazed back up at her with her big brown eyes, her head cocked to one side. Then, as if deciding that everything was okay and this was a person to be trusted, she laid her head on Nedda's foot.

Nedda smiled at Morgana. 'I'm okay with this dog,' she said.

'Oh, don't be fooled. She can be a little terror when she wants to be. Can't you, *trisoru*?'

Luna flopped over on her back and presented her tummy for Nedda to tickle.

'I'm sorry about Gianmaria,' she said.

'Thank you,' said Morgana. She paused for a moment, and then looked directly into Nedda's eyes. 'He wasn't a friend, you understand. I felt I should be here, but Gianmaria wasn't really somebody who did friends.'

'I see.'

'And so, is this going to be in the newspapers?' Again, Nedda was unable to stop herself from starting. Luna gave an aggrieved little yap. 'You're the nervous type, aren't you?'

'Well now, I'm just wondering how you knew I was a journalist.'

'Oh, I'm a witch, that's all.'

'Oh, I know you are.'

'I'm impressed.' Morgana smiled. 'But I'm wondering just how you knew?'

'I'm a journalist. It's my job. But to go back to my question, Mater Morgana, put me out of my misery. How did you know?'

'Well, it might be my mystic powers. But mainly it's because there were people at *U pisci a mari* who spoke of the young red-headed reporter who was there when they pulled Gianmaria from the sea.' She smiled. 'So, nothing witchy at all really. But to go back to my question. Is this going to be in the papers tomorrow – Nedda?'

'You know my name?' She furrowed her brow for a moment and then her expression cleared. 'Ah, of course, my name was in the papers. Witches read them, then?'

'We have to keep abreast of the times, my dear. Crystal balls will only take you so far.'

'Anyway, yes, there probably will be a feature. I mean, it won't be big news or anything. But yes, there'll be a feature.'

'I'm not sure you'll find much to write about.'

'Maybe not. Maybe so.'

'Oh. Really? What makes you think that?'

Nedda shifted uncomfortably in her seat. Was this the sort of thing one should really be discussing at a funeral? But then again, as she kept saying, she was a journalist, wasn't she? 'It's just that – well, I kind of got the impression that *signor* Lombardo wasn't all that popular.'

Morgana chuckled quietly. Then she cast her eyes about the church. 'Well, the number of mourners would hardly give the lie to that, now, would it?'

Nedda heard footsteps from behind her.

'Good morning, Salvatore,' said Morgana.

Nedda turned to see the bald-headed man from the video, his shirt open perhaps one button more than necessary and a chunky gold medallion around his neck. 'Morgana,' he said.

'I thought you'd be here. Come to pay your respects?'

'Of course. He was a pal. And you?'

'I would never have described him as such. But I didn't like the idea of him setting off on his final journey on his own.'

'And her?' He jerked a thumb in the direction of Nedda without bothering to face her.

'This is my new friend, Nedda. You want to be nice to her. She's a journalist.'

Salvatore turned to her and looked her up and down. 'Really?'

Nedda fixed her brightest smile to her face. Punching someone on the nose in church, she knew, was still frowned upon by traditionalists. 'Yes, really.'

He grunted. 'Well make sure you write something good about him.' He raised his eyes to scan the rest of the church. 'He's not here then,' he said, lingering on *He's*.

'Did you really expect he would be?' said Morgana.

'Just as well. If he'd turned up, I'd have punched the fucker out.'

Inevitably, of course, the priest chose that precise moment to enter. There was an awkward silence, and then he processed to the sanctuary, indicating that the congregation should rise.

Salvatore slipped out during the sermon, where the well-meaning *padre* thought of nice things to say about a man he had, in all likelihood, never met. Nedda looked across at Morgana, who raised an imaginary cigarette to her lips as she inclined her head towards the door.

He didn't return for the rest of the service, although Nedda caught sight of him as the coffin was carried from the church, ready for Gianmaria Lombardo's final journey to the cemetery in Aci Castello.

Nedda shook her head. 'You've got to be really desperate for a smoke to head outside during your friend's funeral.'

'I'm not sure they were ever exactly friends. Gianmaria was just one of those people that Salvatore didn't actively dislike.' Morgana smiled. 'That's not a long list. Besides,' she nodded at the priest as he passed by, 'I know this one. He's good for a twenty-minute sermon. Thirty if he's had a good night's sleep. Salvatore probably thought he had time for both a cigarette and a drink in the bar down the road.'

Nedda looked at her curiously. 'I'm not sure I'd have tagged you as a churchgoer.'

'You expected I'd be more comfortable hanging around in graveyards, communing with the dead, that sort of thing?'

'Well. Yes.'

'Well, I do quite a lot of that, of course, but sometimes it's nice to have a day off.' She paused, trying to read the expression in Nedda's eyes. 'Joke,' she said, helpfully.

'Who was the *he* that Salvatore was talking about? The one he said he was looking forward to,' she cast her eyes heavenwards, 'punching.'

Morgana chuckled. 'Calogero Maugeri. Also known as the Magus.'

'Oh, him. I've seen him.'

'Really?'

'I saw a tape of that TV show you did together. The late-night talk show.'

The older woman smiled. 'My goodness, I should think that makes you a member of a very exclusive club.'

'I understand it was never broadcast.'

'So I heard. I left before the end. I could tell it was only going to end one way and I didn't really feel like being stuck in the middle of a melee between a group of overgrown schoolboys.'

'You don't have a very high opinion of them, then?'

'I suppose I feel sorry for them, if truth be told. They've been at this game for so long now they've almost forgotten the line between fantasy and reality. It's like they're starting to believe they really do have,' she wiggled her fingers in the air, 'special abilities.'

'And the Magus?'

'He's a strange one. He's basically doing what they're doing only he makes it obvious from the off that it's all stage magic. Cold reading and the like. His point being that any clever professional can do what Salvatore and Gianmaria do. Getting them all together on the same show was deliberately done in the hope of a fight starting.'

'I don't understand what you were doing on there, though?'

'I thought it might help to have one grown-up in the room. It seemed I was wrong.'

Luna gave a big yawn and flopped over. Morgana looked down at her, her expression softening. 'Well, look at you. You've been very patient. Time to get you home, is it?' Luna jumped up and into her lap, and Morgana got to her feet as best she could. 'Well, it's been nice to talk to you, my dear.' She paused. 'I don't suppose you've got a car. There won't be a bus for an hour yet and I don't think Luna's little legs are quite up to the walk.'

'Sorry. Just my motorbike.'

'Oh, that'll be perfect. Come on, Luna.'

She turned and walked from the church, not waiting to see if Nedda was following her.

Chapter 23

Morgana looked over the Royal Enfield, approval in her eyes.

'Proper bike,' she murmured.

'You ever have one yourself?'

'Nothing like this. I have a 1968 Vespa Primavera, however.' She sighed. 'Vanity purchase. Silly of me. Can never get it started. Which means using the almost-non-existent public transport. Which means one day I'll be found dead of starvation, the first victim of inadequate moped construction standards.'

Nedda looked at Morgana and the small dog nestling in her arms. 'Erm, you're very welcome to a lift but where are we going to put Luna?'

'You have a tank bag?'

'Sure.'

'There we go then. Just zip her in and leave her head poking out.'

'Are you sure?'

'Of course. She'll love it.'

Nedda unzipped the tank bag and Morgana placed Luna inside, zipping the little dog up until just her head was showing.

'Are you sure about this?'

'Quite sure, my dear.'

'I don't have a spare helmet.'

'Then you'll need to be very careful.'

'And I don't know where you live.'

'I'll tell you along the way. Now. Off we go, eh?'

Nedda didn't like taking pillions without a helmet, but Morgana didn't seem to be in the mood to argue. She'd also seen Sicilians transporting their entire families around on a single scooter, but a dog in a tank bag was new to her. Luna didn't seem to be complaining, but nevertheless Nedda thought this was probably not the occasion to get her knee down.

'Thank you, Nedda. That saved me a lot of trouble. Cup of tea?'

'Yes, thanks. That'd be nice.'

Morgana unzipped the tank bag and Luna jumped out, yapping happily. Morgana swept her up into her arms. 'Naughty Luna, can't have you breaking the circle, can we?' She looked over at Nedda. 'Do mind where you step.'

Nedda looked down at the semicircle of crystals outside Morgana's front door. 'Salt?'

'For protection, dearie. Come on.'

Nedda stepped over the circle, and into Morgana's front room.

'I've just thought, would you prefer coffee?'

'Well, I would if that's an option.'

'I'm afraid it isn't. I never have it in.'

'Tea will be perfect then.'

'Then tea it shall be.' The older woman stepped closer to her and stared into her eyes. 'Oh, you look tired, my dear. Bit of a late night, was it? But not to worry, a cup of green tea will sort all that out. Just take a seat.' Nedda made to sit down. 'Not that one. That's Menocchio's. He'll be most displeased if you take his seat.'

'Your husband?'

'My owl.'

'Oh.' There didn't seem to be much else to say. Nedda looked around. 'Is here okay? I mean, I don't want to take Luna's seat or anything.'

'Luna will sit where she's told. But Menocchio has a profound sense of territory and is forthright in expressing his opinions. Now, make yourself comfortable. I'll be back with the tea.'

Nedda sat down and looked around her. The painting of a severe-looking woman was reflected in the mirror in front of her, together with her own image, and the juxtaposition bothered her. Then a large brown owl, presumably Menocchio, flapped into the room, perched himself on the chair opposite, and stared at her.

She attempted, and failed, to stare him down as his big amber eyes gazed back into hers.

Unhappy at being intimidated by an owl, Nedda poked her tongue out at him. Then she got to her feet in order not to be stared at anymore. She wondered what Mater Morgana's taste in reading leaned towards and went to the bookshelves.

Morgana's filing system might best have been described as 'random access'. She seemed to have quite a predilection for cheap romance novels, which lined the shelves together with weightier tomes on herbalism and history. And witchcraft. Lots of witchcraft. But then again, Nedda thought, Morgana was a witch. Of course she was going to have books on the subject.

There was a scrabbling sound from behind her, and she turned to see Menocchio, who had shifted in his seat in order to be able to better stare at her.

I'm being stared at by an owl. This is what owls do. The fact this is a witch's owl in a witch's house makes no difference at all. Even if Morgana is a real witch, which of course she isn't.

She decided that she liked Luna better. Then she turned back to the shelves and took down a hefty leather-bound tome.

Henricus Institor. The *Malleus Malificarum*. 'The Hammer of Witches', she thought. The title rang a vague bell. She opened it halfway and then shook her head. Latin had never been her best subject at school. She replaced it and took down another.

Margaret Murray. *The Witch-Cult in Western Europe*. Also of limited use. English had not been her best subject at school, either.

'Have you found something interesting, dear?' Morgana had re-entered the room without a sound. Good slippers, Nedda imagined.

She held the book out. 'Sorry, just being nosey. Other people's bookshelves are addictive, aren't they?'

'They most certainly are. A lot of these were my mother's. I couldn't bear to throw them out.' She looked at the book in Nedda's hand. 'Margaret Murray? Mother had strong opinions on that book. Didn't hold with it at all.' She traced a finger across the spines on the shelves and looked with distaste at the dust that gathered on it. 'I really must have a proper clean. Here, now, this one is of far more interest. She pulled out a book and passed it to Nedda, who frowned when she saw the cover.

'*The Night Battles: Witchcraft and Agrarian Cults in the Sixteenth and Seventeenth Centuries*,' she read. She looked back at Morgana. 'I have to say, it doesn't sound like a blockbuster.'

'You'd be surprised. It revolutionised thought on witchcraft in Italy when it was published.' She stroked Menocchio's feathers, and the bird shivered with delight. 'You've been introduced, I see.'

'We have. Can I ask what he is? Beyond being an owl, I mean.'

Menocchio hooted gently. Nedda turned to him. 'Sorry, I know I'm making assumptions with the "he".'

'He's a tawny owl. I believe the Latin name is *Strix aluco*.' Morgana smiled. 'They were birds of ill-omen in the past. They would, it is said, be seen in the house three days before a death. However, our word *strega* – witch – comes from the Latin *strix*. So when Menocchio decided to move in with me, I took it as a good omen and not a bad one.'

'I didn't realise it was allowed. To keep an owl as a pet, I mean.'

Menocchio turned his unblinking gaze upon her. Morgana gently placed her hands over his ears, as if in fear that Nedda might have caused offence.

'Pet? A pet? Menocchio chooses to live with me when it pleases him. No more, no less. He and his kind made their home in a petrified orchard on the slopes of Etna.'

Menocchio shifted his gaze from Nedda to Luna. The

little dog held her ground for as long as she could, but then whimpered and curled up behind Nedda's legs, out of his unblinking gaze.

She looked down at her. 'Do the two of them get along?'

'Oh, perfectly well. Luna is far too large for Menocchio to take any interest in her.'

Luna whimpered again, as if to indicate that she had heard this before but that neither she – nor, for that matter, Menocchio – were one hundred per cent convinced.

'Now then. Why not sit down and drink your tea?'

Nedda sat down and cast her eyes around the room.

'Is there something wrong?'

'No, it's just,' Nedda laughed awkwardly, 'I'm sure you've been asked this hundreds of times, but—'

'You're asking if I believe all this? If I really am a witch? My dear, I don't believe it. I know it.'

'I'm sorry, but I don't think I even know what that means.'

'Well now, child. For that we need to go back several hundred years. To the time of the witch trials.

'The men of Sicily are relatively civilised, you know? As they were back then. By the standards of the Inquisition, that is. No women went to the fire, very few even went to jail. Some were sent into exile abroad – I imagine that must have been hard. A barely educated Sicilian woman would hardly have spoken much Italian in those days. But all-in-all, although we were disapproved of, we were not treated badly. Now, does that mean that good Sicilian men were simply more tolerant than their counterparts on the mainland?' She shook her head. 'I think not. I think it was because, at heart, there was still a belief in *faerie*. In the other. And over the years we'd managed to integrate it with Christianity. In some ways, we saw no difference between them.

'You saw that the other day, in Aci Trezza. *U pisci a mari.* A pagan pantomime side by side with the veneration of a Christian saint. These things have gone hand in hand for centuries. And scratch the surface of Sicily, and you'll find they still do.

'I used the word *faerie,* because that's what we were. The Spanish called us the *doñas de fuera.* The *donne di fuora.* The ladies from outside. Our magic was in healing, and in dancing, and in communion with the fairy world. And what harm could there possibly be in that? Well, those were different times, and ladies from outside were always seen with more than a touch of suspicion.' She sighed. 'Perhaps those times were not so different after all.

'But that's what I am, child. I'm a lady from outside. So why not sit down, drink your tea and tell me why you think Gianmaria Lombardo was murdered?'

Nedda managed to stop herself from starting. All of this, she was starting to think, was something of a test.

'Well now, Mater Morgana. Why would you think that?'

Morgana smiled. 'What else would have brought you to San Giovanni Battista this morning?'

'I'm a journalist, remember? The funeral of a man who died in bizarre circumstances last week is still a little newsworthy.'

'And maybe it is. But I didn't see you take any notes. Or any photos. So, either tomorrow's story is going to be a little sketchy, or you never had any intention of filing it.'

Nedda sat down and inhaled the vapours from her tea. She sighed.

'Better?'

'Much. Thank you.'

Menocchio was still staring at her. 'Does he always do that?'

'Only with strangers. He likes you, though. I can tell.'

'Oh good. I wouldn't like to think he didn't like me.' She paused. 'There's something I was meaning to ask you. Back in church. You greeted Salvatore before you'd even seen him. I had my eyes on you all the time. You didn't turn round.'

Morgana smiled. 'Well, perhaps I should say it was a sixth sense. But remember, I'd told you we wouldn't be expecting a huge number of mourners. Salvatore has never been the most punctual of men. There was also the faint smell of stale cigarette smoke and grappa. So, it was a reasonable guess. And if it hadn't been him, you wouldn't even have remembered that I said it.'

'It was a demonstration, then? Or a test?'

She smiled again. 'If you like. Then she frowned. 'Mind you, that's the sort of thing Calogero likes to do. But he'd have been ever so *theatrical* about it. That's the difference between him and me.'

'So, what do you think happened to Gianmaria Lombardo?'

'I think there are two possibilities. One is that a man with no particular interest in swimming decided to take it up on the busiest day of the year. The other possibility is that,' she sipped at her tea, 'he was, indeed, murdered.'

'But why?'

'It's very easy to make enemies in their line of work, Nedda. Somebody loses their life savings, their inheritance, their job. All this can happen.'

'There was someone in Acireale. I won't give you his name,

but he called himself *"AngryinAci"*. He said there were plenty of people around who would have been celebrating the fact he'd died.'

'Mmm. Of course, there's quite a difference between wishing someone dead and doing it. And it's not that easy to kill someone. Empathy keeps getting in the way. For a normal person, of course. And even if you can overcome that, then actually getting away with it is even harder.' She smiled and sipped her tea again. 'At least, so I believe.'

'So where would you start?'

'Well, you already have this angry man in Acireale. Although I wonder if an actual killer would be telling everyone how happy they were on what I understand they call the social media. No, I think perhaps we need to look closer at Gianmaria's circle. The two other people on that panel show. I wonder what they might have to say.'

Chapter 24

Calogero paused outside the apartment block on the *Lungomare dei Ciclopi* and looked upwards. Lombardo's apartment, he understood, was on the third floor. The view towards the *Ciclopi*, or, in the other direction, to the fortress of Aci Castello, would be spectacular. In contrast to some of the other blocks along this stretch, where the plasterwork crumbled and the shutters were chipped and faded, the apartment building itself looked shiny and sparkling, the paintwork clean and white, the shutters a fetching shade of deep-sea blue and the glasswork shining. The restaurant on the ground floor looked good, and the aroma of grilled meats and fish made Calogero wonder if he should stop for lunch first.

This was, of course, Aci Trezza, where property prices might not be those of Rome or Florence or Venice. Still, Gianmaria Lombardo had evidently done very well for himself.

Calogero hung around outside the front door waiting for someone to exit, and snuck in to the entrance lobby before the door could close, taking care to turn his face away from the security camera.

Lift or stairs? Stairs, he decided. Easier to avoid people. The lift ran the risk of close proximity to residents and enforced conversation.

Only three flights of stairs, yet the heat left him panting. *Calogero, my boy, you need to start looking after yourself a little better.*

He ran his hands over the lock. Scratch marks. It could be that Gianmaria was just a little clumsy with his keys. Or it could be that someone else had been here before him. That, he supposed, was only to be expected.

It was a standard Yale lock instead of a five-bar *porta blindata*. Good. That would be near-impossible to open without professional gear. He checked both left and right and then took a card from his pocket. The door clicked open within seconds. He smiled. The old trick still worked.

As he stepped through and made to close the door behind him, he heard a noise from the landing. He pushed the door shut as quietly as he could. Again, he heard the sound of footsteps from outside, and he stood dead still. Then he heard movement again, the sound of the lift arriving, the doors opening, and then the lift descending. One of the other residents, of course.

Time to get to work. Well, almost time to get to work. He took a look around the living room. The sort of classy, minimalist space that one might associate with Stockholm or Copenhagen instead of Aci Trezza. A large-screen TV was fixed to the wall. The air conditioning model looked new and sophisticated. Sicily might be burning in a few weeks' time, but Gianmaria Lombardo would not have felt it. Of course, Calogero thought to himself with a smile, it was entirely possible that Lombardo was burning somewhere else right now.

The picture window looked out over the bay, and the view was as spectacular as Calogero had imagined. He shook his head. Even if Gianmaria's tax declarations to the *Guardia di Finanza* had been creatively adjusted, he found it hard to imagine how he could have accumulated the sort of money for a place like this. Or rather, he could imagine it, and the thought made him smile, bitterly. Gianmaria's dossier must be a substantial one.

The only thing that seemed out of place were the cotton sofa covers, ragged and torn around the edges. The explanation for that came when a *miaow* sounded from around his feet. A ginger cat scratched at the sofa, and then looked up imploringly. Calogero bent down to scratch it behind the ears. It nipped at his finger but only gently, as if its heart wasn't really in it.

'Poor kitty. I wonder who's going to look after you now.' The cat looked up again at the sound of his voice, but Calogero shook his head. 'Sorry, but I've never really been a cat person.' He walked through to the kitchen in search of cat food, and noticed that its bowl was still half-full.

He scratched his head. Gianmaria, as far as he knew, had no close relatives although he thought he remembered a cousin in Catania. He supposed they might have come around to feed the cat, but why wouldn't they just take it away with them and try and find it a proper home? He supposed it was possible they were coming back.

He shook his head. No time for that now. Slowly, methodically, he went through every cupboard in the kitchen. Then he repeated the process in the living room. And then in the bathroom.

Nothing.

He checked his watch. No need to panic. He had a show that evening, but that was hours away. No need to rush. Just find it, however long it took.

A ceramic fruit bowl, in gaudy red and yellow, sat on the living room table, the one splash of light in the otherwise spartan room. It held a set of keys on a leather keyring, and a small business card.

Calogero scratched his chin. Should he take the keys? It would, he supposed, make it that much easier to get back in should he need to. He picked them up and dropped them in his pocket. He picked up the card. *Stefano Gallo. Giornalista.*

Odd. Psychics tended not to speak to the press. Late-night cable TV shows were one thing. A journalist that might start asking awkward questions was another.

There was only the bedroom left to search. If that failed, he'd have to come back another day. Or think of somewhere else.

Immediately it was obvious that someone had been there before him. The rest of the apartment was immaculate, Gianmaria Lombardo seemingly as obsessively tidy in death as in life. But the bedroom had been disturbed.

Disturbed, but not torn apart. A large signed photograph of the Catania football squad had been taken down off the wall, and propped against the wardrobe. Behind it lay a wall safe. An open wall safe.

Calogero fought down the panic that was rising within him. He pulled the door open as wide as it would go and ran his hand around the interior. Nothing.

Empty, now. But had it always been so?

He shook his head. Wrong place, wrong time to be trying to make decisions on something like this. Better to go home, do tonight's show, and then think it over in the company of a drink.

He got to his feet and moved to the door. A plaintive *miaow* came from the kitchen. What to do about the cat? He didn't want to take the damn thing home, but what was the alternative? To come back here every day to feed it for the rest of the cat's – or his own – natural life?

He sighed and went through to the kitchen. He could, at least, leave sufficient food for a couple of days. Maybe Gianmaria's cousin would have decided to take it in by then.

He searched through the cupboards until he found something that looked as if it might be dried cat food. Then he looked down at the bowl, where the cat was happily foraging. Gently, he pushed it aside, in order to top up its food.

There came a sound from the living room. Calogero darted back inside. The front door was still closed. Surely he'd have heard that opening and closing? As he looked around the room he noticed the curtains blowing in the breeze. The door to the balcony had been opened.

He moved outside, trying to keep half an eye on the door the whole time. He risked a quick glance downwards. No. Too far, way too far for anyone to risk climbing, let alone jumping. The balconies to the left and the right seemed beyond the possibility of reaching. Upwards? He took a glance and shook his head. You'd have to be insane. Or really desperate.

He turned back to the living room. The door was still closed. The table still bare, except for the bowl. That left the bedroom, bathroom and – how many damn rooms did

Gianmaria have in his apartment anyway? Was there anywhere he'd yet to check?

He was still thinking that over when the floor came up to meet him at high speed.

Calogero got to his feet, ever so slowly. He put his hand, gingerly, to the back of his head. No blood. That, he assumed, was a good thing. His stomach churned and he fought down the urge to vomit.

He'd been knocked out three times in his life, and hoped this would be the last. Water. Water would definitely be good. And then what? *Pronto soccorso*? Or go home and hope for the best? Was that a stupid idea? Again, he gently rubbed the back of his head as he headed for the kitchen.

So, Gianmaria's dossier was now in the hands of someone else. What did this mean? That, of course, might have been easier to work out if he'd known exactly what the damn folder contained in the first place.

He splashed water across his face, his head throbbing.

Best possible case: whoever now had the file would set fire to it and Gianmaria's whole filthy business would be gone forever.

Worst case: whoever had the file was now picking through it with increasing delight. And Calogero would soon be seen as a potential income stream.

Police? Impossible.

Don't panic.

Keep calm and feed the cat. Then what? Go through the apartment, top to bottom, in the hope of finding something useful? Or just head back to Acireale and prepare for tonight's show?

He made his way, a little unsteadily, back into the living room. Something was wrong.

He looked down at the fruit bowl. The business card – Stefano someone-or-other – had gone. And something had replaced it. A card with the image of a cloaked figure over-looking a river, with five cups at its feet.

A Tarot card. The one card that was missing from the deck left outside Salvatore Sipala's house.

He suddenly became aware of two cops standing in the doorway, hands on hips and smiling at him.

He raised his hands above his head and smiled back.

'Okay, guys, I guess there's two possibilities here. One is that I finish feeding the cat,' he nodded towards the kitchen but the cat, awkwardly, had decided to become invisible, 'and I'll be on my way.'

The bigger of the two cops shook his head, his smile widening.

Calogero sighed and shrugged his shoulders. 'Well in that case, I suppose this means we need to have a conversation. . .'

Chapter 25

'So, child.' Morgana paused and frowned. 'My apologies, I can't keep calling you that. What should I call you?'

'You could use Nedda if you like. On account of it being my name, and all.'

'Very well then. Nedda it is. The two other people on the panel show. Calogero Maugeri and Salvatore Sipala. What do you make of them?'

'I've seen the video – the complete video, as I said – of the programme. Maugeri had a fight with Sipala on camera. Do you know what that was all about?'

'I'd walked out by then. But it was obvious the producer wanted an argument at worst and proper fisticuffs at best. Salvatore is the worst kind of charlatan and easy to goad into violence. So was Lombardo for that matter.' She smiled again. 'They say one should not speak ill of the dead. I prefer to think one should only ever speak honestly of the dead. And Gianmaria Lombardo was not a good man.'

'And Maugeri?'

'The Magus, as he likes to be called. He's been in this region less than a year. He has some success as a stage magician. I suspect that's why he was on the panel. To have a sceptic there, someone who could reproduce all the cheap tricks from Salvatore and Gianmaria without having to pretend there was anything other-worldly about it. Because that's all it is. Cheap trickery.'

'And why were you there?'

'Oh, to be the mad old woman, of course.'

'Didn't you mind?'

'They offered me some money and being a witch doesn't pay as much as it once did.' She looked over the top of her glasses at Nedda. 'If you want me to help, I'm not sure if I can. I'm afraid I can't actually commune with the outside and ask them a direct question. Or summon up the shade of Gianmaria Lombardo and ask him directly.'

'That's a shame. I was kind of hoping for something like that.'

'I'm sorry. But there are rules, you know.'

Nedda could never be quite sure when Morgana was joking.

'There was something else on the video. The last thing Lombardo said before Maugeri walked out. He said the viewers would like to know where he'd been this time last year. Does that mean anything to you?'

She shook her head. 'Not a thing, I'm afraid. Prison, perhaps?'

'Does that seem likely?'

'For a peripatetic entertainer, associating with mountebanks and charlatans? Not uncommon or unlikely. Why don't you ask him?' Nedda was about to speak, but Morgana wagged a finger at her. 'Now, you be careful here. Especially of Salvatore. I don't know much about him, but what I know I don't like. He's not a good man. As for Maugeri,' she shrugged, 'I have no idea if he's a good man or not. But he, I think, would be worth speaking to.' She frowned. 'If, that is, he wants to speak to you.'

Nedda's phone rang, but she pointedly ignored it until Morgana nodded. 'Go ahead.'

'Stefano?'

'Nedda?' His voice was excited. 'I've got some news. Are you in Acireale?'

'Yes. Well, near enough.'

'Great. Get to the *Questura* as soon as you can. They won't let you in, but just hang around outside. I've had a tip-off. . .'

Nedda hung up and smiled at Morgana. 'You know, *Mater*, he might just want to speak to me after all.'

Chapter 26

'I'd been expecting something a little different,' said Calogero.

The policeman on the other side of the desk stared at him.

'I mean, it's perfectly nice and everything, I'd just been led to expect something a little more. You know, like in *Montalbano*.'

The cop rubbed his forehead. 'If I had a euro for every smartarse who comes in here and says "It's not like *Montalbano*." No, it isn't, and for the record, no, I do not live in a house like his either.' He tapped a pen on his desk. 'I'm *ispettore* Gori.'

'Pleased to meet you. I'm Calogero Maugeri.'

'I know that. Good Sicilian name. Unlike mine.' He tapped Calogero's identity card on the desk, and then stared at it. He'd been doing a lot of that, and it was starting to bother Calogero.

'You know, you look younger in the photo?'

'Well, I use a lot of stage makeup, you know?'

Gori looked at the card again. Calogero wished he'd stop doing that. 'Oh yes. Your profession is down as "Performer".'

'Yes.'

'What do you perform then? Who knows, maybe I've seen you?'

'I'm a magician.'

'Ah. Okay, maybe I haven't.'

'In my line of work, people expect you to give them the full Doctor Strange in photos and the like.'

'Even your ID card?'

'I'd probably just come off stage.'

'Just as well you're not wearing a cloak, I guess.'

'Yes. You know, you're lucky. If I was twenty years older they'd be expecting Gandalf.' He sighed. 'I expect that's in my future.'

Gori merely nodded. 'So, this is the first time you've been in here, then?'

'It is.'

'We'll be checking that, you know.'

'I'd be disappointed if you didn't.'

'So, for the benefit of the tape, you're here because you were found breaking into the house of one Gianmaria Lombardo, now deceased but previously resident at 13 Lungomare dei Ciclopi, Aci Trezza.'

'No.'

'What do you mean, no?'

'I mean, I wasn't breaking in. I had a key.'

'Why would you have a key?'

'He gave me a set, some months ago. Just in case he needed someone to drop by and feed his cat.'

Gori stopped scribbling in his notepad and looked up. 'He has a cat?'

'Yes. It'll be there somewhere in the house. Probably under the bed. You didn't think to check?'

He scribbled away again. 'Okay. Maybe we need to do

that.' He looked at the papers in front of him. 'It says here that you live here in Acireale?'

'That's right.'

'We're five kilometres from Aci Trezza. You mean to say you were the nearest person he could find to feed his cat?'

'Sure. I don't think he had many friends.'

'But you were one of them?'

'No. We heartily disliked each other.'

'So,' Gori rubbed his forehead, 'why would he ask you to look after his cat?'

'I'm very good with cats.'

Gori leaned back in his chair, and put his hands behind his head. 'You ever heard of Paolo Rossi, Maugeri?'

Calogero shook his head.

'Italian football player. One of the greatest.'

'I'm not really into football.' He thought back to the signed Catania FC photograph in Lombardo's apartment and couldn't suppress a chuckle. 'I'm not sure Lombardo was for that matter.'

Gori let it go. 'Paolo Rossi. Scored a hat-trick against Brazil in the 1982 World Cup. Then twice in the semi-final. And once in the final. National hero.'

'Wow.'

'Died back in 2020.'

'I'm sorry.'

'And do you know what happened on the day that Paolo Rossi, national hero, was buried?' Calogero shook his head again. 'During his funeral a couple of scumbags burgled his house.'

'Shit.'

'You know what I think, *signor* Maugeri? This is something

we see all the time. Someone's death gets reported, it's in the papers, the time and date is announced for the funeral, and some unscrupulous little bastard takes advantage of that and goes round to burgle their house when they know no one's going to be around.'

'And you think that's what I did.' Gori nodded. 'But I have the keys, remember?'

Gori picked them up and jangled them in his face. 'You have these, which we found in your pocket. You could have picked them up after breaking in.'

'But there's no sign of breaking in. Is there?'

Gori sighed. 'No. But maybe you're very good at breaking in. Just like you're good with cats.'

Calogero put his head to one side and nodded, as if weighing up what the cop was saying to him.

'Who called you?' he said. 'One of the neighbours?'

'What?'

'Somebody must have called you. Your guys didn't arrive there by accident. Now it could have been a neighbour, but I don't think so. I think whoever attacked me called you and said, oh sorry to bother you, *ispettore*, but I've seen somebody breaking into the late *signor* Lombardo's apartment.'

'Which you say you weren't doing.'

'Which I indeed was not doing. Because I had the keys. Incidentally, can I have them back?'

'In good time, and when I say so. Continue, please.'

Calogero rubbed the back of his head and winced.

'It's as I said. I went round to feed Gianmaria's cat. I guess at some point somebody is going to have to look after it.'

'Why not you? You're good with them, remember?'

'I don't lead a very cat-friendly lifestyle. As I was saying, I was there, somebody was either waiting for me or entered the flat without me noticing and then,' again, he rubbed the back of his head, 'goodnight, Aci Trezza.'

'Mmm-hm.' Gori tapped a pen up and down on his pad. 'And that was it. Nothing taken? From you, I mean.'

Calogero shrugged. 'Not as far as I can tell.'

'You checked your pockets? Wallet still there?'

'The only thing that's been taken are the keys. By you.'

'Mmm-hm,' he repeated. The tapping was starting to irritate Calogero, and he rubbed his temples.

'You okay?'

'Headache. As you might expect. You have any paracetamol?'

'No.'

'Glass of water?'

'Still or sparkling?'

'Sparkling would be nice.'

'I'm sorry. I think we're out.'

'A shame. On a hot day, that's almost as good as a beer. Tap water will be fine.'

Gori nodded at the young cop keeping watch by the door. 'A glass of water for our guest, please.' He turned back to Calogero. 'Ice?'

'That'd be nice.'

'You heard the man. Ice.'

'Of course, sir.' The cop grinned. 'I'll see what I can find.'

Calogero and Gori sat in silence for a few minutes, the *ispettore* rhythmically tapping his pen against the desk.

The young lad returned with a glass of water. 'You're in

luck,' he smiled. 'There were just two ice cubes left. Now, normally the boss saves that for his end-of-day martini, but I felt in this case I could make an exception.' He turned to Gori. 'Was that the right thing to do?'

'I think we all need to make sacrifices at times, Enzo. This is one of them.' He nodded at Calogero. 'Please.'

Calogero picked an ice cube from the glass, and pressed it to the back of his scalp, sighing with pleasure.

'Better?'

'Much.'

'Good. Okay, let's get back to basics. You went round to the late Gianmaria Lombardo's in order to save his cat from starvation. Whilst you were there, an unknown assailant knocked you out, and called the police while you were unconscious. Is that correct?'

'Correct.'

'Yet, as far as you can be certain, nothing was taken from the apartment. Correct?'

'Correct.'

'And none of your personal effects have been taken apart from this set of keys? By us.'

'Correct.'

'And while you were unconscious, your assailant dropped a,' he stared more closely at the papers in front of him, 'a *Tarot* card into a fruit bowl?'

'The Five of Cups. Correct.'

Gori replaced his pen with the keys and, again, began to rhythmically tap them up and down on his desk. Calogero scooped the other ice cube out of his glass and pressed it to the back of his head.

'No,' said Gori, finally.

'No what?'

'Makes no sense, does it? Somebody waits around in Lombardo's flat for you to come calling, knocks you out, and then leaves without anything. Oh, and then they leave a Tarot card as a calling card. Nonsense, isn't it? Why would anyone do that?'

Calogero sighed. 'I don't know. Maybe to frame me for something. I don't know what.'

'To frame you for something?' Gori chuckled. 'We really are going the full *Montalbano* now, aren't we? But, okay, let's run with that as an idea. *Signor* Maugeri, in your opinion, who would want to frame you and what would they be trying to frame you for?'

'I don't know. But I do know that Gianmaria was not exactly the most popular man in Catania. There are any number of people with a grudge against him.'

'*Any number of people with a grudge.* Okay, let's have some names.'

'I don't have any names. The guy was a medium. They tend to attract enemies. Ask anyone who's lost an inheritance recently, if that narrows it down.' He pressed the glass of water against his forehead.

Gori nodded. 'Okay. I can see you're suffering a bit.' He looked at the papers in front of him. 'Go and get that head checked out. I'll see you back here tomorrow morning.'

'What?'

'Still plenty of things to talk about, *signor* Maugeri. Bright and early at nine o'clock, shall we say? I'll make sure there's coffee.' He smiled. 'Get a good night's sleep in the meantime.'

Calogero, wearily, got to his feet. Gori was still holding the keys. 'I'll hang on to these for the time being.'

'But—'

'No, don't worry. We'll make sure that the cat – if we can find it – is fed and watered.' He raised his hand in a mock salute. '*A domani, signore.*'

Calogero pulled on his jacket. The cop by the door held it open for him. There might just have been the hint of a little bow as he passed by. Terrific. A pair of smartarse policemen who evidently wanted to be in show business. That's what the world needed.

He looked at his watch. And talking of showbusiness, he needed to be on stage in a few hours when all he really wanted to do was go and lie down in a darkened room, with the air conditioning turned up to max.

The heat was the first thing to hit him, as he left the station. The second was the sight of a young red-haired woman snapping away with a phone camera.

She dropped the camera into her handbag and waved at him. '*Signor* Maugeri?'

He nodded. There seemed little point in denying it.

'I'm Nedda Leonardi, from *Catania Nuova*. I wondered if you might have time to chat.'

He looked her up and down. '*Mizzica*. Journalists really are getting younger these days, aren't they?'

Nedda smiled. 'We are. And do you know what, I've heard even girls can do it. Now, how about a talk over coffee. I'd suggest a spritz or a negroni but you probably think I'm far too young for one of those.'

'A chat over coffee, eh? That sounds nice.' He rubbed his

forehead. 'Oh wait. Wait. No, it doesn't.'

'Have you been arrested?'

'No.'

'No. That's great. Now we're communicating. Did the police want to talk to you about the death of Gianmaria Lombardo?'

'No. They wanted to check with me if adequate provisions had been put in place with regard to the long-term survival of his pet cat.'

Nedda stopped smiling. 'You know, maybe you could just stop being an asshole for a moment?'

'Maybe I could.' Calogero turned and walked on. 'Maybe I'll stop being one when you stop asking me questions.' He heard her footsteps behind him and turned to face her. 'Or is that not going to be possible?'

'No.'

He sighed. 'Look. I've been hit on the back of the head. It's a baking hot day. I've got to go to work in a few hours while all I want to do is sleep. Actually the thought of throwing up is also an attractive one at the moment.'

She nodded. 'Too much information. We probably won't print that.'

'Thank you.'

'But I know you need to go to work. *Teatro Giovanni Verga*, Acireale, right?'

He frowned. 'How do you know that?'

Nedda tapped the side of her nose. 'That would be magic.'

Chapter 27

Calogero had never liked scooters and was now coming to the conclusion that he liked motorcycles even less. In the absence of a spare helmet, Nedda had promised him that she'd take it easy, and the journey from the *Questura* to the theatre was a short one. It seemed to him, however, that she could perhaps take it a little easier than she was; whilst, at the same time, the distance seemed a little longer than it should.

She parked outside the theatre, kicked the stand down and dismounted. Then she removed her helmet, shaking her hair free.

Calogero dismounted, his limbs now feeling leaden and shaky.

'You okay?'

'Fine.'

'Sorry. Did I step it out too much? I'm not used to having a pillion.'

'It's okay. Just my head aches a bit, that's all.'

'Mine too. Coffee? Or something stronger?'

'I don't drink before a show.'

She looked at him more closely. 'You look rough. Are you sure you're okay?'

'I've been in a fight and I've been down the police station. No, I'm not really okay. But losing my job isn't going to make me feel any better, and so,' he flung his arms wide and declaimed, 'the show must go on.'

'Okay. I understand.'

'Thank you.'

'Just maybe don't do that again. I think people were looking.' She looked around. 'Okay, there's a decent *gelateria* near here. We could treat ourselves to a *granita* and brioche and call it dinner.'

He shook his head. 'I need something more solid.' And then for the first time, he smiled. 'And I know just the place. Come on.'

It was barely five o'clock but *Toast of Aci* was already busy. The *barista* waved at Calogero, raised an eyebrow upon seeing Nedda, and then winked.

'They seem to know you here,' she said.

'They certainly do. It's only five minutes' walk to the theatre. I'm here pretty much every day.'

'Wow. You must think a lot of it.'

'Well, if it wasn't for this place I'd have to buy proper kitchen equipment and do actual cooking and all that "looking after myself properly" thing and I'm not sure I'm quite ready for that.'

'So, you eat here every day?'

'Five o'clock. Pretty much on the hour.'

'What's good?'

'*Toast.*'

'Eh?'

'*Toast. Toast of Aci.* That's what they do. *Toast.* It's not just a clever name.'

'That's all they do? Toasted sandwiches?'

'Yes. That's the genius of it.'

'We're in Sicily. You know, *arancini, caponata, pasta alla Norma, sarde a beccafico* – all that sort of stuff. And you come here to eat *toast*?'

'What can I say. I've never been an adventurous eater. When I find something I like, I tend to stick to it.'

The *barista* came over and clapped Calogero on the shoulder. '*Ciao,* buddy, how's it going?'

'Not too bad, Dante.'

'Good to hear.'

'Actually, that's not quite true. I've been knocked unconscious, spent the afternoon trying to explain to a policeman that I'm not a burglar, and when I thought things couldn't get any worse, I had a lift on a motorbike.'

'Oh, thanks for that,' muttered Nedda.

Dante smiled a broad smile and clapped him on the back again. 'Okay. So you know what will make you feel better?'

Nedda raised an eyebrow. 'This might be a wild guess, but is the answer *toast* by any chance?'

'*Sisignurina!*'

She looked over at Calogero. 'What's good?'

He ran his fingers down the menu. 'Hmm.' He turned to Dante. 'Any specials today?'

'My friend, we do thirty different variations on the toasted sandwich. Chef says he can't make them any more special.'

'Okay then. Well, given it's Saturday,' he rubbed the back

of his head, 'at least, I think it's Saturday – I'll just go for something simple. *Fior di latte*, tomato and basil.'

'You sure that's all?'

'That'll be just fine. How about you, Nedda?'

'Mozzarella, mortadella and grilled *melanzane*. At least that'll get some vegetables into me.'

'Excellent.' Dante scribbled away at his pad. 'And to drink?'

'Sparkling water.'

'A *birra Messina* for me,' said Calogero.

'I thought you said you didn't drink before a show.'

He looked confused. 'I don't.'

'But you're having a beer?'

'Beer doesn't count.'

'Oh.' She turned to Dante. 'Scratch the water. I'll have a beer as well.'

'Well now,' said Calogero once Dante had scurried away, 'I imagine you want to know why I was called in to help police with their enquiries.'

'That'd be good.'

'In exchange, you tell me what your interest is.'

Nedda paused. 'Okay. Deal.'

He smiled. 'You go first.'

She smiled back. 'Why don't you read my mind?'

'Okay.' He pressed two fingers to the bridge of his nose, and screwed his eyes shut. 'You think the death of Gianmaria was something other than an accident, of course.'

'Yes.'

'Well, I didn't have to be a mind-reader to work that out. He was a man with a number of enemies.'

'Including you?'

He shrugged. 'Didn't really know the man, to be honest.'

'Really?' Nedda paused. 'I've seen the tape, you know? The whole tape. Of that TV show.'

Calogero gave an embarrassed little chuckle. 'Oh. That.' Then he frowned. 'That never went out. How do you know about it?'

Nedda tapped her nose. 'Sources. Try reading my mind again. But in the meantime, why not tell me just why the police wanted to talk to you this morning.'

'A misunderstanding, that's all. I went round to Gianmaria's apartment to feed his cat.'

'Seriously, now.'

'Seriously. And the cat's fine, just in case you were worried. Oh, and then somebody hit me on the back of the head. After which' – he shrugged – 'explanations, you know?'

Nedda put her head to one side. 'Mmm. Thing is, though, I'm having trouble believing that.'

'You can believe what you like, Nedda. It happens to be true.'

'Okay.'

The two of them sat there in silence. Calogero was the first to break.

'What do you mean by *okay*?'

'Nothing. It's just *man feeds cat* isn't much of a story, that's all. I'll have to spice it up a bit.'

'What do you mean?'

'Well, I'll have to write something that's worthy of the front page, or Aldo Lentini – that's my boss – will have me straight back on baked goods duty.' She took out her phone, flicked through some of the photos, and turned the screen to Calogero. 'That's a nice one of you there. Close-up. So I was thinking something like, *On the day of Gianmaria Lombardo's funeral, what secrets lie behind the haunted eyes of Calogero Maugeri?*' She put the phone down on the table. 'What do you think?' she said, brightly.

Calogero shook his head. 'I think you're not the sort of person who would do that.'

Nedda folded her hands and rested her chin on them. 'Try me,' she said. 'Oh, wait a minute, there's also the video of the TV show. We might put a link to that on the website.'

Calogero had long since ceased even trying to smile. 'I don't want to get lawyers involved, *signurina*.'

'Of course not. Thing is, though,' she said, glancing around her, 'you're a man who eats every night in a restaurant that specialises in *toast*. So I'm thinking perhaps the money isn't there to fund the best lawyers in Catania.'

'Or maybe I'm fabulously wealthy, and just happen to like *toast*. And cats.'

'Maybe so.' Nedda sighed. 'Look, Calogero, I don't want to be a shit about this. But you might just be my ticket out of shit job hell. And so, if that means I have to write a headline that makes you look like a killer, then that's what I'll do. Or—'

'Or?'

'We help each other out. There might just be a story in this that's good for both of us.'

'Good for our careers, you mean?'

'Absolutely. I get a proper job at last. You – I don't know – get to play bigger theatres. Whatever you want.'

'Mmm. And just maybe when I came in here I could afford the special double-decker *toast*.'

'Absolutely. You'd be living the dream.'

Calogero nodded. 'Okay then.'

'Good.' She passed him a business card. 'Take this. How can I find you?'

'Look in the mirror and say my name three times. Alternatively, just turn up at the theatre. I'm usually around.'

Dante arrived with two beers, and two enormous toasted sandwiches.

'They make bread that size?' said Nedda.

'We have a special supplier, *signurina*,' said Dante, and winked again. 'Oh, and a really big toaster.'

Calogero and Nedda clinked bottles and set about their sandwiches.

'You ever been to London, Nedda?'

She shook her head. 'Never gone any further than Naples.'

'Oh, it's a great place. You know what they call *un toast* over there?'

She shook her head.

'A *toastie*. Isn't that a lovely word? But,' he wagged a finger at her, 'here's the thing. It's just cheese. Or cheese and ham. Imagine that.'

'I'm – trying.'

'Our English cousins, eh?'

Nedda put a hand to the back of her head. 'You are okay, aren't you? I mean, you don't think maybe you need to get checked out?'

'I'm feeling better by the minute, Nedda.'

She munched on her *toast* and couldn't stop herself from smiling. 'You know, this is actually really good.'

'It is, isn't it? That's why I never eat anywhere else.' He

checked his watch. 'Okay, I'll get these.' Nedda was about to protest, but he shook his head. 'No, no. My treat. Just to say thanks for the lift. Well, for getting me here alive, at any rate.'

'Thanks.'

'No worries.' He smiled. 'You can pay next time.'

'Next time? Ah. You know this is just work, right?'

He looked puzzled. 'Of course it is.'

'It's just I wondered if there'd been some kind of misunderstanding. I mean, not that there's much to misunderstand, it's just *toast* after all.'

'Just *toast*. Of course. What is there to misunderstand?'

'Nothing, really. It's just—' Her phone buzzed. 'Sorry, I need to text back.' She jabbed away at the screen. Thirty seconds later, it buzzed yet again and, once more, she tapped away at it. 'I should turn the bloody thing off.'

Calogero smiled. 'Boyfriend?'

'No.' She could feel herself flushing and hated herself for it. 'Just a colleague.'

'Just a colleague?'

'Just that.'

'It's just that your phone's buzzed four times in the time needed to eat a single *toast* and each time you look a little bit cross, but you also smile a little bit and flick your hair out of your eyes.'

'Wow. You really are very good at this, aren't you?'

He shrugged. 'It's my job. Gamblers call it a *tell*.'

'And he's not my boyfriend, not that that's any business of yours. He's just a colleague, as I said, although I suppose he's a friend as well, and so that just makes him a friend who happens to be a boy and—'

Calogero held up a hand. 'I think maybe you ought to stop speaking now.'

She flushed. 'Maybe.'

'As I said, I'll get these. If we ever go for a romantic *toast* for two again, you can pay. No strings attached. Promise.'

'Well, there's an offer I can't refuse. In return, how about you tell me about your relationship with Gianmaria Lombardo?'

'I don't have one.'

'Uh-uh.' She waved a finger at him. 'No fibbing.' Then she smiled. 'It's just that you've got a bit of a *tell* as well.'

Chapter 28

'You know how tough the pandemic was? Well, I didn't work for eighteen months. Theatres were closed, and the cruise ships just sat there in dock. And, strangely enough, stage magician wasn't seen as being a valid reserved occupation.'

'I'm sorry. It wasn't too bad for journalists.'

'Anyway, as I was saying, I was verging on broke. And then the cruises started up again, and I got lucky. Just seven days' work, round the Med, but I was told that if I did my job properly they'd keep me on their books for more work. Seven days. Free holiday. Some money in my pocket. Of course I was going to do it.'

He smiled. 'A week round the Med. Taormina, Malta, Barcelona, Marseille, Naples and home again. Of course, it's Messina really, not Taormina, but they seem to think Taormina plays better with the tourists.'

Nedda frowned. 'What's wrong with Messina?'

'Search me.'

'Anyway. Going forward. Tell me about your role on the ship.'

'I'm a magician. I did magic. One session every afternoon in the lounge. One late-night show in the theatre.'

'They have theatres?'

'You'd be amazed.'

'Sounds like a nice job.'

'Oh, it was. At least for a bit. Three days in, I've finished my show for the night. We've left Valletta and we've got a whole day at sea the next day. This means I do an extra show just after lunch.' He shrugged. 'That's no real problem. Anyway, I'm having a drink at the bar when a woman taps me on the shoulder. I recognise her, but I've not spoken to her. She's a croupier at the casino. Pretty girl, from the Philippines or Thailand. Somewhere like that.' He chuckled. 'And I'm thinking that maybe it's my lucky day.'

Nedda frowned.

'Sorry. I'll carry on. She wants to talk to me about a guy who comes to play the tables every night. Do you know the sort of people who gamble on cruise ships, Nedda?'

She shook her head.

'I'll tell you. People who really shouldn't be gambling at all, that's who. Imagine a tourist who's been lying in the sun all day, he's had a few martinis because he thinks that makes him look like James Bond, there's a pretty girl working as croupier and – hey presto – he's living the dream. And the next morning he wakes up next to his wife, he's got a hangover, and there's going to be a difficult conversation over breakfast as he attempts to explain that holiday spending money isn't quite what they'd been budgeting.

'So, the *signora* asks me to sit in on a few games. Because some guy is winning more than he should. Nothing ridiculous, nothing that should attract too much attention, but more than he should. And she's starting to get suspicious.

'I sit in on a few games that evening. We play a few hands of blackjack and I'm pretty certain he's not counting cards. Nevertheless, he keeps making regular gains. He's walking away with good money. There's no evidence of collusion because there are different people at the table every time. And I'm doing my damnedest not to stare at the guy so he doesn't twig why I'm there.

'I notice the medallion around his neck. Big. Chunky. Gold. A bit vulgar. I'm trying to make out the design, but – like I said – I don't want to stare.

'I lose an amount of money that I can afford to lose. But I still haven't worked out how he's doing it. Anyway, later on, I see the croupier in the bar again. I offer her a martini, which she turns down, but we get chatting anyway. Turns out her name's Pia, and she's from Manila. I ask her if she's noticed that medallion around our friend's neck.

'She giggles and tells me I'm not to laugh. She says she's a good Catholic girl – like I said, she's from the Philippines – and she's worked out what the image is. And it's St Agabus.'

'Saint *who*?'

Calogero grinned. 'That's what I said. St Agabus. Patron saint of prophets.' He paused. 'Prophets and seers and fortune tellers.'

'We have a patron saint for *that*?'

'Who knew? Apart from my friend Pia, that is. I've got just two more nights left to nail this guy, and I'm starting to get an idea of what's going on. Because that medallion isn't perfectly round. No, our friend Agabus is holding a small Bible with its pages open. And the edge is just a little bit pointy.

'I spot it almost immediately, the following evening.

Sometimes when he's got the cards in his hands, he raises the medallion to his lips and kisses it. And while he's doing that, he makes the tiniest of movements. Because he's marking the cards with the pointed edge.

'And I smile to myself, because now I know I've got him. Because I'm pretty good at that game myself. I play a few games that evening, and I make sure that I'm losing steadily. I've always got a drink to hand and I'm appearing to be having just a little bit too much of a good time.

'And then, that final evening, I mirror his technique. I start marking cards myself. And immediately I can see he's starting to panic. None of his little tricks are working anymore. So, it's just him versus me.

'And I take him to the cleaners. I take everything from him except his trousers, and one more hand and I'd have had those as well. I take his chips, cash up and the next day I get off the boat at Naples and fly back to Turin. Just in case he turns out to be a sore loser.'

Nedda frowned. 'Turin? What were you doing there?'

'This and that. Why?'

'Oh, it's just that my. . . my colleague is from there.'

Calogero smiled. 'Maybe I know him?'

'His name's Gallo. Stefano Gallo.' She caught the expression on his face. 'What's wrong?'

'Oh, nothing. Just a common name, isn't it? I don't think I ever met him. Anyway, this was all before I moved to Catania. And I didn't think anything more of it. Until earlier this year, when I appeared on a low-budget TV show with a witch and two pretend psychics. One of whom was wearing a flashy gold medallion. With the image of St Agabus on it.'

Chapter 29

Calogero had never cared for wands. Yes, you could whip them around with a nice thwippy sound but that risked damaging delicate internal circuitry. And it was all, perhaps, just a little bit too Harry Potter. No, better to go with a staff. There was something reassuring about the feel of a good solid piece of wood in your hands. And, who knows, it might always come in handy in the event of a tough crowd.

'Thank you, Aci. You've been a great audience. And remember – it's only magic if you think it is.'

At short distance the noise would be deafening and he'd already taken care to insert the near-invisible ear protectors. He raised the staff with a flourish, felt for the button under the insulating tape, pressed it and waited for the flash and the explosion that would tell him it was time to get running for the back row.

Nothing.

He pressed it again. And again. And again. And then he looked out at the audience.

There was an awkward silence. Then there came a smattering of polite applause and the odd whisper, point and chuckle.

Oh bugger.

Best to bluff it out then. 'And sometimes, ladies and gentlemen, the magic just doesn't happen. Something I'm sure all the gentlemen in the audience know about.' He winked.

It was enough. A roar of laughter made its way round the crowd, and Calogero waved, bowed and backed off stage.

A close call.

'Something not right tonight, *maestro*?'

Santo, the stage manager, fussed and fretted around him.

'No, Santo. Lots of things not right.'

It hadn't been a vintage performance. Maria Giulia hadn't been able to join him. The basketball player was teaching her to shoot hoops, whatever that meant. Besides, people were starting to recognise her by now. He'd run through his usual repertoire, but the cold reading hadn't worked as well as usual. Applause had been polite, at best, and there'd been a couple of walkouts.

He'd offered Nedda free tickets but, it seemed, she had a better offer. Probably Stefano Gallo. He frowned and then shook his head. At least she'd missed a poor performance.

No doubt about it. The act was getting stale. Ah well, his contract was up at the end of the following week. He'd need to give it a complete rethink. Perhaps he should go on the road again. He had sufficient contacts with the cruise companies to find a job for a few months. He could treat it as a holiday whilst he thought about the future.

He yawned and shook his head. 'Lots of things not quite right. Listen, could you get someone to take a look at my staff for me?'

'They'll be queuing round the block, Calogero.'

Despite himself, Calogero grinned and patted him on the back. 'I might have known I'd get an answer like that. Seriously, though. Nothing happened tonight. The capacitor didn't discharge. All a bit of a damp squib, as you could see.'

Santo frowned. 'When was it last charged?'

'Must be a couple of days. My fault. I'm getting lazy, Santo, I completely forgot about it.'

'Mm. Okay, don't you worry. I'll make sure it's properly charged for the next one.'

'Thanks.'

'Would a grappa be good?'

'It would be very good. Trouble is I gave the last of it to that idiot Salvatore the other day.'

Santo grinned. 'I'd thought of that.' He proffered a shopping bag and Calogero heard a cheery chink from inside. 'And no supermarket rubbish. "Cleaning grappa" my dad calls it. No, this is the proper stuff.'

He poured out two measures. Calogero took a generous sip, closed his eyes and sighed. 'Ah, you're a good man, Santo.' He opened his eyes again. 'But you're right. This isn't supermarket stuff. I should be paying for this.'

'No, you shouldn't and don't be silly.'

'I won't hear otherwise. At the very least we need to go *Romana.*'

Santo shrugged. 'If you insist.'

'I do.' He pulled his wallet from his jacket and swore, gently, as something fluttered to the floor. He bent to pick it up, and his expression darkened.

'The *fuck* is this?' Santo frowned. 'Sorry.'

'What is it?'

It was a playing card. Calogero laid it on the table and turned it to face him.

The image showed a burning tower, struck by lightning, against a dark background. Two figures, their faces stretched in horror and disbelief, plummeted towards earth.

'Tarot?'

Calogero nodded. 'The Tower.'

'Meaning?'

'Lots of things. Nothing good.'

'So, er, could I ask why you carry it around with you?'

'I don't. Surprising as it might sound, I don't carry random Tarot cards around with me. Neither do I have a magic wand, a top hat or a rabbit.'

'So, what's it doing there?'

'Somebody must have slipped that into my wallet when I was out cold.'

'What?'

Calogero waved the question away. 'Another time.'

'What's it mean, then?'

'Maybe nothing. Maybe everything. But Salvatore found a deck on his doorstep, with just one card missing. The Five of Cups. A hooded figure overlooking a river in front of a castle.' He stared at the card, and knitted his brows.

'Something wrong?'

'I think so. There's something about this card that isn't right. And I don't know what it is.' He smiled. 'Fortunately, however, I know somebody who will.'

Tomorrow was shaping up to be a busy day.

Chapter 30

Salvatore Sipala's apartment was almost the polar opposite of Mater Morgana's. If the witch's had given an impression of a kind of organised chaos, his was spartan to the point of dreariness.

It had been a dreary morning, to be fair. Calogero had sat in Gori's office for an hour, answering the same questions as before, only this time with coffee and a less-aching head. There had been veiled threats and some finger-pointing but, at the end of the day, Calogero had had Gianmaria's key in his pocket and that was an end to it.

Yes, there was a safe and it was open. But there was no sign of a break-in, and Calogero had little more on him other than the clothes he was standing up in.

More sighing. More finger-pointing. And, finally, the suggestion that they might need to speak to him in future.

Today was his day off. Time for the stage crew at the theatre to take a look at his staff. It was tempting to go for a leisurely lunch and, perhaps, a few drinks but there was work to be done.

He made his way down to Salvatore's apartment on the outskirts of Catania. Again, no serious lock protected it.

Calogero frowned. Both Salvatore and Gianmaria lived in apartments that were, at best, badly protected from those who might arrive with ill intent. Were they just depending on fear to keep burglars at bay?

Oh well. That was another problem for another time. He fished a plastic card out of his wallet, set to work, and let himself in.

Dreary was indeed the word. It didn't look as if Salvatore spent much time here. He cast his eyes around. Packing cases everywhere. Either they were doubling up as furniture or Salvatore was planning on moving out.

There were few books on the shelves to speak of beyond a few dog-eared bestsellers, and a couple of classics. Giovanni Verga's *I Malavoglia*, which had blighted Calogero's school-days. A few English novels. A battered *Fahrenheit 451*. A seemingly pristine *The Girl on the Train*. A couple of Harry Potters.

Calogero frowned. Salvatore hadn't seemed to be a man of hidden depths. For that matter he hadn't even thought him to be a man of hidden shallows. Nevertheless it seemed he was a man capable of reading a complete novel in English.

A small flat-screen TV stood on top of a metal stand in the corner. The artwork on the walls consisted of anonymous views of the sea and of Etna erupting that likely as not had never been seen by the artist. Or, if they had, Calogero feared for their safety. He sniffed. He didn't know much about art, he thought, but he knew what he didn't like. And he didn't like this.

The kitchen consisted of a few cabinets, a Baby Belling and a small microwave. The bathroom held a half-size bath with a rubber shower hose slipped over the taps. The bedroom, smelling strongly of cigarettes, held a single rumpled bed and wardrobe. Calogero checked. A few shirts. Trousers. Underwear. Otherwise empty.

The curtains were closed and a thin sliver of sunshine penetrated through the gaps, illuminating the dust motes that swirled in the air. Calogero ran his hand around his collar. It was getting hot now. He scanned the walls. No air conditioning. Not even a free-standing fan. Evidently, Salvatore was living a rather spartan life.

He took another turn around the flat, carefully opening and checking cabinets and drawers. He checked under the bed. He moved aside the paintings. Nothing.

He flicked through the books, and a business card fluttered out of Harry Potter, where it had been serving as a bookmark. *Stefano Gallo. Giornalista.*

Why was that name turning up again and again?

He shook his head and replaced it at a random page.

There was, it seemed, nothing to be found. In which case he'd just have to settle down and wait. A coffee in the meantime might be nice. A shiny Nespresso machine in the kitchen seemed to be by far the most modern piece of equipment in the flat. He found two espresso cups bearing the legend 'I ♥ Catania', and set them aside. A half-empty packet of brown sugar was secured with a clothes peg.

There was something missing. Ah yes, capsules. Try as he might, he couldn't find any. Not even a packet of instant coffee. Calogero poured himself a small cup of water from the tap, drank it, and then poured another.

He heard the rattle of a key in the lock, and braced himself.

Hopefully Salvatore would be reasonable. It would, he admitted to himself, be the first time that the words *reasonable* and *Salvatore Sipala* had been seen to cosy up together, but you could never tell. The alternative, he imagined, would be violence but he hoped that wouldn't have to happen. All the more so if he were to be on the receiving end of it.

Salvatore stood in the hallway, looking through to the kitchen, a look of disbelief creeping across his face as he saw Calogero standing there.

Calogero gave him a little wave. 'Hi there. I was just about to make some coffee. Are you having one?'

'The actual *fuck* do you want?'

'Right now, coffee. Only I can't find the capsules. You know where they are?'

'You get out of here right now, you prick, or I'll call the police.'

'No, you won't. Maybe you need decaf?'

'I'll count to five and then I'll throw you out myself and I'll hurt you on the way.'

'Well, you're welcome to try. But you haven't managed that in the past and I don't think it's going to happen now. It's practically noon. It's a hot day. You've probably been spending a few hours in a bar somewhere. You're not really in a fighting shape or mood. Neither, for that matter, am I. So let's just have a coffee, eh, and talk like old friends.'

Salvatore stood, flexing his fingers, and then nodded. 'In the cupboard above the sink,' he growled.

Calogero slapped his forehead. 'Ah. Didn't think to check there. Thanks.' He slotted a capsule into the machine. 'Single or double?'

Salvatore held two fingers up in a V-sign.

'I'll take that as a double.' He placed a cup under the nozzle, pulled down the lever, and the machine hummed away. He nodded in satisfaction and smiled. 'First time. I'm not very good at working these things, you know? I still use a Moka. I know they're a pain to clean and wash up and all that, but I prefer them. The pod machines aren't very good for the environment, I understand. But I know that's not your fault.'

The machine beeped, and the smell of fresh coffee filled the room. Calogero slid the cup on to a saucer and passed it to Salvatore. The thought came to him that the other man might hurl the scalding liquid into his face, but he forced himself to keep smiling.

Salvatore took the coffee from him, and looked down at the cup, as if the same thought had occurred to him. Then he growled again, 'What the—'

'Fuck do I want?' Calogero turned the smile off in an instant. 'I want to know where it is, Salvatore.'

'What do you—'

Calogero waved a hand. 'No, no. You know what I mean. I want to know where it is.'

'I don't know. How did you get in here?'

'I'm good with doors. Just like you're good with cards. And safes. And this place wasn't difficult to get into. How long are you staying here, by the way?'

'What do you mean?'

'How long are you staying here? You're obviously moving out.'

'This is my home, you prick.'

'It obviously isn't. Look at it. Generic art on the walls. Barely any furniture. Hardly anything to cook with beyond the coffee machine. Oh, that reminds me.' Calogero clunked another capsule into the Nespresso, and waited as it hummed away. He sipped at the freshly brewed coffee, and frowned. 'I really do prefer a Moka, I have to say. I'll buy you one for your next place. Moving-in present. Oh, and the reading material?' He chuckled. 'Salvatore, forgive me, but I don't think you've ever read *I Malavoglia* in your life. And you certainly haven't read Harry Potter in English.'

He looked around. 'No, this is just a cheap rental, isn't it? Can't have been much fun here, I imagine. But it seems like you're moving out. Somewhere a little more desirable perhaps? Somewhere like Gianmaria's place? But that wouldn't come cheaply, of course. Unless you've come into some money, that is?'

Salvatore was stony-faced. 'How did you find me?'

Calogero tapped his nose. 'Magic. Or, if you remember, I dropped you off here a few months ago. You remember, just after our TV special. Now, as I was saying, all I want to hear from you is the answer to: *where is it?* Gianmaria's dossier.' He put a hand to the back of his head. 'There's still a bruise there, you know? From when you hit me the other day.'

'I hit you on the back of the head? Sounds more like you were dropped on the head to me. Get out of here, Calogero. I've got nothing to say to you.'

Calogero's arm lashed out as he made to grab Salvatore's shoulder, but the other man grabbed his hand before it could make contact. Calogero could see the sweat on his brow, smell the booze on his breath, but he'd never let Salvatore get this close before and he was stronger than he expected. He squeezed Calogero's fingers mercilessly, making him wince with the pain, before dragging him closer.

'Listen here, you piece of shit. I know what you want and guess what – you are never getting your hands on it. I'm going to squeeze you like an orange. You understand that? Now you let go and fuck off before I start deciding how much extra interest I'm going to be charging you.'

He dropped his hand. Calogero thought about punching him in the face but his throbbing fingers made him think that might hurt him more than Salvatore.

He made his way to the door and turned around. 'This isn't over, Salvatore.'

'As I said. Fuck off before I start counting.'

Calogero turned and slammed the door behind him.

Chapter 31

Lentini put down his copy of *Catania Nuova*, smoothed it out on his desk and smiled. '*Mystery Man held while friends and family mourn*. You've done well, Nedda. Doesn't mean I approve of you skiving off your actual job to pursue this, of course. But well done, nevertheless.'

Nedda was about to say that it had been Stefano who'd called her with regard to Calogero's arrest whilst she'd been at the funeral, but, out of the corner of her eye, she saw him making a cautionary movement with his hand. *No.*

She looked over at Lentini. 'Thanks.'

'I was just wondering, however, how you knew where to go?'

'It was the woman I met at the funeral,' Nedda began, a little hesitantly. 'We were talking about people who might have had a grudge against Gianmaria Lombardo. Then I started thinking about – who was that football player who died a couple of years back? Played in the World Cup final or something? Sorry, I'm not really into football.'

'Paolo Rossi,' said Aldo and Stefano as one.

'Yeah, him. Anyway, I remember his house was burgled during his funeral. Because everybody knew it would be empty. And so I started thinking – for someone with a grudge, the funeral would be exactly the right time to do,' her voice trailed off, 'you know. Something.'

Lentini looked puzzled. 'Well, I wouldn't have thought the Mystical Lombardo—'

'Lombardo the Mystic.'

'Whatever. I wouldn't have imagined there being quite the same outpouring of grief as there was for Paolo Rossi. Anyway, if it was a guess, then well done.' He paused. 'When I say it's brilliant, of course, it's brilliant as far as it goes.' He took off his glasses. 'Do you have a name for the person involved?'

It seemed pointless to lie. 'I do.'

'Uh-huh. Are you going to tell us?' She said nothing. 'Nedda, you can keep silent if you like. But the other papers are going to find out within days. That's just what journalists do. So give me the name now, and we can be the first to break it and – and this might be important to you, I'm guessing – put our spin on it. We won't do a hatchet job. That's not the way *Catania Nuova* works.'

'I can't do that, Aldo. He had my word.'

Aldo looked for a moment as if he were on the verge of losing his temper, but then he just shook his head. 'Okay. I understand. I'll give you some time on this. But as soon as I get a sniff of some other paper pre-empting us, you tell me the name and I'm putting it out there. Deal?'

She nodded.

'And so who is he? In confidence, of course.'

'His name is Calogero Maugeri. Also known as the Magus. He works as some kind of stage magician – he has a show up in Acireale at the moment. He's the one where we have footage of him getting into a fight with Lombardo and one of his friends on a late-night chat show.'

The thinnest of smiles broke across Lentini's face. 'My word. You really have done well.' He turned to Stefano. 'Okay, Gallo, I'd like you to go along to the *Questura*. Get a quote from anyone you can. We'll keep it anonymous. For now.'

There was silence for a moment, until Nedda spoke up. 'And me?'

'I need you online. Dig up whatever you can on Maugeri and Lombardo. And be ready to take a call from Gallo.'

Stefano broke another awkward silence.

'No,' he said, shaking his head.

'Eh?'

'I mean it's not fair, Aldo. Nedda's done all the work on this. So she should be the one doing the legwork.'

'I need her for research.'

'I can google as well as anyone, Aldo. I'll do it.'

Lentini stared at them both for a moment, and then nodded. 'Gallo. Give us a few moments, would you?'

Stefano nodded, and flashed a quick smile at Nedda before leaving. Lentini drummed his fingers on the desk for a few seconds. She opened her mouth to speak, but he shook his head.

'Don't say anything, Nedda. Not until you've counted to ten. I really don't want to have to sack you.'

They sat in silence as she silently counted.

'Why are you doing this?' she said.

Lentini furrowed his brow. 'More to the point, why is Gallo doing this? He's not one to turn down a big juicy story.'

There might – just might – have been the faintest trace of a smile around his lips. 'No. No, I can't possibly think why he might be doing this.'

Nedda flushed. 'Stefano's just a friend, Aldo. Nothing more than that.'

'Sure.'

'And I still want to know. Why are you doing this? If I'm just going to be fetching and carrying *cannoli* for you every day—'

'And research.'

'If that's what we have to call it. If that's all I'm ever going to be doing for you then,' she took a deep breath, 'then I'm afraid I'm going to have to go elsewhere.'

'My goodness. Is that a resignation?'

She closed her eyes. 'If that's what it has to be, then yes.'

'Well, don't be ridiculous. I'm not accepting it.'

'You can't just keep me here forever as your *pasticceria* correspondent.'

'*Catania Nuova*'s a good place for a first job, Nedda. In a few years' time, your experience here will look good on a CV.'

'You mean I might work my way up to senior *gelato* correspondent?'

Lentini smiled. 'Would that be so bad? It sounds quite fun to me.' He sighed. 'I wish I'd had the opportunity to do something like that.'

'You're going to tell me that you spent your years as a cub reporter working on marriages, deaths and refilling inkwells, aren't you?'

'Refilling inkwells? You had to work up to refilling ink-wells. That wasn't just trusted to anybody, you know.'

'You know what I mean, Aldo.'

He sighed. 'Yes.'

'All this stuff. It just isn't for me. You know what I want to do.'

'I do.'

'*Cronaca nera*. Crime. Proper investigative reporting. Not lifestyle shit.'

'Lifestyle shit is important as well, Nedda. It's what people want to read.'

'But it's not what I want to write. You know that. And for some reason there's a lack of trust and I don't know if it's just because you don't like me or because I've done something to piss you off or there's some unknown macho code that I've broken without even knowing about it. And I just—'

Lentini held up a hand, and she broke off. 'I know what you want, Nedda. You want to be like your mother.'

The two of them sat in silence. 'Yes,' she said, eventually.

'And I don't want to you to do that.'

Nedda slammed her palms down on the table. 'And just what the FUCK has it got to do with you?'

Lentini said nothing. He just removed his glasses, and polished them on the cuff of his shirt. Nedda could see there were tears in his eyes.

'Your mother was a fine reporter. A fine investigative journalist. I knew her, Nedda.' He paused. 'And I pulled her body from the car.'

Chapter 32

'I don't understand.'

'Your father never said anything?'

'No. Nothing. I remember him saying that he'd known you back in Palermo, but nothing more.'

'I think he was trying to protect you.' Lentini sighed. 'And so was I.'

Nedda felt the blood rush to her head but forced the anger down. 'That wasn't a decision for you to make, Aldo.'

He shook his head. 'No.'

Nedda sat back in her chair and brushed the hair out of her eyes. 'Okay. Well this is big. Why don't you tell me about it?'

'There isn't much to tell. I mean that. I didn't know your mother very well. We both worked at *Giornale di Sicilia*. That was a good job for two young reporters. Except Rosa was brilliant in a way that I wasn't. She was all about organised crime, corruption, proper *cronaca nera* stuff. And I – well, I wasn't. In all honesty, I'd have been happy enough to see my career out with births, marriages and deaths.' He gave a thin smile. 'And all that "lifestyle shit", as you might put it.

'So, I could never really say we were friends. But we knew

each other and got along fine. Except that I could see she'd be heading off to the mainland sooner or later, to *La Repubblica* or *La Stampa* or the *Corriere della Sera*. And I'd be staying in Palermo, and that was fine by me.

'She was so unlucky, you know? What happened to her. It wasn't even anything she'd been investigating. She was simply in the wrong place at the wrong time. And me – well, I was just there and I pulled her from the car before it exploded. But I knew she was already gone. I'm sorry. In some ways I think it was the bravest thing I ever did.'

Nedda sat in silence for a few minutes, trying to take it all in. 'Thank you,' she said, finally.

'You were the little red-haired girl. The one being held in that woman's arms – I never did find out her name. There was nothing about me in the papers at all. I called in some favours with a few friends. They kept my name out of it. And that suited me fine.'

'I don't understand. Why? You, a journalist.'

He sighed. 'Because I was frightened, Nedda. Properly frightened. Your mother had a courage that I didn't have. When she died, I took a long, hard look at my life and asked myself if this was really what I wanted. And I decided that, no, it wasn't. And so I left the *Giornale di Sicilia* and moved to this second-division little paper in Catania.'

'I don't understand. I know this might not be Palermo. But we've got proper crime, serious crime, organised crime here as well.'

'I know. And I just keep my head down and keep away from it as best I can. We're Sicilians, Nedda. We're very good at ignoring elephants in rooms.' He smiled. 'Even in Catania.'

'And you thought you were doing me a favour by keeping me away from it as well. Both you and dad.'

He nodded.

Nedda shook her head and got to her feet.

'Where are you going?'

'Outside. First I'm going to buy a Smash the Patriarchy T-shirt. Then I'm going to buy you a final box of *cannoli*. And then I'm going to clear my desk out.'

He shook his head. 'No, you're not.'

'You try stopping me.'

'You're not doing it, because I need you to be down at the *Questura* on the Maugeri story.'

'You what?'

'I need you to work on the Maugeri story. Gallo can do any research he might need to back here. Call him if you need to know anything. Or me.'

'Seriously?'

'Seriously.' He smiled. 'Of course, if you're still willing to go out and buy *cannoli*—'

'I am. Oh, I am.'

'Good. That's settled, then. *Buon lavoro,* Nedda.'

'Aldo.' Nedda's voice broke, just a little. 'We're going to need to talk about *mamma* at some point.'

He nodded. 'We will.'

'And then tonight, there's going to have to be a difficult conversation with *papà.*'

'Go easy on him, Nedda.'

'I will.' She sighed. 'But, flattering though it is to have so many middle-aged men telling me what's good for me, I think it's time I introduced him to the concept of the twenty-first century.'

'Well, good luck with that.' She was about to leave when he called her back. 'Oh, and Nedda?'

'Yes?'

Lentini removed his glasses and pointed them at her. 'You just be careful, okay? Don't do anything stupid. You promise me that.'

'I promise.'

'Good. Because I don't want to have to send Gallo out for *cannoli*.'

Chapter 33

Stefano and Nedda clinked bottles in the shadow of Nedda the Elephant. In truth it was more of a dull thunk as his *birra Messina* clashed with her plastic bottle of water.

'So, everything sorted then? You and the old man best pals?'

She smiled. 'I think so. Look, I just want to say about – back there – what you said to Aldo. I just want you to know that I appreciate it, that's all.'

'No worries. Just seemed the right thing to do. Anyway, you've earned it.' He sipped from his beer. 'So, what's he like then? This Maugeri guy?'

'He seems all right. Eats too much *toast*. But I think he's okay.'

'Hmmm.' He grinned and jabbed her gently in the shoulder. 'Not a murderer, then?'

'I don't think so.'

'Think so?'

'He just doesn't seem the type. He seems like a regular, if slightly odd, guy.'

'That's the thing about serial killers. They look like everybody else. Seriously, though, just be careful around him.'

'Oh, I will be. Any particular reason why?'

'Nedda, he was caught on film having a fight with a guy who was murdered.'

'No, he wasn't. He was having a fight with the friend of a guy who *might* have been murdered. Officially this is an accident, remember?'

'Whatever. He was also arrested for breaking into a dead man's house on the day of his funeral.'

'He tells me he wasn't arrested, that he had a key and that he was there to feed the cat.'

Stefano shook his head. 'You can believe what you want. I'd be careful, that's all. Very careful. No matter what he's telling you about feeding cats.'

Nedda tried to swallow the irritation that was rising within her. Stefano was, in all probability, right. That didn't make it any better. 'Tell you what, Stefano, why don't you ask him yourself?'

'Well, normally I'd do just that. But this is your story, remember. Just be careful, that's all I'm saying.'

'Nedda? Nedda?'

She looked up. Calogero was standing there looking tired and drawn.

'Calogero? What are you doing here?'

'I called your office. They said you normally came here after work.'

'You called my office?'

'Well, you gave me your card. I assumed it would be okay?'

Stefano gave her a dark look and shook his head. Just a fraction. 'You gave him your card?'

Calogero shrugged. 'Sure. That's what people do with

business cards, isn't it?' He smiled and stretched out his hand.
'I'm Calogero. You must be Stefano Gallo?'

'Must I?' Stefano hesitated but shook his hand.

'Well, it's a guess. But they told me at your office that
you'd most likely be together.' He turned to Nedda. 'I need
to speak to you. It's important.'

Stefano glanced at his watch. 'To be honest, I'm not sure
this is the best time.'

Nedda shushed him. 'We've got time. Sit down, Calogero.'

He pulled up a chair and joined them at the table. He
waved at the *barista*. 'Small beer, please.' Stefano opened his
mouth, but Nedda shook her head at him. 'I'll just be five
minutes and then I'll be away and everyone can get back to
having a lovely time.' He looked over at Stefano. 'I've heard a
lot about you.'

'Really?'

'Don't worry, it's all good.'

'*Stuzzichini, signori?*' The *barista* returned with a tray of
snacks. Stefano nodded, and the barman arranged the trays
on the table. Peanuts, *pizzette*, crisps, mini *arancini*, olives.

Calogero reached a hand towards the peanuts, and then
pulled it back. 'May I?' he said.

'Go ahead.'

'Thanks. I haven't eaten much all day.'

'And why is that?' said Nedda.

'I've been helping the police with their enquiries again.'
She said nothing. 'Nedda, I've done nothing wrong, but it's
something to do with that damn TV programme I was on.'
He took a deep breath. 'And I think they really want me to
have had something to do with Gianmaria's death.'

'What do you mean?'

'They know I didn't get on with him. Given I had a fight with him in the studio.'

Stefano speared an olive with a cocktail stick. 'I understood it was with the other man?'

'It was. But I don't think they care. It would be really convenient for them if I'd done it. Nedda, I've got nothing to do with this, I swear.'

'Then you've got nothing to worry about,' said Stefano.

'What do you mean?'

'Well, this was an accident, right? Nothing more. So, no reason to worry. I mean, feeding the cat seems like a good reason to be in Gianmaria's apartment during his funeral, right?'

Calogero stared at Nedda. 'You told him?'

She couldn't meet his gaze. 'He's a colleague.'

'Oh. I see. A colleague.'

Stefano looked at his watch. 'I guess now might be a good time to head off.'

'Nedda,' Calogero's voice was pleading, 'I need you to help me on this. Please.'

Stefano got to his feet. 'People will be wanting the table.' He looked down at Calogero. 'Nice to meet you. Look after yourself, okay?'

'Sure. I'm sorry I barged in. Have a good evening, yeah?' He stood up, clumsily bumping into the table and sending the remains of Stefano's beer spilling over his jacket.

'Sh—' Calogero noticed diners with small children staring at them and he choked back the expletive. 'I'm sorry, man. Here, let me.' He grabbed a pad of napkins from the metal container and made to pat Stefano down.

'Leave it. Just leave it, you dickhead.'

'No need to be rude.' He lowered his voice. 'And there are kids here, so mind the language.' He patted away at Stefano's jacket as the other man tried to swat his hands away.

He grabbed Calogero's hand. 'I said leave it, okay.' Calogero stepped back. 'Come on, Nedda. Drop me at home and I can get changed before we head out.'

She got to her feet, and Stefano took her hand. 'The bike's in the garage,' she said. 'Perhaps I'll have to look at getting you an actual helmet.' She turned to Calogero. 'Call me tomorrow, okay. First thing.'

Stefano tugged at her hand. 'Nedda, I'm standing here stinking of beer. Can we go, please?'

She gave Calogero a wave with her free hand. 'Tomorrow, yeah?'

Calogero sat back down in the chair and had a go at swabbing the table, which was still awash. The *barista* arrived with a cloth and started to mop up.

'Sorry about that,' said Calogero.

'Not your fault, *signore*, sometimes these things they happen.'

'Yeah, but I seem to have annoyed one of your regular customers.'

The *barista* furrowed his brow. 'Who?'

'The gentleman who was just here. With the young woman.'

'Oh him. He's not so much a regular. He hasn't been here long.'

'Ah. My mistake.'

The *barista* smiled. 'Still, regular or not, we prefer it if people don't throw beer over our customers.'

'I'll try and remember that. You know, maybe I'll have another myself. Oh, and you have one as well.'

'Thank you, *signore*.'

Calogero patted his jacket pocket. He nibbled on a mini *arancino* as he waited for his beer to arrive. For a moment there he'd been worried that Nedda would want to stay. But he'd read Stefano right, and the beer trick had worked. He smiled to himself. He could be a pretty good actor when he needed to be. Then he slipped a hand into his pocket and took out Stefano's wallet.

There were the usual things. Bank cards and a driving licence. Banknotes, perhaps a hundred euros in total. An ID card. And then there was something else, a small disc that had evidently been there some time as it had left a circular imprint in the leather. He worried away at the wallet, winkling it out.

It was a small silver coin, imprinted with a stylised 'GA' logo and the words 'One Day At A Time' printed underneath.

He raised an eyebrow. Well, now.

He slipped the wallet into his pocket. It had been a good evening's work.

Chapter 34

'Will I do?'

Nedda looked Stefano up and down, trying and failing to keep a straight face.

'What's wrong?'

'Nothing. It's just I didn't realise the double denim look was back.'

'I've only got one suit. You know, the one your friend spilled beer over.'

'He's not my friend. Anyway, aren't you going to be hot?'

'I guess so. But as I said, I've only got the one suit.'

Nedda smiled. 'It'll be fine. But just turn around a moment.'

He spread his arms wide and turned in a full circle. 'Everything okay?'

'Yes. I was just checking for patches. Or if your mum had stitched the words "Iron Maiden" on the back or something.'

He looked cross for a moment, but then his expression cleared. 'Oh. Would that have been a deal-breaker?'

'I don't know. Let's not push it, though.' Then, suddenly, she reached out to him and quickly kissed him on the cheek.

'Gosh.' He blushed. 'I must get beer thrown over me more

often.' He rubbed the side of his face. 'Be a long time 'til I wash that cheek, I can tell you.'

'As I said, don't push it.' She linked her arm in his. 'Come on then. Time for a drink. Hopefully none of them will be thrown.'

Stefano led her past the metal fence that separated Piazza Luchino Visconti from the road. Nedda had always thought that the word *piazza* was pushing it a bit, it being little more than a large terrace.

But what a terrace it was, the view looking out over the harbour stretching out into the Ionian sea, the *Ciclopi* and the tiny island of Lachea. The entire space, however, was sealed off with a wire fence.

'This makes me sad,' she said. 'I can hardly remember it being open.'

He nodded. 'I've never known this as anything else. How long has it been going on for?'

'Feels like forever. Pushing ten years, at any rate. Thing is, it's not really a piazza. It's the roof of the old coastguard building below and the *Comune* was worried about it collapsing. There'd been a survey, or something.

'Anyway, they closed it for three years while they wondered what to do about it. Which, I think, meant hoping that people would forget about it or just stop noticing. Then they spent three years trying to raise the money – half a million or something like that. And then there was Covid.' She sighed. 'Five years ago this would be regular front-page news. But now Aldo just shakes his head and says nobody cares anymore.'

She stuck her fingers through the wire. 'This is the problem with this country, you know? Everybody's given up on caring. Just because it happened a long time ago. It's like the entire country is living under a statute of limitations.

'When I first came here – I was just a little girl – people used to hang out here, sit on a bench, look at the view. Maybe they'd buy a beer from a kiosk and sit here to drink it. Or they'd just enjoy a quiet smoke. Maybe kids would be playing, and their parents would go crazy in case a ball went over the side and down into the street. Maybe there'd be music playing in one of the bars and people would dance. Or flirt.

'But now it's just depressing. It all closed a long time ago and people have given up caring.'

'This is a deep conversation for this time of the evening, Nedda.'

She closed her eyes for a moment, her hands curling and tightening around the metal links. Then she looked up and smiled. 'You know, it is, isn't it? Drink needed.'

He led her across the road to *Bar Eden*, dodging a scooter along the way, and they grabbed a table.

'What's it to be?' he said.

'I'll have a *granita*. And a brioche on the side, of course. If they're still doing them at this time?'

'I don't think they ever stop. And to drink?'

'What goes well with a *granita*? Maybe a Frangelico over ice.'

Stefano gave the *barista* a wave and a smile, and he approached them.

'*Signurina?*'

'A chocolate and pistachio *granita*, please. With a brioche. And a Frangelico with ice.'

He nodded and smiled. This, evidently, was a combination of which he approved. '*Signore?*'

'Just a beer, please. *Birra Messina.*'

Nedda frowned. 'Hang on a moment, you can't just have a beer.'

'Well, a beer's what I want.'

'I don't care. You can't sit there with just a bottle of beer as I sit here with an enormous *granita.*'

'Why not?'

'Because,' she flapped her hands, 'I'll just look like a proper girly girl, that's all.'

The *barista* coughed. 'You want me to come back later?'

Stefano smiled at him. 'No, no, it's fine. Just bring us two spoons as well, please.'

Nedda shook her head. 'No. That won't do at all. You'll just have one tiny scoop and then say that's plenty.'

'Okay then.' Stefano turned to the waiter. 'I'd like a Blue Hawaiian, please.'

'Of course, sir. With pineapple?'

'Absolutely.'

'Maraschino cherry?'

'Bring it on.'

'Flaming?'

'You can do that?'

'To be honest, sir, I'm not sure. But I can ask, if you'd like.'

'Hmm. Maybe not. Just cherry and pineapple then.'

'Of course.'

The *barista* departed.

Nedda looked at Stefano. 'What on earth is a Blue Hawaiian?'

'To be honest, I've got no idea. But I'll be disappointed if it's not blue.'

'Did you just order the campest drink on the menu, just to keep me company?'

'Yes.' He smiled.

'You're quite mad. But thank you.'

'Not at all. I'm sure it'll be worth it.' He drummed his fingers on the table. 'Trouble is, it's going to take a while to arrive. They're very good at taking orders for complicated drinks here, but it does take them a bit of time to actually make them.'

'Do you make a hobby of complicated drinks then?'

'No. More of uncomplicated ones. But my hand's been forced.'

'So. What do we do in the meantime?'

'We could talk, I suppose?'

'Okay. The Lombardo story?'

Stefano pretended to bang his head gently on the table. 'Oh hell, no. Not work. I'm not talking about work.'

Nedda sighed and rolled her eyes. 'Okay then. Tell me about your family.'

He raised his head from the table. 'What?'

'Your family. I don't think you've ever mentioned them. Are they still up in Turin? And, well I don't know what's going to happen, but I hope I won't have to cook for them because I'm not much of a cook and so—'

He raised a hand. 'Nedda. Nedda. Stop.'

She saw the expression in his eyes. 'Oh shit. I'm sorry.'

'No need to be.' He sighed. 'But as we're doing this, I

never knew my father. *Mamma* said he left when I was very little. Never wanted to be a dad apparently. He blamed my mother for that. And then there were times when she blamed me for that. And then, one day, when I was thirteen, I came back home from school and she told me I was moving out. Not her, you understand. Me.'

'Oh God. I had no idea.'

'Why would you? I never talk about this.'

'So, what happened? To you, I mean.'

'Uncles. Aunties. Grandparents. Some of them were nice enough. And some of them weren't.' He shook his head. 'I'm not in touch with any of them. I don't even know if they're all still alive.'

'And your mother?'

'Dead this last year. We rebuilt some bridges. Eventually.'

'I'm sorry. Maybe this was a bad idea. This isn't a conversation for this time of night.'

He nodded. 'You know what? Maybe we should talk about work instead.'

Nedda reached for his hand, but the *barista* chose that moment to re-appear and the moment was lost.

'*Signurina*.' The *barista* deposited a tray with Nedda's *granita*, brioche and Frangelico. '*Signore*.' He smiled as he placed Stefano's drink in front of him, a symphony of blues, yellows and reds. Two straws and a little umbrella at a jaunty angle jutted out from the top.

Nedda looked down at her *granita* and then across at Stefano. 'Okay. I think you win this one.'

The two of them burst out laughing, and the awkwardness was forgotten.

He took a slurp via his straw.

'So, what's it taste of?'

'Blue things.' He twirled the second straw around so that it faced her. 'Try it.'

She bent her head, and he did the same, so that their noses nearly touched.

'Wow,' she said.

'Good?'

'I'd say that if you like blue things, there's probably nothing better.' She broke off a corner of her brioche, and then dipped the long-handled spoon into her *granita*, scooping up a mixture of chocolate and pistachio before smearing it on to the brioche and popping it into her mouth. She closed her eyes, as the chocolate blended with the savouriness of the pistachio and the spiciness of the bun.

'Oh, wow,' she repeated. 'Okay, we have to keep coming here.'

'I've never tried a *granita* here.'

'You're kidding.'

'Never had much of a sweet tooth.'

'Well if you're going to stay in Sicily you need to acquire one. Try this.' Again, she scraped up a mixture of the two *granite* and held the spoon out to him.

'Mmm. You know, this is good. This is very good indeed.' He waved at the *barista*. 'Maybe you need to bring me a second spoon after all.'

Of course, they needed more blue things. And in the warm haze of the late evening, Nedda had to admit that perhaps things were going pretty well. Calogero could wait. Aldo

Lentini and his *cannoli* could wait. Gianmaria Lombardo could wait, although, to be fair, he had little choice in the matter. For now there was the night, and the chatter of happy people, and blue things. Oh, and Stefano. He was good as well, she thought. Well, pretty good. He'd have to lose the denim, but she could see that as a project.

Stefano looked at their empty glasses. 'Another?'

She shook her head. 'That probably wouldn't be wise.'

'I know. But are we going to anyway?'

'No. I really don't think so.'

'Probably right.' He waved to the *barista*. 'Can we pay over here?'

The waiter arrived with the bill. 'Card or cash, sir?'

'Card, I guess.' Stefano reached inside his jacket. And then reached for his other pocket. 'Oh shit.' He looked up at the *barista*. 'Sorry.'

'What's wrong?' said Nedda.

'I've come out without my wallet. I must have left it in my other jacket.'

Nedda put her hand on his. 'I'll cover this, don't worry.'

'I can't ask you to do that, Nedda.'

'It's not a problem. Really. And better this than having to do the washing up.' She hoped the joke would at least raise a smile, but he scowled.

'This is embarrassing.'

'Don't be silly. These things happen. This is my treat. You can pay next time.'

'Are you sure?'

'Of course. Except next time I'll order something fabulously expensive.' Nedda took a card from her purse, tapped it on the machine, and the three of them smiled as the receipt printed off and the tension in the air drifted away.

***

Stefano linked his arm in Nedda's as they walked back through the streets of Aci Trezza.

'Sorry about that.'

She squeezed his arm. 'Don't be silly. It's the twenty-first century. Girls are allowed to pay now.' She paused for breath. 'On another note, why do you think everything in Aci Trezza has to be built uphill?'

'We're on the side of a volcano. It kind of goes with the territory. Your ancestors might have thought of this when they moved in.'

'You know, they might. I guess you have to admire their confidence, though. Building on the slopes of Etna.'

They stopped outside the door to his apartment. Stefano looked at her and smiled. 'Well, here we are. You know where everything is. And you know how to unfold the sofa bed.'

'I think I can remember.'

'It's just that, well—'

'Yes?'

'The whole seven years thing.'

'Yeah, that I remember. How could I forget that?'

'Well, I think there's two weeks to go. Except, of course, there's been a couple of leap years in between and that knocks a couple of days off. . . and also. . .'

'Oh, for Christ's sake.' Nedda pulled him towards her and kissed him hard.

Seven years, minus a couple of weeks. She reckoned it was worth the risk.

Chapter 35

Nedda was woken by a cold blast from the air-conditioning unit, as the bedclothes were yanked away from her.

For a moment, she thought it was Stefano's idea of a joke, or perhaps he was trying to wake her up, with breakfast or something else on his mind. But he was asleep, his feet tangled in the bedsheets and his legs thrashing around.

She touched his shoulder, gently, and whispered into his ear. 'Hey. Calm, now. You're having a dream.'

He shook off her hand, his legs continuing to flail at the sheets as a drowning man fights against the water that drags him down. He half-rolled over, his head thrashing from side to side. Words, unintelligible to her, spilled from his lips in a dreadful half-gargle, as if his throat were thick with phlegm.

'Stefano.' She shook him. 'Stefano.'

He took a deep breath, wheezing horribly. She shook him again, more violently this time. Should she call an ambulance? Was he having some kind of seizure? Was there something he hadn't told her?

'Help me.'

He latched on to her hand, squeezing it painfully.

'Stefano, what's the matter? Do you need a doctor? Is there medicine you need?'

'Help me.'

His head whipped from one side to the other and a terrible, high-pitched wailing came from his mouth. Surely, she thought, the neighbours would hear. One of them would be hammering on the door or calling the police any moment now.

Then his eyes flashed open.

'*Mamma.*'

Nedda felt as if the blood had frozen in her veins.

'*Mamma.* Help me.' He moaned again, that awful high-pitched whine.

She grabbed his shoulder and shook him again. How did you wake someone from a nightmare? *Papà* might have known but, on the other hand, she was quite glad *papà* was not there.

'Stefano. You must wake up.' She shook him and shook him. 'Wake up, please.'

He stopped wailing and spoke, very clearly this time.

'I. Am. Awake.'

'You're not awake, *caro.* You're having a nightmare. You're sleeping.'

'I am not sleeping.' He flapped at her hands, pushing them away, and then he was slapping at her, properly slapping, and she couldn't stop herself from screaming.

And then he stopped. His eyes cleared, and he slumped back upon the pillows.

'Very sleepy,' he murmured, and smiled. He reached for her hand and squeezed it. 'Sleepy,' he repeated.

He rolled over on to his side. 'Silly dream,' he murmured. Then, within seconds, there was silence, broken only by his rhythmic, gentle breathing and the hum of the air conditioning.

Nedda lay back in bed, breathing deeply. Then she drew her legs up, bending her head forward and hugging herself as her heart, slowly, stopped pounding.

Was this what she did when the nightmares came? Poor *papà*, she thought. How many times had he had to deal with that?

She slipped out of bed, and padded barefoot to the kitchen, where she poured herself a glass of warmish water from the tap. The air in here felt clammy and humid, and she could feel her arm sticking to the table as she rested it there.

She hadn't smoked in months but Stefano, she knew, always seemed to have a packet on him. 'For emergencies,' he said.

Where? she asked herself. Jacket pocket? Where had he hung it? She looked around and saw it lying on the floor in the hallway. She blushed yet smiled to herself. They hadn't been in a hanging things up frame of mind. She picked it up, intending to hang it on the back of the door, when something fell from the pocket. A packet of cigarettes. And something else.

A watch.

Strange. She could only ever remember Stefano using his phone when he checked the time. She picked it up and looked closer.

Rolex.

She dropped it back into his pocket and, with shaking hands, wiggled a couple of cigarettes from the packet.

What the actual *fuck*?

So my boyfriend has a Rolex. So what? Nedda, what a lucky girl you are.

She lit the cigarette off a gas ring and smoked away before chaining the second off the first. The first one, as ever, was unpleasant but, by the second, she'd smoked her way back into the habit and it was ever so slightly better.

My boyfriend has night terrors and didn't tell me.

That kind of made sense. *'Do you fancy staying over at my place? But I have to warn you I might wake up screaming uncontrollably and try to kill you'* was, perhaps, a line best held back to a second date.

My boyfriend has night terrors and a Rolex in his pocket. She looked around. *And a very nice apartment.*

So, he had an expensive watch. It had probably belonged to his dad or his grandad or someone. Something which you couldn't possibly sell and so was effectively worth nothing.

Why would he carry that around in his pocket, though? Cigarettes made sense, yet he'd forgotten his wallet but not the Rolex.

Why was she analysing this to death?

She sat there in her T-shirt, her sweaty arm sticking to the table, smoking horrible cigarettes that did nothing other than remind her why she gave up in the first place.

Love really is a many-splendored thing, isn't it?

She shook her head. Enough of the L-word. 'Like' it was and no further.

She filled another glass with lukewarm water and went back to bed. Stefano lay there, muttering to himself, but with a smile on his face. Whatever had happened, the nightmares were over.

She stroked his hair and kissed the back of his neck. She thought about snuggling up to him but, even with the air conditioning, it felt too hot and the sheets were unpleasantly stale and sweaty.

Again, she kissed the back of his neck and gently tapped the top of his head.

'What the hell is going on in there?' she whispered. But Stefano muttered to himself once more, smiled that mysterious smile, and started to snore, ever so gently.

Chapter 36

'You've been smoking in here?' Stefano looked pissed off.

'Sorry. I didn't realise that wasn't allowed. You being a smoker and all.'

'I don't smoke at home. Stinks the place out.'

'Sorry,' Nedda repeated. 'I'll try and remember next time.'

'Oh, you're assuming there'll be a next time?' He smiled and gave up trying to look cross. 'Just go outside, eh, that's what I do.'

'I didn't have any trousers on. That'd really give your neighbours something to talk about.' She took a deep breath. 'Stefano. You had a bad night last night.'

'Really?' He tried, and failed, to stop himself from grinning.

'I'm being serious. You had a nightmare. It was horrible. I couldn't wake you up.'

'A nightmare.' He rubbed his eyes. 'Sorry. It happens sometimes, but I haven't had one for ages. Didn't scare you too much, I hope?'

'You were thrashing around. I couldn't stop you. You were hitting and slapping at me.'

'What?' His expression changed. 'Christ almighty. I didn't hurt you, did I?'

'No. But it was frightening. I thought you were about to start screaming. I was afraid the neighbours might think someone was attacking you.'

He shook his head. 'I'm sorry. I'm so sorry.'

'It's not your fault. But seriously, have you seen a doctor about it?'

He shrugged. 'Never felt the need. After all, I'm always asleep at the time.'

'Stefano, just stop joking for once. I thought you were going to hurt yourself. Or me.' Nedda rubbed the side of her face.

He put his arms around her, kissed her cheek and stroked her hair. 'I'm sorry. I've never done that before. At least, I'm pretty sure I haven't.'

She gently, but firmly, pushed him away. 'You said something about your mother.'

His face darkened. 'I did?'

She nodded. '"*Mamma*. Help me." Stuff like that.'

'Stuff like that or just that?'

'I don't remember. I'd just woken up and I was trying to stop you hitting me. You never mentioned her until last night.'

He sighed. 'No,' he said. 'As I told you, I didn't know her for long. But it's something you carry with you, I guess. That your mother will always be there. Will always be able to help you. I guess that's why I still have dreams about her. Looking down on me. Taking care of me.' He took a photograph down from the bookcase. 'This is her.'

Nedda smiled. 'She looks nice.' But at the same time she wondered why parents always looked so much older in photos.

'It's the only one I have of her.'

'She has a kind face.' She couldn't think of much else to say. 'She looks like you.'

'Do you think so?'

She nodded. 'What about your father?'

'I don't have any photos.'

'I'm sorry.'

'I'm not. It seems you're lucky with your dad, though. I envy that.'

'I know. I might complain about him at times but I'd be lost without him.' She replaced the photo on the shelves. There was another, on the adjacent bookcase, that she hadn't noticed before. Three people, one of whom was Stefano, with his arms around a young woman and a small girl.

'My sister and her daughter,' he said, anticipating her question.

'They look lovely. Both so beautiful,' she said. 'Are they in Turin?'

He nodded. 'Still there. She's doing something very clever with the University, as I understand. Don't ask me to explain what it is.'

'Do you see them often?'

'Not as much as I'd like.'

'A shame. I'd have liked a sister. Not a brother, though, they sound horrible.'

Stefano smiled, and she replaced the photo. Then she paused, just before setting it down.

'Something wrong?'

She shook her head. 'No. Nothing at all.' But she took the quickest of looks just to confirm what she thought she'd seen.

There it was. On the third finger of Stefano's left hand. The one around the young woman. A ring.

'I'll make coffee,' she said.

'Nedda?' There was a strange note in Stefano's voice, something she hadn't heard before. 'Could I ask you something first?'

'Sure.'

'It's just . . .' He paused. 'Fuck, this is awkward. It's just – I'm having trouble paying the rent this month.'

'I don't understand.'

'Stupid of me. Cashflow problem.'

'Stefano, you earn more money than I do.'

'I know. But this place, well, it doesn't come cheap. I do freelance stuff on the side, you see, and kind of depend on that. But,' he spread his hands, 'sometimes invoices don't get paid on time. Or people still try and pay by cheque and you've got to wait for them to clear. Hell, I still get people sending post-dated cheques. So, yes,' his voice trailed off, 'sometimes stuff happens. And I was wondering if you could help.'

Nedda stared straight into his eyes but he couldn't hold her gaze. 'How much?' she said, quietly.

'I was hoping, maybe, a couple of thousand.'

She blinked, unable to quite believe what she'd heard. 'A couple of thousand?'

'Or thereabouts. But only if you've got it.'

'Stefano, I still live with my dad. What makes you think I've got that kind of money?'

'Okay. Okay.' He held his hands out. 'Silly of me to ask. Forget about it.'

'Stefano,' she looked around the flat, 'I don't understand.

I know this place is nice but how can you owe a couple of thousand on it?'

'It's been a couple of months and I've fallen behind. That's all. And my landlord's been good about it up until now but he's starting to get impatient.'

'Of course he is. So why did we go out last night if you're short of money?'

'It's because,' he sighed, deeply, 'it's because I wanted you to have a nice time. Especially after that whole business with Maugeri and my jacket and – well – if we're a thing now, I just wanted everything to be nice.'

'Things were nice. And, yes, I guess we're a thing now.'

'You guess?'

Nedda smiled and tried not to show how tired she was. 'We're a thing, okay. But you don't have to do things like that.' She sighed. 'Look. I can't get hold of this sort of money at short notice. You understand that?'

He nodded.

'And I don't think you'd be happy with me asking my dad, would you?'

He threw up his hands. 'Hell, no.'

'But I'll do what I can.'

His entire frame seemed to shudder, and his shoulders slumped. 'Thank you,' he whispered. 'Thank you thank you thank you. I'll make it up to you, I promise.'

'I know you will.' And then she pulled him to her so that he couldn't see her face. 'Look, can I borrow your computer for a moment?'

He drew away from her. 'Why so?'

'I can transfer some money now, if that'll help?'

'It really will.'

'Give me your landlord's details then, and I'll set it up.'

'Can't you just pay me directly?'

Nedda strove to keep her voice neutral. 'Why should I do that, Stefano?'

'It's just easier, that's all. You see, it's not just my landlord. There's the electricity board, bills, things like that.'

She nodded. 'Uh-huh. Okay, just log me on and I'll make a payment now.'

'You don't have a phone app?' She shook her head. 'You should get one. It makes everything so much easier. Never mind, I'll log on for you.'

The computer was a newish iMac Pro, much nicer than anything they got to use in the office. He looked at her apologetically. 'Sorry, there's an operating system update.' He tried to smile. 'It never does this at a convenient time, does it?' He yawned. 'Any chance of a coffee? There's a jar in the cupboard next to the fridge, and a Moka on the hob. '

Nedda tried to smile. 'Okay. Give me five minutes.'

The Moka, of course, was still full of yesterday's dregs. *Men*, she thought. She searched for a bin, found one under the sink, and banged the filter against the side until the grounds fell out. Then she rinsed out the pot as much as she could be bothered and topped the filter up with coffee from the jar.

'Sugar?' she called through. There was no answer. 'Stefano, sugar?' she called a little louder.

'No thanks. Although I quite like you calling me *sugar.*'

'How are you getting on?'

'Nearly there, I think. Ninety-five per cent done, if you

can believe that.' She heard him clattering away at the keyboard. 'Ninety-six, ninety-seven, ninety—'

'It's okay, you can spare me the countdown. I was only really interested in the sugar.' She heard the Moka starting to bubble and poured out two cups.

'Here we are,' she said, kissing him on the back of the neck.

'You're a star,' he said, patting her hand.

'Okay. Just scribble your bank details down for me.'

'I've done it already,' he grinned, passing a scrap of paper to her with an IBAN and branch code.

'Thanks.'

She tapped away at the keyboard. Stefano stood opposite, smiling, and then, as if thinking that perhaps a degree of gratitude and, indeed, humility might be appropriate, turned away.

Nedda clicked on the 'History' tab.

There was nothing.

'Thank you, *cara*.' He hugged her and kissed her on the cheek. 'You are an absolute star, you know that?'

He'd called her that twice in ten minutes. Any more and she'd have to start twinkling. He picked her up and twirled her around, nuzzling into her neck. 'You know, you don't have to go just yet, do you? What do you say?'

She gently, but firmly, pushed him away. 'I say I need to go. I need to see my dad and think of a clever way of avoiding an awkward conversation.' He opened his mouth to protest, but she placed a finger on his lips. 'And, above all, I've got some money to move around. Okay?'

He smiled and hugged her. 'Thank you so much. I mean that.'

She touched his cheek and kissed him. 'Yeah.' And she wished with all her heart that it was twelve hours earlier.

Chapter 37

Stefano was either a heavy sleeper or pretending to be one, but Calogero had noticed the curtains twitching and was sure it was the latter.

It was a nice place to live. From the terrace, you'd be able to look over the roof of the church of St John the Baptist, with its little angel clinging to the cross, and out over the sea to the island of Lachea. On the other hand, the steps leading down to the centre of town were steep and the return journey would be punishing on a hot day. Like today.

He checked his watch. There'd be a bus back up to Acireale in thirty minutes. He'd better get on with it. He buzzed again and again. He was prepared to stand there all morning with his finger resting on the button if need be.

He heard muffled swearing from inside, and footsteps approaching. The door shuddered in its frame as Stefano yanked it open. He was bleary-eyed with sleep and rubbed his eyes as he stared at Calogero.

'You?'

'Good morning, Stefano.'

'If you're looking for Nedda, she's not here. Probably at her dad's.'

'Why would she be here?' His eyes widened. 'Oh.'

Stefano yawned and stretched. 'I was asleep on the sofa. Just woken up. Is there anything I can do?'

Calogero took out the wallet and held it up. 'Sorry, I'd have brought this back earlier but I was busy all last night at the theatre so this was the earliest I could manage.' He held it out, but Stefano made no move to take it. For a moment, it almost appeared as if he shrank back.

He said nothing, but his eyes continued to flick from Calogero to the wallet and then back again.

'I thought you'd be pleased?'

Stefano shook his head. 'Where did you get that?'

'Last night. You remember. I kind of intruded on your evening – sorry, that was thoughtless of me – and then your beer got spilled all over you. My fault entirely, I'll pay for that jacket to get cleaned.'

'Thanks. It's not necessary.'

Calogero shrugged. 'If you're sure. Anyway, after you'd gone, I saw this lying on the ground.' He turned it over in his hand. 'I took a look inside. Sorry, I hope you don't mind too much. But I thought it would speed things up. And, well, there's a driving licence in your name. Business cards and the like. So, I knew it was yours.'

Stefano gave a dry little chuckle. 'You know, I hadn't even noticed it was missing. You know how we use our phones for everything these days? I thought it was still in my jacket. The beery one, I mean.'

'Of course. You want to be careful, though. You never know, one day the cops will ask to see your ID card. And you don't want one of those to fall into the wrong hands.'

'Absolutely not. Well, thank you.' He smiled at Calogero in a way that clearly stated he was grateful but no coffee was going to be offered and he'd like him to go.

'I was just wondering. Could I take a business card perhaps?'

'A card?' He shrugged. 'Sure. If you ever need a journalist, I don't know, for publicity or whatever, give me a call. It's not really my thing, but I'll find someone who can help.'

'Thanks.' Calogero turned the card over. He took a deep breath. Now or never. 'Thing is, Stefano. I've seen one of these before.'

'You have?'

'I didn't know you knew Gianmaria Lombardo.'

'Lombardo.' He frowned. 'I didn't.'

'Oh. Maybe I'm wrong. It's just that I saw one of these in his apartment. You know, when I was feeding the cat.'

Stefano laughed. 'It's possible. I give a lot of these out. They can end up anywhere.' He yawned and stretched. 'And now, I think, I'm going to lie down on the sofa again and watch some rubbish on television. I'd ask you in for a beer but the flat needs a bit of a clean-up.'

'No problems.'

Stefano made to close the door but Calogero, gently but firmly, stretched his arm out to stop him. 'What's going on, Stefano?'

'I don't understand?'

'Something's wrong. It involves you and Gianmaria Lombardo.'

'Maugeri, it's the middle of the afternoon, I have plans, and I have no time for this.'

'You're in trouble. I know you are. And I might be able to help you.'

He laughed. 'Help me? Maugeri, what do you think you can help me with?'

'I'm serious, Stefano. Let me in. Let's talk. I can help.'

Stefano shook his head, almost imperceptibly. He seemed to shrink in on himself and, for a moment, looked ten years older.

'No,' he said. 'No, you really can't.'

And, with that, he closed the door in his face.

Chapter 38

Early morning, in that blissful and all too brief moment before the sun shone down unbearably on Acireale. By midday the streets would be baking, and those bars and restaurants with the misfortune to be on the wrong side of the road would be closing up their outside seating areas; even tourists being unwilling to spend more than a few minutes in direct sunlight. But for now, it was early morning, the air was fresh, the sky was clear and Calogero Maugeri was enjoying a pistachio *cornetto* and a coffee.

He checked again the address he'd scribbled down on the back of Nedda's business card. He was pretty sure this was the place. And if there had been any doubt, then the yellow Royal Enfield parked outside was a clue.

Good place to live, he thought. The *caffè* where he was currently seated seemed nice, likewise the pizzeria opposite. He wasn't quite sure what to make of the puppet museum, currently closed. Perhaps he should take a look sometime. It might give him an idea for the act. On the other hand, he'd never been quite comfortable in the company of puppets. There was something about their eyes. They were impossible to read, and that bothered him.

He heard a door slam as Nedda, helmet in hand, headed for her bike.

'Nedda? Nedda, wait up.'

'Maugeri?' She had switched to his surname. 'Have you been waiting for me?'

He thought about quipping that it was just magic, but the expression on her face told him that would be a bad idea. He decided to be honest. 'Yes. I needed to speak to you. So, I took the opportunity for breakfast.'

'Okay.' She folded her arms. 'What do you want to talk about?'

He ran a finger across his goatee. 'First of all, am I clear?'

'Clear?'

'*Cornetto* crumbs. Traces of pistachio. Green facial hair has never quite caught on.'

'Oh.' She gave him the most cursory of glances. 'Yes, you're clear.'

'Good. About the other night. I just wanted to say sorry. For getting in the way and spilling beer everywhere.'

'Okay. Is that all?'

'Oh.' He smiled. 'I guess you mean Stefano's wallet.'

'Well now. And how might you know about that, Mr Magus?'

'I found it under the table. He must have dropped it when we had the beer and jacket incident. I returned it to him yesterday afternoon.' He took a deep breath. 'Nedda, there's something I need to ask you.'

'Yes?'

'Stefano. Has he ever asked you for money?'

Silence fell between them. 'Why would you ask that?' she said, quietly.

'There was something I found in his wallet.'

'So, you went through it?'

'Yes.'

'You find anything good?'

'Yes. As it happens. Tucked away amongst everything else. A *Giocatori Anonimi* – Gamblers Anonymous – token.'

'What?'

'It's a coin they're given at meetings. To show they've been clean for a certain period of time. Which is why I'm asking if he's ever asked you for money.'

'No. Why the fuck would you even think that?'

'It's just a question. You ever noticed him gambling? Even little, insignificant things.'

'No.'

'Scratch cards. Slot machines. Even things like that.'

'No.'

He shook his head. 'You're lying.'

'Oh, don't tell me, the Magus has read my mind?'

'No need to. I've said this to you before. You have what gamblers call a *tell*. Which means it's obvious when you're bluffing. Or lying.'

Her hand cracked across his face. 'Fuck you.'

He rubbed his cheek. People on the other side of the road were staring at them. Two young guys leaning against a scooter were, he thought, laughing a little too openly.

'Nedda, I'll be honest with you. Stefano is lying to you. He has a problem. And I hope it's just gambling because maybe that can be sorted.' He sighed. 'I'm sorry, Nedda. I think he's in trouble.'

For a moment he thought she was going to slap him again, but her expression changed. 'What do you mean, trouble?'

He lowered his voice, practically hissing the words out. 'Gianmaria Lombardo. His money wasn't coming in from the psychic circuit. He was a blackmailer. He held a dossier on his victims, it's out there somewhere and I think Stefano's name is in there. I also think I can help him, but you've got to let me. And I want you to be careful. I think he's a good guy but I just can't be sure.'

'And I sure as hell know you aren't.' She turned to walk away.

'Nedda, you can storm off if you like. But just hear me out. Two reasons. One, if you ride when you're as angry as this you'll do something stupid and kill yourself. Secondly, just tell me this. Why would Gianmaria Lombardo have Stefano's business card?'

'He's a journalist, you idiot. You know, he has an actual professional fucking job? Remember those? So don't you dare come near me again. Oh, and if you think there's a chance of me going to your crappy show tomorrow evening you're even more of a creep than I thought you were.'

'You what?'

She reached into her jacket and shook a ticket in his face. 'This.'

He grabbed it from her before she could snatch it back. There it was. A complimentary ticket for the following night's show.

'Nedda, where did you get this?'

'Where do you think? *Papà* said it dropped through the letterbox Sunday morning.'

'On Sunday?'

She was about to make another grab for the ticket but he

just offered it to her, and she took it from his fingers. 'I don't understand.'

'Nedda, I am not the Ticket Fairy of Acireale. I don't flit from house to house giving out free tickets. And even if I were, I wouldn't do it on Sunday morning. So whoever sent you that ticket, it sure as hell wasn't me.'

Her expression clouded. 'Whatever.' He thought for a moment that she was going to screw the ticket up, but she folded it neatly away inside her bike jacket.

'Nedda. What are you going to do?'

'I'm going to go to work. The ride will clear my head. It always does.'

'Okay. Just take care, right?'

She nodded, turned and walked back to her bike.

'I meant what I said, you know? I might be able to help.'

She said nothing. But then she turned and nodded. 'Thank you.'

Chapter 39

'What's going on?' said Lentini, looking down at the box on his desk.

'Nothing at all,' said Nedda. 'I just knew you liked them, that's all.' She opened the box, and turned it to him, the smell of sweet, fresh pastries filling the air.

Aldo looked down at the *cannoli* neatly packed inside.

'Okay,' he said, 'now I'm really worried. What are you after?'

She did her best to look affronted. 'Can't a girl buy pastries for her favourite boss without being accused of asking for favours?'

He shook his head. 'No. Particularly when they've spent weeks complaining about it. What's going on, Nedda?'

'Okay, this is going to be difficult. But keep the pastries anyway. It's,' she took a deep breath, 'it's about Stefano.'

'What's the matter? You two not working well together?'

'No, it's not that.' She looked down at her hands. 'I think maybe we've been working too well together.'

Aldo had been in the act of taking a *cannolo* from the box, and stopped, holding it, cigar-like, halfway to his mouth. 'Oh hell,' he finally said.

'It's okay, Aldo.'

'It's not okay. I've had this before. Reporters start getting together and within a few weeks he starts thinking he's Cary Grant and she starts thinking she's Glenda Farrell.'

'Who?'

'Doesn't matter. What's gone wrong?'

'Nothing's gone wrong.'

'It must have done. That's the only reason people come to me in cases like this. *"Aldo, I can't work with this guy anymore." "Aldo, you've gotta find me someone else to work with, this is killing me."'*

'Aldo, it's not like that. I'm – I'm just worried about him. I think he might be in trouble.'

Lentini sat there in silence, looking at her. Then he nodded. 'Tell me why you think that, Nedda.'

'I don't need to give you the whole story, Aldo. It's just that the other morning – well, he asked me to lend him some money.'

Again, the two of them sat there in silence. 'I don't understand,' he said, finally.

'Me neither. Sure, he's living in a great apartment but I don't see how he can be so short of money he can't pay the rent. Or why he should be asking me for it.'

He shook his head. 'No. I don't pay you enough for that.'

'Oh, thanks.'

'I'm being serious. I don't understand what's going on.'

'Aldo, can I ask – I know Stefano hasn't been here all that long, but – where did you get him from?'

He sighed. 'Turin,' he said. '*La Stampa.*'

Nedda shook her head. 'I don't understand,' she said. 'I

mean, why? He's still a young guy and – with all due respect, Aldo – *La Stampa* is pretty much the best gig a reporter's ever going to get.'

'He said something about wanting to downsize a bit. I told him we couldn't pay him anything like *La Stampa*, but that didn't seem to bother him. It might just be that he's not got used to what we're paying him.'

'You haven't seen his apartment. It's nice, yes, but there's no way rent in Aci Trezza is going to be anything like Turin.'

'Nedda, there are all sorts of reasons he might be a bit short at the moment. Credit cards. Still paying off the cost of relocating. All sorts of things like that.' He frowned. 'Strange, though. Aci Trezza, you said?'

'Uh-huh.'

'When he moved here, he took a small place on the outskirts of Catania. He had a moving-in party there. I remember we were all sitting on packing cases because he had almost zero furniture. Perhaps he thought he'd downsized just a little too far.'

'I think there's more to it than that, Aldo.'

He raised an eyebrow. 'Oh yes?'

She blushed. 'Kind of difficult to talk about, though.'

'Oh hell. Look, Nedda, he came with first-class references. That's all I was interested in. Getting a senior reporter for next to no money. But I'm sorry you've been put in a difficult position. Tell you what, I'll have a word with him, see if I can help out a bit.'

'No.'

He frowned. 'I don't understand.'

'If you say anything, he'll know I've been speaking to you.

And I don't want that. Not yet anyway. Just give me a couple of days on this, Aldo, okay?'

He nodded. 'If that's what you want.'

'It is. Thank you.' She got to her feet.

'Oh, and Nedda?'

'Yes?'

'You can leave the *cannoli*.'

Chapter 40

'No, I don't want a cup of tea. Or a cup of coffee. I'll have a beer from the fridge if that will make you happy. And only if you promise to sit down afterwards.'

'Sorry. I just don't seem to be able to settle.'

'You're not joking. You've been up and down all evening since we finished dinner. You've been pretending to watch football, which you never do. You've even been pretending to enjoy it.'

'As I said. I'm just finding it hard to settle.'

'Right. It's half time. Go get me that beer, and then I'll have precisely fifteen minutes to sort out whatever is wrong with your life before the second half.' Angelo clapped his hands. 'Go on. Fifteen minutes as I said.'

Nedda got to her feet.

'And get one yourself. If we're going to do the whole father–daughter thing, I think you might need it.'

She returned with two bottles of *Messina*, and two glasses. Drinking from the bottle was, according to Angelo, a sign of retreating into barbarism, and even though young people down at the beach seemed to do it, it was on no account to be encouraged.

He turned the volume down on the television. 'Come on then. I'm missing Marco Tardelli for this.' Then he frowned. 'Actually, that might not be a bad thing. Come on then. What is it? Is Mr Wonderful not calling?'

'He says he's got work to do tonight. Freelance stuff.' She hesitated. 'And I'm not so sure if he's Mr Wonderful. Truth be told, I always thought he was more of a Mr You'll-do-for-now.'

Angelo winced. 'You didn't need to tell me that, *trisoru.*'

'Sorry. It's just that, well, stuff has happened and,' she took a deep breath, 'I think he might be in trouble.'

Angelo sighed. 'Okay. Prospects of the second half seem to be receding.'

'Look, we can do this another time.'

'No, we can't. There'll be another tournament in two years. I can afford to miss this one.'

'Okay, there's no easy way to say this but – Stefano asked me for money yesterday.'

Angelo raised his eyebrows. 'I see,' he said, after a long pause. 'You said no, of course?' She said nothing. 'You said no, of course?'

'Not exactly.'

He sighed and looked at his beer. 'Sometimes I wish these came in bigger bottles. How much?'

'Okay, first things first. I didn't give him what he asked for.'

'Which was?'

'A couple of thousand.'

'*Gesù,*' he said, immediately followed by a wag of the finger and 'You're not to say that, of course. Tell me how much you actually gave him.'

'A couple of hundred.'

'Mm-hmm.' His eyes sharpened. 'Why?'

'Because I think he's in trouble. But more than that. If I hadn't given him anything I think he might just have asked me to get out or we'd have had a good old row. A couple of hundred euros buys me a bit of time to find out what's going on.'

Angelo grinned and leaned over to ruffle her hair. 'That's my girl,' he said.

'More than that. I left the room to make us coffee. He told me his computer was updating.'

'Is that when you get that annoying circle that just goes round and round forever, giving you time to go to the shops and back before it finishes?'

'Exactly that. But here's the thing. I heard him typing away. He wouldn't have been able to do that if it was updating. And when I sat down to send him the money, I checked his browsing history. It was empty. He'd cleared the cache, everything.'

Angelo stared at her. 'Okay. I thought I was doing ever so well knowing about this "updating" thing. Now you've lost me.'

'Basically, he cleared all the information relating to every website he'd ever visited before he let me on to his computer.'

'Okay. Gone for ever?'

'Not for ever. But it's beyond my ability to retrieve.'

He nodded. 'And what do you think was there?'

'I don't really like to think about that.'

'I can imagine.' He sipped at his beer. 'I can imagine,' he repeated. 'So, what now?'

'Dad, I think you might be able to help me.'

'If you're talking about the two hundred euros, *trisoru*, I think you might need to chalk that up to experience.'

'Not that. It's about Stefano. You still know people in the *Guardia*. Can you, you know, run a few checks on him?'

'The *Guardia*? Tax records and the like?'

'Criminal records, financial information. Anything that might demonstrate why my boyfriend of a few days is asking me for money.'

'Hmm. Highly irregular. Possibly actually breaking the law. Maybe putting careers at risk.'

'But will you do it?'

'Of course.' He leaned over and ruffled her hair again. 'But what do you want to find out, Nedda?'

'That he's waiting on being paid by a bunch of clients.'

'And what do you think you will find out?'

'I don't know. But I need to.'

'Of course you do. Now, with that settled, shall we get back to the match?'

'That'd be nice.'

'Well, it might be. They say hope springs eternal, after all.' He looked down at his glass. 'Oh, and we seem to have finished our beer.'

Nedda smiled. 'I'll get them.'

He looked up at the screen, and a broad smile broke across his face. Italy had scored. 'Maybe we might just be getting lucky,' he said.

'Oh, and *papà*?'

'Yes?'

'There's one other small thing.'

'Yes?'

'I think he might be married.'

Angelo sighed, and switched off the television. 'I think perhaps I'll just watch the highlights later,' he said.

Chapter 41

'Calogero Maugeri?'

'That's me.'

'Also known as the Magus?'

'That's still me. Can I help you?'

'Yes. We do know each other. Sort of. I'm Toto Licata.'

Calogero hesitated for a moment, and then frowned at his phone. 'Oh yes. Toto. How are you?' he said in that tone of voice reserved for those conversations when you have no idea who the other person actually is.

Toto chuckled. 'From *Bella Catania*. The TV station. Remember, you were a guest on our late-night psychic special a few months ago.'

'Of course. Otherwise known as Fight Night. Yes, I do remember now.'

'I thought I'd give you a call. Just to say thanks.'

'Right. Well, no problem.' He laughed. 'I mean, nobody got too badly hurt, did they? And if you want me to appear again, then just call my agent and we'll sort something out.' He paused. 'I don't actually have an agent, but you could always call me directly, that's what I'm saying.'

'I'm sorry, I don't understand. That's not why I'm calling.'

'It isn't?'

'No. As I said, I just wanted to say thanks. For the ticket.'

'Okay. So now we're having one of those conversations where neither party understands the other. What ticket?'

'For your show tonight. The complimentary one that arrived this morning.'

'Wow. Well, I have to say I'd be delighted if you can make it. But it really isn't from me.'

'It wasn't?'

'No. Listen, could you just describe it to me?'

'Not much to say. Printed ticket for this evening and a slip with "With compliments" on it.'

'Nothing handwritten?'

'No.'

'What about the envelope?'

'Slipped into my letterbox this morning. Hand delivered. Listen, what is all this?'

'I'm not sure yet. Just one more thing. What's the price on that ticket?'

'I don't know, I didn't really look. Let me check a moment. Here we are. Twelve euros.' Calogero said nothing. 'Is there anything wrong?'

'No. No. Just checking. Anyway, I hope you can make it. Perhaps we can grab a drink and a bite to eat after.'

'That'd be nice. See you later.'

Toto hung up, and Calogero stared at his phone.

He knew about complimentary tickets. He'd given away enough of them. In the early days of the show it sometimes felt as though members of the audience who'd actually paid were in a minority. And complimentary tickets from the

Teatro Giovanni Verga never had a price on them.

Somebody must have bought them and hand delivered them to both Nedda and Toto. Now, why?

Chapter 42

'Not like you to come into Catania, *papà*.'

Angelo smiled. 'Well, if I can't buy my favourite daughter lunch, what can I do?'

'That's nice of you.'

'I say my favourite daughter. I mean my only daughter, of course.'

'Don't spoil it.'

'So, inside or outside?'

'Inside. Air conditioned. And the smell of fish becomes a bit too much outside.'

Angelo smiled at the waiter, who nodded as if to indicate that he quite agreed and ushered them inside.

Nedda took her seat and stared out of the window at the bustling fish market down below. 'I'll never understand how people can do this, you know? The entire morning. In this heat. Working with fish.'

'Perhaps they really like fish?'

'*Papà*, I really like fish. I just wonder if anybody can possibly like it that much.'

'Well anyway, I'm glad you mentioned fish. I was starting to forget why we'd come here. What are we having?'

'How about we share a raw seafood platter. Nice and refreshing on a hot day?'

'Perfect. And to drink?'

'A half-bottle of *Falanghina*?'

'Only a half?'

'That's for you. I've got to go back to the office, remember?'

'Of course. That's a shame.'

Nedda smiled and reached across the table to take his hands. 'Okay then, *papà*. Why don't you tell me just how you're going to ruin my life?'

'What?'

'You never come into Catania. So it must be important. Out with it.'

He sighed. 'Ah, your mother really would have been proud.' His eyes grew misty for a moment, but then the waiter arrived to take their order.

'So,' said Angelo. 'I've got some information back from the *Guardia*.'

'That was quick.'

'Yes. Still got a few friends there who can pull some strings. It's going to cost me a few beers, mind you. I'll be taking that out of your allowance.'

'I've not had an allowance for ten years, Dad.'

'Haven't you?' He peered over the top of his glasses. 'Well, in that case I'll add it to this month's rent. Now then. Stefano Gallo.' He licked his thumb and flicked through the notebook in front of him. 'Born Turin, 1989. Hmm. That makes him a bit older than you. Anyway, graduated in *giurisprudenza*, University of Turin Department of Law. Journalist's card obtained in 2016. Joined staff of *La Stampa* that same year.' He nodded. 'Good job, that. Very good for a first position.

'He was there for a few years. Very promising up and coming young reporter. And then, he moved from Turin to Catania a year ago. To join *Catania Nuova*, which,' again he looked over his glasses at her, 'with respect, *trisoru*, does not seem like a step up.'

Nedda said nothing, but merely made a 'hmph' which was short for 'I understand and basically agree with what you're saying, even if perhaps you didn't need to say it.' She restricted herself to 'So maybe he just wanted a quieter life. I mean, that's what you wanted, wasn't it? After – what happened.' She immediately wished she hadn't phrased it like that, but Angelo merely nodded.

'True enough, perhaps. Now, here I had to call in some favours with the *Guardia* and also with the *Anagrafe* to check where he was living. Again, a few more beers. Again, a little more on the rent next month. Anyway, he moved from Turin to the outskirts of Catania.'

'Cheaper part of town.'

'It is. Although it turns out your Stefano had quite a bit of money.'

'I don't understand.'

'His mother died. Just over a year ago. Just before he moved to Catania. She left him a very generous *patrimonio*.'

'Except that now he's moved on up by moving to this place in Aci Trezza.'

Angelo shrugged. 'Why not? Take a cheaper place for a few months while you try and find where you really want to be. It makes sense to me.'

She sighed. 'You're probably right. I don't suppose you know who the landlord is?'

'I did make a note of that. And this is where it gets interesting.' He took off his glasses. 'It is – or was – our friend Gianmaria Lombardo.'

'Really?'

'Absolutely.'

'Oh *papà*.' Her face cleared, and she reached over to hug him. 'That's wonderful.'

'It is? Have I done something good?'

'It explains – well it explains a lot of things. It explains why Lombardo had a business card of Stefano's. It makes perfect sense. He was renting an apartment to him, why wouldn't he have one?'

Angelo nodded. 'That's true.' He coughed gently. 'But it doesn't explain why he's asking you for money, *cara mia*.'

'All sorts of reasons. Maybe there's some sort of financial confusion now that Lombardo's dead. Something like that.' *Something like that* sounded weak, but she was prepared to let it go for now.

'Something like that. I guess so.' Angelo had been smiling, but his expression changed, became serious again. 'But there is something else I need to tell you, *trisoru*. And I don't want you to be sad. Or to be angry.' He gave her a pad of paper with a telephone number scrawled on the top.

An area code of 011.

Turin.

There was a name scribbled underneath.

'*Papà*, what is this?'

'It's the phone number of someone called Mariana Giordano.' He sighed, deeply. 'Stefano Gallo's wife.'

Chapter 43

'You don't seem to be settling this afternoon, Nedda,' said Lentini.

She shook her head. 'Head's all over the place today, Aldo. Sorry.'

He nodded. 'Okay. Anything to do with our little chat yesterday?'

'Maybe. By which I mean, yes.'

'Okay. Tell you what, let's have another one. In my office.'

He sat himself down behind his desk and turned the air conditioning up a notch. 'Humidity's going through the roof, isn't it?' Then he spun his chair around to look out of the window. 'And there's rumours that Etna's due to start acting up again.'

'Really?'

'I've got a contact at the airport. They always seem to be informed about this sort of thing earlier than anyone else. Anyway, I was thinking about our little chat yesterday. And I really shouldn't be telling you this, but I went back to check out Gallo's references again and—'

'And?'

'Well, there's nothing wrong with them. Nothing at all.

It's just I've written enough of these in my time to know when something's not quite right. His is just, well, bland. Not much more than a list of his dates with the newspaper and basic duties carried out.' He took a deep breath. 'The sort of reference you write when you don't want to say anything bad about someone but can't afford to be completely honest.'

'You still took him on, though?'

'My fault. I was just a little bit too excited at the prospect of poaching a journo from *La Stampa*.'

'I can understand that.'

'And he is a good journalist, Nedda.'

'I know he is, Aldo. Okay, I'll get back to work and try and straighten my head out. First things first, though. There's a phone call I need to make.'

'Okay. Anything I need to know about?'

'I don't think so. Not yet anyway. And then later on, I'm going to the theatre.'

'Oh right. Anything good?'

'I don't know yet. A magic show.'

Lentini wasn't able to keep a straight face. 'I didn't think that was your thing.'

'I don't think it is. But it's a free ticket. And it's from Calogero Maugeri.' He looked blank. 'The guy who was questioned on the day of Lombardo's funeral.'

'Really?' He smiled. 'Proper investigative reporting. I remember that. Is Gallo going with you?'

'No. I think that might be a bit awkward.' She frowned. 'I haven't seen him in a few days as it happens.'

'He phones in every morning. Unwell with a "fever", he says.'

'Oh. He just told me – well, that he had stuff to do.'

'I see. Well, I'm sure it'll sort itself out, Nedda. Have a good time tonight and forget about it all. Just don't let him saw you in half.'

For the fifth time, Nedda's hand hovered over 'call', and then hung up. And then, taking a deep breath, as if she were about to plunge into the Ionian Sea in the middle of January, she retyped the number and hit the button with her thumb.

'*Pronto.*' The voice was young, much younger than she'd expected.

'Hello. Am I talking with Mariana Giordano?'

'I'll fetch her. *Mamma.* Someone on the phone.'

Ah. That explained it.

'*Pronto.*'

'Mariana Giordano?'

There was a long pause. Then, 'Who's calling, please?'

'My name's Nedda Leonardi. I'm a journalist with *Catania Nuova.*'

Another long pause. 'I'm sorry, where did you say?'

'*Catania Nuova.* In Catania. Sicily.'

'I know where it is. Why are you calling?'

'I have a work colleague called Stefano Gallo. I believe you know him.'

By now, she was used to the long pauses. 'I do, yes.' Then, 'Is he all right?'

'He is, yes. Don't worry, it's nothing like that.'

'Is he in trouble?'

To be honest or to not be honest. Nedda bit her lip. Truthfully, she hadn't imagined getting this far. 'I don't know,' she said, finally.

There was a deep breath at the end of the line. 'Is it money again?'

'I don't know, but—'

'Did he ask you to ring me?' The questions were coming ever quicker now.

'No, he didn't. Can you just confirm to me – I'm sorry to be blunt, but am I speaking to his ex-wife?'

'No.' Nedda took a deep breath, before all the air was knocked out of her. 'I'm his wife.'

There was nothing she could think of to say.

'Don't call me again. And tell him I don't want to speak to him or see him again, ever. We're getting on with our lives now. I won't let him drag us back down. You tell him that, you understand?'

Nedda hung up, without replying.

She bought a double *macchiato* from the coffee machine and drank it with shaking hands. Then she went back to her desk and sat in front of her computer, the monitor reflecting back her image, grey and distorted.

She checked her watch. There was, she supposed, one more thing she could productively do before heading off to watch Calogero pulling rabbits from hats.

There was no doubt about it now.

Stefano had moved from one of the most venerable newspapers in Italy to a small provincial one.

He'd left a wife and daughter in Turin. Who no longer wished to speak to him.

He'd started all over again. As if wishing to erase his past.

It was time to go. Suddenly the prospect of being sawn in half didn't seem quite so bad.

Chapter 44

The *Teatro Giovanni Verga* was a pretty good space, for the third best theatre in Acireale, Nedda thought.

She'd only been here once before, when she was very little. A travelling group of British actors had thought it might be nice to introduce Italy to the concept of the traditional British Christmas pantomime. However, Nedda, like the rest of the locals, had struggled with the concept of 'audience participation' and the company had never returned. *Papà* had told her that children in London got taken to the pantomime as a special treat every Christmas but that, to Nedda, just seemed like a cruel and unusual punishment.

The man on the door had smiled and waved her through on seeing her ticket and given her a programme as well. Or, at least, a four-page folded sheet of adverts for local services together with a short biography of the Magus. There wasn't much to read, much of it being taken up with just how mysterious he was and, like all the best mysterious people, he didn't seem to have much of a backstory. *Toast of Aci* had a quarter-page advert. By now, she imagined, Calogero's patronage must surely more than have covered the advertising fees.

She felt a hand on her shoulder from the seat next to her. 'Hello there?'

There was something familiar about the face, she just couldn't quite place it. Then it came to her. 'Toto?'

'I thought you'd forgotten me.'

'No, sorry. Of course I remember. Not working tonight?'

'We're putting a lot of repeats out to cover it.'

'The dentist guy?'

'Yep. His fans are in for a bit of a treat, frankly. But I thought I needed to be here.' He reached into his pocket and smoothed out a ticket. 'I got one of these in the post.'

'A complimentary ticket?'

'Absolutely. I'm feeling like a regular VIP.' He looked around. 'Although I have to say, I was rather hoping for a private box. Not the very back row of the stalls.'

Nedda took her own ticket out. 'And I got the same.'

He smiled. 'Damn. Now I feel a bit less special. Maybe we're all VIPs. Maybe nobody paid for their tickets and the Magus has been scurrying around handing out freebies.'

'I don't think he has, you know. I asked him about it. He says it wasn't him.'

'Must be the theatre management then. Probably for publicity. You know, you might be able to give them a good write-up. We might be encouraged to do a feature on them.' He looked around. The *Teatro Giovanni Verga* had probably been a fine building once upon a time, possibly in Giovanni Verga's day, but now it seemed in need of a lick of paint and a bit of care. 'I think they might appreciate the publicity.'

'So, have you actually seen him in action?'

He shook his head. 'How about you?'

'First time.'

'Well then,' said Toto as the lights dimmed, 'here we go.'

'Thank you, Acireale. You've been wonderful as ever.' The theatre was half full. That wasn't bad.

Calogero stepped back, waving. He raised his staff in the air, pressed the button and realised, too late, that something was wrong. There was a flash of light, the smell of burning, and a scream that might have been his own.

There was silence for a moment. Some nervous laughter. Then the lights came up, revealing Calogero sprawled face down upon the stage, and the laughter turned to screams.

She turned to Toto, who sat there, stunned.

'My God.'

The audience were on their feet by now, blocking her path to the stage.

There came a cry from the front. 'We need an ambulance here. And a doctor.'

She tried to force her way through, but arms were out, holding her and blocking her path.

'Let me through, please.'

'*Signurina*, are you a doctor?'

'No.' She paused. 'I'm his friend.'

The crowd parted and she kneeled down at his side. 'Calogero?' She looked up at the people around her. 'Is he alive? Can we move him?'

'Nedda?' His voice was weak.

She grabbed his shirt collar and tore it open.

'Why are you doing that?'

'I don't know. I think I saw it on television.'

'Oh. Carry on then.' He looked up at the faces staring down at him. 'But could I have a proper doctor, please? I think that might be nice.'

And, with that, he closed his eyes and fell asleep.

She looked back at the audience. Toto was slumped over in his chair, his head almost resting on his shoulder. How the hell could he sleep through this? And then the screaming began again, and a cry went up.

'There was a man with a knife.'

Chapter 45

'How are you feeling, *signor* Maugeri?'

'Rough as hell. They tell me I'm lucky to be alive. Could have been severely burned, killed even. As it is,' he held up his bandaged hands, 'I just have some light burns. Too early to tell if there are any long-term effects.' He smiled. 'Amnesia, I'm told, is one.'

Gori looked pained. 'Well, let's hope you can fight that off for the next few minutes at least. Let's start with what happened to you.'

'There's a device in my staff. It generates a high-intensity flash and triggers pyrotechnics from the stage. You charge up the capacitor beforehand and it's normally good for a couple of days.' He looked at his hands. 'It has to be well-insulated. There's two hundred volts across it. On a bad day that's enough to kill you.

'I was stupid last night. I should have double-checked the staff. The insulating tape had been stripped away from the button that activated the charge. As soon as I touched it,' he wiggled his fingers, 'two hundred volts. Through me. I've been lucky.'

'I take it we're not talking about an accident here.'

'I doubt it. Thing is, I'm not sure it was really aimed at me. I think it was a distraction, which allowed someone to knife poor Toto Licata.'

'You knew him, then?'

'That's a stretch. I'd met him, just the once.'

'Are you sure about that?'

'He produced a TV programme I was involved with a few months ago. You won't have seen it.'

'Try me. When I can't sleep at night, I'll watch almost anything.'

'It never went out.'

'And why was that?'

'I don't know.'

'Uh-huh. This would be the TV programme with your-self, Gianmaria Lombardo, Salvatore Sipala and,' he checked his notes, 'someone calling themselves Mater Morgana.'

'So, you have seen it?'

'Not yet. But my boys have requested a copy. Which might now be difficult to find. Given the producer is dead.' He spread his fingers wide. 'Why don't you tell me about it in the meantime?'

Calogero sighed. 'Well, I suppose it all started when some-body decided it would be fun to film a bunch of middle-aged people fighting on camera.'

Gori finished scribbling in his notebook.

'So – and correct me if I'm wrong, *signor* Maugeri – but two people involved in this programme are now dead?'

'That's right.'

'And, on air, you had a fight with one of them.'

'Not with Gianmaria, I didn't. With Salvatore Sipala. And, strictly speaking, *he* had a fight with *me*.'

Gori folded his hands together. 'We know you didn't like *signor* Lombardo.'

'There are plenty of people I don't like, *ispettore*, the vast majority of whom are alive and well.'

'Only the majority?'

'I was never a big fan of Berlusconi. But you'll have a hard time pinning that one on me.'

'Okay. Reasonable point.' Then he shook his head. 'What was your problem with Gianmaria Lombardo?'

'I thought he was a fraud. And a leech. Nothing more.'

'Mm-hmm. Are you sure that's all?'

'Absolutely.'

'How about *signor* Toto Licata?'

'I met him precisely once. Months ago.'

'You were angry with him, maybe? Because of the way that TV show ended?'

'I honestly didn't care either way. I suspected a local TV station most famous for its dentist was never going to break me as an international star. But I still got paid. For what it's worth, I'm sorry he's dead.'

'You knew he was going to be there last night?'

'No.'

'But sometimes you know people in the audience, yes? "Plants", you call them?'

Calogero sighed. 'That's true. Toto was not supposed to be there, though. That seat's kept empty. It's where I reappear at the end of my act.'

'Why that seat in particular?'

'Can we just call it the magic of theatre? Let's just say it's the quickest one to get to.'

'The young woman he was sitting next to. You know her, I understand?'

'Her name's Nedda Leonardi. She's a journalist. With *Sicilia Nuova* or *Catania Nuova* or whatever it is. One of the papers that I don't get.'

'How long have you known her?'

'A few days, no more.'

'How do you know her?'

'She was waiting outside the *Questura* the first time you pulled me in. You remember, the time I was hit on the head instead of being electrocuted?'

He nodded. 'You like *signurina* Leonardi?'

'I don't know her well. I like her well enough.'

'She's a pretty young woman.'

'She is. And quite a bit younger than me.' Calogero sighed. 'Okay, so last night I was electrocuted. A man in the audience was murdered. And now you're suggesting I'm an ageing creep as well. Terrific.'

Gori smiled. 'I'm not suggesting anything, *signor* Maugeri. I called you in here because I thought you might be able to help us.'

Calogero blinked. 'Okay. I wasn't expecting that, I have to say.'

Gori placed a card upon the table. 'Could you describe this to me?'

'Sure. It's the Three of Swords. Three swords piercing a heart. There's not much more to it than that. It's one of the most negative cards in the Tarot deck.' He looked up at Gori.

'Where did you find this?'

'In Licata's pocket.'

'You think somebody slipped it there?'

'Probably. I was wondering if it's connected with this. The one from Lombardo's apartment.' He laid another card upon the table. 'Again, can you describe this to me?'

'It's the Five of Cups. Also from the Tarot.'

'A little more, if you can.'

Calogero shrugged. 'It shows a cloaked figure, head bowed, overlooking a river. A castle stands in the background. At his feet are five cups – goblets, if you prefer – three of which are overturned.'

'And what does it mean?'

'It can mean two things. Disappointment, sorrow. Yet it can also mean a blindness to what is still good – three cups are overturned but two still remain.'

Gori scribbled away furiously. Calogero had no idea how he could possibly be finding any of this useful, but the ways of the police, he was coming to learn, were frequently impenetrable.

'Have you found any more of these?' he asked.

Gori shook his head.

'Okay. Well in that case you need to see this. One of these was slipped into my pocket the other day. While I was unconscious.' He raised his voice. 'And in case anyone's watching, I'm reaching into my jacket for my wallet. Not for a gun.'

Gori winced.

'Sorry. Just trying to lighten the mood.'

'Please don't. Continue.'

Calogero laid the card down.

'So what's this, then?'

'The Tarot, again. The Tower.'

'Meaning?'

'Nothing good. Interesting, though, that it shows a bolt of lightning, don't you think?'

'Anything else I should know?'

'These are all from the same deck. Beautifully produced. Can't be too many of these around, I'd have thought.'

'Okay.' Gori folded his hands again. 'Gianmaria Lombardo, drowned. Within sight of the castle at Aci Castello. Toto Licata stabbed through the heart. You, electrocuted on stage. Does this suggest anything to you?'

'Oh, you mean the presence of Tarot cards prefiguring each event?'

Gori thumped his fist on the desk and looked him straight in the eye. 'Exactly.'

Calogero grinned. 'No. It's nonsense.'

Gori's expression darkened. 'What?'

'It's utter rubbish. Whoever's doing this wants us to think there's a serial killer running around killing people according to symbols found in the Tarot deck.'

'And you don't think that's likely?'

'I think it's very, very unlikely. Why would you do it? It's a stupid person's idea of a clever idea.' Gori frowned. 'No offence meant,' Calogero said, and then wished he hadn't. 'Why would you make things so complicated? Why make things more difficult than they need to be?'

Gori smiled, thinly. 'I believe you and your people call this the art of misdirection.'

Calogero couldn't help but smile back. 'Exactly that. This is misdirection. Nothing more.'

'Maybe. Maybe not.' Gori pushed a photograph across the table. 'You know this man?' Calogero shook his head. 'His name is Elio Caruso. Guardian at the *Fortezza*. He's a man known to have a grudge against people in the psychic community. He's made threats online. And he's done occasional work at the *Teatro Giovanni Verga*. He knows the layout of the building. He knows how things work.' He narrowed his eyes. 'Are you sure you don't know him?'

Calogero shook his head wearily. 'I've never heard of him. Really. Do you mind if I go now? I just want to have a lie down in the dark and then do my show.'

Gori laughed, genuinely surprised. '*Signor* Maugeri, there's not going to be any show tonight.'

'What?'

'Of course there isn't. There was a murder there last night. It's a crime scene. More than that, there's obviously a potentially lethal electrical fault with some of the equipment. The place is a death trap.'

'Oh.' Calogero rubbed his forehead. He had to concede he had a point. 'Tomorrow?'

'And tomorrow and tomorrow and tomorrow.' Gori smiled. 'I did Shakespeare at school, you know? I wouldn't plan on going back any time soon, that's all I'm saying.'

'I've got a lot of my gear stored there.'

'And we'll let you know as soon as you can have it back. You're not in any hurry to leave, I take it?'

'No.' Calogero got to his feet. 'Perhaps I'll just have a quiet night in, then.'

'I think that would be good.' He leaned across his desk and, to Calogero's surprise, shook his hand. 'Have a pleasant evening off, *signor* Maugeri.'

Chapter 46

Nedda was waiting outside the *Questura*, leaning against the
Royal Enfield.

'How did it go?'

Calogero ran a hand around his collar, and wiped his forehead with the back of his hand. 'Good, I think.'

'Really? Because you look like hell.'

'Oh, that'll be the electrocution, I imagine. Remember
that?'

'No, completely slipped my mind. I was sitting next to a
man who was murdered, remember?'

'Oh yes. That.'

'And I rubbed your hands. That might have saved your
life.'

'Thank you. Anyway, *ispettore* Gori seems to believe me
when I say I'm not a serial killer. That's a winner, right?'

She nodded.

'I mean, being electrocuted and yet somehow managing to
make it to the back row in order to stab Toto Licata. Pretty
good trick, even for me.'

'Calogero, this isn't funny.'

He sighed. 'Yeah, I know.'

'I phoned his sister today. Just to get a quote we could use. I'm not proud of that.'

'I'm sorry. I imagine that must have been difficult.'

'It was. So, what else did the police have to say?'

'That's the thing. They almost sounded as if they wanted my help. Kept asking me about the three Tarot cards that have turned up. He thinks there's a link there and I think it's all nonsense, except,' he rubbed his temples, 'there were six people involved in that show. Two are now dead. I could have been. And there's no denying there was a Tarot card linked with each of us.'

'And so?'

'And so I'd be very nervous if my name happened to be Salvatore Sipala. Or Mater Morgana.'

'Or Calogero Maugeri?'

'Sorry?'

'I was just thinking whoever it is might have another go, that's all.'

'Yes, there's a cheery thought. And the day had been going so well.'

'So where do we start?'

'Well, firstly, I still don't really buy the Tarot theory. Way too complicated. There must be another reason behind the deaths. Having said that, there are other people who know more than I do about Tarot.' He smiled. 'And so, we need to go and talk to a witch.'

'Morgana?' He nodded. 'Okay, let's go.' She patted the seat of the motorcycle. Calogero's face fell, and he wiped the sweat from his brow.

She looked him up and down. 'Hot?'

'Just a bit.'

'You could always, you know, take your jacket off?'

'No thanks. I'll feel better knowing that there's something between my body and the tarmac if I come off.'

'You're not going to come off. Stop being a baby.' She patted the seat behind her. 'Come on, hop on.'

Calogero got on.

'Oh, and we need to talk about hands. Specifically, where they go.'

'I haven't done anything!'

'Hold on to the grab rail. Not me.'

'I'm sorry. I wasn't trying to be. . . you know. . . *familiar* or anything.'

'Not that. If you hold on to me, you'll slam into the back of me if I need to brake suddenly. Not fun for either of us. If this is going to become a regular thing, you're going to need to know how to properly ride pillion. Lean into the corners when I do. Don't try and stay vertical. And use the grab rail.'

'What's that look like?'

'It's a rail. Grab it.' And Nedda set off.

Calogero sipped at his tea, and looked down at it with distaste.

'What is this?'

'Valerian,' said Mater Morgana.

'It's horrible. I mean, thanks and all that, but this is foul.'

'It relieves anxiety and anger. I thought it would be good for you.'

'I don't want to be relieved of anything. It's only the anxiety that's keeping me going. That and coffee.'

'Then I should switch to decaf if I were you. How about you, Nedda?'

'Valerian will be just fine, thank you.'

'Look, can I just say that in the past twenty-four hours I've been electrocuted, been asked to help the police with some half-arsed theory about a Tarot-obsessed serial killer and – worst of all – I've been on a motorbike again. And now we're discussing herbal teas.'

'Hmm. I understand. Maybe I should have let it stand a little longer?'

'Morgana, there's not enough valerian in the world. And what's more, tell your owl to stop staring at me.'

Morgana shook her head. 'Menocchio is not the sort of owl to whom one *tells* things. Polite suggestions may work better.' She sighed. 'So, come on then, Calogero. If a nice cup of tea won't calm you down, why not just tell me why you're here?'

'The Tarot deck. The one that Salvatore left with you. Do you still have it?' She nodded. 'Okay. Could you lay the cards out for us?

'Now, one card is missing. The Five of Cups. Found in Lombardo's apartment. I found the Tower in my wallet, and the Three of Swords was in Toto Licata's pocket. And, yes, I know what the cards mean but there's a lot about Tarot that I don't know and I keep thinking I'm missing something.'

'And so you came to me,' said Morgana.

He took a deep breath. 'Yes.'

'I thought you thought I was a terrible old fraud?'

'I do. I thought you thought I was a charlatan and a con man.'

'I do. But now that's out of the way, let's continue.'

'Morgana, you know more about Tarot than I do. I want to

know if there's anything about this pack. Anything unusual. Anything at all. Something that will lead us to the owner.'

She nodded, and moved towards him, pausing to scratch the owl behind the ears. 'Ah, Menocchio, we've got a bit of a troubled soul here, haven't we?'

She spread out the pack and smiled at him. 'Nothing coming to mind?'

He shook his head.

'Come on, Calogero, it's easy with a moment's thought.'

'I've taken several moments. It's not easy.'

She sighed. 'It's obvious. This isn't a Sicilian deck.'

'What?' Then his expression cleared, and a smile spread across his face. 'Oh, I see.'

'This deck isn't for playing *tarocco*. That's for gaming and gambling. This is the Rider-Waite deck. For *divination*. If nothing else, this narrows things down. You'll find packs of the *Tarocco Siciliano* in almost every tourist shop in Sicily. But for a Rider-Waite deck, you'd be better off going to an actual magic shop.'

'Or Amazon,' said Nedda.

'Or Amazon. But that complicates things, so let's not worry about that until we have to. Now, there a good number of shops that would sell a Rider-Waite deck. But these are unusual. The design on the back. The gold foil effect.' She smiled. 'It's quite a lovely deck. It would make a fine present for someone. In fact, I'd go as far as to say these are cards to have more as a keepsake, as a display item, than for serious divination.'

'Morgana,' said Calogero, 'you help me find the place that sold this and I'll buy you one myself.'

'It's a deal. Leave it with me.' She got to her feet. 'More tea?'

'Thank you, no.' He smiled. 'You know, I think I do actually feel better for that.'

'Good.' She looked at Nedda. 'Just ride carefully. Valerian can make one a little tired.'

'I'll grab a coffee when I get back to Catania.' She checked her watch. 'And I need to be there right now. There's someone I need to see in a couple of hours' time, and I think I'll need to brace myself for it.'

Morgana sighed. 'Coffee will undo all the good.'

'I'm prepared to risk it.'

'As I said. Be careful. And not just riding. Someone is playing a very interesting little game with us and I'm not quite sure where it's going.'

'Maybe I should draw a salt circle around my front door for protection?'

'Maybe you should.' Menocchio hooted, and Morgana bent to scratch him behind the ears. 'He agrees, you see. And if there's one thing I've learned, it's always to take his advice. Oh, and Calogero?'

'Yes?'

'There's something you might like to see.'

He was about to say he didn't understand, but then his expression cleared as Morgana took an envelope from the desk and withdrew its contents. 'This arrived yesterday.'

A single card. She smiled at him. 'There is no card for a witch in the Rider-Waite deck. Different times, perhaps.' She turned the card over. A woman, enthroned, with an ornate crown and blue mantle, the moon at her feet. 'The High Priestess. The best they could do, I imagine.'

Nedda shook her head. 'I don't understand. You had Salvatore's deck. Was that card missing?'

'No.'

'And neither was the Tower nor the Three of Swords. So, whoever's doing this has at least two decks. But why?'

'That remains to be seen.' Morgana smiled again. 'But as I said. Ride carefully.'

Chapter 47

Nedda drummed her fingers on the table and looked out at her namesake the elephant.

'Something to drink, *signurina*?'

'A sparkling water, please. Although I'm not feeling very sparkling.'

'*Signurina*?'

'It's okay. Really. I've got my bike with me. Water will be fine.'

Her phone rang. She was on the verge of hanging up without even looking at the screen, but then she checked it and sighed.

'Calogero?'

'Nedda. Morgana's been in touch. She might have found something. Are you at your usual place? By the elephant?'

'Yes.'

'Great. I'll be there in ten minutes.'

She saw Stefano approaching, waved, and did her best to smile. She lowered her voice. 'Make it thirty.'

She hung up. Stefano kissed her on the cheek and hugged her. She returned it as best she could. He turned to the *barista*. '*Birra Messina*, please.'

'How's your day been, Stefano? Back at work, I see.'

'Yes. I've been feeling a bit out of sorts over the past few days. But that's okay. It gave me a bit of time to get some other things worked out. Anyway, the old man's very pleased with us both. With you in particular. That *Theatre of Blood* piece was marvellous. Imagine how thrilled he was having a reporter right there on the spot when that poor guy – what's his name—'

'Toto. Toto Licata.'

'That's him. When he was killed. Sometimes in this job, Nedda, you've just got to be lucky. And that's something you've got.' He frowned. 'You're not listening to me.'

The *barista* set his beer down, clocked the atmosphere, and retreated hurriedly.

'You're not listening to me,' he repeated. 'What's wrong?'

She sipped at her water. 'Why didn't you tell me?'

'Tell you what?'

'About Turin. About why you left. About your gambling problem. About your wife and daughter.' He was on the verge of laughing and she shook her head. 'Please don't try to deny it. That really would be most disappointing.'

'Nedda, I don't know where you've got this from, but none of it is true. I swear to you, it isn't true.' He made to take her hand, but she snatched it back. 'Come on. We've been having a good time. Haven't we?'

'Yes, we have. And that's what makes it so sad. You left Turin leaving a string of angry creditors, yes?'

'Nedda, this is not—'

'This *is* true, Stefano.'

'Where did you get this from?' He laughed. 'Oh, I get it,

it's the Mighty Magus, isn't it? Now I wonder what his interest could possibly be in making me look bad?'

She ignored him. 'And there's a woman called Mariana,
living in Turin with your daughter. Your wife. The one in the
photo. You know, the one that shows a wedding ring on your
left hand.'

'Oh, that?' He laughed again, but it sounded strained.
'Okay, I admit that was stupid. But I kind of panicked. We'd
been having such a good time and then you saw that photo
and I thought – well, I thought I really didn't want to get into
explanations. So I told a little white lie about how they were
my sister and my niece.'

'Stefano, that is stretching the definition of a white lie to
breaking point. You have a wife and a daughter.' She sipped at
her water. 'Oh God, that makes me both "the other woman"
and a home breaker.'

'Nedda, this was all over years ago, I swear.'

'What happened to you, Stefano? What spoiled
everything?'

'I—' He tried, and failed, to find the words.

'It was the gambling wasn't it?'

'I—'

'And it's still going on, isn't it? The scratch cards I could
have overlooked. But then there was the lack of money and
asking your girlfriend of twelve hours to bail you out.' She
paused. 'And what were you going to do with the Rolex?
Pawn it?'

'You've been going through my stuff? How fucking dare
you?'

'I was looking for cigarettes, if that helps.'

'That was my father's. It's the only thing of his I still have.'

'And you just carry it around in your jacket pocket?'

'It's – complicated.'

Nedda sighed. 'I know it is. Might have been less complicated if you'd told me all this at the beginning, though.'

Stefano bent over the table, running his hands through
his hair. 'A few weeks, Nedda, just a few weeks and I'll be
straight, and we can put all this behind us.'

'Oh. Does that include Mariana as well?' She looked at
his beer, which had disappeared. 'Probably best not to have
another one of those before going back to work. I'll see you in
the office tomorrow, Stefano. I've got things to do this afternoon. Make my apologies to Aldo. Tell him I'll call him.'

He reached for her hand. 'What about later?'

'I'm sorry, am I buying you dinner again? No, Stefano,
that's not going to happen. I've got a lot of stuff to think
about.'

'Nedda, we need to talk.'

'We've been talking. Now I have stuff to think about and
things to do. And, strangely enough, neither involves you.'

'Nedda—'

'Don't go overthinking your importance, Stefano. I'll see
you in the office tomorrow.'

He got to his feet. 'Okay. I'll be heading back. But the
watch, Nedda. I do need to tell you about the watch.'

She looked up at him.

'It *was* my father's. It's the only thing I have of his. And
it was the last thing my mother gave to me. And you know
what? Yes, I was prepared to take it to the nearest pawn shop in
Catania and take whatever money they'd give me for it.

'Because that's what this is like. Addiction. It takes everything from you. And I hope to God you never experience anything like that, Nedda.'

And, with that, he turned and walked away.

Chapter 48

'You don't seem happy, Nedda.'

'Is it that obvious?'

'It's just that you seem to be taking a more relaxed attitude to observing the laws of the road than I remember.'

'I apologise. For what it's worth, it's not your fault.'

'Would it help if I asked who?'

'No.'

Apprendista Stregone was situated behind the botanical gardens, in a cluster of vaguely alternative shops selling everything from vinyl records to art supplies to herbal remedies. The sign in the window was that of a hooded figure with a lantern in one hand and staff in the other, standing on top of a rocky outcrop. Calogero recognised it as the figure of the Hermit from the Rider-Waite deck. Nedda thought it perhaps seemed familiar from her father's record collection but couldn't quite place it.

'Are you sure this is the place?'

'It's called *The Sorcerer's Apprentice* and there's a bloody great Tarot card in the window. Yes, I'm pretty sure.'

Nedda sighed. 'Not that. Even I can see that. I mean, are you sure that this is the actual place we're looking for? It's not just another weirdy occult shop?'

'Morgana seemed to think so. She did a lot of work on it. Divination, that sort of thing. I suspect she might even have asked her owl. But ultimately I think the *Pagine Gialle* and Google were the most useful.'

'Couldn't we have done that?'

'We could. But the thing about Morgana is this. She may or may not be a witch. I honestly don't know. But I do know that we want her on our side. We need to involve her. And now we know there must be two decks, at least.'

'I understand. Now, have you got the cards and the photos?' He nodded and patted his pocket. 'Okay then. Let's go.' She paused. 'You go first.'

'You're the investigative journalist.'

'And you're the wizard. Therefore, it's your home ground.'

He shrugged and opened the door. There was a tinkle of wind chimes, and the faint scent of cannabis tickled his nostrils. He noticed an incense stick burning in an ashtray and smiled.

He cast a practised eye around. He'd been in shops like this all over Sicily, all over Italy. Crystals, incense sticks and jewellery. Herbal teas and healing draughts. Harry Potter memorabilia. Rubik's cubes. Well, he thought, these places had to move with the times. A cat sat on one of the shelves, curling itself around a shining crystal skull. What was it about cats? he thought. Were magic shops a guaranteed source of employment for them?

'Can I help you?' The speaker was a little bald man, painfully thin with sunken cheeks, and with full finger rings on both hands that gave the resemblance of talons. And yet it was, Calogero had to admit, a pretty good look for somebody who worked in a magic shop.

'Maybe you can. It's about a pack of Tarot cards.'

The Little Magician shrugged. 'Got lots of those, my friend. Gaming or divination?' His voice, excitable and cheery, seemed at odds with his appearance.

'Erm, not sure.'

'Sorry?'

'It's for a present.'

'Oh right. You mean you just want something that looks nice.' He looked disappointed. 'I mean, we've got all sorts here. Rider-Waite deck, Sicilian deck, Piedmontese, Bolognese, Swiss, Spanish, all sorts of French. So, yeah, I reckon I can find you something that looks nice.'

Nedda looked over at Calogero. 'Okay. Do you want to explain all those to me?'

He shrugged. 'I could. If you want me to. Would it be easier if I just said it's kind of a magician thing?'

She nodded.

'Great. Excellent.' Calogero turned back to the Little Magician, reached into his pocket and pulled out the Tower card. 'Have you got a deck that looks like this?'

He nodded. 'Think I've still got some in the back. We don't sell many of them, coz they're expensive. They're more for display than actual play, you see. But they do look nice. So nice that you wouldn't want to risk getting them all dirty or bent by actually using them.'

'Uh-huh. So, do you think you might remember some-body who did buy a deck off you? Maybe a couple of weeks ago.'

He laughed. 'My friend, I might be a magician but remembering everyone who's bought a Tarot deck is beyond me.'

'But you said you don't sell many of these. Is there any chance you might?'

He shrugged. 'Maybe so.' Then he frowned. 'Now, is there any particular reason you might want to know?'

Calogero nodded towards Nedda. 'My friend here's a journalist. She's doing some research.'

'Journalist, eh?' he muttered. 'Don't like journalists. Researching what?'

Nedda cleared her throat. 'It's a piece I'm writing for *Catania Nuova*. I'm calling it "The new mysticism". After the pandemic, are we seeing ourselves as a more spiritual people? That sort of thing.'

'Sounds like bullshit to me. Someone with too much money wants an expensive deck of cards. Don't see much more to it than that.'

Calogero sighed and reached into his jacket. He took out two photos and a twenty-euro note, which he let flutter to the desk. 'Oops,' he said, but made no attempt to pick it up.

The Little Magician stared down at it. Calogero pushed the photographs over towards him. 'Do you recognise either of these men?'

He picked up the photograph of Lombardo. 'I know him. The one that died, right?'

'That's him. He ever come in here?'

'Sometimes. Just for crystals, incense, stuff like that.'

Calogero smiled. So far, so good. He tapped the other photo. 'And him?'

The Little Magician picked up the photograph of Salvatore. 'Yeah, this guy I know,' he nodded.

'He's been in here?'

'Lots of times. *Salvatore the Seer* or something like that, isn't he? You get to know people in that line of work in a shop like this.'

'And he wanted a deck like this, am I right?'

He nodded and then did a double take. 'How do you know that?'

'Indulge me. When did he come in?'

'About two weeks ago.'

'But Salvatore is a professional mystic and these cards aren't for serious professional use.'

'Like you said, my friend, he wanted them for a present. Thing is, he said he needed them urgently, only we didn't have any in stock. Said he'd pay more if I could turn it round quickly.'

'And did you?'

'Within forty-eight hours. Very efficient service.'

'That's good to hear.' Calogero paused for a moment. 'And then he came back for a second packet. Some time before Saturday the twenty-ninth?'

'What?'

Calogero rubbed the back of his head. 'Yes, it would have to be before then. That was the day I was knocked unconscious.'

'What?'

'Sorry, I'm just thinking aloud here. But he did, didn't he? He came in sometime between the twenty-sixth and the twenty-ninth to order another set.' He placed another ten euros on the counter, and the Little Magician snatched it away.

'He did, yes.'

'When?'

'I can't be sure. It was the middle of the week. He said he'd lost the pack and needed another one. He'd pay me extra, he said, if I could get him one in time for the weekend.'

'And you did?'

'I absolutely did. Turned a nice little profit as well.'

Calogero grinned and turned to Nedda. 'We've got him,' he said.

'We have?'

'Absolutely we have. Now, could you accidentally drop some banknotes on the floor?'

'Me?'

'I did it last time.'

'Oh, very well.' She took out a ten-euro note and let it flutter to the floor. Then another. Then another. The Little Magician looked up at her, his eyes glittering. 'Don't push it,' she said.

He dropped to his knees and gathered them together, before scurrying back behind his desk.

Calogero turned to Nedda. 'Come on. We need to celebrate. I'll buy you an expensive *toast* and I promise I won't complain about your horrible motorbike.' He turned to the owner. 'Thanks for your time. Anything else you want to ask, Nedda?'

She shook her head.

'Am I going to be in the papers?' said the Little Magician.

'Would you like to be?'

The smile never left his face as he shook his head. 'No.'

Chapter 49

Nedda worked her way through the menu one more time, and then smiled up at Dante. '*Un toast*, please.'

'*Toast* is what we do, *signurina*. Could you be more specific?'

'Just cheese and *prosciutto cotto*.'

'Just that?' She nodded, and he looked disappointed. He turned to Calogero. '*Signore?*'

'With *prosciutto di San Daniele*, a little *rucola*, mushrooms and the merest scattering of *parmigiano*. Perhaps a light drizzling of olive oil.' He smiled at her. 'See. That's how you do it.'

'Look, I'm not familiar with the concept of *toast* as an evening meal. I'm having to work my way into that.'

'Trust me, you'll never go back. Anyway, I thought you might like to know what I've been thinking.'

'Uh-huh. Go on.'

'The whole Tarot thing. You know, each card is linked to a particular murder. And one's first thought – like the police – is, "Oh, that's clever." But it isn't clever. It's actually very stupid. Why complicate things? Why leave clues? And so, as I said, I thought it was a stupid person's idea of a clever idea.

'But then I started to think some more. What if that's

what the actual assassin *wants* us to think? What if it's actually a clever person's idea of what a stupid person thinks is a clever idea?'

Nedda frowned.

'Do you get what I'm saying?'

'I think so. I'm trying not to think about it too hard. My brain keeps kind of sliding off the words.'

'Okay. Murderer smart, not stupid. Can we go with that for now?'

'I guess so.'

'You've met Salvatore?'

'Briefly. At Lombardo's funeral.'

'And what did you think?'

'Smelt of booze, cigarettes and too many late nights. Good suntan. Kept mentally undressing me. Typical macho medallion man.'

Calogero grinned. 'Okay. I think that sums him up pretty well.' He frowned. 'Hang on. *Medallion* man?'

'Yeah, sure. He was wearing a chunky gold medallion. Like he'd come out of some terrible seventies porn film or something.'

'Could you describe it?'

'I didn't want to get too close. But it was a big, heavy thing. Definitely religious. There's a guy, he looks like a monk or something and he's holding up a book. A Bible, I guess. So it was oval, but the book gave it a spiky edge.'

Calogero grinned. 'Of course. That was Gianmaria's medallion. And now Salvatore has a similar one. Or the very same one? Now I wonder just how he got that. Remember, I told you about it. St Agabus.'

Nedda looked mildly interested. 'Oh yes. The one I'd never heard of before. So what do you know about him?'

He shrugged. 'Well. He was a prophet.'

There was silence for a moment.

'That's it?'

'Pretty much. Sorry, do you think it's important?'

'Patron saint of psychics and prophets. Mysterious medallions. Yes, I think it probably is. Whereabouts in the Bible is he?'

There was another long pause. Nedda sighed and took out her phone. 'Never mind, I'll do it myself.' She tapped away. 'Only two verses.

'Acts 11:27–28 *And in these days came prophets from Jerusalem unto Antioch. And there stood up one of them named Agabus, and signified by the Spirit that there should be great dearth throughout all the world: which came to pass in the days of Claudius Caesar.*

'Acts 21:10–12 *And as we tarried there many days, there came down from Judaea a certain prophet, named Agabus. And when he was come unto us, he took Paul's girdle, and bound his own hands and feet, and said, Thus saith the Holy Ghost, So shall those at Jerusalem bind the man that owneth this girdle, and shall deliver him into the hands of the Gentiles. And when we heard these things, both we, and they of that place, besought him not to go up to Jerusalem.*'

She frowned. 'Does that mean anything to you?'

'Let me think.' He shook his head. 'No.'

'I mean, is it some sort of code?'

'It's got to be. Somehow. Lombardo had a medallion of St Agabus. His boat was called *Agabus*. There must be a link, somewhere. Is there any sort of link between Agabus and the area around here? Come on, you're local, you must know.'

'If there is, he must be one of the few saints without a feast day. Otherwise Aldo Lentini would have told me to cover it.' She tapped away at her phone once more. 'No. St John in Aci Trezza. Agatha in Catania. Venera in Acireale. Maurus in Aci Castello. Nothing about an Agabus at all.' And then she broke off, and smiled. 'Except—'

'Except?'

She turned the screen to Calogero. 'Look. There he is.'

He screwed up his eyes, peering at the image in front of him. A pale, sun-bleached statue of a bearded prophet, behind a rusted metal gate.

'I don't understand.'

'St Agabus. There's a roadside shrine to him down in Santa Maria la Scala.'

'What?'

'It's about a kilometre outside of the town.'

'You've only just thought of this?'

'We've got hundreds of shrines. Sooner or later, every prophet gets one. I'm sorry, I never thought to memorise them all.'

'His medallion. His boat. And now you're telling me there's a shrine to the man himself down in Santa Maria la Scala?'

She raised an eyebrow. 'You think it's linked?'

'Do you have any better ideas?'

'No.' She cast her eyes heavenwards. 'Can't you, you know, do some magicky things and just have a word with them "up there"?'

'What, you think I can just call up Sherlock Holmes and ask him? It doesn't work like that.'

'Oh, that's very convenient. Also, he didn't exist.'

Calogero frowned. 'He didn't? Okay then, what about that French guy?'

'He was Belgian. Also didn't exist.'

'No?'

'No. What sort of Magus are you?'

'A very good one. Now, could we stop bickering for long enough to solve the mystery?'

She took a bite of her *toast*. 'Okay. Let me see if I've got this right. Gianmaria Lombardo has acquired a dossier of information on various people which allows him to blackmail them. Salvatore Sipala knows this. And so he works out that if he can get Lombardo out of the way, then he's set up nicely and can carry on raking in the money all for himself.'

'Makes sense, doesn't it?'

'He goes out with Lombardo on the day of *U pisci a mari*. Hits him over the head. Throws him overboard. Swims to shore, it's not too far. Everybody, but everybody is watching the pantomime. Or John the Baptist. A small boat drifting on its own has nobody's attention.'

'Yes, but the trouble is that Salvatore hasn't thought this through. Just exactly where is this dossier? Without it, he's worse off than before. More than that, now he's killed someone and needs to make sure the police are looking elsewhere. So he comes up with the Tarot scheme. To buy himself time. To throw some shade elsewhere. And the police will, I imagine, be looking very closely at people like Elio Caruso – Mr Angry in Aci – on the back of it.'

'So you think the dossier is, what, in this shrine?'

'I think it's worth a look.'

'Why not just in a secure box at a bank?'

'He's a crook, Nedda. Crooks live in mortal fear that one day the *Guardia* will take a close look at their affairs and everything they have in the bank will be impounded. No, it won't be there.'

Nedda hesitated for a moment and then nodded. 'Okay. It sounds crazy. But there might be something in it. But are you sure it's Salvatore?'

'He's got a motive. More than that, he's got Gianmaria's medallion. He had the opportunity. We know he bought the Tarot decks, and we know he pretended to Morgana that one of them had been left for him on his doorstep. The trouble is he'd already had a few drinks by the time he went to see Morgana and so he left the deck there.'

'So why didn't he just go back and ask for it?'

'Morgana's very clever. Salvatore knows that. It might have raised her suspicions. Easier just to buy another deck.'

'So, we take that to the police.'

'We could do. But I don't want to do that if there's another way.'

'Okay. Now tell me why I should do this.'

He sighed. 'Because there's something you need to explain to me. The TV show that I was on. How did you find out about it?'

'Stefano told me.'

'Uh-huh. And how did you know that the police had pulled me in on the day of Lombardo's funeral?'

'Stefano.'

'And how did he know?'

'He said something about a "tip-off".'

'Okay. And when your boss – the guy who makes you go out and buy *cannoli* – was going to pass this all over to Stefano, it was Stefano who told him that it should be you that followed it up. Wasn't it?'

Nedda held his gaze, and then nodded. 'It was. Yes.'

He sighed. 'Oh Nedda, I'm so sorry. But this guy's been playing you. He's been feeding you just enough information, sending you on this crazy trail of Tarot cards and psychic serial killers.'

'But why would he do this?'

'Ah, come on, Nedda, you know why.'

She took a deep breath. 'Okay. Stefano Gallo is a hopeless gambling addict who's left a string of debts and a wife and daughter on the opposite end of the country and set up in Catania to make a new start. And maybe, just maybe, his name is also on the list of Gianmaria's compromised people. And he didn't want to be seen to be getting too involved in the affair himself and so ever so gently kept prodding me in that direction. In the hope that I might lead him to the dossier that Lombardo was holding on him.' She sighed. 'Bastard.'

'Nedda, it strikes me that at some point there's going to have to be a tricky conversation with your boyfriend.'

'We've had several. But I guess there's always time to fit in one more. . .'

He coughed, gently. 'Would you – I mean, don't take this the wrong way – but would it be useful if I was there?'

'I don't think so, Calogero. I think magicking all this away is beyond even your powers.'

'I understand.' He paused. 'I'm sorry.'

Nedda reached out and squeezed his hand. 'Yeah. Me too. Thank you.'

'But if we can find that file and destroy it – then everyone's in the clear.'

'Everyone?'

There was silence between them for a moment.

'I'm in there too, Nedda.'

Silence, again. 'Oh. I see,' she finally said. 'And so, what do we do now?'

'First of all, I'm going to finish my *toast*. And then,' he smiled, and lowered his voice, 'we're going to have a proper think about the best way to break into a shrine.'

Chapter 50

Nedda had fussed and fretted her way through the evening and Angelo, a master at this sort of thing by now, had decided that the best solution was to let it be and, most certainly, not to mention the man who may or may not be boyfriend material.

The two of them had shared a pizza and, like always, had argued over the fact that what they'd ordered wasn't exactly what either of them actually wanted; and split a couple of beers whilst they watched an old *Montalbano* repeat on the television. Angelo, as he always did, made acerbic comments on just how someone on a policeman's salary was supposed to be able to afford a house like that.

Nedda retired to bed early, and tried to clear her mind of villainous magicians, blackmail dossiers and gold medallions of obscure saints. She also tried to clear her mind of disappointing boyfriends with complicated backstories.

The night was hot and stuffy, and sleep was hard to come by. She switched on the fan at the end of the bed with her toes, which left her feet feeling icy cold and the rest of her as hot and uncomfortable as ever. She considered reading a dull book. If only she'd brought one to bed. Then she closed her eyes and started counting down from one thousand. When that proved too easy, she tried doing the same but in English. And when that proved too difficult she thumped her pillow into shape, flipped it over, closed her eyes and just hoped that sleep would come upon her.

She awoke, hours later, to the sound of a motorcycle passing by. She leaned over to look at the time. Barely four o'clock. She rubbed her eyes. Shit. What were her chances of getting back to sleep? Perhaps she should just get up and have an early breakfast?

The sound of the motorcycle returned, a low bass throb. A Harley-Davidson perhaps? No. It wasn't a bike. Too low, too bassy to be a car. An aircraft? Perhaps? The sound continued. No, it was nothing mechanical. This was almost like air being blown across the neck of a bottle.

The windows rattled and she got out of bed in order to open the curtains and look outside. Tiny flecks spiralled in the street lamps, like fireflies or mosquitos or even flakes of snow. Except, these flecks were black as coal.

The distant roaring continued and Nedda heard Angelo calling from the other room.

'Are you all right, *trisoru*?'

'Yes, *papà*. I'm just going back to bed now. Did it wake you up?'

'Yes, *cara*. Don't worry. I'll take a little *grappa* from downstairs and I'm sure I'll drop off again.'

'Don't make an excuse of it, *papà*.'

She smiled to herself and watched the flecks dancing in the streetlights. Tomorrow, she knew, there would be a lot of work to do.

The low, insistent roaring and whistling continued to sound, as the black flakes piled higher and higher in the streets.

Etna was angry.

Nedda awoke feeling tired and crabby, as though there was sand in her veins. She fixed herself a disappointing coffee and went outside to look at the streets.

The ash cloud, they were saying, had reached ten kilometres into the sky. Flights into Catania had either been cancelled or diverted to Trapani or Palermo. Black ash had settled over every exposed surface in the area.

She went outside to see the extent of the damage. The waiter across the road gave her a tired wave as he swept ash from every chair and every table into a neat pile on the corner. At some point, emergency vehicles would be dispatched. In the meantime, it was everybody's duty to dispose of it responsibly.

Hosing it away or washing it down the drain was an impossibility as the ash would solidify to the consistency of a thick mud. Neither were you allowed to put it out with normal domestic waste. No, the only solution was to clear your area as best you could and wait for the professionals to clear it away.

And this is what Catania did, what Sicily did, every time Etna chose to erupt. Over the centuries it had become part of the pattern of life. It was just something you did if you chose to live there. She looked at the Enfield, sighed, and got to work.

It could be a five-minute job. Nedda took thirty. There

was no sense in rushing it. When it was done, she sighed and stretched, and flicked a rag across the now spotless surfaces of the bike. A proper polish would still do it the world of good, but better to wait and see if Etna had anything else in mind before doing that. She became aware that Angelo was standing behind her.

'More coffee?'

'That'd be good.'

'Do you want to go and pick us up a couple of *cornetti* from the bar?'

She looked over across the street. The same waiter was still wearily sweeping up.

'I think they've got bigger problems, Dad.'

'Trust me, they'll appreciate doing something normal. And they'll appreciate the money even more. Even if it's only a couple of euros.' He looked at the Enfield. 'That almost looks like new. Very good job. But don't think about going out on that thing today.'

'What do you mean?'

'The Mayor's just announced emergency measures. Thirty-kilometre speed limit throughout the whole province. And absolutely no bikes or motorcycles. The roads are too slippery.'

'Ah shit.' She pushed her hair out of her eyes. 'That was a waste of time.'

'No, it wasn't. It looks lovely. And don't swear.'

'Sorry. I'll get those *cornetti*, eh?'

'That'd be good.'

She smiled, and made her way across the road, her shoes crunching and leaving trails in the ash.

She wasn't sure what Calogero had planned for the day, but one thing was certain. Everything had just become a hell of a lot more complicated.

Chapter 51

'That's your plan?' said Nedda. 'It's just I thought you might have had a bit of a rethink in the last twenty-four hours.'

'You got a better idea?'

'Nothing at all. I just think yours sounds a bit hopeful, that's all.'

Calogero sighed. 'Look, it does kind of make sense. Let's game this through.

'Gianmaria Lombardo kept a dossier of information on a number of blackmail victims. One of which might just be Stefano Gallo. And another of whom is me.'

Nedda was about to speak, but he shook his head. 'Another time. Now, if I'm right, Salvatore killed Gianmaria to get access to the file. And hence a very nice little income stream. His problem is, he doesn't have it. Or, at least, it wasn't where it was supposed to be. Gianmaria's last little laugh from beyond the grave. Salvatore's all geared up for moving out of his cheapo apartment. Trouble is, without that document, where's the money going to be coming from?'

'Could it be online?'

'It could be, but that doesn't help Salvatore. Getting access to a deceased account is incredibly difficult. For someone like

Salvatore – not a relative and not even anyone who could be recognised as a legitimate business partner – it would be impossible. So if it physically exists, where could it be?'

Nedda shrugged. 'Might it have been on his boat?'

'Possibly. In which case it's safely destroyed. We can be pretty certain it's not in his apartment. I couldn't find it. And, trust me, I had a very good look. And neither could Salvatore, assuming he was the one who belted me on the back of the head when I was there. It can't be in a bank vault. Way too risky. But there's another possibility. The shrine to St Agabus.'

'That just seems a lot of hard work to conceal something, that's all.'

'Oh, he'll have a copy online, somewhere, I'm sure, but that's lost to us for ever. But think about it – if the *Guardia* suddenly took an interest in him – there's nothing in his bank, nothing on his boat, nothing in his apartment – it was a useful little back-up, that's all.'

'Why not just leave it if it's that difficult to find?'

'Because sooner or later somebody is going to find it. Even Salvatore will work it out eventually. And then – well, then there'll be trouble.'

She shrugged. 'Okay. I've got nothing better to do than poke around a shrine looking for documents. But I can't risk being on the roads on a bike. Not for the next few days.'

'You can't? Oh good.' Nedda playfully slapped him around the head, and he rubbed his ear. 'Ow. Okay, well Santo says he needs the car tonight, so we'll take the last bus down. And then we'll have to walk back up the path. Very slowly.'

'There's a pub right at the top. The *Mescan*. Irish place. *Papà* says the Guinness is good there.'

'We'll be needing one. Even late at night that's a tough walk.'

She checked her watch. 'So, what sort of time are we leaving?'

'Let's leave it 'til after nine. It needs to be dark. I'm not sure how much time this is going to take.'

'And if we do find it?'

'Then I'm in the clear. And so, I imagine, is Stefano. And, of course, all the others.'

'And that's what we want, right?'

He frowned. 'Sure it is.' But Nedda's face was difficult to read.

'I don't get it,' said Nedda. 'Why have a shrine to St Agabus in Santa Maria la Scala?'

'Fishing village, isn't it? It would have been important to know the best time to put to sea. The patron saint of prophecy might have been useful.'

He tilted his head back and looked up at the imposing bulk of the *Fortezza* looming over them. 'Long way up, isn't it? So, where's the shrine then?'

'Pretty much at the base of the footpath. There used to be a small dock there, a century back. St Agabus, it seems, wasn't deemed worthy of an actual chapel and so a roadside shrine was the best they could do.'

Nedda looked out across the bay, to the lights shining in the distance.

'How long are we going to give it?'

'As long as it takes. Until we're sure there's nobody around. But that probably won't be long. It doesn't look as if anyone lives along this stretch.'

'And what are we going to do in the meantime?'

'Stimulating chats, I suppose.'

'Or we could go back into town for a drink?'

Calogero shook his head. 'Better not to. Just in case people remember us if we have to come back.'

'Stimulating chats it is then.'

They sat in silence for a while, until the distant sounds of traffic fell silent and all that remained was the sound of the sea.

Calogero nodded. 'Let's go.'

The shrine to St Agabus had seen better days. A whitened, worn figure of the prophet stood behind a rusted metal gate holding up a Bible in supplication. Some faded flowers were strewn around – Agabus, clearly, was not completely lacking in followers – but cigarette butts and crushed beer cans were more common.

Calogero tutted and shook his head. He tugged at the gate, which refused to budge, and then yanked at it harder and harder until it yielded and opened with the scraping of metal against stone.

The two of them looked around, but the sudden noise did not seem to have attracted any attention.

Calogero nodded. 'Okay then. Give me a hand with Agabus, eh?'

'What do you mean?'

'Let's shift him.'

'How do you know it's going to be there?'

'I don't. But it looks as if there could be a space behind him.'

She shrugged, and the two of them wrestled the statue to

one side, enough at least to be able to shine a light into the space beyond.

Calogero grinned at the dusty metal object within. 'A safety deposit box. Now, who would hide a cash box under a plinth in a roadside shrine in a tiny village miles from anywhere?'

'A crazy person. Someone with way too much time on their hands.'

'Or someone who knows that their very livelihood depends on this not being found.' He tapped his nose. 'Clever, eh?'

'Then why leave us clues? He could have picked any old roadside shrine.'

He frowned. 'I don't know. It still feels to me like he's playing a game with us.' He leaned inside and pulled out the box, grunting with the effort. 'Fair old weight on this.'

'Can you open it?'

Calogero rested the box on the base of the statue and rubbed his chin. 'Of course I can open it. I'm great with locks. Just give me some light.'

Nedda held her phone up as Calogero took a selection of small picks and files from his jacket. He worked away for ten minutes, occasionally pausing either to swear or sweep his hair back from his eyes. Then he sat back on his haunches, breathing deeply and shaking his head.

'Impossible,' he said.

'I thought you said you were great with locks.'

'I am great with locks. I'm just not great with this one, that's all.'

'So now what?'

He got to his feet, and hefted the box in his hands, raising it high about his head. 'Brute force?'

'Don't be stupid. You'll just damage the lock and then we'll never get in.'

'Look at it. That's thick, thick steel there. And cutting our way in isn't an option without some seriously specialised gear.'

'So the only way is to guess the code?'

'Six digits. Two dials. So, I make that 999,999 possibilities for each side. Which is quite a lot. I guess it might take a while. Shall we start with 000000?'

For a moment, Nedda feared that he might actually be serious. Then she stretched out her hand and pulled his away.

'No,' she said.

'You have a better idea?'

'Perhaps. Have you got a Bible on you?'

'Yes, I never leave home without one. Of course I don't.'

'Okay. Can you find one on the internet?'

'What?'

'There'll be loads of copies. It's out of copyright.'

'And why?'

'Think about the medallion. Agabus holding the Bible. More than that, he's pointing to it. Gianmaria's leaving us clues. Playing with us. But that's where the answer is. Think of it. How many of us have even heard of St Agabus? Where is he in the Bible?'

Calogero tapped away at his phone. 'Acts 11:27–28. Acts 21:10–12.'

'Exactly. Just two verses. That's it.'

'Seriously?' Then he smiled. 'Let's try.' He swivelled the numbers on the left dial. '112728. And on the other. 211012.'

The locks clicked open. Calogero turned to Nedda and grinned. 'You're a genius.'

'So, what have we got?'

He reached in and pulled out a thick padded envelope. 'Just this.'

'I hope it's worth it.'

'Oh, it will be.' Calogero and Nedda whipped round to see Salvatore standing behind them, his body silhouetted in the moonlight and a knife in one hand. 'I'll take that.'

'You bloody won't.'

Salvatore grabbed Nedda, twisting her arm up behind her back and making her gasp with pain. 'I will, or I'll cut the girl to pieces.'

Calogero shrugged. 'Well, that's not really a choice, is it?' He looked inside the envelope and a smile spread across his face. 'If you're sure, that is?'

'I'm very sure.' He waved the knife. 'And no tricks.'

'No tricks, Salvatore. I promise. Let me guess, you weren't able to follow Gianmaria's clues yourself and so you've been following us?'

'Letting you do the hard work. Thanks for that. I might even let you have a month off payment.' Then he frowned. 'Oh, wait a minute. No, I won't.'

Calogero made to toss him the envelope, but Salvatore shook his head. 'Uh-uh. Just pass it to me nicely.' He twisted the knife so the tip was under Nedda's chin. 'Don't get this wrong, Magus. I only have to move an inch and it's bad news for girly.' He stretched out his other hand and took the package.

He pushed Nedda away, sending her sprawling to the

ground. He grinned, weighing the envelope in his hand. 'My retirement plan. Thank you both.'

He looked inside and his expression changed to one of bafflement.

'What the fuck is this?'

Calogero started to laugh. Gently at first and then almost uncontrollably.

Salvatore turned it upside down. A fine stream of ash trickled out.

'What?' said Nedda.

Calogero wiped tears from his eyes. 'Gianmaria, you magnificent bastard. The ultimate trick. It was never here at all. All that nonsense with amulets and Bible passages and some obscure saint no one's ever heard of. All just a distraction. An illusion. And we all fell for it.'

Salvatore shook his head, violently. 'No. It's got to be somewhere. He wouldn't have destroyed it. It makes no sense.'

'Well, wherever it is there's no finding it now. Come on, Salvatore, give it up. You could always get a proper job. Let's let bygones be bygones, eh?'

'There are the murders, of course,' said Nedda. 'I don't think we can just let that go.'

'Oh yes. That slipped my mind. What happened, Salvatore? You just got jealous of Gianmaria and took him out for one final boat ride? On the one day of the year when literally everybody's attention would have been elsewhere. Clever. Good magical practice. But you're right, Nedda. I don't think we can let that go.'

'Yeah. Good luck making that one stick.' Salvatore raised the knife. 'You tell me where the file is now or I'll cut you both into ribbons.'

He lunged at Nedda, but she rolled out of his reach as Calogero threw himself upon him, grabbing at the medallion around his neck and twisting.

Salvatore gurgled, saliva drooling from his mouth as the chain cut into his throat. Calogero saw his eyes rolling back in his head.

'Got you, you bastard.'

One more twist, just a few more seconds, and he'd have him. One more twist.

Just one more.

And the chain broke.

Salvatore dropped to his knees, gasping.

Calogero reached into his jacket, pulled out an envelope and thrust it into Nedda's hands.

'Run.'

Then Salvatore was upon him and Calogero punched him in the face, sending him reeling backwards. Nedda looked at the two of them, unsure what to do.

'Nedda. Run like hell.'

Then she looked down at the envelope in her hands and ran.

Chapter 52

Calogero thought he was in reasonable physical shape, but his shoes were slipping on the lava path and blistering his feet within them. Even at this hour the air was sticky and hot and his lungs burned as he laboured to breathe. Nedda – younger, fitter – had disappeared into the dark.

He was probably in better shape than Salvatore. If it came to a normal fight he could, he suspected, give a good account of himself. But this would be no normal fight. Salvatore had a knife, at least.

The punch to the face had bought him a few seconds. Enough to give him a lead. He risked taking a look back. The last time he'd checked, Salvatore was three lengths behind him. Now he'd cut it to two. For a moment, they gazed at each other in the moonlight. He could not see the expression on the other man's face but could hear his breath rasping.

Acireale was barely two hundred metres away. It might as well have been two hundred kilometres. Salvatore would be on him long before they could reach the safety of lighted streets and houses and people.

And then what?

'Nedda.' Calogero's voice was raw. 'Keep running.'

He stopped for just a moment as he tried, and failed, to catch his breath.

'You'll have to go on. Get help. I'll hold him as long as I can.'

That wasn't going to be very long at all. Salvatore's footsteps and his laboured breathing were ever louder. Calogero's one bit of good fortune was that the other man, evidently, wasn't in any better shape than him.

The shadow of the *Fortezza* loomed into view. Perhaps another one hundred metres to go. He forced himself to drag one foot in front of the other, his chest burning.

And then a figure moved out of the shadows, and a hand clamped itself over his mouth.

He struggled for a moment but could only manage a muffled 'Mmph!' Then a voice whispered in his ear.

'Quiet.' And the hand was gently taken away.

'Nedda?' he whispered.

'Shhh,' she said. 'Follow me. Be as quiet as you can.'

The gate was ajar, thank all the gods of Sicily, just enough to let them squeeze through. Nedda dug him in the ribs and pointed towards the abandoned museum. 'In there.'

They picked themselves over the rubble and squeezed through the entrance. Calogero pressed himself into the wall, trying to control his breathing as his heart laboured painfully in his chest.

Nedda dragged a table over to the wall, hauled herself on to it, and pulled down the hunting rifle.

'What are you doing?'

'Saving our lives.'

'Do you know how to fire a gun?'

'No.'

'Is it even loaded?'

'Don't know. Don't even know how to check. But he won't know that.'

She heard footsteps crunching against the fragmented lava path. For a moment, she thought she heard them directly outside the entrance. They stopped, and she held her breath. The footsteps moved on, but now it sounded as if there were two sets of them on different sides of the *Fortezza*. She shook her head. There could only be the one. But where?

'Salvatore.'

The footsteps stopped.

'Salvatore, I have a gun.'

A throaty chuckle came from nearby. She could hear his breath wheezing. For all his *braggadocio* Salvatore was in worse shape than her. And there were two of them. Even if Calogero was barely able to stand.

Salvatore wheezed some more. She heard his footsteps receding. But to where?

'Girly's got a gun, has she?' she heard him chuckle.

'I have. And I'll use it if I need to.'

Footsteps again. But from where?

'I can see you, Salvatore.'

More shuffling.

'I don't believe you, girly.'

'Try me. I'm going to count to three. And then two things will happen. Either I hear you running away as if the devil himself was after you. Or I'm going to fire.'

He wheezed some more. Frankly she didn't think he was in any shape to do any more running.

'One.'

Footsteps. But she couldn't place where. She'd have to fire blind.

'Two.'

A low chuckle and then a voice. 'I can see you, girly. And guess what? I've got a gun too.'

'Three.'

Nedda closed her eyes and squeezed the trigger.

There was a click from the rifle. And then the roar of a gun, and a scream that died away within seconds.

Chapter 53

'One hundred metres, straight down,' said Gori. 'Well, straight-ish. I'm told he bounced a few times along the way.'

Calogero winced.

'You were very lucky, you know?'

'Nedda saved us. No, that's not fair. She saved me. She knew that the museum at the tower was the one place where we could make a stand. I was all in. There was no chance I could have made the last stretch to Acireale.'

'And she had the idea of taking and using the gun on the wall?' Gori raised an eyebrow.

'I think she thought she could just bluff it. I doubt she's ever fired a gun before.'

'Well, this one was never going to work. It seems it was deactivated years ago. But we found one at the base of the cliff face with the prints of our friend *signor* Salvatore on it and one empty chamber. That most certainly worked. As I said, *signor* Maugeri, you've both been very lucky.'

'I know. What do you think happened?'

'That section of the wall is crumbling. It's barely there in some places. No wonder they're closing the damn thing down. I imagine he stepped back to steady his aim and,'

Gori fluttered his hands in the air, 'the whole thing collapsed behind him.'

Calogero nodded.

'I'm just wondering what exactly led you and *signurina* Nedda to that spot at that time of night.'

'I – she – we – had a theory. Lombardo seemed to be a wealthy man. Salvatore less so. They seemed to spend a lot of time together. I think it was just two crooks falling out. Salvatore simply pushed him off his boat. The whole Tarot thing was just a distraction to shift blame on to anyone who might have a grudge against psychics. But Lombardo was always one step ahead of us all. He laid a false trail, all linked around St Agabus. The medallion. The name of his boat. The shrine. Sending us on a treasure hunt for his money, but ultimately leading us to an envelope filled with ash. It's a good joke. Even better, of course, if he'd been around to enjoy it.'

'And his money?'

'Who knows? If it's in his apartment, you'll find it. If it's in a bank vault, you'll find it. Or maybe it's at the bottom of the sea with his boat.'

Gori nodded, and drummed his fingers on his desk. 'You're assuming it was money, then?'

Calogero shrugged. 'Sure. What else could it be?'

'Oh, there are stories about *signor* Lombardo. He was a man who made enemies. A man who collected information about people. Information that could be useful to him.' He stared at Calogero. 'You know the sort of information I mean?'

Calogero held his gaze unblinkingly. Eventually he smiled. 'I can well imagine,' he said.

'You and *signurina* Nedda seem a strange couple to be on a treasure hunt in the middle of the night.'

'She's a journalist. And I had a vested interest. Salvatore had tried to kill me, remember? So not so strange at all really.'

'Mm-hmm. Okay. That's almost everything. Whatever he had is lost for ever, I imagine. A shame. It would have been most interesting to see exactly what it was.'

Calogero smiled back at him. 'It would indeed.'

Chapter 54

'You've got a visitor,' Angelo said.

'Stefano? Tell him I'm busy.'

'No. Another gentleman friend.'

'Oh right. Well, I probably know who that is. You want to show him in?'

'Sure.' Angelo showed no sign of going anywhere. 'You want me to hang around?'

'No, it's okay.'

'You look busy.'

'I am.'

'Can I make a coffee first?'

Nedda reached into her purse. 'Here you are, *papà*. Go over to the bar and get yourself a beer or a spritz or whatever. And I'll see you in thirty minutes, okay?'

'That's kind of you.' Then he frowned. 'He's not that sort of gentleman friend, is he?'

'No. Certainly not.'

'Good. Because I'm not too old to kick his arse.'

'I know.'

'Not that I want you using language like that.'

'I won't. I promise. Can you show him in before he dies of old age, perhaps?'

Angelo shrugged, and wandered off. 'She says to go through. I'm just heading out for thirty minutes. Only thirty minutes, mind you.'

Calogero walked in, smiled, and tossed that morning's *Catania Nuova* on to the table. 'Hello, Nedda. You seem to have become a bit of a star overnight. *Intrepid girl reporter battles Lombardo murderer.* It's all very exciting.'

'Yeah. Well, I didn't write the headline.'

'And thanks – sincerely – for keeping my name out of it.'

'Oh, that was easy. Given I don't actually know what it is.' He was about to protest, but she shook her head. 'I'm fed up of being lied to by disappointing men. So please don't bother to deny it.

'You see, I was thinking. About that trick you pulled down at the shrine. The sleight-of-hand with the envelope full of ash. That was very clever. But the thing is, you couldn't have known Salvatore was going to be there. That fake envelope was for me, wasn't it? You were going to pocket the original and no one but you would ever have known about it.'

He sighed. 'Perhaps. But at the end of the day, Nedda, I trusted you with it.'

'Only because the alternative was Salvatore. So. Were you ever planning on telling me who you really are?'

'There never seemed to be the right moment.'

'Perhaps not. It's a difficult conversation to have. "Excuse me, but just to make everything absolutely clear, my name is not Calogero Maugeri and before being a stage magician I was—" *What* exactly?'

'I didn't think it was a conversation to have over a *toast*.'

'So, you're a crook?'

'I'm not sure I'd consider myself one.'

'That always works well in court.' She patted the envelope on the table. 'So why shouldn't I go to the police with this?'

His expression changed and, for a moment, she thought she saw genuine fear in his eyes. 'Nedda, if you do that, I'm in trouble. Big trouble.'

'Okay then, *Calogero*.' She leaned into the name. 'Tell me about just how much trouble you'd be in. And be honest with me.'

'I've been using a false ID. I even gave it to the police. If they find out, then I could be looking at two years for that alone.'

'Uh-huh. Anything else?'

'There's a man in Turin who doesn't wish me well.'

'Someone you conned? Someone you robbed?'

'Someone I cheated at cards because he was trying to cheat me. I was just better at it, that's all.' He ran his hands through his hair. 'Nedda, if he finds out where I am, I'm in trouble. I could do the two years, I reckon, but this guy will try to have me killed. And the other people on the list? Have you looked at the names on there?'

She shook her head. 'Not yet. I wanted to see you first. To hear what you have to say.'

'Nedda, this could make your career, I know. But are we really talking about gang bosses, corrupt politicians and *mafiosi* here? Or are we talking about a bunch of sad sacks like me who've just made a couple of mistakes? Oh. And there's Stefano, of course.'

Nedda was silent.

'Have you checked his file yet?'

She shook her head. 'I don't want to. I don't need to. Whatever he's done, I don't really care.'

He sighed. 'Well, I'll be going. I need to clear out my stuff at the theatre.' He paused. 'Thirty minutes, your dad said?'

Nedda felt a chill on the back of her neck as she looked around the kitchen. The knife rack was fastened to the wall directly behind him.

He saw the direction of her gaze and shook his head. 'Oh, you needn't worry about me trying to grab a breadknife, Nedda. I'm not that sort of person.'

She said nothing.

'The thing is,' he continued, 'if I were, I could have done it by now. Couldn't I?'

Her throat was dry, and so she merely nodded.

'So, I'll be on my way. I'll leave the documents with you. It's your choice. But I think I know what sort of person you are. Because I trusted you with them.'

He got to his feet and made his way to the door.

'Aren't you even going to tell me your real name?' she asked. 'If trust is so important all of a sudden?'

He turned and shook his head.

'What would be the point?''

Chapter 55

'You seem out of sorts, Magus.'

Calogero sighed. 'You noticed, Santo?'

'You don't seem to be quite firing on all cylinders tonight. If you don't mind me saying. Anything wrong?'

He nodded.

Santo pulled out a bottle of grappa. 'Want to talk about it?'

'I'll take a grappa. But, no, I don't really want to talk about it.' Santo looked offended for a moment, but Calogero just motioned him to sit down. 'Come on. I'll have a drink. One for the road.'

Santo poured a generous measure into a plastic cup, and a half-measure for himself. They clinked cups, as best they could. Calogero took a drink, and grimaced. 'Always hated grappa,' he said.

Santo looked at the label. 'I'm not sure this is the best stuff, to be honest. So come on, Magus, what's up?'

Calogero sighed. 'Just end of show blues.'

'Oh, I see.' Santo sipped at his grappa. 'Is that all? Nothing to do with a woman by any chance?'

'Yes. But not like you mean. I'm just sad, that's all.'

'Cheer up. Come on, tell me. What's next for the Magus?'

'Don't know. I might go back up north for a bit. There's a few things I need to sort out.'

Santo knocked back the remains of his drink. 'You want to take the rest of the bottle with you?'

'Better not. I'm not sure it'll do me any good. And don't worry, I'm sure I'll be fine tomorrow.'

'Can't you look into the future and check?'

Despite himself, Calogero grinned. 'Thanks for everything, Santo.'

'No problems. I'll lock up everywhere. Just switch off the lights when you're done, and I'll see you downstairs?' He nodded at the bottle. 'Have yourself another for the road in the meantime, eh?'

Another for the road. He grimaced again at the lingering taste of the grappa; an unlovely combination of cigarettes and burning tyres. Maybe a half for the road would have been better? Or even a none for the road?

He took his remaining stage clothes from the wardrobe and folded them away inside his suitcase. He took one last look around and nodded. Time to go.

The air outside was no cooler and, for a moment, he felt a pang of nostalgia for the less oppressive climes of Turin. Then Santo wound down the window of his Cinquecento and gave him a wave. 'Magus. Over here.'

'You sure about the times, Magus?'

'Absolutely. I'll get the last train to Messina. And then I'll get the late ferry to the mainland. That'll get me in early tomorrow morning and then, well, then I can have a think about where to go next.'

'You know the trains are all messed up because of Etna, though? What happens if they just cancel it? There's going to be no one around at the station at this time of night.'

'Well then, Santo, I'll just have to give you a call and you can come and drive me.' He clapped him on the back. 'Joking. Seriously, it'll be fine. I'm feeling lucky.'

'If you say so.'

'I do.' Santo drew to a halt and jumped out of the car, pulling Calogero's suitcase out of the back seat. 'No, no, Magus. Easier if I do it. There's a knack to getting a suitcase in and out of a Cinquecento.'

'Thank you, my friend.'

Santo looked at the deserted platform. 'You sure you don't want me to wait?'

'No. If you don't mind. I've never liked that. I think it goes back to the days when *mamma* would see me on to the train when I was heading off to school. And I'd look back and see her standing there and she looked so sad.'

'I promise not to cry if that helps?'

Calogero laughed. 'Be off with you! Seriously.' He spread his arms wide. 'But give us a hug, eh?'

'*Ciao*, Magus.'

'*Ciao*, Santo. Maybe next time you can start using my actual name, eh?'

Santo smiled, gave him a thumbs up, and jumped back into his car. He gave him one last wave, and then he was gone, leaving Calogero alone on the platform.

Railway stations are melancholy places. Perhaps because they're neither here nor there. Or because they're associated with leave-taking. Or maybe because, in a place like Acireale, you might find yourself waiting a long time for the next train, and inevitably short by ten cents of being able to get something from the vending machine.

He heard footsteps along the platform. Santo, back again? No, he'd have heard the car. Another passenger. He sighed, inwardly, and braced himself for the small talk.

'Hello, Calogero. Or would you prefer Magus?'

The face was hidden by the glare of a torch, but Calogero nodded and patted the seat next to him.

'Hello, Stefano.'

Chapter 56

'I can't say it's a pleasure, Stefano. But it's not unexpected.'

'No?'

'Don't try and con a con man. That's what they say.'

Stefano grinned and tapped his forehead. 'Unless he happens to be better than you, that is.'

'I suppose I should be insulted. But really, I've met so many people like you over the course of my life, Stefano.'

'Oh. And I thought I was special.'

'Oh no. Not at all. I've met so many compulsive gamblers. The ones banned from every casino in Italy. From every private club. Where does that leave them? It leaves them scratching the itch with scratch cards. It leaves them having to play with the card sharks. The unlicensed games. And people who might just be a bit better at cheating than they are. People like Salvatore and Gianmaria.

'Salvatore didn't fall from that tower. You were there. You pushed him. The final problem removed. Salvatore knew he had to buy himself as much time as possible with the Tarot scheme. He needed to find a scapegoat like the sad little Angry in Aci man. Didn't have to be for long. Just long enough. Killing Toto was a way to do that. But the thing is, that gave you an opportunity. Killing Salvatore and making it look like he'd fallen – and that was the easy part – would neatly close the case off and give you a free run at the dossier.

'Except even that didn't help all that much, did it? Because that file is still out there somewhere.'

'With all your details in it.'

'Indeed. Which is the reason I can't let you have it.'

'You're not really in a position to say that.' Stefano reached into his jacket and, before Calogero could move, had taken out a switchblade and pressed it into his thigh.

'Femoral artery. You'll bleed out before the train arrives. And nobody, but nobody, is coming to help. I'm going to give you more of a chance than I gave Salvatore. I'm going to give you a count of ten. So just tell me, Magus. Where is it?'

Calogero nodded downwards. 'In my luggage.'

'You're lying.'

'Why would I do that? There's no way I'd be leaving town without it. Those names are going to be very lucrative for me.'

He clicked the suitcase open. Five minutes, perhaps, until the train arrived. He just needed to keep Stefano talking to buy time.

'So, you want the file, I can get it for you. And you can do what the hell you like with it.' He paused. 'I haven't seen the names. I don't know who's on there. But I imagine you'll do very nicely out of it. Lombardo found blackmail paid much better than the fake psychic scene, after all. That's why you and Salvatore got rid of him. Trouble is, you then fell out. Crooks do that. Events have a habit of catching up on you.'

'Only if you're not smart. And I'm very smart.' He paused. 'Do you think I like having to do this?'

'In all honesty, Stefano, if you don't, I think you're doing a pretty good impression of it.'

'And that's where you're wrong. I didn't want any of this. Those sad bastards in the casinos and the private clubs. They could have been me. They are me.

'I have a wife, you know? And a daughter. I don't see them anymore. I can't see them anymore. My mother – my blessed mother – died penniless. She gave me everything to help me out.

'And within months of her dying, I was back in the same state. Broke. Penniless. Owing bad people a lot of money. I lost my job, of course. I was never around. I was too busy chasing the big win that would make everything right. They told me to leave and that they'd give me a good reference.

'Thing is, I'd been covering a story about illegal gambling in the city. About a local boss who'd been stung and was very, very keen to get back in touch with an old friend. An old friend who went by the name of—' He leant over and whispered into Calogero's ear.

Calogero nodded. 'Very good.'

'Do you know, the next time I heard that name was a freelance job I worked on, about gambling on cruise ships. And about a man called Gianmaria Lombardo who'd been taken for a ride by a man from Turin. And the more I looked at Gianmaria Lombardo, the more I discovered about how he actually made his money. And I thought he might be willing to pay well if I could slip him a name.'

'Which is how you ended up working for a tiny local paper in Catania.'

'Aldo thought it was strange. But he bought my story about

wanting to downsize. About wanting a new start. And in a way, that's what I wanted too.' He ran his hands, damp with sweat, through his hair. 'Christ, do you know how irritating that stupid fucking girl got, complaining about delivering *cannoli* to Aldo? I'd give anything for my life to be as uncomplicated as that again. Anything for a clean slate, anything for a new start.'

'Including murder and blackmail,' said Calogero.

'I can't turn the clock back, and believe me there is nothing I'd like more. But this is my chance. When the money starts coming in from Gianmaria's *clients*. A new start. Somewhere else, maybe outside of Italy. A chance to begin again.'

'Oh Stefano,' Calogero sighed. 'I think you really believe that. But the minute you're debt free and living somewhere where your photo isn't in every bookmakers, you'll be back chasing the big win again. It's what junkies do and that's what you are.

'Tell someone you're an alcoholic and you'll get sympathy by the bucketload because so many of us are secretly more than a little worried about overstepping that line ourselves.

'Tell someone you're addicted to cocaine and you'll get sympathy but maybe also a bit of a look and the odd whisper behind your back. Because now you're not just an addict but you're also a lawbreaker. You've crossed a line now. You're no longer quite one of us. You're an addict, yes, but you're not a *good* addict, and that's the difference.

'And then you tell someone you're addicted to gambling. And perhaps there's a bit of an awkward silence. Because everyone is thinking, *How could you be so stupid? Why don't you just, you know, stop? How can it be that in a set-up that everyone knows is always going to work in favour of the book-maker, you – and you alone – have found a way to buck the system?*

'But it's not stupid, is it, Stefano? I understand. And so, trust me when I say that blackmailing people to clear up your debts is not going to sort out your problem.'

Stefano was about to speak, the knife still pressing pain-fully into Calogero's thigh, when the sound of an engine broke the stillness. A low rumble, the screech of tyres and the glare of a single headlight.

Calogero smiled. 'In fact, I'd bet my life on it.'

Chapter 57

Nedda took off her helmet, her red hair shining in the glare of the headlight as she shook it out.

'Nedda?'

'Stefano. Calogero.'

'I'm very pleased to see you, I have to say.'

'You ought to be. I'm breaking the law by doing this. And risking my life. The streets are slippery as hell with all that ash.'

'You took your time.'

'I know. But I needed to get hold of Santo. He told me where you were. But I also had things to think about. And I had a few things to check out.' She turned to Stefano. 'You see, there are a lot of names in that file. But there's one important name missing. Yours. And that means you were never doing this just to save yourself. If you had been, I could almost have understood. But no, it was just for money. Along with everything else in your life.'

'Nedda, this really isn't what you think.' Stefano spread his arms wide.

'Look at you, Stefano. You're sitting on a railway platform jabbing a knife into the man sitting next to you. What am I failing to understand here?'

She moved towards Calogero. 'Come on then, useless. Let's get going.' She turned to Stefano. 'And you'd better leave him alone. This is one of my good tops and I don't need him bleeding on me.'

Stefano moved to block her off and held up a hand. 'Nedda, I don't want to do this. But if you're going to try and stop me then I'm going to have to kill you as well.'

'How are you going to do that, Stefano? You're going to try to make it look like some bizarre lovers' suicide pact? Nobody's going to believe that.'

'Oh, thanks,' said Calogero. 'I'm still here, you know?'

Stefano rubbed his chin. 'But he could have killed you and then himself in a fit of remorse. I think that could work. Long enough for me to call in every last debt and be on my way, at any rate.'

'He's got a point, Nedda.'

She ignored Calogero and turned back to Stefano. 'You know, I did genuinely think you quite liked me.'

'Just a little. Sorry if I broke your heart, sweetheart.'

'You were just another vaguely disappointing boyfriend, Stefano. And at least none of the others had actually killed someone.'

'Well, I'm afraid I'll be a hard act to live up to.'

'Just one thing, though. The seven years of bad sex thing. Maybe we really should have waited that extra couple of weeks?'

Calogero sniggered.

'You, shut up,' said Nedda.

'Yes, shut up,' said Stefano. 'Come on now, Nedda. We know how this ends. It ends with me walking out of here with the file. And I don't see you stopping me. So be a good girl and tell me where it is.'

Nedda looked from Stefano to Calogero and then back again. 'Okay. But you move away from him.'

Stefano hesitated and then shrugged, shuffling along to the other side of the bench. Calogero thought for a moment about making a break for it but decided against it. The moment wasn't quite right. Not yet.

Nedda took out a thick padded envelope. 'Gianmaria must have been a very busy man over the course of his illustrious career,' she said. 'And also a very organised one. Everything's here, A to Z.

'Now, I had a good old think about this before I came over here. I seriously thought about destroying it.'

'Really? That wouldn't make you any sort of reporter.'

'I admit I haven't gone through all of it yet. But I've seen some of the names.' She squinted at the page in front of her and whistled. 'This one, for example. My goodness.'

Stefano stretched out his hand. 'Come on then.'

'The trouble is, the three of us will know about this. I don't think that would be good for my long-term health.'

Stefano nodded and grinned. 'Okay then. Let's make a deal. We take this to Aldo. It'll blow him away. I'll give you all the credit. I promise. No more *cannoli* runs for you. Just proper, serious reporting.'

She nodded. 'I could do that. The trouble is that he,' she nodded at Calogero, 'might well be a clown and a charlatan. But I'm not convinced he's done anything that bad.'

Calogero looked up at her, a glimmer of hope in his eyes.

'So, as I said, I thought about destroying it. But then I

decided I couldn't do that.' She took a step towards him. 'No. If you want it, you're going to have to take it from me. Prove to me what kind of a man you are.'

Stefano grinned. He was about to raise the knife when Nedda swung her helmet at him with all her strength.

A flash of crimson sprayed across the platform as the knife skipped and skittered across the concrete and on to the track.

She breathed deeply, looking down at the helmet. 'They're right, you know, these things really can save your life.'

He swayed unsteadily on his feet. 'Bitch.' Then he threw himself at her, flailing more than punching, his hands clawing at the envelope. As she staggered back under his weight, she felt it drop from her hand. He made a grab for it, but Calogero was there to kick it away.

To kick it away from him and on to the track.

The rails hummed with the sound of the approaching train. Stefano looked first at Nedda and then at Calogero, and jumped.

He landed awkwardly on the track, sprawling on the line, his hands scrabbling for the envelope.

'Jesus, Stefano, *no.*'

He knelt there for a moment, his face illuminated by the lights of the oncoming train. There might even have been a look of triumph in his eyes.

Calogero crouched down. 'Give me your hand. Quickly.'

The tracks were slippery with ash and Stefano's feet skidded and slithered as he tried to push himself off the line and out of the way. From the train came a terrific screeching of brakes, and before she hauled Calogero away, Nedda could see the horror in the face of the driver.

Stefano had no time to scream at all.

Chapter 58

'Nedda!'

'Aldo?'

Lentini sprung from his chair and threw his arms around her. Then he held her face between his hands and kissed her on the forehead.

'I love you. Did I ever tell you how much I love you?'

'Er. No. But thanks.'

He sat back down in his chair and spun it through three hundred and sixty degrees.

'You want to know why I love you so much?' He picked up a newspaper from his desk and tossed it to her. 'Because of this. Because of your story. You know, we outsold *La Sicilia* yesterday. First time ever.'

'Wow.'

'So, this means big changes are going to happen. First of all, we've got a vacancy now. Because of Gallo, obviously.'

'And so?'

'Well, I was thinking of offering it to Belardo.' He paused for a moment, to enjoy the expression on her face. 'Who do you think I'm going to offer it to? You, of course.'

'So, no more lifestyle features? No more *pasticceria* of the month columns?'

'You can still keep doing those. If you like.'

'No. It's okay. Really.'

'Then consider those days over. No more fading pop stars. No more cake shops.' His face fell. 'Which is a shame, though.'

'Proper *cronaca nera* stuff, then?'

'If that's what you want, Nedda. I need to protect my prime asset now, before those vultures from *La Sicilia* come circling. Or even from Rome or Turin. *Repubblica, La Stampa*, they'll all be after you.' He frowned. 'I shouldn't be giving you ideas.'

'I hadn't thought of it like that, Aldo.'

'Well, stop thinking about it.' His frown deepened. 'Hey, none of those guys have been calling you, have they?'

'No, Aldo.'

'You'd tell me if they had?'

'Of course, Aldo.'

'Well, then there's nothing more to be said. I'll get the paperwork sorted out this afternoon. You can move your stuff into Gallo's office in the meantime.'

'I will do. And thanks.'

'Oh, and Nedda? Could you go out and get some *cannoli*? Just one last time? And maybe some prosecco. I think we all have some celebrating to do.'

Nedda smiled and nodded. It might have to be done in easy stages, but Lentini was changing.

Chapter 59

'Cold, isn't it?' said Nedda, as they watched little Luna happily scampering amongst the rocks.

'Never gets above eleven centigrade, even in July. I used to come up here from time to time back in the day. When the temperature became unbearable down below. Not so much recently.'

'Give me a call anytime. You know, if you just want a lift up here. You and me and Luna.'

'I'll do that.' Morgana smiled. 'So, you're a famous girl now.'

Nedda laughed. 'Oh, I'm enjoying my moment in the sun. The most famous reporter on the third most read paper in Catania.'

'You should be proud of yourself. Proper journalism there. Your mother would have been so proud of you.'

'I hope so.'

The two of them sat in silence looking out at the view, down the slopes of the volcano and to the Ionian Sea. The *Ciclopi* were mere dots at this distance. He might not have had much of an aim – for which, perhaps, he might be forgiven – but Polyphemus must have had a hell of a strong right arm.

'Any tea left?'

Morgana held up the Thermos and gave it a shake. 'I don't think so. I've got something stronger, though, in a hip flask.'

Nedda shook her head. 'Not very wise for me. Probably not for you, either. I like pillions to be relaxed but not too relaxed, if you see what I mean.'

'I do.' Morgana got to her feet and stretched. 'Ah, but it's so good to breathe the air up here. The smell of sulphur.'

'You like that?'

'I'm a witch, remember. It goes with the territory. You ever been to Vulcano?'

'No. Never been to any of the Aeolian Islands.'

'We should go. The two of us. And Luna, of course. It's wonderful round there. Although the stink of rotten eggs will cling to you for days.'

'Hmm. How did that job with the Sicilian Tourist Board work out?'

Morgana smiled. 'I wasn't there long.' Luna came scampering over and looked up imploringly at her. Even under the winter jacket she was wearing, the little dog was shivering. 'Oh, come on then. Let's get you back into the warmth.' Morgana zipped her, uncomplainingly, into the tank bag.

'I was thinking about what you were saying,' said Nedda. 'About my mother. Being proud and all that. But at the same time, I wonder what she might have done with the dossier.'

'Doesn't matter what she might have done, girl. Only matters what you did. And are you okay with that? Because that's all that matters.'

She nodded. 'Yes. I think I am. Perhaps *mamma* would have handed it straight to the police. But I am Nedda, I am the only other red-haired girl in Sicily, and I am not my mother.'

'Then that's all that needs to be said.'

Luna's head emerged from the tank bag and she yapped at them impatiently.

Nedda smiled, swung a leg across the Enfield and kicked the engine into life. 'Time to go, Morgana.' She turned to look at her pillion. 'I was thinking about something you said. It seems like a long time ago now. When you were talking about the *donne di fuora*. The Ladies from Outside. And that's what we are, isn't it, Morgana? We can do anything. Because we're the Ladies from Outside.'

Chapter 60

Nedda sat on the sofa, her legs curled under her, zapping from station to station with the remote control. She heard the door creaking open behind her and turned to see her father standing there.

'The dreams again?' he said.

She shook her head. 'No. Nothing like that. I just couldn't sleep.'

He sat down in his usual chair. 'What are you watching?'

'Nothing really.' She frowned. 'There always seems to be football on, doesn't there? I think just now it was something from Argentina.' She clicked away with the remote, and then stopped as she reached a cheap-looking channel where a man in a suit that was just a little bit too shiny was speaking into a telephone.

'Your husband wants you to know that he's happy and that he loves you very—'

Click.

Nedda tossed the remote control on to the other side of the sofa. 'I'd never realised how much of this stuff is out there.'

Angelo nodded. 'Me neither.'

'It's out there, and it's hurting people.'

He shrugged. 'Is it, though? Perhaps it gives people comfort. And is that so bad?'

'But it's all a lie.'

'Is it?'

'Come on, dad, you know it is.'

'Do I?'

She sighed. 'I see we've reached the "answering a question with a question" stage of the evening, then.'

'I'm being serious. It would have been a great comfort to me.' He smiled. 'But I know your mother would have kicked my arse.' He wagged a finger. 'Don't say that. I wonder, though, how many of these people,' he pointed at the screen, 'believe it themselves.'

'Oh, I think Calogero's always known it's all a scam. But as for Mater Morgana, I'm not so sure. I think she might really believe it.'

'So, you think she's crazy?'

Nedda shook her head. 'No. Well, I think she might be crazy. But not in that way, if you see what I mean. I think I could learn a lot from her, you know.'

'Oh yes?' He raised an eyebrow. 'Such as?'

'Well, I think lesson number one is *never, ever fuck around with a witch.*'

He tried to look shocked, failed, and then pretended to cuff her across the head.

They sat in silence for a while.

'Do you want to watch television, Dad?'

'I don't think so.'

'It doesn't have to be Psychic TV. I'm sure I could find you some football you'd recognise. Or an old film, or something.'

He shook his head. 'No, I don't think so,' he repeated. Silence hung in the air between them.

'I'm sorry,' he said, finally.

'What about?'

'About Stefano.'

'Oh. Him.'

'You quite liked him, didn't you?'

She nodded. 'I did. Quite like him.'

'There are better people out there, you know?'

'I think there must be.'

'And you deserve someone better.'

'Thank you, *papà*.'

'By *someone better*, I mean someone who isn't a psychopathic killer, of course.'

'Of course.'

'So what's he like? This Calogero fellow?'

'He's,' she grasped for the words, 'intensely irritating. But—'

'But?'

'Also kind of quite nice. I think. In a strange way.' She looked over at him, as he tried and failed to stop a smile creeping across his face. 'Not like that, okay?'

'I understand.' He wasn't even trying to stop the smile now.

'I mean it. Don't make me come over there.'

Angelo threw up his hands. 'Okay. Okay. I understand.' He yawned and stretched. 'So,' he said, 'you know what would be good right now?'

'Warm milk, honey and grappa?'

'The very thing.'

'You know what would make it even better?'

He shook his head.

'Why not hold on the warm milk and honey?'

Epilogue

Calogero sat on the edge of the stage, swinging his legs out over the orchestra pit and looking out at the rows of empty seats. With the house lights up, the red plush of the seats and the curtains looked shabby and faded, and the gilt of the boxes worn and tired. He'd never noticed that before. All part of the magic of theatre, he supposed.

He smiled to himself. But, of course, magic was exactly what it was. All of it just an illusion, aided by the willingness to suspend disbelief.

A bored-looking cat sat on the back of one of the seats and gave itself a good scratch behind the ears.

'How are you feeling there?'

He started, thinking the cat had spoken for a moment. All part of the magic, all part of the illusion. He scanned the rows of seats. Nedda was seated at the back, her legs crossed and arms folded. He hadn't seen her come in.

'Sorry, I didn't mean to startle you.' She smiled at him. 'How are you feeling?' she repeated.

Calogero rubbed his chin. 'Not too bad, all things being considered. How are you?'

'Sort of okay.'

'Sort of?'

'Yes. I wouldn't go any further than that. Because everything's just a little bit weird. Did you really do a show today?'

'I did two of them. They couldn't wait to have me back. Santo tells me they couldn't sell tickets fast enough. It seems there really is no such thing as bad publicity.'

'That's nice for you.'

'Well, mustn't let my head swell too much.' He smiled down at her. 'Right now it seems I have an audience of two.'

'Two?'

He nodded at the cat. 'You and him.' The cat gave a yawn and stretched before half-jumping, half-toppling from the back of the chair and stalking towards the exit.

Nedda raised an eyebrow. 'Tough crowd?'

'I guess so. Anyway, how have things been for you? I imagine your editor was most pleased.'

'He was.'

'Bit of a career-changer for you, I imagine. You'll be off to Rome with *La Repubblica* then, I guess?'

She shook her head.

'Turin, with *La Stampa*?'

She shook her head again.

'Ah, Milan. *Il Sole 24 Ore*.'

'No. God, for a Magus you're rubbish at this. I'm staying here. Just for a while. Or at least that's what I keep telling myself.'

'With *Nuova Catania*?'

'I keep telling you it's *Catania Nuova*.'

'I thought you hated it?'

'I did. But only sometimes. And Aldo's a good man at heart.'

Calogero stroked his goatee, weighing his words carefully. 'And I suppose that there's now a senior reporter vacancy.'

'There is.'

'Well, I guess that's – convenient?'

'Oh, I see. And you think I'm the kind of person who'd shamelessly profit from the death of a colleague.'

'I didn't say anything.' He drew a finger across his lips. 'Not a word, see.'

'Stop laughing.'

'I'm not laughing.'

'You are. And for a magician your poker face is terrible.' She paused. 'But, as it turns out, Aldo did offer me Stefano's old role. On a six-month trial, he says.'

'Well, that's wonderful. Congratulations. No more *pasticcerie* then?'

'It seems not.' Nedda's stomach rumbled. 'Tell you what, though, I could do with some of those *cannoli* from the Buscemi Brothers right now.'

'So could I.' He glanced at his watch. 'How about dinner?'

'I knew you were going to say that.'

He grinned. 'Now who's the Magus? But no *toast*. Pizza and beer okay?'

'That's more than okay.'

Calogero paused. 'There were other names in that file, Nedda. Names that could really have made your career.'

She nodded. 'I imagine there were.'

'You weren't tempted to look?'

She gave a thin smile. 'Can't you read my mind?'

He shook his head and smiled back. 'No.'

'There may have been some big names in there, who

knows? I only looked for Stefano, you see. Maybe there were some seriously bad people to be found. Or perhaps not. Seriously bad people don't react well to blackmail. But there might also have been people who maybe just made a mistake or two along the way.' She paused. 'People like you. And so it's shredded into a million bloody fragments fluttering alongside the railway line. And I'm not sorry that it's gone.'

He sat there on the edge of the stage, his legs swinging. 'Thank you,' he said, finally.

'So, what are you going to do now?'

Calogero shrugged. 'Hadn't really thought. Take the show on the road. Maybe on to the mainland. Or maybe back on the cruise ships. That's not a bad life. But maybe I'll stay here for a bit. I think there's enough work around here to keep me going for a while.'

'Well. I'm glad.'

Calogero jumped down into the orchestra pit, and hauled himself up the other side, wincing with the effort. 'Don't suppose you'd fancy being a magician's assistant?'

'I'm not sure I'd trust you sawing me in half, to be honest.'

He grinned. 'Ah well.' He offered her his arm. 'Come on then. Perhaps we could slip in a negroni before pizza?'

'Perhaps we could. But before that, there's something you really do need to tell me.'

'Yes?'

'And I want you to be absolutely honest with me this time. Just who the hell are you?'

The Magus smiled.

'I'm Calogero,' he said.

Glossary

A list of words in the text that might need translation, either in Italian or in Sicilian.

Albo dei Giornalisti	the list of official registered journalists, essential for legally working as a journalist in Italy
Arancino	deep-fried risotto rice, formed into a ball or pyramidal shape and filled with a *ragù*, mozzarella, swordfish or any manner of fillings (*arancina* in the west of Sicily)
Bianconero	black and white
Birra Messina	Sicilian beer from the city of the same name, notable for the addition of salt crystals to the brew
Buon lavoro	literally 'good work'. A better translation might be 'Have a good day's work'
Cafone	plural *cafoni,* boor, oaf, imbecile
Campanile	the bell tower of a church
Cannolo	plural *cannoli,* typical Sicilian pastry, a tube-shaped crispy shell of pastry enclosing a sweet ricotta-based filling

Caponata	tasty sweet-and-sour Sicilian dish, typically based on chopped fried aubergines, with the addition of tomato, celery, olives, capers and, ideally, pine nuts and raisins
Cazzo	expletive, roughly equivalent to *fuck*
Centro storico	the historic centre of a town or city
Che minchia	what the hell, what the fuck
Che vergogna	shame on you
Chi è?	who's there?
Chiaroveggente	clairvoyant
Chiosco / chioschetto, plural chiosci / chioschetti	stall, kiosk
Cinecittà	the legendary Italian film studio, still the largest in Europe
Cinquecento	Fiat 500 car
Citofono	door intercom
Comune	in this case, the nearest equivalent would be *council*
Corna (sign of)	the 'devil horn' hand gesture beloved of generations of heavy metal fans. In Italy, the horns pointing skyward is offensive. Pointing the horns towards the ground, however, is protection against the evil eye
Cornetto, plural cornetti	the Italian version of a croissant (confusingly called a 'brioche' in Venice/ the Veneto)
Cornicello	a charm, in the shape of a twisted

	horn or chilli pepper, believed to be a defence against evil
Cosa Nostra	literally *our thing*, the Sicilian Mafia
Crodino	non-alcoholic Italian beverage with a slightly bitter, herbal taste
Cronaca nera	literally 'black story' or 'black chronicle'. The crime pages in a newspaper
Faraglioni	sea stacks
Gingerino	Italian non-alcoholic beverage
Granita	a typically Sicilian semi-frozen dessert, often served with a sweet brioche bun
Guardia di Finanza	the Italian financial police
I Malavoglia	notable, if rather depressing, novel by Giovanni Verga, concerning the lives of a group of fishermen who live in Aci Trezza
Mano figa	another charm against evil, this one in the shape of a hand, the fingers curled, with the thumb interposed between the forefinger and middle finger
Mediaset	the largest Italian commercial broadcaster, majority owned by Silvio Berlusconi's *Fininvest* group of companies
Mizzica	the Sicilian equivalent of *Caspita!* Which might be translated as *blimey* or *crikey*
Moka	the classic Italian coffee pot, typically made by Bialetti
Molo	wharf, the area surrounding a pier

Motorino, *plural motorini*	motor scooter
Nero	to be paid *in nero* is to be paid in cash
Ordine Nazionale *dei Giornalisti*	the Italian national association of journalists
Pagare alla Romana	to split the bill, to go Dutch
Pagine Gialle	Italian equivalent of the Yellow Pages
Pasta alla Norma	a classic Sicilian pasta dish involving tomatoes, aubergine, ricotta and basil; named in honour of the Catanese composer Vincenzo Bellini and his opera *Norma*
pasticceria, *plural pasticcerie*	pastry shop
U pisci a mari	perhaps the best translation would be 'the Sea Fish', a part-pantomime part-ritual staged in Aci Trezza on the Feast of St John the Baptist, in celebration of the town's links with the sea
Porta blindata	reinforced, burglar-resistant door
Pronto	Italian greeting upon answering the phone, along the lines of 'hello, I'm ready to talk now'
Pronto soccorso	the A&E department of an Italian hospital
Questura	the main police station or local headquarters of the Italian state police
RAI	the Italian state broadcaster
Ràis	ship's captain
Sagra	a feast day or festival

Sarde a beccafico	sardines stuffed with raisins, breadcrumbs and pine nuts, and baked until crisp on a bed of bay leaves
Scribacchino, plural scribacchini	pejorative term for a journalist, a hack
Signurina	young or unmarried woman (Sicilian equivalent of *signorina*)
Stuzzichini	snacks served with drinks
Tabaccheria	a shop licensed to sell cigarettes and tobacco
Tavola calda	literally 'hot table'. A bar or café serving hot snacks. Usually sufficient to remove the need for dinner
Toast	a toasted sandwich, pretty much identical to what the British might call a 'toastie'
Torta cassata	a sponge cake filled with ricotta and candied fruit (or chocolate chips), then covered in marzipan, fondant icing and topped with candied fruits
Trisoru	darling (Sicilian equivalent to the Italian *tesoro*)
Vecchiu	old man

Acknowledgements

First of all, my thanks to all of you who've read this far and didn't hurl the book across the room upon discovering that Nathan Sutherland wasn't in it! Fear not, Nathan will be back, and his adventures will, I hope, alternate with those of Nedda and Calogero.

All characters are, of course, invented, with the exception of the brief references to Camilleri, Pirandello, Paolo Rossi, Marco Tardelli and the late Paolo Bucinelli, known professionally as *Solange*.

Sicily is the part of Italy I love the most, apart from Venice. I always hoped that, at some point, I'd set a novel there. All I can say is that I hope you enjoyed it.

My thanks to Hannah Wann, Rebecca Sheppard and everyone at Constable. And to Colin Murray, my agent John Beaton, my wonderful wife Caroline and, of course, to all of you.

Philip Gwynne Jones, Venezia / Aci Trezza 2024
www.philipgwynnejones.com